Colleen G. Lowe

I0655460

People at play.......

FAMILY foibles...kerfuffles and

lifelong scars....

Treachery, deceit, invasion and

abandonment from most unlikely

sources.

Some suggestive language & patois snippets///

A look at life & people, where fiction dons the cloak of

truth....... by gifted Jamaican Raconteur & Author

Colleen G. Lowe

Family foibles and Lifelong Scars

Revised Fifth Easy Read Edition

Publishers: Lignum Vitae Investments, a dba of Import-Export Solutions, Inc. P O Box 831896, Miami-Dade Fl. 33283-1896 Email: Muteelegance@bellsouth.net

Volume purchases and distribution. Contact Publisher at above address. Printed in the United States of America. First printing June 2019. Fifth revision and printing, April 2022. Reformatted EasyRead edition.Times New Roman 11 point.

Read excerpts and buy online at: Theglenwoodcollection.com.

Also sold on Amazon/Kindle. Search: Colleen G. Lowe

Delivery confirmation & USPS tracking data: 305-794-4820

ISBN-13: 978-0999122952 ISBN-10: 0999122959

Dedications..

....my mother, Fredricka who gave me gift of life. God grant her eternal rest.....

....my grandmother, Louise. Loved and mothered me. Proving at times, love is a hurting thing......

....my father, Henry. Taught me wisdom to live life by. I still miss someone....

....the Darby's, Tom and Rhoda. Sheltered our family from ravage of hurricane Charlie, sparing three lives. Friday August 17th, 1951

....the "Bunchie-genuine as sunrise." Loved me without parameters as only a woman can.....

.....every woman who unselfishly gave of herself. Sustaining life and civilization. You are indeed, God's gift to mankind....

Contents..

Autographs and Observations:

Family foibles...People at Play. Fifth revision and reformatting, March 2022. Fifth printing April 2022. Peace, love, courage and positive vibes in your earth runnings.......Colleen G. Lowe

Introduction

The good book declares. 'If the blind leads the blind, they shall both fall into the ditch.' Used to be, us the nearsighted and even them with untrammeled vision, but marginally learned in some things. Relied on elected leaders for guidance in our areas of deficiency. You see, we came to recognize and endow them with superior intelligence. Entrusting to them, an ability to always direct or steer us in right direction. Rarely were their utterances and motives questioned, because "they knew." All life forms have one thing in common, no matter what specie their classification. That connective strand is, rule of self preservation and by extension, our own. In alpha life form, which is man. It is called 'common sense.' It has been proven, more 'educated' a person is, their reservoir of common sense diminishes. Giving rise to us at times, questioning utterances and intentions of them whom we had come to regard as geniuses. An educated fellow would use 'genii' instead of geniuses. If only to prove sojourn within ivied walls of academia. Having lost faith in abilities of them to whom we had looked for guidance. We are now assailed by conflicting idioms, skewered gospel and lies. As we ponder and try to assimilate, words of Joseph Addison comes to mind. He, in his 1713 play "Cato," declared. 'He who deliberates is lost.' Indeed we are, and must now revert to inherent knowledge, common sense. Although embodied and moulded into our persona, alas, there are limitations.

Common sense doth not demystify our financial systems vagaries or overwhelming fields of science, which affects our existence on planet earth. Which brings us to 2019 and Covid pandemic. Our world and people has always been victims of epidemics and pandemics. Going back to 'Black Death' which demised an estimated 200 million. Flu of 1918, demised 20-50 million. Asian Flu 1958, tolled 2 million. There's been Cholera, and in our time, 2005-2012. HIV/AIDS, tolled 36 million. Massive death tolls assigned diseases, have always been occasioned by. Time elapsing between, science defining, disease's nature and structure.

Next hurdle is, developing medicines to neutralize and eradicate. Trial confirms effectivity, disease is conquered, vanquished to history tomes, and life goes on. Until next unknown malady comes to fore. We have, all of us during our lifetime. Been required to take numerous vaccinations, without which we are not allowed admittance to schools. Less than four years old, I was pricked with a needle, then told to stretch tongue out. Glob of syrup was dropped on, followed by. "Swallow quickly." Never knew why, but in later years, suspected this might have been poliomyelitis intervention. It has been confirmed, Covid is airborne, necessitating face masks. This to prevent, those afflicted, passing it on to those unafflicted. This is where common sense should appease and embolden all to be so guided. But alas, the educated have taken to airwaves and social media. Denouncing scientific research and conclusion, as flawed. Some say, scientists have ulterior motives. Their advice to all and sundry? Vaccines are dangerous and everyone has the right to wear a face mask or not. No One can force others to obey, vaccine or face mask mandate. Meanwhile, Covid not only rages on, but creates new variants by mutation. There are people in regions of our world where this disease is out of control. They would consider, vaccines and masks access, heaven sent blessings.

Now to unveil the big hypocrisy. Elected leaders who seize every format and opportunity to remind citizens. They cannot be forced to do anything they don't want to. It being their right to make decisions as seen fit. Then enact legislation that takes away women's right, to decide whether or not she should abort a pregnancy. Now, she's an imbecile. Can't be trusted to make her own decision. The state has to do that for her. Under threat of severe penalties, should she dare refuse to be guided by this edict. It is gratifying to hear naysayers, on bed of affliction with penultimate breath. Imploring others to avoid their fate, by wearing masks and get vaccinated. Brings to mind, poignant lyric by Hilaire Belloc. "Cautionary tales for Children." Published in London, 1907. 'Chief defect of Henry King, was chewing little bits of string. At last he swallowed some which tied. Itself, in ugly knots inside. Physicians of the utmost fame. Were called at once, but when they came. Answered, as they took their fees. There is no cure for this disease. His parents stood about his bed, lamenting his untimely death. When Henry, with his latest breath. Cried, Oh my friends! Be warned by me. That, breakfast, dinner, lunch and tea. Are all the human frame requires. With that, the wretched child expires.' Any One, knowing his demise is at hand, and takes his last breaths. To nobly admit errors and warn mankind against doing same, has earned etching of his name on pillars of life.

I have been piqued by an observation, and am led to ask the wind. You do know, that's where answers are. Blowing in the wind. Where will this take our nation and it's citizens, and how soon or how long. One of many privileges enjoyed in this country, was denied me in my birthplace. It is that of freely casting vote, to elect aspirants to offices of governance at all levels. Mid 1970s, I went out early, bent on beating the rush to cast my vote. Would get home and relieve my wife, sitting our children. She too would go do her civic duty. I would then take off to my day job. Entrance to polling venue was guarded by two strange goons. One of whom, stuck an arm across my path. Embraced my shoulder whilst steering me direction I had come. Called me by name and said. ***"Nuh worry youself. We take care of things areddy. We making sure, good things happen for you and you daughters them."*** He also made sure, I saw the gun, stuck in his waistband. I meekly walked home, told my wife of the event and never tried voting again. Cannot explain inner euphoric experience, when I walked into and voted for first time in Florida. In recent times, political leaders at every level in this country. Have constantly introduced legislated measures, to frustrate and disenfranchise citizens from free and fair access to participating in the elective process. Seems we had come to accept subtlety of gerrymandering, as par for course. Efforts to stymie are now brazen, constitutional guidelines are ignored and changes enacted by majority. All of which, beggars question. Are we no longer ascribing to democracy? Are those who bulldoze through and trample our voting rights. Seeking to establish society as exists in regions of Asia and East Europe? Them that lives longest, will see the most.

In a lifetime interacting with people of different religious, racial, ethnic and social persuasions. I find truism in belief that people are same. However, corresponding truth, exposes an ever widening chasm of difference. This because, when knowledge essential to survival was propagated among ruling class echelons of society. Passed on to working class minions. Options of sifting fact from fiction were non-existent. Another truth is, even them that were exposed. Were being fed assumptions and beliefs as wisdom. Eventually proven to be illiterate, as science and technology disproved myths. Who would believe, knowledge quite often creates conflicts? Yet it does. Look around and see countless examples of someone going amok, without definable rhyme or reason. Asking why? Because decades old fact or truth has now turned out not to be. Conflicts arise at times, because it is now being revealed. A people, family or person, were wronged eons ago. Those who now wear descendant's gilded mantle with pride. Have been armed with cudgel and raised voices, demanding redress. Whichever way this goes, for certain it will demise peace on earth, goodwill towards men. It is said in adage. 'Ignorance is bliss.' We will, for as long as we live, learn about our past, present and future. New drugs and medical discoveries, conquering diseases and prolonging life will come. As will knowledge for man to annihilate himself from and ruin our planet. See glaring conflicts, truths sometimes creates? Quote by Konstantin Josef Jirecek. Austro-Hungaria Czech citizen, June 24th, 1854-January 10th, 1918. Now attributed to Mary Teresa Bojaxhiu. Born Anjeze Gonxhe Bojaxhiu, more commonly known as Mother Teresa. August 26th 1910-

September 5th, 1997, very aptly reads. 'We the willing, led by the unknown are doing the impossible for the ungrateful. We have done so much with so little for so long. We are now qualified to do anything with nothing.' This is indicative of man's intolerance for progress' pace, and threat of cessation. By those who forge selflessly without tangible recognition.

I must admit, if it's not already blatantly obvious. Being an unrepentant idolater and dedicated observer of women. Thus empowering me to state another proven truth. Females have always been smarter than males. More creative, resourceful and calculating than males can ever come close to being. Quality that makes her superior being is, inherent maternal capacity to love and nurture. Which, when she does. Men have abandoned kingdoms and treasures they hold dear. But be not lulled into comfort of complacency. She has hidden potency to be viciously lethal. Having studied women of varying ages. Girlfriends, sweethearts, wives. Have peered into souls through eyes of women. Who kept their innermost selves deeply vaulted. It frightened when the unconscious began meandering through labyrinthine hallways of their minds. This then is a look at people's behaviour, in quest of ultimate goals. To detriment of others, near, far or dear. Focus on women is by their being fount of human creation and bowl of ongoing sustenance. Women have been tagged. "The weaker sex." Stroke of female brilliance, lulling egotistic male into false invincibility. Note well, she has never raised dispute or denial. A friend was in habit, always saying his wife was stupid. Hence he could sing her any song and she would dance. Told him, I think a woman is only as stupid as she wants a man to believe she is. More stupid a woman appears to be, could indicate height of creative brilliance. Siren's lure. Granny called it. "Playing fool to catch wise." We sat in her garage, jawboning to rhythm of buttons clicking inside dryer drum. She said, with just a tad too much nonchalance. You got to listen keenly, pay attention or miss essence of. *"I did not know, when you bought a new Toyota truck. You had to change all tires?"* "**Where you got** that from?" I asked, after flash hashing for unspoken meaning. *"Your friend bought set of tires on our credit card. I asked, why he would buy new tires for a brand new truck. Know what he said to me?"* **"Then Marcia, you never know Toyota's are made in Japan. And Japan's roads not smooth and level like ours. Tires that come on their cars have to be changed out, before we can drive them?"** She replied, mimicking husband's basso. Not wanting to create angst or upset apple cart, I replied. **"Oh, truck probably came with terrain or snow tires. He had to change them for regular ones."** She instantly leered at me. Lips pursed, brow furrowed and contemptible eyes. *"You too? You can find your way out. I am busy. Would have been best you kept your mouth shut. Shrug your shoulders, as you do many times. But don't sit in my house and take me for idiot. He bought them for his woman's car!! This idiot went to the store. Got copy of the bill, with make, model and tag!"* **"Whoa! Mama Mia! Sheath your dagger."** I said, as I hugged her and went on. **"Youse is both my friends. So as not to sow discord, I have to be hypocritical. Come on Mia Cherie, say you understand."** Just for a minute, look into her eyes. See lurking hatred and turmoil. Asking her husband, about this big ticket charge on their card. He giving her baloney whilst she's looking at him and knows different. Makes you think, she could have killed him. As is often said, in cold blood, for this deception. It really hurts when you know someone is taking you for an idiot. My father Henry called it, insulting his intelligence. I was in this instance the lucky one. Being and wanting to stay in good graces with both. Many women detests husband's male friends, more than his female friends. Especially if male friend has traits she detests, or spouts arguments that rankles her sensitivity. In her mind, it's only a matter of time before her husband gets corrupted by his friend. Of course, there are husbands who experience similar angst, regarding wives female friends. Recently a wife asked her husband. *"What do you and Steve* *talk about, so often and for so long?"* **"Oh, man stuff."** He replied. She rejoins. *"I thought you were going to say woman's stuff. He's so hooked on that one organ, God saw fit to not bless him with."* He let's the discussion die. His neighbour to whom he was relating, asks. **"She let it float away, just like that?"** He says. *"She's trying to be slick. Got to think before saying anything to her. But not to worry, I've got her by the balls."* Neighbour finds that funny and chuckles heartily as he asks. **"I thought you had the balls?"** He quickly replies. *"Oh no my friend, we got nuts. Women are Ones with the balls. At least, that's how it is in these United States. Women will chew you up and spit you out, without taking a sip of water my friend."* Women study their mates for subtle behaviour changes, which mate might not even realize, he's exuding signals. If there's question of lost fervency, however minuscule. She begins suspecting, another woman has caught his fancy. Else, she can readily identify, aping his friend's behaviour. There's no denying we outsmart each other or try to, as part of life's ritual. We should however take care, observing first rule of self preservation known to all living creatures. Never imply someone else's inferiority, by mistaking our schism for superiority. In this book, I will examine facets of our existence. Personalities of people, women and men. Union of husband and wife, going to making a family. How some children develop into adults. Support given or got by whom. Treachery and hate that's sown and prosper. Most times nourished by greed, lust and or envy. Same motivation gave rise to Cain killing his brother, is still rife within our persona. Only difference being, we have more and better tools with which to commit crimes and at times, successfully hide it. Yes, people do get away with crimes, especially murder most foul. Having exorcised myth of women being weaker sex. Let's take a glimpse at male's fortitude. As with everything that's part of our earthly existence, there was a beginning. June 7th, 1381. Priest John Ball, open air sermon in Blackheath England, asked poignant question. *"When Adam delved and Eve span, who was then the gentleman?"* Good book tells, Adam hid, on hearing creator's footsteps. Vainly tried covering his nudity, ashamed of physical transformation. Asked reason for having eaten of that which was forbidden. He replied. The woman gave him of the fruit and he did eat. "Did" in this context is indicative of intensity, fervour and zeal. What an overtly awesome, exhilarating experience that must have been. Both had been warned to not partake of the fruit. Let's say, the woman got curious and used her persuasive skills on the man. He could have said, no. Then walked away, instead of being weak. Succumbing to curious temptation and blaming the woman for his deed. By observation and personal experience. There are occasions, man admires female form. Or finds himself in tight embrace, as at courtesy dance. If we peer through dimness, there will be seen rising distention. As happened at cookery class in school. Thus evidencing, endemic strength of male's weakness. It is testament to woman's strength, unlike a male. She has never decried this tag of being weak. She wears it with smiles and pride as she does her Easter bonnet. Comfortable in knowledge of who she is and what she's capable of. It gives her opportunity to overtly arm her cannon with smile of acquiescence. Lulling male into false sense of security and superiority. So, we asks the wind and listens for it's whisper. Will man ever concede being weaker of sexes? If he does. How will that dictate gender relationship? Man is born of woman, whom as nature prescribes. Nurtures and infuses him with life's sustenance and comforting when he aches. This becomes enduring embodiment of his psyche in times of unrest and despair. His weakness leads him to find succor in woman's strength. Like tap roots, going deep down to anchoring Sequoia to higher heights. We could agree, he's trapped in vicious cycle of dependency. By very nature of his origin and entry to life. Unable to break free of that ordained, when he lost a rib. A gorgeous, spellbinding creature, called woman was created. Bringing him succor and blissful contentment. For this, I'm so thankful. Life without woman, would not be, couldn't be. Look at her, be silently grateful.

When you are family friend-1

I loathe visiting former sweethearts, who are now married or in committed relationships. Moreso, husband is aware of our history. Men find it hard being "also ran." Priscilla's husband was unaware, assuming me to be co-worker. So, I heeded her beckon and stopped by. Husband, she said, was creating angst in their marriage. She was quite beside herself, asking advice on dealing with mother-in-law. Who was coming over, supposedly for lunch. Told me. *"I just know she's coming to rasp my first, last and those in between nerves. Her ugly son, done ran to her, crying. She's coming to rebuke, make new rules and chastise. Would not put it past her to declare, if I don't straighten up and fly right. She's going to tell him toss me to the kerb and come home to her. Which will suit me just fine. Best of both world's situation. He will have to meet financial obligations to children and myself. I will be spared contact with him, and her wretched, debilitating, conniving persona. Oh, happy day!"* She exulted, both hands upward stretched as in kindergarten or church. I said. **"Wow! You got a heavy load out there girl child. That sounded like chronic indigestion. From that, all-you-can-eat, game-stop session. However, before you spewing bile on that woman, and her slapping you silly. Just remember, her son is as pretty to her, as your children are to you. Mothers always see their children prettiest, dares anyone to say otherwise. So go easy on "ugly son" theme. You can listen and not comment or commit. Don't hear the acerbic. Try focusing on mutual positivity you and your children find so heart warming. Acknowledging, ugly son's role in that tranquil existence."** She silently stared ahead, before saying. *"What if I told you. That lying piece-o-shit, doesn't know I know. Last Tuesday when he "worked overtime." He was at gyal*

Dahlia Fenton's house, screwing her senseless. Hope and pray he breeds her." "Who, she be?" I asked. *"One of many part time whores, working at Pacifick Energy and Gas. Wanna join me in payback? Serve him dish of his own sauce. Dying to see how he enjoys it."* I'll admit being roused by the suggestion, but let Bighead dominate on this. **"First of all, this would have to be "Meat eaten in secret" session. He would not have knowledge of, or ability to compare dishes. Second, me too old for jumping through window. Back in old country. I would be daring young Buck, sprinting from Ebenezer and his machete. Today, Messrs. Smith and Wesson guards turf. Though enthused, must reluctantly say, count me out this grand sexcapade."** She stared at me, long and hard. What'd she expect?

If there's a most fertile ground for breeding and thriving of deadly sins, 'twould be within family circle. Greed, envy or gluttony, covetousness and lust. Ensures, embracing all others, to some degree. Some argue, this is older than the hills. Good book doth record numerous instances of. Notwithstanding, it grates inner sensibilities being spectators. Witnessing, dastard trespassing and trampling by kin against kin. Treachery, if pursued. Should never be among kin. There were brother and sister, Maud and Tobias. In era when commonwealth citizens, migrated freely within territories. Tobias went to and settled in London. Two years after marriage, it was proven his wife could not carry pregnancy to term. Denying his silent quest for white children, and reason marrying white woman. Sadly lamenting deep disappointment to his sister. It was agreed, her only child, Dinah. Would join him and advance herself scholastically. Dinah was agog, excited, going to England. She left daughter Sylvia, with Maud. All was well within the family circle. Or, so One took for granted. Before long, seeds of lust and greed were sown and bloomed. No One being aware of developments. Adage reads.'Bad habits are gathered by unseen degrees. Just as brooks makes rivers and rivers run to seas.' Dinah found work in a white bloke's Pub, who was Tobias' friend. Seeing his niece being over friendly. Tobias warned her, bloke was married. If we assumed, Tobias was protective of Dinah's welfare, we would be wrong. It was simply jealousy and lust. Dinah had twins. Boy and girl, both coloured. Which, prior to their birth, created anxiety for Pub owner, but now brought relief. He being under radar of suspicion by his wife. Not to prove he was not gallanting, he just got lucky or took precautions. Dinah confessed to Maud, on tear blotted pages. Uncle Tobias was her children's father. Naturally, Maud was righteously upset. Shared news of Tobias' slack behaviour, with relatives and close friends. She further made it known, if her brother ever came home. First step taken on solid ground, she would stone him to death. As good book declares, should be fate befitting his shameless, sinful deed. ***"One lieth not with flesh of thine own flesh."***

Office maid Maud, and messenger, Ruben. Were co-workers at same company, engaged in larcenous cahoots. Her being self appointed exchequer, kept miser's grip on returns. To which, Ruben often voiced weak discontent. Fridays, Sylvia came for market money from Maud. Quite unawares, having caught lusting eyes of Ruben. Verbatim discussion between both adults would not be gleaned, but gist confirms. Ruben was attracted to fifteen year old. Who, in all fairness, could pass for a young woman. In equal fairness, Ruben was in his sixties, about to become an old fool. Maud began writing to Ruben, purportedly from Sylvia. Asking for presents and money, which was quite often sent with grandma. He was emboldened, felt encouraged. Maud approved of this budding

April November relationship. Each monied letter he sent to Sylvia, invited her to visit his home. Sylvia wrote back, made excuses why they could not rendezvous. Yet, asking monetary favours. It could be said, bit was in Ruben's mouth, and he followed that rein whenever it was pulled. You see folks, each letter held out hope. His wishes would come to fruition in less time than expected. One missive quoted old adage.'Patient man will ride donkey.' Had he not been blinded by lust, he would have recognized. That old quote would not be used by a young woman. No matter how old he thought her to be, not knowing she was fifteen. Metaphor was reassuring, there was in store for him. Day of rewarding surprise, if only he could be patient. We can imagine, old coot salivating and visualizing. Moment of ecstatic sexual joy, when morning and midday sun came together. Yearning, he took day's unpaid leave from work. Reason? Family illness. Early morning, braved peak vehicular traffic. Bicycling over ten miles thru busy streets of Kingston to St. Andrew, under tropical morning sun. Found him in state of ecstatic trance, rapping Maud's door. Breathless, rivulets of sweat streaming down his face, he uttered amid panting. ***"Beg you, some water, now. You look, ten time better, than you letter. Me can leave, bicycle outside. Nobody, won't thief it?"*** His eyes beamed, as if he had stumbled on El Dorado. Seeing him for first time, bewildered Sylvia asked. **"Who, you come to, Sir? Grandma, not here you know."** She had never seen Ruben, prior to this. Did not know who he was, from where or why he was at the home. Assumed he had to be visiting grandma. Of course, reaction took Ruben aback. He began mounting steps towards her. She yelled. **"Stop! Where you going?"** A young Buck stepped forward. Machete in hand, he asked. **"Who you, Dads? You at wrong house, nobody here don't**

know you." Safari brochures, shows Silverback defending the prize. Not so in our civilized existence. Certain there was misunderstanding. Ruben enjoined Buck, be calm. Begin dialogue to unravel mystery, saying. *"Me old, but not mad yet. Bear with me."* Caught between anticipation, embracing Sylvia and threat of Buck's firmly gripped machete. He pleaded for rational accommodation. First, he brought out three or four letters received from Sylvia. Handing them to Buck, he quickly said. *"These is what come to me since this month, but me have whole heap more."* Buck had childhood deficiency, in that he never learned to read. He coaxed and got Sylvia to join them. Perusing letters and reading aloud in disbelief, her jaw fell. Averring, to marginally skeptical Buck. She had never written letters, or received money and gifts alluded to. Feeling clueless and helpless, she resorted to tears. Afraid to face grandma's and Buck's wrath, who dared ask. **"You have any of the money? Me won't vex, you can tell me."** A closely guarded secret, no One knew. Was that Buck, ten years her senior, was Sylvia's lover. Often, slapped the teen around. Accused her of smiling with shopkeeper's son, staying at school too late after dismissal. Sylvia ran away, sought and was given refuge with relatives. Grandma, faced with dearth of domestic skills. Visited and did try, getting Sylvia back in her household. She would not know, she was merely one half of Sylvia's nemeses. Kinfolks were surprised when Sylvia's letters to Ruben. In grandma's semi-literate scrawl were shown. Baring facts of deception brought on by greed. Out of evil, came good results. Sylvia escaped Buck's tyranny and grandma's scheming. It cannot be said. 'They lived happily ever after.' Dinah is in her eighties, still living in England. Maud, uncle Tobias and Ruben died of old age. Buck died in prison riot fire, preceding breakout attempt. Sylvia in her seventieth year, can never forget grandma's greed and deed. So we ask ourselves, and the wind. What caused Maud succumbing to temptation, putting her oldest grandchild in such dangerous situation? GREED, plain and simple. Ruben, overcome with LUST. Was led as is said, like a lamb to slaughter. Was minded to reek vengeance, at whose quarter it is not known. But, let the matter die quietly, quite rightly so. Not all garden's blooms, whose odours rides the winds. Are as welcome to senses as that of the rose. Or chirps of songbirds to One's ears. Ruben reluctantly gave up option to be rambunctious. Feared being a laughing stock. Should things come to knowledge of co-workers and friends. These things have tendency, proliferating like plague gone viral. And Maud? Old Tactician that she was, recognized Ruben's impotence. Taking comfort in that zone also. Sword that's keen edged, also has blunt heel. Told Sylvia years later, quite dismissively when questioned. ***"Child, what gone bad at morning can't come good, evening. Makes no sense crying over spilled milk. What don't kill you, makes you strong."***

No Gratuity?-2

This brief glimpse at segment of Flavia's life. Mirrors many others, taking first step in working world. Might come as eye opener, giving cause to pause and think. Lest one goes down similar path, unawares. She was out high school, listening to excited peers. Discussing college invitations received. Possible study or boarding grants at their disposal. She smiled with them and. ***"Oh! That is so great."*** She got a job, inhaling cholesterol from burgers and fries grill. Whilst taking part time classes in medical billing and coding. Her mom worked in medical field, and advised. This vocation had endless possibilities for autobahn advancement, if luck had it.

Mom told Sebastian, about her daughter, just out high school. Very motivated and quick to learn. He was setting up practice and needed qualified staff. Unable to pay going salary, he asked to meet Flavia. Was immediately taken by an attractive, flirtatiously outgoing young woman. He figured, with a little push she could be moulded into an efficient workplace asset. Exacting patience, her incompetence often bristled his last nerve. Sensing disquiet, she initiated appeasement, to which he succumbed like block ice block on summer's pavement. Us men are so easily bribed and distracted. It's nothing short of miraculous, we survive to be old men. But, it's part of "People at Play." With guidance from mom, Flavia quickly learned how to engage and cope with business routine. Soon had aspects of client records, appointments and collections. Running, like Swiss clockwork. To aid her getting to office on time, or more so to facilitate their rendezvous. Sebastian bought her a used compact car and life was just for living. Most men will swear, playing in mittens. Robs them of half game's pleasure. Leaves it to women to employ appropriate safeguards. You know, it's always woman's responsibility to protect herself. Some women, by dint of instinct or goading. Can see gleam at rainbow's end. Leaves field wide open, encouraging hit or miss, home runs. Was no surprise when. Flavia had their child, having stridently and in tears. Denounced Sebastian's offer of safe abortion. Named the child to honour it's maternal grandfather. She had been told, some women who aborted first pregnancy. Had difficulty conceiving later, if they wanted to. Often accompanied by life threatening, 911 trip to hospital. Sebastian was uncomfortable with developments, but far from distressed. No doubt, soothed by balm that calmed. He sat her down for a pow-wow and got assurance. She would take steps to ensure, her child did not have a sibling by him. Quid pro quo, he bought her a new mid sized sedan. Moved her and baby into an exclusive pied-a-terre apartment. Enrolled their child in better private school. Smiles and grins teemed. In situations as we have here with these two. It's safe to assume, one is wheeler and other is dealer. It is a barely detectable kind of coercion, that might take on resemblance of blackmail. But please, let's not dress good intentions in cloak of dishonour. Still very uneasy, Sebastian took Flavia viewing model homes. Shortly after, mother and child moved into a cozy townhouse. By this time, amorous passion of One. Other or both, had slowly vapourized. Love nest and trysts were abandoned. Flavia's mom came to live with daughter and granddaughter. Them who knows, will not tell, but it's taken. There was now, relationship reversion. To strict employer employee conduct, between Sebastian and Flavia. So, we ask. What's next? Flavia's child graduated college, a lettered alumna. Flavia's mom, in silent reflection on years and events past. Quietly praised Sebastian for all good gifts abounding. Said to friends in sworn secrecy, he was a good man. However, there was financial void, on brink becoming abyss. Time on the move. Thirty, office thanksgiving parties later. Sebastian entered another life phase, sought buyers for his business. Wanting to enjoy fruits of labour, taking his family on extended world tours. Without albatross of practice to run back to. What with Flavia directing cadre of staff. All of whom were more qualified than her. But, as was PanAm's byline. You can't beat experience. What a travesty. Minor matters aside, the business was quickly sold. Transfer of ownership imminent, Flavia got overly anxious. Began wondering if new owners would retain her position. After all, she had been doing this a number of years. Could manage the business, eyes closed. On other hand, owners were corporate investors with network of offices. Quite likely would want, person in office manager's position. To be lettered and extremely knowledgeable, on their organizational methods and operational functions. Given size and scope of operations. They probably had qualified staff, raring for chance of upward shift. Rather than trying to retrain someone, more than likely set in her way of doing things. She thought long and hard on possible outcome, but was not comforted with gut feeling on the matter. Dinner deliberations with mom, that stretched into late night, did not alleviate the stress. Question would arise, whether or not she was given gratuity or redundancy purse, from profits of sale. One could truthfully argue. She was rewarded during her tenure, with unprecedented generosity by Sebastian. Could also be convincingly argued. His generosity was borne out of wanting lovechild. To enjoy existence, close to that of his nested children. Even if she was given gratuitous sum. That would have quickly melted to mere smear, like butter against warm palette knife. Had it not been for loans taken often, against equity in her townhouse. Mortgage would have long ago been fully satisfied. Grandma saw compelling need, taking lovechild on cruises and sightseeing excursions to foreign lands. Whenever Sebastian and his brood, took to oceans or sky, on expeditions of discovery and pleasure.

She would never admit, such trips, did more to tickle her fancy, than that of the child. Flavia and grandma, both experienced a void for the child. Which she did not, at any stage of her life. Always, happy contented child. Grandma and Flavia insisted, excursions were necessary. Broadening, child's development, in cultured growing experience. Made vexed point, unlike Sebastian's brood. Child was at no time, ever exposed to music instrument training. Ballet, creative dancing or extra curricular activity to enrich her youth. Flavia existed in present, with nary a thought on future. Nothing, it is said, lasts forever. She might have had foresight, or been encouraged by someone who did. Look ahead to life's autumn years and make efforts to consolidate and secure. First step should have been, furthering her marketability. She must have seen Sebastian age before her eyes and figured. *'This pumpkin will soon be cut from the vine. It's time I made my own chariot if I'm to attend the ball.'* In all of this, she lost grace with her child over years. Having refused to disclose, top half of her parentage. Obediently, maintaining pact with Sebastian, to never under circumstance. Comes hell, high water or Armageddon. Divulge lineage or allow to become fact. Someone whispered, grandma disclosed to kin in secret to grave. Receiving substantial cash bribe from Sebastian, keeping his identity unknown. Of this, Flavia had no knowledge. Although, not confirmed, it makes sense. Grandma, being in thick of events, from start to finish. How could Flavia be prevailed upon to hush. Whilst mom was left, free to gab. Every child or person knows it takes two, and barring adoption. There's always curiosity to identify parents. If one or both are deceased, child moves on to next kin. Wanting to know cousins, grandparents, aunts, uncles. Anyone, who can give insight into what their biological parents were like. It is one of those human curiosities that flames, until extinguished by death. I see lurking ghost of blackmail and silencing a wagging tongue. Am certain, many are times when Flavia asks. Should I tell and be done with it? After all, Flavia has a right to know. On other side of town, Sebastian questions to assure himself. Can Flavia and grandma be trusted to keep their secret? Horror of horrors. What could happen if they don't? Well!….Books have been written and movies made on outcome of similar situations. Plots not always pleasant. I will aver there is no perfect marriage. People accept unions for what they are, including imperfections. Once it is established. Neither One of us, wants to say goodbye, or can afford to. Just break bad news already. Introduce outside child to siblings and family. If only to ensure, they do not meet and innocently become lovers. Storm will abate after gusting and one event is guaranteed to not happen. That of brother and sister getting romantically and intimately involved with sibling, neither One knew existed. It happens. Girlfriend and I had been going for close on a year. Took her home one evening, after a movie. Her mom greeted me with a grin and asked how was her sister. I stuttered a response. Girlfriend, faced with our inevitable breakup, began crying. Island life can be like that. We revel in. "No problem." "Don't worry, be happy." That's our theme.

Francine, Roxanne, Al & Them?-3

Belinda was not mine…and I did not find her holding Jim and loving him. She had itch that could not be scratched. Would not give up efforts to. Took pains correcting most everyone, on pronunciation of her name. ***"It is Belinda, not Blinda. Do not eat the E."*** Average Jane or Joe does not stress pause in speech to pronounce in that manner. It calls for conscious pause to create emphasis. That's not how everyday people talk, as a rule. Coworkers adopted nameless dialogue, like. ***"Hey, ACD meters came in."*** Her obvious delight came, when others used her surname with Miss. Most now agreed, that was her ultimate goal. One could understand if her's was situation similar to Petagaye. Whose button people prodded, calling her name as question. "Peta Gaye?" She simply had a name change to Peta. Her ID badge reflected new name. Al Parsons met Belinda when he joined staff of Pacifick Energy & Gas. She spoke ever so often about her "little girl." Kept everyone in loop on scholastic milestones. Coworkers whispered on photographic absence. Normal go with, what by intent should be show and tell. At company sponsored function celebrating safe working, injury free over extended period. Everyone was introduced to Belinda's "little girl," Francine. Now a young, very attractive woman. Told that Al Parsons is Jamaican by birth, she stuck by him. Asking for tips, on where to go and how to avoid being overcharged on souvenirs. Having already planned first Jamaican vacation. Just as she took Al to be her first Jamaican friend, treasuring his acquaintance. He an older man, found gratification in company of young women. Not necessarily in pursuit of intimacy. If it came knocking at his door, he beamed with ecstasy. Frannie often sought favours of Al, and he gladly obliged. Her trips to Jamaica became frequent, she found love in the tropical isle. Not having volunteered, details of how they met, and respecting her right doing her thing. He always looked at her with stifled yearning and rue. *"What a waste."* Roxanne stayed weeks in Florida, and Frannie reciprocated, in Jamaica. Today is Thursday, late evening after taking both to FLL. Roxanne boards Montego Bay bound, flight.

Frannie and Al are relaxing, under wispy vines and broad leaves of Yellow Yam hills. Making lush canopy of Ackee tree branches. Bent to create shaded alcove. Frannie sat on a stool, while Al sat on trunk of an Otaheite Apple tree, brought down by hurricane Michael. Balancing platter on her palm, eyes and face reflected gastronomic satisfaction. ***"This is so….so freakin' unbelievably earthly. Know what I'm saying?"*** She asked Al. **"Yes, I do. Indescribably fulfilling pleasure."** He replied, as she went on. ***"You're close. I mean, this takes me back to holiday in Virginia with my Hillbilly cousins. An heavenly childhood experience. Until a cousin*** *played doctor nurse with me."* "How old were you?" Al asked. With veiled annoyance, she said. *"Why didn't you ask, how old he was? He was fifteen, I was eight. That creep "examined" me every chance he got. I knew that shit was not right. But he always told me to not tell, or else. One day, Uncle Beck, his father. Put me to sit on his knees and coaxed me to tell what we did in the barn. I told him truth, so he went in the barn and hollered for Steven to come to him. Next thing, I saw Steven running like typhoon. Uncle Beck close on his heels, cracking that mean looking whip. Boy went and shacked up with kinfolk, cross county. Never came back until Uncle Beck's funeral, twelve years later. Seeing him made me so angry, I tried avoiding him. Sat by the bird house, admiring them. He came, all smiling and said something, which I still can't say I heard. But I stood and spat on him. Knew where Uncle Beck kept an old gun. I was ready to blow him to paradise with Uncle Beck, if he ever dared make aggressive move. He grimaced and walked away. I still felt urge to look for the gun....but."* "Was this Virginia holiday, your turn off event?" Al asked Frannie, who asked Al. *"Where did you learn to cook?"* "Evading the question?" Al gently prodded. *"Yes, I am. Trying to extend beauty of this hour."* She retorted. "You went overboard "Love Boat," minute you recalled childhood foray in Virginia." Al timidly reminded her. *"Maybe, but it hasn't sunk in yet. So, indulge me, please. You always do. Although I wonder why, with much gratitude. So don't go having change of heart. Lord knows, sometimes I am overly spontaneous, but you are sweetly accommodating. Cooking, come on."* Frannie urged Al, who began. "Cooking is kind of second nature to some Jamaicans. Especially them who were ghetto raised." She cocks her head at an angle and asks. *"So, if One is raised, say middle class. Then, One can't cook?"* He hems, then says. **"Less likely. Middle class homes generally hire servants. Children are spared scullery duties. Us Hood Rats sometimes scrounged for food, trapping birds and rabbits or fishing. We learned to cook with newspaper, twigs and brush wood. Going into early teens, we were all professional hustlers and….. "** Frannie interrupted. *"Hustlers?! Isn't that another word for small time thieves? I am sorry, don't be touchy. For me, hustling is like tricking and numbers. Just want to confirm and understand. Pardon the interruption, I lose thought track if I don't. So once again, indulge me please. Don't get all sour pussy. See? I knew that would thaw your chill."* Al asked. **"Does it not occur to you. I also lose my thoughts when you suddenly interrupt? Think about that, Mama Mia."** He went on. **"As I was saying, once we begin earning a little bit here and there. We pool resources and "run a boat." That's term for bush cooking. Each person brings something to the pot. No stowaways taken on board. Meaning, who can't ante, will be denied partaking the grub. One fellow hired his mom's pots, which he washed before she came home. Thus earning share of vittles. I would define cooking, as second stage in food preparation. After seasoning and spices are added, before or during the boil pot boil stage. Most foods are bland and unappetizing. First step to change that, is adding salt, to taste. Guided by cuisine traditions we add, condiments, spices and herbs. In pursuit of an ooh la la gastronomic experience. Different peoples have specific tastes and at times, will only savour foods with which their taste buds are accustomed. Your enjoying this meal as you are, is a not so rare feature of Jamaican foods. Being widely accepted by Americans, once spice content is lessened.**

Will say though, for some foods. Spicy, enhances true flavour." Frannie said to Al. *"If you must know, I was tempted to get pizza, whilst you took an eternity, shredding and chopping. Jeezaloo. Person could drop from hunger, waiting on you to....but will say, this was worth the wait. What is this called?"* Al told her. "I call it, "chicken ahwhadis." She made to say. Changed her mind, then did say. *"Tell me all about.....Explain what you did just after you.....Okay. You turned the burner off and threw bowl of chopped onions in. Stirred briefly and covered the pot but the stove was already off. I expected onions to be raw, but it is not. So, just heat of the stuff did the cooking? Come on! That smile means conceit."* Al told her. "Onions are raw. Barely par cooked for ten minutes. You expected acrid tang of ordinary onions. What I put in that pot my dear, are "Vidalia" sweet onions. Reason for par cooking, is to give added crunch to your chicken. You do love that crunch and sweet flavour. Don't you?" She gave him a coy glance and said. *"I love lots about you, not just crunch of sweet onions. When Roxy gets back, I must tell her about my weekend."* She pauses, thinks, then adds. *"Then again, maybe I won't. Mentioning your name, gets her uptight. Can't for life of me, figure out why. Says, she knows Jamaican men in ways I don't, and older ones are more kind.....cannot recall word she used. Like fox sly or something. It's a jealousy thing with her, why she was not happy, your agreeing to my staying here with you. Said I should check-in a hotel, for four nights weekend. I told her your Best Buy is very close, so you are harmless. Know what she replied when I said that?"* "No. What did she?" Al asked. *"She said, she's heard of road kill snakes that will get you with venom if you get too close. Let me ask you. Don't you find it tough on your ass, sitting that log? Or discomfort is offset, by pleasure of a gander up my thighs? Maybe your Best Buy is not as close as I thought. You taking me Miami Beach and Aventura like I asked?"* **"I told you, yes. Didn't I?"** Al asked, slightly peeved being accused, ogling her thighs. *"You did, but I've been just grating your every nerve. I was kind of hoping you would not change your mind. Why you do for me? You think, by slowly working your psycho thing on me, I will let you f... me? I see how you look at my tits and my ass. You know, it's not gonna happen? So, if you want to change about Alton Road. Say something, anything. Your silence unnerves me."* Al was tempted to prolong her misery, but asked. **"You got eyes in back your head to see me ogling your ass?"** *"No, I feel your eyes burning through my shorts, and my nipples tingle when you look at them."* **"Wear a bra, that should end your tinglin.' Did Roxanne tell you, in Jamaica, you are called a "Cock Teaser?"** She tittered. *"Cock Teaser? Now I get it. Roxanne said, you are cunning. You old Ones are like a big Jamaican spider.*(Brer Anancy)*I like being with and talking to you. Because you are a straight shooter. So tell me. You would love to f... me. Wouldn't you?"*

Al demurs, she goads. *"What's to think about? Say, yes or no. Although, I think you would be lying if you said no. Old Jamaican male, close to your Best Buy. Not gonna say no to a young woman. Unless you've got vaginal prejudices. White, Black, Native American or Gypsy, it's same. And it's not true what they say, about Eskimos being mighty cold. That's made up by horny army recruits, confined to training camps. Now, I'm not saying I would let you. But would you love to? F... me, I mean. Too graphic? You looking at me like a child who just said "shit" or something unexpected.*

You're not gonna lie to me now." Al glanced skyward and said."**Graphic? Isn't that indicative of picture or drawing? Someone said a picture is worth thousand words, not words making picture. So? There."** *"How then would you describe my question?"* Fran asked and Al replied. **"One could say, sexually explicit."** *"Okay, that's settled. And I'm still waiting on your answer."* She insisted, as Al replied. **"Frannie, I am unrepentant admirer of, addicted to pleasures of fully developed female. Aware as I am, of your lifestyle and sexual preference. Why would I yearn for, or have expectations sharing your warmth? Days of yore, I would be Fool rushing in where Angels dare not tread. Hoping older does make One wiser. I now know and accept life's limitations."** Next, they verified ages by Frannie asking. *"How old are you?"* **"I am, mid seventies. How young are you?"** *"I am thirty-two. Darn it. I had you fixed at fifty-ish."* Al went on. **"Funny, how I had you, twenty-six, twenty-eight. And not once did it cross my mind, we could get romp going. Even if you weren't. You know? What you are."** *"What! You can't say, "Lesbian?" Could be you'd rather say something real trashy, being an Islander and all. I don't accept the term, myself. So, if you hesitate to say it, I understand."* Al told her. **"I was going to say, left handed."** *"Left handed?"* She echoed and continued. *"What makes you think I am left handed? I am right handed. You do not observe as well you should."* **"Well, you're ambidextrous then."** Al replied with a smirk. *"No! I am not, for crying out loud. Well, come to think of it. I could land a good slap with my left hand. So, maybe you're right. I never gave it a thought. Now wipe that smirk off your face. Looking like circus mannequin."* Al said. **"Frannie, in Jamaica, being left handed. Does not necessarily have anything to do with physical dexterity or** handicap. Just as being called a fruit cake, does not mean you'll be sliced and served. You might get "eaten," but not on a platter." Mouth agape, she thought a while, then said. *"You know something? A group of us rented a book. "Languages within Language," which explains what you are saying. An entire speech can be given in phonetic, syntactic and semantic forms. With or without intent to confuse the limited. Brilliance of it all is, an observer would discount. By seeing speaker in a semi-literate class. So, I'm a left handed fruitcake. Anything else?"* "Hmm, a "Pot cover" and "You love your mother's side of family." Al ended. Frannie seems mentally lost, breaks long silence and asks. *"What's deal with a pot?"* "It means, instead of a pot going with a cover to produce something edible. In your case, you and yours being two covers. Naturally, nothing gets cooked or served, no production." Al told her with a laugh and both went silent, ruminating their thoughts.

Quite unexpectedly, she began. *"After Charles, I stopped wearing bra and underwear. Except when feminine days neared. Love ungirdled feeling of carefree abandon. First time taking off my bra in front a mirror. Was horrified by strangulation welts. No matter, experimenting with different fabrics and designs. Most underwear, migrate into your butt crack like jump rope. Cling to and stretch pubic hairs like rubber bands. Heaven forbid you attempt a fix, and all eyes are on you, in silent rebuke. Sometimes, I get out shower. Climb into bed still dripping, perched on all fours. Let cool air swirl into, up over and under my Coney. Feels heavenly peaceful, like praying. Call it, mantis interlude. You should try."* "I'd love to. Maybe, a session together." Al teases. Frannie eyes him a startled, annoyed leer. He quickly goes on.

"You know? To be certain I grasp finer points." Frannie retorts. *"Visualizing, as you have. I know you have the knack down perfect."* She guffaws and laughs out loud. Stares at him with mocking eyes, goes on. *"Summertime, things are different. Then, I need layers. My apple makes it's own cyder."* "Seconds ago it was your Coney. Now, it's your apple? Why the..?" Al is interrupted. *"Coney! What the hell is this thing, Coney?"* Al tells her. "Tropical rodent, like Guinea Pig, Mongoose or Rabbit from the...." She shakes her head in a tremor and tells him. *"I said, "Cunny!" My cunny. Please, don't ask me to be more vulgar. Let's go in, I feel a chill coming on. Don't you?"* "Not really. I wear underwear, long pants and shirt. Kind of a bit more insulated than you are." Al teases, with a smirk. Both indulge a brief silence, Al snuffs it. "In Jamaica, today is Ben Johnson's day." *"Who is he? Kind of folklore figure, like Guy Fawkes?"* She asks and Al replies. "Oh no, Guy Fawkes was a person. Ben Johnson is persona created by old folks lore, origin unknown. Akin to Mr. Rainy Day, although, latter has more substance." *"Do share the lore, since we can't share the love."* Frannie teased. "We could share both, if you want." "Horny Al," eagerly replied. *"I don't wanna do it, sir. I'm very picky choosy."* "You really are...I forgot your..." A now befuddled Al, tried recapturing run away thoughts. Overtaken by anticipation, sharing love. Came back to senses and said. "But lets do the lore. Day before payday, larder runs dry." *"What ladder going dry?"* She asks, with hand gestures. "Not ladder, larder, where groceries are stored. A cupboard or pantry. It was Thursday, when old mother Hubbard. Went to her cupboard, to get her poor dog a bone. But alas, the cupboard was bare." She stares at him, but does not interrupt. Seems she took his comment seriously. Al went on.

"So, on Thursday the fridge is cleaned of leftovers. Each person gets little of this or that. In lesser home sweet homes, others take to scrounging cupboards. For a little rice, flour, cornmeal, a bit of salt fish or salt pork. Blended with, maybe a coconut, into a one pot meal. Small dumplings, cooked in rice or turned cornmeal, makes contented bowels. No more griping, growling. May not meet, minimum daily nutritional requirement. Does keep worms contented. Till Friday's paycheck brings renewed abundance, such as it is." Frannie seized the break and said. *"Well, don't think your experience is unique. Pretty much mirrors, a greater period of my childhood in Colorado. Moreso when I stayed with kin in West Virginia. Shoot, I'll tell you now, and don't be surprised. But up them West Virginia backwoods, folks don't have regular jobs. Every freaking day was Ben Johnson's day. When you sat down to eat, you dared not ask, what's the meat. Because you did not want to know. See? Got a bit of rhyme going there. And that wasn't worst part of life. But, know what? I don't want to relive those memories. I'll say this though. When you're in it, you never see it until you come out. Then you look back and tremble in fear and disbelief, that's where you've been. That's when you believe there's a God, and prays to him or her. Never to let you find yourself in similar situation ever again. Saw yer eyebrows dance, back there, because not once in your life. Did you think God can be female. Why is everyone sold on God being male?"* Al gave this some thought, then opined. **"Because, "God" is male. Female, would be goddess. So we would begin our prayers. Our mother, who art in heaven. I pray to thee for my daily bread."** Frannie sighed and said. *"You're a cynic, but there's much I learn from you. Next topic, Mr. Rainy Day.*

Want I get you?....Let me get you water, do not protest. My throat is dry from listening. Yours should be parched from talking." She goes and returns. *"Here, your tap water and for me, Zephyrhills. Both from the fridge."* Each, swigged from their cup. She gives a sigh of refreshed relief, then urges Al. *"Come on, sun is going down. Soon it will get gloomy under here. Insects begin coming to their condo and find us here. They pester intruders relentlessly, some will make us their... Mr. Rainy Day, please, pretty please."* Al churned with desire, staring at dimples of her nipples. *"God, she is so desirable when she lets out her woman in her. I could..."* Caught his thoughts, began. **"Mr. Rainy Day, is metaphor symbolizing rainy season. During which fields could not be worked. Labour confined. Compromising production and income. Hardy folks braved monsoons, eventually became ill. Necessitating urgent doctor's visit. From income earned, a portion was saved for Mr. Rainy Day. Being future expenses, unexpected, but, just in case. Bail money, doctor's fees or budget balancing. You know? A cushion to fall back on, in case. My granny kept a rainy day stash under bed, guarded by Panya Mashate. A Spanish machete, keenly sharpened both edges. Designed to slash, on forward and backward sweeps.** Frannie, seated slack jawed. Shook her head, sideways and said. *"That story could come from my kinfolk, when our antenna got blown down. Or an adult was not there to slap the TV into showing something. One of us kids had to go in black of night to get it working. People are just people, there's no reason they should not love One another. Not your definition, loving One another, so don't get excited. I'm going in, insects are setting their tables and gathering for a feast."* They settled on the sofa. She sipped wine, then said. *"I can tell, this piss is supermarket wine. You buy groceries at supermarket, and* *fine wine at a liquor store."* Al did not disturb the hush, until. *"When I left high school, I already had four boyfriends. After number four, decided to call it quits. Got tired being invaded, and big long dicks like broom handles. Being thrust up my vagina, like a friggin' chimney sweep. Asked myself. Where in this, was my pleasure. Game days, you saw them with huge front end loads. Coming at you with broad grins. Once they bait you with a dog and soda pop. Begin massaging your ass and mashing your breasts. You think they're heroes, let them screw you. I mean, everyone's doing it. You don't want to be odd Jane. First timers are good Ones. Afraid the vagina sucks them in and smothers them, they are real carefree.* (careful?) *The pros? They splay you real wide like a freakin' picnic blanket. Make you an acrobat and. Oh! My God. Why was it ordained, women should suffer because of that apple incident. That was eons ago. What happened to forgiveness and all that Bible stuff? Elton John sings about it. Trying to go in your vagina and out your mouth. In moment of conquest. They thrust and poke, frenzied and fast. Oh my God. A cow! Would not stand still for that shit, I tell you. She would have bull's balls dangling from her horns. Women do though, and then say. The cow is a dumb animal. Really? Next, comes the insult. You're hurting all over and the Sons-of-Bitches can't spend two minutes, comforting you, or trying to. Tells you. "I gotta get home, before my brother notices the bike gone." Or some shit that don't make sense."* Frannie was steamed up, nostrils flaring, lips pursed. Al sought calming inner tempests. **"I am sorry to hear, your teen years were an era of sexual abuse and unrequited pleasure. It has been said, regarding sexual intimacy. When you give, you also get your share."** She did an eye roll cross swirl, Al quickly added. **"Oscar Toney Jr. Seemed you were forgotten pilgrim at the table. So, times we pause to assess situations like these and see ourselves shortchanged. When I get with a woman, I try giving what I know a woman wants. Most times am able to hold out until she's sated. Of course, this comes from age honed experience. Possibly, lacking in Eager Beavers and young Bucks. Although, I was trained at early age by an adult woman. Whom some declares, should have been jailed for crimes. I am certain, there are girls and women. Whom at some point, in reflecting. Felt about me, as you do about boyfriends. There are girls in my teens, and women I went with just after. Made me sit and rue. If only I knew then, what I know now. Our sexual encounter, would have been so much more ecstatic, for us both."**

Frannie asked. *"You say, when you engage with a woman, you give her what you know she wants?"* **"I said, I do try. That's not saying, I always succeed. And I vowed, not sucking anything else."** Frannie stared at him and asked. *"Say, what's that now? Who's sucking….what did I say to get sucking in this little gabfest? I am having the wine, not you. So why are you talking crazy?"* **"Never mind, Frannie. It's inane play on words."** Al tried recouping calm. Frannie slowly embraced, saying. *"Okaaay, I'm not sure I follow, but you did say it's inanity. So, it's forgotten, but not buried. For now, that is."* She added, after a pregnant pause, then went on. *"I don't want to forget what you said about satisfying a woman. You talk in present tense as if you are.. …What's the word? Invincible and all that. Older than I figured, as you are. Your Best Buy date has got to be damn close or expired. So, whatever you're now capable of, to be understood. Should be prefaced with. "Once upon a time."* Confused, Al blurted. **"You keep talking about Best Buy. I** thought you wanted me to take you there. Because it's closer than one you always go to. Now you bring date and expiry in conversation, which just doesn't makes no sense at all. Could be, you have had too much of that inferior supermarket wine, for which you should be thankful. Had you imbibed real liquor store stuff, you would be out and open to being at disadvantage." She lapsed into a laughing fit, before saying.*"I am not talking about Best Buy, as in electronics. It's "Best By" in expiry of groceries, medication and such. Sometimes, when I think of those boys, now men. With their mighty broomsticks stoking and prodding. I want to find worst of the light. Throw urine in his eyes, hoping he goes blind. But then, I think. No. I will wait. Wait until his best by date expires, and mighty broomstick lies, flopped aside. Good only as waste drainpipe. Know what I'll do? Give to him, that which he cannot have. This, never loses its ability to function.*(Slowly massaging pubic area) *No best by expiry date. If I live to be hundred, it will always be receptive to anything that comes calling. A probing finger, or if fortune comes knocking. A gently, velvet coated, rigid broomstick. Must retire for the night, hastened by cheap wine and chase of sweet dreams. Take no offense, please sir. Don't mean to be, and tomorrow is a workday. So, I must drag myself away from pleasant, charming company. I say that with all sincerity. Not smoking your ass, like they do Honey Bees to get in the comb. Men! Devise tricks and traps to get what they want. Especially if it's honey, whatever hive it's in. Assholes!! Up there too, deviants with their fetish. Fu..ers!! Oops! That's not very ladylike. Is it? Is Saturday good for North? A yes, would be very nice. You can think on it and tell me later this morning. Ciao."* He was honestly caught off guard, by that last minute's rant.

Seeing her walk away, her sashay had him doing circles. Later Friday morning, she called out to Al from the kitchen. *"I cannot find a vessel to spoon the chicken, and my ride will be here in eight minutes. You hate plastics and have tons of Pyrex without covers. What good are they without covers? Use them for soup or finger bowls?"* He comes to top of stairs and softly calls. **"Frannie, where are you Sweety? Ah! there you are. Looking so irately desirable."** She scolds. *"Al, this not time for your psycho pill. A hive of honey is not gonna get me swallowing. Why can't I find one cover for any mid sized Pyrex bowls you have here?"* Al tells her. **"Designed obsolescence broke plastic covers while still new, long ago. Replacements cost same as first price of bowls and covers."** Wanting to push buttons, he went on. **However, I do believe those are Corning. Pyrex are larger ones with glass covers."** Pursing lips, she sighed hard then asked. *"Do you have any self adhesive wrapping foil?"* **"No, of course not. You would not find that here. This is a Cowboy's ranch, not a family home. But you can look in those drawers, maybe retreating wife left some. I am coming down to help you, all is not lost. Do not despair, you're taking chicken to work today. Who knows, this could be big break, making me next Colonel."** He comes downstairs. Mesmerized and traumatized by fleeting body contact, and whiff of perfume as she hurries by him, upstairs. He looks around for problem to solution. She comes back to the kitchen, mouth pouted and says. *"Well?"* He turns to her. **"Looky here, Poochy Lou. This is an Atlas Mason jar. See markings there? Up to this point, it holds twenty ounces. Has metal cap with inner gasket. What says, Madam now?"** She smiles acceptance. He seeks confirmation. **"Is that smile, a Yes?"** She says. *"Two minutes to my ride and you're having fun. Going from Pyrex to Corning and now*

Mason." He stuffs the jar. Hands it to her as her phone rings. She listens, ends the call without comment. Then, says to Al. *"She is six minutes away and apologizes for unexpected traffic congestion. That's so much BS. If you use city roads anywhere. You expect traffic delays and make allowances for. Miami, New York, LA and Amish country. It's greed, that's what it is. She hogged the call and now she can't make it happen."* Raising her voice she went on. *"You know, they charge for waiting? Tells you to make it up in the tip. As if tip is a given. Watch me and her when she does get here."* Al warns. **"Let it be. If you can't be nice and pretty please. A man will indulge, or simply ignore you. But a woman will unsheathe her talons. Having recently had yours done, you will naturally want to keep them safe from a fray. Also, bear in mind. She's in driver's seat."** She stares at Al, long and hard before breaking her silence. *"I promise you, if ever I decide to try a broomstick again."* Leaving rest unsaid, she walked to the door, turned and said. *"Come here, give me a hug that goes with the fire in your eyes. I could dare kiss you, but you'd be tempted to get overly amorous. Then I would have to instantly regret bashing your head with this jar. So just hug me like you mean it. Don't sag in! I'll prop out. Jeez!"* They were still in a tight embrace, when a horn tooted at the gate. As she hurried out the door, he called after her. **"Have a lovely day and put that jar in the fridge, first thing after reaching work. Bring back orders. Let's start something big."** Stood, staring at her rump going…Invigorated by that parting embrace, he traipsed upstairs to the bathroom. Medicating his eyes, aided by expansive wall mirror. Stared at reflection, conjuring methods to possibilities, then began a Paul Anka song.*"She's so young and I'm so old. This my dear friend,* *you've been told. I don't care just what she says. It's gonna happen one fine day."* Dick Whittington stirred, a mite. Al grinned at his image, began new song. *"Imagination is funny, sure makes that cloudy day sunny. Makes a Bee thinks of honey."* Obsessed with verses after brushing, he asked mirror mate.*"What happened to him? Paul Anka. Boy from Ottawa, Canada. His girlfriend was, Diana. Old when he made the song. She's now over the hill, or maybe under it. Shiiit, sooner or later we all go under a hill. If we are lucky."*

Then he skipped downstairs to his computer. It is said, talking to Self is first indication of madness. I ask. If One can't talk to Self, then who else can One talk to? We got to reason pros and cons with Self. Try on a course of action, before taking it to someone and be ridiculed. That's how you hear someone ask. *"He really said that, and expected you to say. What?"* Al figured he had done everything, intimately worth doing with women. Had never thought of, much more tried bedding a Lesbian. Frannie read him correctly, when she said he was trying to psycho infuse her. Which he figured would be his undoing. Her being aware of and putting up resistance. However, if he could pull this off, he would die smiling at his conquest. Late afternoon, he drove to Doral and took her for dinner. Went to Island Restaurant in Hammocks Shopping Centre. Since closed, with clientele regret. Had been going there, since single shop opened by Bloomfields. Expanded to two, making for dining room. Jamaica Kitchen, Sunset West Shopping Centre, 8736 SW 72nd Street. Would be must go to, for jerked pork and other delights. Thing was, they did not have dining room. Al opted for Island. Server already knew his usual fare. Oxtail with boiled banana and vegetables. After much indecision, he ordered for Frannie. Special dinner, rice and peas, with mini portions of curried goat and jerked chicken. He would share his oxtail, satisfying her yen to sample as much as she could. He played an old joke and asked her. **"You ever had colic?"** Her brow and eyes reflected deft concentration. Moving her head left, right, up at the ceiling, down to the floor and askew sideways. He smiled and said. **"Never mind, it's another Jamaican lore story."** She replied. *"No, I'm trying to unravel where I heard this cowlick before. But it had nothing to do with a menu. Or did it? I am certain I can make something of this. If you just be quiet a spell and bite your tongue, zip your lip. So, hush while I think."* Al said. **"Let me ease your confusion, if I might be allowed. Cowlick, is block salt, placed in cattle pen as dietary supplement. What I said was, colic."** Changing topic, to give her brain cells much needed rest, he said. **"Can you imagine? I did not ask, how taste fest at work went today."** *"Oh! It was poorly received. Far from what I had at your house yesterday. Kind of like, soda losing fizz and goes flat. Onions lost crunch, for one. Tantalizing juices that saturated inner mouth's recesses, bringing delight to One's palate were not there."* She paused, eyes glinted with instant realization. *"It's that darned microwave. That's it, the freakin' microwave. I zapped it too long. Trying to heat entire thing through and through, all at once. I'm sure that's what it was."* She ended in triumph. Having solved riddle, of chicken ahwhadis let down. Al told her. **"You have to be careful with microwave ovens. Better units have heat level controls, timing options. Unlike cheaper workplace models. For warming that chicken, you needed big platter, so you could spread your stuff. Put it in for a minute, take out and sample how much has been absorbed. Then you can gauge how much longer you need to zap it. Important thing is, the food gets heated uniformly when it's evenly spread out instead of......."**

"Excuse me, sir." Said server, plopping the plate down impatiently. Al thought. *'There goes your gratuity ole chap.'* *"What is that."* Frannie asked. **"This is oxtail."** Al replied. *"Pass it here, let me have a go at it until the rest……"* **"No, let's wait until your din n e r c o m e s."** His voice trailed off, as he tried diffusing her anxiety. Too late. She already vacated her seat, took hold of the platter and sat herself down, with satisfied smile. Staring at the food, she asked. *"What is this thing, oxtail?"* Al told her. **"Bovine animals. Cows, bulls, it doesn't matter, it's their tail."** Now, wide eyed apprehensive, she began. *"But, you said 'Ox' before. Now, you're saying, cows and bulls. I don't know if... What's next, horses and buffaloes?"* He laughed, seeing other diners amused by her curious outburst. Tried calming her anxiety. **"Frannie! Frannie. Remember what you said when you ate and did not want to know what it was? Same thing applies here. It smells good? Taste and see if you like."** She retorted. *"Back then, stew could have been any animal or combination of. Rabbit, possum, snake or owl. Here, I am given menu that clearly reads. Goat, chicken and oxtail. Element not knowing, and not wanting to know, does not exist. Come on."* Her plate was served, with respect, almost genuflecting. *"Do enjoy mam. Anything else I can get you? Juice, water?"* In an obvious afterthought, he looked Al's direction. *"And you, sir. Anything else?"* Al told him. **"Water please, thanks."** Fixing Frannie a big grin, he rattled off juices available. She said. *"I'll have carrot. That's only thing I recognize. So it can't be that bad."* Turning to Al, she went on. *"In event it is bad, I am sure you won't let it waste. Why are you having water? Watching your pennies? I can go Dutch. Or better yet, I could treat you."* He told her. **"I would never take a woman out and go Dutch. Since today is not my birthday, I won't let you treat me. When that**

date comes around, if offer still stands. I will graciously accept. How's that?" Frannie did well at tasting, enjoyed curry and kept saying cow tail. Found slight similarity in taste, between jerk chicken and Al's concoction day before. He told her there was a smidgen of jerk seasoning in his chicken. Did not care to explain difference in cow tail and oxtail. Knowing this would confuse her, unending. In any event, he would not have patience. Explaining something he knew, she'd never get. Many Jamaicans don't know there's difference, much more what difference is or would be. Meal remnants were boxed and taken home. Frannie vowed having them before her stay was up. They drove in silence with their own thoughts. Frannie began dry coughing. Rummaged for her bottle, took a sip, then asked.*"Why are you quiet when driving, afraid being distracted?"* He slowly explained.

"Single backwoods lanes, as we are now doesn't bother me. Multi-laned highways would likely do. Moreso if there were raucous, gabbing, untrained tykes. They should be given distracting gadgets as a rule, for road tripping." *"I find it difficult to not talk."* Frannie began a slow response. Seeming to choose words, before continuing. *"You see, I was going to a fair with this boy from school. His licence was just upgraded to solo, he drove his mom's car. Moron began hugging me. I told him. "Cut it out, the light has changed." He still kept doing crap, rubbing my thighs. Doing spider crawl to my crotch. So, I whacked him ten times harder in his ear. Next thing I knew, the car rear ends a van. We were taken to hospital, where his parents came and police took statements. I don't know what story he told. But his dad ups and said to me. "Young lady. Don't you know better, than forcing someone to make out. Whilst* *that someone is in control of a motor vehicle?" I tell you now, I lost it and yelled at his dad. Your horny moron was trying to get his hands in my panties. I slapped Silly Willy, so he'd understand and stop!! You should have been there to watch his parents' face free fall. Cop smiled a 'Good for you, girl.' Told me he will finish the statement for me to read and sign. Shit like that, made me hating broomstick bearers. Broomsticks ever rigid, they're stupid ass morons. Since that accident, if I am riding front seat in a vehicle. I brake hard, every time it nears another vehicle. Sometimes, find myself shifting to one side. If like, a vehicle is merging on my side. I try to avoid these unconscious reactions, but soon as I am relaxed, it happens. If I am seated in back alone, then I am out of scrutiny. Other times when I am up front. I distract myself talking to the driver. It's even better when there's other riders. I can turn and speak to them. That way, I only look ahead if there's sudden braking. I'm damaged for life. If we had not put off our wedding. Frankie was going to get me professional help, through his job insurance. But that didn't happen either. So here I am all cracked up."* "Why did you guys plan on getting married, then call it off? How far along were the plans, or I should ask. How close was the date?" Al pried. *"We were less than a month from the date. I called it off, don't want to talk about it."* Frannie stridently declared. A silence was born and kept growing until she said. *"Now would be good time to tell me the cowlick story."* Thinking she meant, cow tail. Al began. **"Yes, it's cow tail or cattle but it's just…."** Caught himself, then said to her. **"Oh! you mean. It's not cowlick, it's colic. I already told you what's cow lick. Man invited woman out to dinner and show. She told friends, she was going to make sure, drain his wallet. Jamaicans say "nyam him out." They go in restaurant. She orders** numerous dishes, adds ice cream and fruit bowl. Surprised and amused. He asked her if she ever had colic before. Thinking it was something edible, she said, no. But will try it, soon as she finished her platters." *"That's it! Where's funny part you promised?"* Frannie queried. Al said. "Frannie, colic is acute indigestion, One gets. Ingesting copious amounts, different foods. Leading to irritable bowels syndrome." Frannie angrily retorted. *"And this guy was encouraging her to eat more?! Some men are just morons, plain and simple."* She guffawed. Al let the matter die. Sensing nothing positive could be achieved, prolonging this subject. *'How could she see it so lopsided?'* He thought, then quickly realized. All she saw, was man distressing a woman. Polish his ego, or find amusement at her discomfort. Strange, he never saw it from that perspective. She began.

"I wanted to do Aventura tomorrow. But a gang from work, going to Key West and I'm invited. Thing is, I don't trust young Turks. Not doing crap on that long, open, over the sea highway. Someone is bound to spider crawl up my thighs, or similar shit. Would you come along? That's only way I feel comfortable, being driven that far. I would fund expenses, if you let me. Please, let me. Please! Say, Yes." Frannie pleaded. This was as is said, a no brainer. Al asked. "Frannie. Why would this here old coot, want to road trip with young Turks? No way. Further, if I was going Key West. I want to be travelling both directions in broad daylight. That requires overnighting at hotel. That distance creates fatigue, and as someone said. "Nothing good happens on roads, after midnight." I say, nothing good happens after sunrise. So, it's a No and a No. We can stop at Haulover and you toe dip the ocean. It's same

water ebbing and flowing, never ending circle. **You could throw message in a bottle. Ask friends to retrieve it when they get there. Or we can go Biscayne Park and you do it there.**" *"I guess you're right, I'm not enthusiastic for it. I hope nothing untoward happens though. I hate losing any of my friends."* Frannie conceded in resignation. Later, she again tackled what was left of curried goat. After warming it, in one minute spots in the microwave. Al asked, what time she wanted to go North. She was undecided. He told her. **"I have to haul that thing to the recycling depot."** She voiced concern. *"That huge thing?! It's massive. How are you going to get it done by yourself? Don't ask me to help, I will not volunteer. I am house guest, not house slave. You know there are places you can call. Like junk people, that says."* **"Just point, and it's gone."** Al told her. **"I got an idea, from watching "Without a Trace." Perps found it hard to move a body intact. So what did they do? Why? Dismember and move it piece by piece."** Al beamed. Frannie's eyes bulged. *"My God!! That's a morbid idea, if ever there was one. You should not have mentioned, cutting up corpses and all that to me, as your house guest. Do you think that elevates my comfort level?"* Al quietly asked her. **"You want a ride to 312 Street? Many hotels down there that should reignite your comfort level. Or you going to call for your ride? Get it together, Frannie. Today is still Friday, but not thirteenth. I am going to unscrew these doors and take out the drawers. It should be light enough for me to slide outside."** Al tried consoling. She relaxed on the sofa in a calm reflective mood. Al went about doing odd things, then turned on the kitchen TV. Not wanting to disturb fragile Frannie. Set came alive in midst of "For a few dollars more." She slowly waltzed in and asked. *"You love those shoot em up movies too? What channel is that?"* **"It's 39-3 or 39-4."**

"Which cable service you subscribe to?" She asked Al, who mischievously replied. **"Channel Master Outback."** *"Never heard of them. Is it pay-per-view?"* **"No, it's watch per view. Gives about fifty-four channels, some in Spanish. Come, I show you."** As they entered the guest room, she gave him that dubious stare. He retracted blinds and pointed to the antenna, swaying gently in a soft breeze. She laughed and said. *"This is it? This is not cable. This went out from I was a child. Oh my God! I don't believe you. That's all, broadcast channels. Tell me you have internet. I need Wi-Fi to do something."* Al gave her the key, she connected and sat at the dining table with her laptop. Al turned TV's off and on, went to sit on the sofa. Later Frannie wanted pizza. Both sauntered cross street and bought. She told pizzeria clerk, reminded her ten times. **"Less cheese, all meat and well done."** Seeing her raise a finger to get clerk's attention. Al took her elbow and walked her outside. Assured her the order was written and given to the baker. He was a bit tiffed, as he thought. *"Give the beleaguered, underpaid woman a break. You did not add a tip, and stressing her on top of it."* He got an idea. Went in and told clerk, he would be watching from outside. Could she wave when the order is ready. She did and Al tipped her, two dollars after she gave Frannie the pie. She chomped heartily and wanted to know what was on TV. Al gave a partial rundown. **"There's Barney Miller, Seinfeld, Hill Street Blues, Twilight Zone, Alfred Hitchcock and Mannix on different channels."** Ever heard your toilet make a sudden thud, whoosh sound that will scare One to run? So it was, in hushed silence without an ahem or.... Frannie said. *"You know what hurt most? Them four chauvinist pigs tried blaming me for the accident. School was going to rescind his licence until he turned eighteen or graduated. Hearing*

was held in gymnasium. Vice Principal, Mr. Dickson and Miss Robotham, our Guidance Counsellor. Skills instructor and school's resource officer, sat stone faced. This was a court martial. I sat, trance like not listening. Because every time I had to relive the accident, it friggin' freaked me out. Next, I heard Dickson asking, what's my response to a question. Said, I'm sorry, I did not hear the question. He repeated. Did I regret my action? Which clearly was cause of the accident. Lord knows I wanted to tell them how I felt, but helpless tears began instead. So I told him. "Yes sir, I am sorry. So very sorry, it brings heartache and tears to my eyes." Miss Robotham raced over and hugged me. She sensed I was on brink getting in deep shit. Led me down the corridor. Said, she understood. I should have my cry, she would be back. She came and hugged me again, stroked my hair and.......gently massaged my back. It felt so gooood. She was only eight or nine years older. Knew her stuff, when it came to soothing. I held tight to her warmth. Refusing to relax my grip, as insecurity drifted away. She got me a pass and offered to take me home. Told her I wanted to saunter at the mall, clear my head. There was clash of emotions going on simultaneously. Hate for those four pigs and attraction to her. Had me in a wanting more mindset. She asked if I wanted to come to her house. She would give advice on dealing with emotional stress. I know, I jumped out of my skin saying yes. Hoped my eagerness was not betrayed. Then relaxed and thought. "So what?" She showered and changed into one of those tennis outfits, sort of. Sat beside me and said. 'Okay, tell me about your frustrations.' Told her about the accident and how I hated them for making it my fault. In the hugging and comforting, we kissed. Lightly at first then deep and satisfying. Oh God! My pleasure receptors came alive, in a way I never dreamed could happen. Soon after, we became lovers with a difference. For me, that is. I never dreamed, sex could be so heavenly. Without a broomstick thrust up my, you know what you call it. Don't look nonplussed. Roxanne told me about Jamaican men. Names they ascribe to woman's privates. Seems there's a never ending catalogue. I began college about three hours away. We were very good for two years, before trouble crept in. Like sidewalk crack that gets wider and wider. High school and college are different. Pace and work volume, deadlines and penalties, are night and day apart. Her having been through this not so long ago. I figured she understood, when I had to pass up a date. Or tell her, I had projects on a weekend. So, spare the trip until. I began seeing an emerging side of her, that was jealous and possessive. I stopped taking her calls, slowly weaned her from my system. Wasn't easy, but if I put mind and effort. It's done. That Thanksgiving, I went to friend's home and was introduced to her older brother, Frankie."

Al's curiosity bulb glowed inside his head. This was Frankie, he asked about and been shot down. Now, story was coming, without prompting. Well, he hoped. What he knew about Frannie, she would clam up without being provoked. Look how she started sharing this latest episode of her life without warning. He wonders. *"Does she fabricate?"* So, Frannie's saga goes on. *"Frankie and I got started. I immediately told him, what Uncle Beck advised as I sat on his knees. No broomstick in the honeycomb until wedding night, if there's a wedding. I needed space and time to think. Find my true sexual identity. This gave me both. I could compare and balance and all that stuff. It feels good to be in control. Start of semester, Monique from Haiti was new roommate.*

She contradicted what I thought I knew about Haiti. Foreign student no scholarship, boarding assistance, tuition. Yet, she wore good clothes. Not designer's, but good clothes. You wouldn't find her joining line at Wendy's or KFC. She was a subject, all by herself. Little by little, we grew on each other. Began our escapades. I am ashamed to admit this, because knew reason why. Inwardly cringed when we kissed. Always breaking free first, even as she clung to and pulled me back in. Saw it, knew why. Did similarly with Frankie, for different reason. Despite having agreed to abstain, until. He ever tried, working a broomstick event. Lord knows, I had to summon mental faculties. Keeping that Bulldog on tight leash. Once you let it slip even one teensy weensy bit. It's all over and beyond your control." Franny changed tack without warning and asked Al. *"Is that your cat or is it a stray? It's sick. See how it's coat moults in patches? And it's neither Hairless Elf or Sphynx. It's got to be suffering."* He replied. **"That puss is my neighbour's. My pussies are two legged like me. You know? Sapiens erectus."** *"Why do you enjoy making up inane stuff? There's no sapiens erectus specie. Why doesn't your neighbour take the cat to a vet?"* Al told her. **"Oh, he said it's nothing to be alarmed. Pussy is just stressed or disappointed."** They argued, long and vexed. *"Would it hurt for you to say, cat, instead of, puss?"* **"It's a Jamaican thing with some of us. We do not say, cat. Just go for, puss. British elementary primers, started with nursery rhymes, like. Pussy cat, oh pussy cat, where have you been. Also, ding dong bell, mama, pussy in the well. So we grew up with fixation on things pussy, including pussy cat. That's puss and pussy is our other favourite pet. But, so you understand, I do care. Said to neighbour, puss leads laid back lifestyle. He doesn't hunt for food, gets Chewy delivered frequently. Enjoys cool** when it's hot out and heat when it's cold in. What the hell has he got to be stressed about. That puss lives way better than some adults and most Jamaican pussies. He looked at me astonished and asked." *'Are you kidding me Al? You know they cut out the guy's balls at the shelter before giving him up for adoption? I don't know bout you, but if they cut my balls out at any stage of my life. And I not even getting chance to score? I'd be hoisting a 747 over my head, throwing it inside that shelter. How you think he feels, seeing girl cats go strolling by. And can't even signal them to hold up, cause he got something to say? I tell you Al. I couldn't live like that. Neither could you.'* Frannie bemusedly said.*"Your neighbour has broomstick disease, but not to worry. His best by date will catch up to him. Where the hell was I before, you and your....? Oh yes."* Al breathed a sigh of relief, swore the saga had come to an end. Was elated she again picked up the thread and went on. Very slowly choosing her thoughts. *"Any who. Frankie boy and Monique gave me rare opportunity to compare. As they say, apples to oranges. He was warm, attentive and, listen to this. You can see, sort of dilemma brewing. That would without doubt, create a situation down the road. I never told him I was a virgin, but if a woman says to you. No sex before marriage, and she's never been married. It's fair and reasonable for you to think she is One. Right? I mean, I told him exactly what Uncle Beck told me. Don't let any man burst your bubble, unless he has gold band to slip on your finger. No matter how you cut the cake. This was not going to be an easy swallow. Because, there's someone who knows something about you. That you don't want anyone else to know. Even if it's silly. My way, would have been to tell Frankie. Yes, I've done it since nursery school. But you're not getting in, unless. Given how I felt about men, generally. I was past caring. But on his side, to be fair. He should have been told from the get go, not a day later. Happens, Frankie began wearing himself down, trying to wear down my resolve. On our way home from a Colorado trip, he ups and said. Why don't we get married and have children, before we're older. Us loving each other the way we did. It was on my tongue's tip. Swear, I almost said. We? But, checked myself in time. Why be cruel without reason? Found myself stalemated. Monique holding out on, me holding out on Frankie. I'm getting older. What is my life going to be? I'm not teenager. Time is slipping away and none of my options guarantees happiness, so far. I'm trying to get Monique where Miss Robotham had me. She wasn't showing enthusiasm. Told Frankie I felt drained, sort of empty. After college and ups and downs bustle. I needed vacation before embarking on responsibility, being married and children. I've seen younger women, go into that family making thing. And bratty kids age them, right before your eyes. Focused getting his broomstick working, he readily agreed. Then added, we should take a cruise. Told him, I am not good swimmer. He said to me. 'You can't fly either but you go on airplanes.' Laughed himself into coughing spasms. With that remark, I decided there and then. It was over for me and Frankie. Honest to God. I was half minded doing vacation, then come back and try married life. That all went up in the clouds with his humourless wisecrack. So, I got this package vacation to Jamaica and it was fun, sort of. Thing was, it kind of took me to high school. When we went afar on Smithsonian educational trips, or bus to Hoover Dam. Maybe, I got a restless streak or something. But here was I, miserable on vacation. For which, I had paid good money. This young woman, with "Roxanne" stitched on her top. Asked if I wanted to participate in water sports activities. She seemed 19 or 20, but had to be older. What with required training and going through certification process. She was fresh, firm and seriously handsome. I gave her signals. She gave some of her own, but you know. She has to be careful on extent socializing with guests. Gave me her number, said she knows safe places. Freedom to kickback, go touring and have an enjoyable time at reasonable price. After coming back, couldn't get her off my mind. Called her up. Said she could get days off. We've been going for over three years. We agreed, she has to see her folks once a month. There are times, she sees them an entire month. I'm left alone, experiencing feeling of abandonment. Although, there are times. Thinks I'm expecting too much. But what the hell, that's way this world turns. Everyone has got to be put out by someone. Miss Robotham, Monique, Frankie what the…….. All this time, I'm getting older. Off to bed, good morning. See? It's almost three o clock. Come here, hug."* They walk away, she calls. *"Hey, just so you know. Lesbians only hug each other that way, not a male. Similarly, homo men hug the way you do. They would not hug a woman like that. Opposites do not always attract. Just letting you be aware. Night, night and do sleep tight."*

That farewell should have been morning, morning. But who in their right senses, says such awkward things and not get an eye roll. Or finger twirl by the ear, suggesting One is going off the rails. As Archie Bunker says, being a Dingbat. So naturally, they stayed each in his her bed later than usual. Reversed order of the saying. Early to bed early to rise. Frannie came into Al's bathroom unannounced and asked. *"Got any swabs here? It's a good wager, you honestly don't know. How do you function among this scattered pile of odds, evens and ends?"* Al, pointedly said. **"Good morning Frannie. Slept well? Did bed bugs keep you awake? You know, that's always an incentive going to bed late? They have less time to puncture and suck. We always rap at a closed door before barging in. How would you like my coming in your room, and it so happens. You're still in state of partial, or maybe total undress?"** *"Oh, you would love that. Wouldn't you Mr. Happy Al? Saw that gleam of anticipation in your eyes as you asked the question. What could I do if you did? It is your house. I am here at your pleasure. Although I sense, you'd love to make it, for your pleasure. Now, if I were down at the Hylton. I would crack your skull, then strip and holler, rape. Management would write me a cheque, fire your ass and yet. Someone said, this world is a happy place. Do you mind my looking for swabs in the garbage collage? I promise, this place will appear way better than it is now."* Frannie found swabs, made herself pretty and left when her ride honked. She returned to find Al laughing at Kramer's antics. His telling a woman, who had a nose job. *'You got butchered.'* Which is just how Elaine and Seinfeld thought, but were afraid to say. **"Hmm, didn't know that was still being run."** Frannie slowly remarked. Al squelched laughter and told her. **"I told you, it was one of my favourites. Cosmo Kramer is funniest guy on that show. Elaine is pretty and witty, she's two for. Like J. Peterman's speech parlance. Could call it an idiolect. Screaming George and Newman. I like soup Nazi and Babu Bhatt the Pakistani restaurateur. Elaine's father is likeable and Uncle Leo is up there in the top three. George and Doug's father-in-law, Arthur. Yells by script for no reason. What's with this neurotic obsession with ranting and raving for comedy and laughs? Not even**

half man yells. I would understand if he did, being relegated to half man. Know something Frannie? The actress who plays, Harper sibling's mother. Is quite a matured looker. I could go for in a serious way. Don't get me started on Charlie's Psychiatrist. Her aquiline face is quite the humdinger. Do these women know they are admired by fans? I say, they do. Hence, steps taken to keep their homes and contact data secret." Frannie stared at Al and said. *"Al, I hope if I live long I can find better ways to tickle my funny bone. Than to be amused by soap operas. Oh, they're situation comedies, sitcoms. Wasted talents, but rents get paid. Some do live grand style. Keep forgetting, you're not bottled water fan. Forgot to snatch a six pack or…I need a good swallow of clean purified water, before I retire. Keeps urinary tract clean, fresh smelling. Woman has to survive work day and not worry about odours. You know what I'm talking about?"* Al snickered and said. **"I don't have that odour problem, that scares you. My structure was not designed to conceal."** Frannie sharply rebutted. *"You are misery with barbed tongue I must ignore. From your mouth to God's ears, if only…."* She scolded with a finger pointed in warning. Before going off to get tap water. Standing still with that tumbler. Al thought. *"Is she praying?"* Frannie went to bed, there were no exchange of wishes. Al went and caught "Alfred Hitchcock presents." Sunday morning came down. Frannie brewed coffee. Al did a pot of old fashioned oats with cranberries, raisins, cinnamon, nutmeg and honey, without sugar or salt. After his meal, he got ready going North with Frannie. She lolled melancholy and easy like Sunday morning. Al urged her. **"Let's be making a move Frannie."** *"Let's wait a bit."* She said. **"What for?"** Al asked. *"Oh, you know that get up and go* *kick you get in your head. When you really want to do something? That's what I'm waiting for. Won't be long now. I can feel it maturing, but it ain't rippling yet."* Al stifled a question, but thought. *"Talking bout your gut or your head?"* **"Come sit beside me, here. You know I like you?"** Frannie said, rubbing Al's pate.They sat silent three minutes, during which his emotions rose, ere Al said. **"Frannie, I have to go in the lull, while Sots are at water holes imbibing. Get us back home before they get over sated. Driving amok through red lights, and straddling two lanes.** There was no response from Frannie. After five minute's silence, he said. **"If you're a good girl."** Knew it was a faux pas that would convey unintended message, but continued anyway. **"I'm going to take you for pepper steak at P.F. Chang's in the Falls. Girlfriend guided me there recently. I have to tell you. I am not beef person. That steak and house made ginger beer went to my pleasure zone. Almost like good bout of sex would."** She just stared at him, not saying a word. He rued. *"I knew it was shit, but once I started, couldn't stop."* He went on. **"Week after, I'm going to another year end PE&G function. If your mom is at work, I might see her."** He had jaw drop moment when Frannie replied.

"She is not my mom. She's my aunt, who was court ordered to adopt me. After my mom was taken from us." **"Oh, I am sorry to hear that. How old were you when she died? Was she ill, or was it an accident, or…?"** *"She ain't dead, my father is. She killed him before I was born. What I know, is what Uncle Beck told, and showed me an old family photo. Uncle Beck is really my grandfather. My parents, were his children in truth and…"* **"Rassclawt!!"** Al unconsciously exclaimed. *"Say what was that now?"* Frannie asked. **"No, nuh, no, is not nothing. I mean. Is not anything."** Al stuttered. *"Yes, it is someth….you said a word there. What*

did you mean?" Frannie pressed for answer. Fearing she would clam up, Al said.**"It's colloquial Jamaican phrase, expressing surprise."** Mollified, Frannie went on. *"Mom went fishing with big brother, who was over eighteen. She was almost fourteen, a pretty child. Uncle Beck said, he loved and took very good care of her, his only daughter. His woman at the speakeasy, kept saying. He was not father of his daughter. She belonged in truth to a Bean Farmer. He used to bring telegrams from Western Union, back in the day before they stopped. He paid no mind and always laughed it off. So, along comes this young man. Shows mom a pond pool, where fishin' was best. He was older than her brother by couple years and began. You know? Trying to do stuff. He be laughing, touching and tuggin' at her clothes. So, she's kickin' and hollerin' for her brother. He comes runnin, she's glad.' Tells her, hold still, not make it harder. Can you believe that crap? Then, when Murty got done. Her own brother, jumped on her and had his way. She was done fightin' for good. Jest laid there and wept her eyes dry. Murty was gettin' ready for another go at her. She ran and met old Dan, the trapper. He let her wash herself some. Then took her home and told Uncle Beck. Them boys done did something wrong. Well now, Uncle Beck lay awake. Trying to figure things out. How he can make one boy be lost, but not other. And kinfolk having things to say. Always knew, the boy was not made up in his head. Couldn't believe he would do this to his sister. That riled uncle Beck pretty bad, but he thinking of a way out to savage his own son. You know, teachers got nose for chronic sadness in children. Questions got asked. Answers came tricklin' from neighbours and kin. Soon, boys were taken to jail. Got sent home on bail, and mom's brother took coaching her. What* *she should say and not say, or else. She cried to her papa, told him, she felt ugly. Only head, belly and scrawny legs. You figure she was mentally distraught, damaged, One would say. Uncle Beck says, way it was shaping up. Mom was farm Hen that squats and lifts her tail, when seeing Roosters coming. His son, now slept outside in the old shed. One night my mom crept in. Took herself a good kindlin' plank and bashed her brother's head in. Tried to hide her crime, for a time, wasn't suspect. But her hand ballooned from the shive. You know, like a splint stuck deep in her palm? Rest was easy. Funny thing is. She never got bailed after Sheriff took her in. Been behind bars ever since. Life just ain't fair overall, but more so when it comes to men and women. It's man's world they say. Well, let them f… each other and be happy. Leave women out of it. Don't bother reminding, I speak only for me. I already know that."* **"I am sincerely sorry to hear of your loved One's travails. You are stronger than you know. I can imagine your pain."** Al said, not wanting to say too much. Leave a tender moment alone, the song sings. Trying to milk her whilst she could be, he timidly asked. **"Your cousin now. One who played doctor. Was he really a cousin or…?"** *"All I can truthfully tell you is. There are lots of questions, I want to ask about kinfolks, but I don't. Know why? Every time I ask. Uncle Beck hesitates, then slowly relates. End up wishing I hadn't asked. With my folks, knowledge brings pain that never goes away. I'm thinking of going to Colorado and be by my mom when she gets released next year. You would think, yeah, and encourage me. Not so fast my friend. That too has it's share of problems. Mom keeps talking about my marrying nice man. Give her grandchildren. She has unspent maternal wealth to lavish and dote on them. She doesn't understand, or know, how I live and why. Truth is, neither* *do I. But things will be revealed one day or night. When we least expect, comes a surprise. You know what I feel? Our stars could be aligned. Were it not for you born too early or me too late. But, stay close to me. I've got an inklin', your wildest dream could come through. Come on, give me one of your cloak hugs. Feels like energy transfusion. Swear, in your heyday you were a flamin' Olympic torch, despite wind gusts and rainstorms. When you gonna tell me about your life? For how long you lived? Island man? You gots to have history. I'll bet you walked on the wild side."* Sunday was going great for Al. Luckily, his numerous pinch spots stayed invisible to the eye. Being coloured has advantages at times. It was shaping up to be, stay-at-home Sunday. Al was not going to seek confirmation in any form. He deemed Frannie a chameleon, which although he focused on. Hoped she was headed a certain plateau. Sensed, she could have trait of an evil instinct. Lurking behind that good girl persona. That joke about cracking his skull, then hollering rape and getting hush money. Is not a scenario to be overlooked. Coming as it were, without study or deliberation. In situations such as this, One should tread lightly. Studies other person's eyes and features generally, for betrayal of intent. Al never hesitated to tell male friends. Women are always smarter than men. Dumber they seem, smarter they be. His dad cautioned him early in life. Listen when someone speaks. Most times, what is meant, but not being said. Comes out clearer than what is being said. Women are as diverse collectively, as men are basically the same. *"You want to go first, or can I?"* Frannie asked. **"Where are we going, dear Frannie. And one leading the other?"** Al seemed genuinely confused. *"I am asking, who wants to shower first, with ten minutes between. So, water doesn't go cold. If both showers run at once."* She explained.

Al told her. **"That has never been a feature of this house, I've noticed. What led you to think it might be?"** *"In our apartment, that's how it is. Figured that was how plumbing worked in upstairs houses, as a rule."* Al showered before bed, had no intent doing so again at this time. Reading Frannie's question as veiled order, he does. Pleasantly agog at assumed reason, he obeyed. Caught in mental flux. In happy belief and scorned disbelief, chiding Self for presumption in extreme. Brushed teeth, again. Asked Self many questions. If Frannie, having abandoned her outing, had significance for him. What ploy should he use to find an answer. He hated it when he assumes and gets rebuffed, as happened with Elaine. He came from bathroom and jumped out his skin. Seeing Frannie propped on two pillows, watching TV. Quite casually said to him. *"I did not know they still showed Barney Miller. I watched reruns and it's being re-rerun again? Characters are more life like and sharp on your TV. Arcade box in your guest room is an insult. Or maybe, it's part of your ace plan, luring guests to your quarters. Well, it worked. Here am I. Do not hesitate to climb aboard, it's your bed. One notch up, for your genius."* Foreplay and fifthplay, were too drawn out, by any measure of intimacy. Call it insecurity or cold feet. Al, of all persons. Found himself goaded by Francine. *"Consider yourself young Olympic hopeful, trying harder to qualify for finals. So give it your best shot, or stay in spectator section."* Frannie whispered, which mode she adopted and he followed suit. Monkey see, monkey do. *"I hate being deep kissed, so don't go past my lips."* **"Hmm, mmm."** Al stroked and massaged. *"You got mitten on? Don't want your pus invading my clean urinary tract. Might be best you doubled up, like grocery stores."* Frannie told Al, who replied. **"It's not mitten, it's boots or nylon stockings. And you don't ever double bag."** *"Why not? Got to be safer having a back* *up. Some of those things are extremely thin. Give the male more satisfied experience. Always about the male and what makes him freakin' happy."* Al feared she was going off track, testily denouncing men. Definitely a mood killer, at this pivotal juncture. Truthfully, he didn't expect in a million years, to be where he was at. Not with a Lesbian. **"Frannie."** Al began. **"Rubbers are made to adhere to skin. Most times they stay adhered, despite vigorous push'n'pull. They are not designed to adhere to each other. Trust me on this. Put one rubbers over another. First stroke, it slides right off. Goes jaywalking over the clean fresh tract. Will quite likely hang around too, enjoying ambience."** She ignores his gabbing and prods. *"You ole dog you, knows all the tricks. I'm not there yet, soothe me till the woman in me loses inhibitions. I know you got tricks up your sleeve. Don't be afraid. Get creative. Working hands can be abrasive and calloused. Nails hold crap. Best you try a little tenderness. Roxanne tells me, some Jamaican men make up for..."* Al interrupted. **"I know what Roxanne told you. I am no musician. Won't get me playing skin flute."** *"Skin flute, what kind of instrument is that?"* **"Opposite of bonophone, played by some women."** He said, smirking aside, unseen. **"You think hands are abrasive? Moustaches and beards are worse than steel wool."** Frannie whispered. *"What beards and...?* Al told her. **"During recital, beard becomes the pelvic pad. Moustache is the womb broom."** Pausing, she asked. *"Are those, Jamaican colloquial phrases expressing something queer?"* **"No, Frannie. Those phrases defines Barbershop Quartets."** *"Do not distract my mental fixation, it's about to work in your favour."* Frannie cautioned Al. He felt a slipping away from his tenuous grasp. Decided, speech is silvern, silence golden. So he worked in that mode and made for an invasion of the pleasure parlour. Frannie seized broomstick with urgency, making light feather like strokes on outskirts. Al whispered. **"I know it's not Christmas, but baby it's cold outside. Mr. Dicky wants to go where it's warm. Helps his circulation, keeps him alive and kicking. Else he withers and wilts."** Frannie laughed. *"And here I was, being considerate. Thinking he's likely to faint from over exertion."* Al tried another tact. **"Used to be, he could stand idle for quite some time, but lately. Quicker he gets into warmth, longer he stays in service. I'm telling you seriously. Take it from me, I should know. He's about ready to wilt like a sunflower at six. Or as Cosmo told his audience. "Like a frightened turtle."** She'd been primed, had sprung many times. Made no response. Simply snuggled her head into half a pillow, shoulders on another. Al used other half of pillow to elevate his head, staving off apnea. Laid on his side facing her on her back. Gently cupped nearest breast in his palm. She sighed and shuffled deeper. A man does not turn his back on a sleeping woman on her back. Having slept some, Al awoke. Immediately traced a hand down her? Which was gently arrested. Clasped firmly with hers, mid chest. Soon, Monday dawned. They laid in abject silence, she said. *"My nipples are heavenly tender. You work breasts like a sundae straw. Can't you now?"* Al barely replied, distracted by persistent, low keyed headache. Brought on by anticipation and disappointment. Mornings after some nights before, should be. Usually is for him, a time of ecstasy and mental reveling. He could not reconcile, having been so close to paradise, and yet been denied entry. Told himself, keep the dialogue alive. Maybe it leads to a revival of latent emotions. Now, he told her. **"Well, I was not an early weaner. Nursed for as long as I could. Years after I got separated from** mama. Miss Candy took me over. I'm glad you got a thrill from." *"Was Miss Candy your sitter?"* "Oh yes, she was. Tell me. You ever slapped a guy during sex?" *"What do you mea…? Why would I slap a man having sex?"* Frannie asked. "A female pastor on TV, says it's done. When the sex is so good, woman goes into a trance. Loses control and starts thinking. He might be tempted, giving another woman a taste. Imaginary anger makes her slap him." *"Don't believe everything you see on TV. Some channels are cable versions of National Enquirer, but. What is your point?"* "You could experience ecstasy that gives rise to. It's not too late. I am ready to oblige and be slapped silly." *"Walk with me, go shopping for breakfast staples."* Frannie urged Al, indicating she was done with that subject. Case closed. Chagrined he gritted teeth, took comfort the day was not done. Could be opportunities ahead. She fixed eggs and bacon, convinced Al. *"One breakfast won't clog your arteries. Fridge the oats, let's enjoy something together. I like essence of us across from each other. Small round table fosters togetherness and eyes contact."* Al made a sandwich and held it up. "This is essence of how I see us. Not across from, but…." Rest left unsaid. As they feasted, Frannie relived night past. *"It's an overused cliche, but in this instance it's true. Last night was not you, it was all me. I could not bring myself into heat with you. You should visit Colorado, super nice with mountains, like those in Jamaica. Thing is, you are stuck in my head, way Uncle Beck is. You know? Older with that frightening air about you. Reading my lie, even if I deny. Uncle Beck put me on his knees and asked a question. He looked at me looking away, and I had to answer truthfully. You scare me, I'm afraid of you. Your eyes, even for brief glance, unsettles me. Mostly, it was seeing you as Uncle Beck. Who might be my father, that worked against us. Know something? I'm glad I was once again in control. Listen up and understand my plight. It's been said. Uncle Beck was, was not mom's father. Did my mother kill her brother? Is Uncle Beck my grandfather? Knowing answers to these questions would mean a lot. Although he's no longer alive. I've been told there's affordable testing that can unearth truth. But as always. Hesitate and I do fear. Truth will also bring unpleasantness. So, what would you say to me in all this?"* Al thought about her situation. Well, he tried very hard. His brain was stuck trying to solve his situation. Having been close to promised land, was loath to keep walking away. Maybe he should try relaxing her mind, ease her tensions. He figured she's, as "Pink" sang. Not broken just bent. Therefore, straightenable. Needs a good Smithy with deft skills. He began.

"You know Frannie, tracing your genealogy. You might find, wanton murderers and dangerous psychopaths. You might find revered saint. One who cared for indigents, or other good, kind hearted folks. But they are gone from this earth. Whilst you would take pride, being descendant of them that society embraces. You would strive, distancing yourself from thieves and pillagers. If I were you, I would focus on now. Make effort at best of what I am and now know. No element of generational history, should be made to impact how you live and shape future existence. I would advise, begin by making your truth known. Rather than hang on until it's no longer relevant. Like with your mom. Visit her. Say, maybe there will not be grandchildren. Because... Courage is always better than cowardice. One, is telling mom truth like it is. So she can have space to adjust expectations. Other, has her hanging to this dream of happy ever after. Whilst you

stare in her face and wonder how best to tell her what she doesn't know. Uncle Beck told you things you had a right to know. But he did so at an age where he thought you could handle it. He was not going to ever keep truth away from you. He just wanted you to develop a resilience to painful truth." Frannie sat deep in thought. Al, burdened with unsated desires, figured the timing was impecca, pecca, peccable for a move. He gently stroked her hair, kissed her forehead. Did an Eskimo nose kiss, then her lips. Taking her forlorn eyes, for absence of mental resolve. He gently laid her down. Lightly stroked tip of each breast in turn. She shuddered, closed her eyes. He kept working, kissed her navel and tickled with tongue tip. As a hand went caressing, slowly, slowly, moving on down. She sat upright like a corpse in rigor mortis and blurted. *"It's just that I think, and know. Someone, somewhere, somehow f…ed up my life and I don't really know who or how. Sometimes I wonder if I am part of my problem."* Al rejoined. **"Stop trying to figure five W's. Who, when, why, what, where. Only thing that matters is simply. You and Self alone has master key, unlocking solutions to your problems. Discovery stage is done, it's time for remediation. You can do this, you are woman."** He trudged in defeat to the kitchen. Began wiping stove top and counter, free of oil splatter and washing dishes. When woman sees man as old family icon. There's no way, she's going to accept him as lover. Foreplay brings sensuous ecstasy. Once he begins making progress. Time to get a grip, smother flaming candle. And so another escapade ends. One person expressing regrets. Other experiencing elation, and disappointment. Finding it hard to believe he got that far, with Lesbian, of all persons. Check mark. Despite not attaining lofty goal of reformation. Having a youthful source of comfort in his corner. Al experienced elation, getting where he did. **"Know something Frannie? I just realized, there's added incentive to visit you in Colorado. Years ago, Clyde McPhatter sang about leaving his girl down in Denver, missing her terribly. Trying to reach her on the telephone. Last time I heard, he was packing his bags and getting there on the double."** Al said to a glum Frannie, in effort at cheer. Seems the effort was lost. She looked up at him with lazy eyes, asked. *"Who is Clyve?"* **"Not Clyve. Clyde McPhatter, was first lead singer of Drifters. When he left, Benjamin Nelson aka Ben E. King took lead."** She resumed her nonchalant demeanour. Trying possibly to get grip on inner fortitude to face adversities. She began. *"I've been meaning to ask, but didn't. Because it might not make sense. I have been revisiting my ears and I heard what I heard. When we walked into the restaurant, a woman said to you. Her sister did not bring the chewing sticks when she came. Then you kind of pretended it wasn't important. Was that something, I'm not to know about, or….?"* Al replied. **"Chewsticks are Neem tree twigs. Cut in about three inches length, sold in small bundles. First, an end is chewed to make a brush and sudsy foam to brush teeth. Some folks use it to avoid chemicals found in toothpaste."** Frannie said. *"Oh! You're talking about faggot packs. Monique used those. I figured it was….How do I put this, this….? Once, Roxanne and I went to fun place in Jamaica. Whilst waiting our bus, we shared a tender moment and someone in a passing car, yelled at us. "Faggots!!" We got into a fight with ourselves, when I asked her. What did we have in common with bundled sticks. She told me, "faggot" is slang for male homosexuals and has nothing to do with sticks. I tried telling her, a bundle of sticks is called a faggot. Having nothing to do with people, but she got….."* Her ride honked, six minutes early. She was ready and truncated her response, ran out the door. Now, Al was confused about this faggot business. He went to usual source, Google. Sure enough, Frannie was right. Next question in his mind was. Why would someone yell "faggot" at two women, embracing and sharing a tender moment? That term is usually applied to males, but who knows. Times and things do change, making our knowledge redundant at times. As Frannie's perfume rode the wind, long after her hurried exit, he again reflected on her persona.When young woman pursues and attains punctuality. One should admit that's huge positive for her score chart. As she bade goodbye, again reminded. Not disappoint, ignoring invitation to visit Colorado. When settled she will send contact information. Al, Roxanne and Francine, frolicking in Colorado highlands? He began anticipating the trip. Curious as to whether or not he could get close to and excite Roxanne, as he did Francine. Thoughts galloping fast apace. Al recalled Seinfeld episode. George asked, girlfriend agreed to menage a trois with him and her roommate. Wondering if he could somehow pull that off. Sanity returned and the idea seemed a script. For another episode of "Dateline's" "Without a trace." Them two would not hesitate to put cement boots on Al and drop him in a frozen lake. Was there not an episode where Elaine seduced a homosexual dude, or came close doing so? Al asked himself and the wind. Is Frannie ever going to be settled? Is she a victim? If so, of what or whom? Herself, maybe? Her troubles were born long before she was. Was mom, Uncle Beck's child, or Bean farmer's? A brother, helping to rape his sister and whetting his Popsicle in the candy bowl? That's frigid. Yet, stranger things do happen.

Chapter Afterword

Readers of previous editions have zeroed in on this particular chapter, citing some level of obfuscation in the family structure and wonders if this is deliberate. Truth is, in any story that's told. What piques curiosity is most times, not what's been told. Rather, it is that iota of detail, left to One's imagination. Read again, Frannie's words as the chapter nears it's end. *'Listen up and understand my plight. It's been said, Uncle Beck was, was not mom's father. Did my mother kill her brother? Is Uncle Beck my grandfather? Knowing answers to these questions would mean a lot.'* There is a work in progress, to develop this chapter into a motion picture manuscript. It all hinges on success of this book, so stay tuned.

Different strokes--different Folks-4

Week and half later, Al Parsons went to PE&G's end of year function. Usual cook out of varying cuisines. Most popular fare was, jerk chicken and festival by master Chef, Carmine. Although recently retired, Al hobnobbed with invited retirees. Introduced to new hires and laterally promoted supervisors. New acquaintances mingled with in festive mood, including Belinda. She corralled Al and others at group table, with overt determination that had him thinking. *'What's Belinda up to?'* Looked across at her with a knowing smile. *'If you only knew who spent a weekend at my house and how much she told me. Oooh la la.'* She gabbed motor mouth, asked for and gave phone numbers. Another week or two went by. Al forgot about party and those he met. Until Belinda called, greeting effusive as if they were ever best friends. All endless gabfesting and hilarious knee slapping laughter. Then she said. ***"I am inviting you to mom's New Year's Eve party. Let me give you the address."*** Al now realized what the grand roundup was about. Said, without hesitation. **"I can't accept your invite. I am unable to attend."** *"Why can't you come?! What's the problem?"* She asked. He asked. **"If I had said, Yes, I'll come. Would you have asked, why? No. You wouldn't. You would have taken my answer and run with it. Having said, No. You should do likewise."** She got agitated and argued. *"I don't understand. What is your problem? You don't have a wife. You're divorced and all alone. What better can you find doing, than among friends on New Year's Eve, for a little celebration?"* Oh, that rasped his last nerve. He told her why. **"Truth is, I avoid places where, in heat of revelry. Folks are likely to start firing guns in air."** She went berserk. *"So, what you saying?! I live in one of them shithouse neighbourhood, and you live where Mr Man? Pine-f...in-crest?"* Al yelled back at her. **"Well, I don't know if where your mom's at is shithole. But Shangri-f...in-la it sure ain't. So, chill being a Bitch."** Then, he abruptly disconnected the call, thinking. *'The gall of her. We weren't friends when I was on the payroll and we just ran into each other back there. So it's nice to be considered for an invitation. But if a person says, no. It means they don't want to be there. For whatever reason.'* Still pissed about the verbal clash, Al decided to call a mutual best friend.

"Hi, Cynthia. I heard Belinda's keeping a New Year's Eve party. Are you going?" *"Hi, Al. How you doing? No, I was not invited. So I won't be there. Even if I had been, I would have to decline. Anyways, Belinda would not have invited me to her party. She's at that stage of life, where she's horny and broke. Ain't nuttin' I can do for her. Were you invited?"* **"Yes, she just called and….."** *"So you're going?"* He related the call and ensuing conversation. Ultimate petulant outburst from Belinda and his response. Al's adult children, all women. Told Al, he was rude. No One wants to be told, they live in a crime ridden neighbourhood. Even if they are aware they do. Like a parent, knows their child is a terror. Yet resents anyone telling them this to their face. It's called diplomacy, tact and consideration of other people's feelings. So there, verdict is in. Al is chastised and shamed. He thinks they are both of kind. Belinda should've exercised tact and diplomacy, after the invite was declined. Gracefully refrained from asking why. He did apply diplomacy by saying, she would not have queried a reason, if he had said, yes. So why query for reason, because he did not accept, as anticipated? She should have, as is sometimes said. "Quit, while ahead." She brandished proverbial knife. Reminding him he was divorced. Living his sad existence, isolated and alone. He took out his Uzi and laid it on the table. Both had bruised egos, and fair is fair. But as one daughter advised. *"Be nice dad. Because, in circle of life you never know."* That ship having sailed without him, brought Mr. Acker Bilk's, "Strangers on the Shore" to mind. Al took out his phone and got the music going, thanks to YouTube.

Later he called Florence to arrange their first meet and greet. Stranger things have happened, but this saga began when she went home. St. Croix, US Virgin Islands. Met neighbours at a party and made photo introductions of families. Opening the phone screen wider she stared, then. *"This gentleman looks like someone I see quite often, walking by the Airbase with purpose."* She was told. **"That's my dad. He lives nearby and sometimes goes power walking that route."** Not believing in coincidence, she said she would like to meet him when she returns to Fort Myers. They exchanged texts, he sent her songs and then he called. Suggesting a Sunday hang out by Biscayne Park. For a *"Getting to know you, getting to*

***know all about you. Getting to like you, hoping that you'll
like me."*** Excerpting song from "The King and I" by Julie
Andrews. Flo said, that suited her fine. He could come by her
house. ***"I live close by the fire station on Asquith Street. I
will text you my address."*** He found the texting effort strange.
Why not tell him? She knows where she lives. Doesn't have
to look it up. It's simple street and number. What did he
know? He never heard from her all week, until Sunday at
twilight. She had been busy with this and that. Come over to
her house. They'll make an evening of it. ***"I am texting you
my address, as we speak."*** Al got to an apartment building.
Right then and there he decided going home. If she called
later, he would say he couldn't find the address. Reneged on
second thought, called from parking lot. She gave apartment
number. Greeted at the door. Feeling piqued, he ignored her
outstretched arm and hugged her. Handed over an all meat,
less cheese, well done pizza he brought. He was not a pizza
person, but having sampled Francine's, he did now and then.
She brought out plates and tumblers. Poured tankard of apple
juice for him, her, a zippy cup. He chuckled, she asked reason.
He told her, in his wild oats era. He'd put mugs of Cydrax,
Peardrax or Babycham at her disposal. Whilst he contentedly
sipped a pip all evening. She looked at him, narrow eyed.
Asked in a soft, reprimanding voice. ***"So you're saying, I am
trying to get you drunk on apple juice. So I can take
advantage of you?"*** Now, he laughed, but made serious
comparison to demijohn versus noggin. She made no
response on that theme, tension crept in. Each chomped on
pizza. They grinned, gabbed about this, that and things
between. Talk, touched a touchy subject, for him. In male
circles, he got grins, fist bumps and. ***"Dawg, when me grow
up, me want be like you."*** Women, mostly made efforts at

synthetic smiles. Faces showed discontent or resentment. She volunteered, having three daughters. Raised by her, single mother. All three went on to great careers, so on and so forth. Y'all remember that drug buy scene. *"I got my stuff close by too. What about you, where you got your stuff?"* This was kinda reminiscent of. I tell, you tell me, and our story continues as Florence asks Al. *"What about you, how many you got?"* Dialogue gets interesting, as Al hems and haws. **"Well, well, jury kinda still out on that."** He replied. *"What do you mean, the jury is out? You don't know how many children you fathered?"* She asks, fixing him glare of incredulity. Undaunted, he soldiers on. **"Well, see now. You know it's been said. Mama's baby, Papa's maybe. There was a father who told his son, he can't marry love of his life. Because 'The girl is you sister but you mama don't know.' Then later, boy's mama told him. 'You daddy ain't you daddy but you daddy don't know. See?"** *"Yes, I've heard that. But come on, you must know how many you acknowledged as your own."* She pressed him, with a smile that he saw was really a frown. He stared her in both eyes, went on. **"It's always at times, difficult. Because, every time I think I got it down pat. Uncertainty creeps in from most unlikeliest of sources. Like presently, young man in Canada. I knew his mom from way back. One of my daughters saw him on Facebook. Told me he resembles my son. Her brother who lives in New York."** *"So were you two dating? Was she at any time, your girlfriend?"* **"Not in the....She was her boyfriend's girlfriend. I was her sister's boyfriend."** *"So, you're saying you were dating both sisters?"* **"No, not really. It was like dating one and doing two."** She lapsed into deep concentrating silence, Al said. **"Director just yelled "Cut!" So, I am doing a bathroom break."** She directed him to bathroom, he went in and tinkled. Cleansed hands with single use alcohol towelette. Came out and said. **"You know. I went to a girlfriend's house once. After hand washing thing. Dried them on a towel, like the triple set you have in your bathroom. Oh, she was vexed stiff. Said those were for show. I should have used paper towel from the box. How was I supposed to know these things? I've been married twice. My wives did not do towels for show. Towels were to be used and changed when soiled."** Sensing reproach on her brow, he hastened to add. **"Oh, I did not use your show towels."** Thought telling her he did cleanse hands and how, but then decided.*'What the hell, she already sees me as large lowlife. Anything else I can say will not be to my credit. No use spritzing perfume over stink. Let stink ride.'* Having never resumed sitting, he told her. **"Look at that, eight-o-clock already. Time does fly when you're having fun. I'm sure, as a working girl. You need your whole night's rest. Unlike me who can sleep all day if needs be, in my state of retirement."** She agreed, too quick. *"Yes, I do have a few things to get done, before going to bed."* He strode over, repeated greeting scene. Her holding out arm, he getting a hug going. Al hasn't heard from Florence since. He kinda half expected he would not. Took this outing as a serious lark. He went to this visit, feeling somewhat cantankerous, because. After making initial contact and promising to text her address. Never did, until the eleventh hour. She seemed hesitant going through with meet and greet. Obviously, had to think whether she should disclose her address. Having decided, she left out a crucial part. So, Al went in, determined to be a coot and not give a dam. I do agree with you. If he felt that way, having reached and found directions incomplete. Should have turned back and if asked, why he did not show. Say he could not locate the address as it took him to an apartment complex. While he of course was searching for a single unit place. Put the shame ball in her court, end the charade. But…people and their foibles. Al is at a happy existential phase, where he doesn't have to lie, pretend. Or use diplomacy and tact with some people. Growing up, he lied like the horse's back foot to escape a whipping. Yearned for day, he could say to someone. "Yes, I ate, said, did it." And not fear being whupped. Diplomacy, he had to use with business clients. Except when he cussed British dude in the restaurant. He thought, being a drug runner and wealthy from. Gave him licence to disparage peons, like Al. Who brought him down a peg, even if there was no substance to. This then was his era of coming into his own. Saying what he meant and meaning what he says. It's not an existence of complete disregard. Situations yet arises, where, as lore teaches. One has to bite their tongue and swallow phlegm, instead of expunging at will. You never want woman you're interested in, asking. "You're married? Why didn't you say, when we discussed relationships?" Goes, without being voiced. Curiosity has now been piqued. Regarding boyfriend's girlfriend and sister's boyfriend. It really was quite conundrum, surpassing what is usually referred to as a love triangle. To extent, it boggles One's mind, participants cooperated, making it real.

Males were, Al, Harry, Devon, old man Rupert. Females were, Beverley, Dawn, Penelope and Aunt Millie, aged late sixties. She was Beverley's and Dawn's, father's sister. Old man Rupert was late seventies, trying hard to win affection of Aunt Millie. She had eyes for him not. All other players aged between, Dawn at sixteen and Al at twenty-four. Beverley was Dawn's sister. Devon and Penelope were siblings. Harry was Penelope's boyfriend, Beverley was Devon's girlfriend. Dawn was secretly, Al's girlfriend, sort of. Dawn's dad was stridently against any shenanigans between her and "old man" Al. When Al visited, he made it appear he was really there for Beverley. Dad cautioned her, against dancing with two monkeys simultaneously. No One of the two can say how intimacy crept in between Beverley and Al. While she was getting it on with Devon and Al was doing similarly undercover with Dawn. Al was sly, had freedom of camaraderie among families. Penelope took shine to him while her and Harry was getting it on. Quite a budding teapot storm, which Al, with wide smirks. Labeled to cronies, his love hat trick. Seasoned women can smell disgrace, even when there's no wind. So it was, Aunt Millie asked Al for a ride to the doctor shop. Silent in thought on outward journey. On way home, she straight up told him. She knew for fact, he was gallivanting with both her nieces. Often had to create cover stories to her brother for younger One. While laying on this charge, it was surprising to Al. Her arm atop the bench seat and hand. Gently massaged his nape, slow grooming his hair. Figuring, best way ensuring someone's silence is. Give them a role in crime. He diverted to the waterfall and persuaded her to skinny dip. She went into fits of laughter, seeing he did not have underpants on. He enjoyed "bowiebat" freedom." ***"Big man like you, walking round without drawers? If me did hear it from someone. Me would have to think is a lie."*** Al ignored and helped her undress. She just would not let trivia rest, kept coming back to it, after short breaks. ***"I really can't believe big man like you, go without drawers on you behine. This is something you practice?"*** Now flaccid, Al put his clothes back on, but regained urge. Goaded by coaxing and smooches. Still feeling rebellious, he diverted her attention. Sent her drawers sailing, like a pink silk horse. Remember how we raced twigs in roadside gutter stream and called them board horses? It was a pretty frilled pink with appliques and lace. He would later in deep afterthought, regret it. Drawers rode the current and bobbed it's way downstream out of sight. She shook him awake, and. *"One bwoy peeping in the car. You did lock it up good?"* Al told her stay as he went down to the lad. Threatened and shooed him on his way. Came back to see her in misery. *"Why me can't find me panty? Is set of three me daughter send from England for me. Only wear them to church or somewhere special."* She stared at Al accusingly, he said. **"Breeze must be blow it away, like how it light. You shoulda put stone on it."** A minute later, she resigned going home without underwear. Al was happy with their encounter and ending. Both were going home with bare behines, without drawers. She was excited and wanted to make this sexcapade a frequent event. Told her nieces, Al asked her to work on weekends at his one room cowboy pad. Neither of two suspected anything other than. She came by bus every Saturday. After chores, they got happy and Al drove her home by evening. A stated sum was agreed on, before first visit. Without defining what was pay and what was play. Having second thought, maybe thinking she had self lowballed. On reaching home, she asked. *"You not giving me offering for church tomorrow? You must learn to give thanks for blessings, it will come in abundance. Although now, you probably can't handle no more. See here. Your breadbasket overflows. Stop it yaw massa."* Her laugh was on again. A reticent Al grinned, bore her humour, adding a tip and self satisfied. Let's see now, how this saga played out. Aunt Millie knows, she and her nieces are gallivanting with Al. Devon and Penelope, thinks Al and Dawn are sweethearts. So does Mrs. Bennett, their mother. Beverley thinks she's secretly homing in on her sister's boyfriend. Harry is happy with his true love. When sifting gets done, Al alone can fit pieces to make a picture. One might ask One's self. What magic wand does Al waves in casting his spell. I would put Al's appeal, to his having a 1964 Ford Consul 315. Painted saluki bronze and matte black. That and willingness to freely taxi friends and adults places. Mrs. Bennett reminded him of her doctor's visit, adding. *"You're such a kind young man. Any woman who get you, will have gold spoon in them mouth. Make sure you don't jump and pick up any and any woman."* Al constantly took people to airport, weddings and what have you, for a smile. Babs asked he come for her. Take her to Terra Nova hotel for her guests, then take everyone to airport. Stay until their flight leaves and bring her back home. At her gate, she says to Al. *"Wish I could give you tip for gas. But good friend better than pocket money. Don't bother look at me with dreamy eyes. Me and you girlfriend is best friends."* A saga of kindness gone amok, is worth telling.

Dawn and Al had a movie tryst, on mark, set and ready to go, coming Saturday. She confided this to Penelope, and when Al came around. There were Beverley and Penelope on board. July 1969, two features billed at separate cinemas. After caucus it was decided, all four would see, Jim Brown's "100 Rifles" and George Peppard's "What's so bad about feeling good." Seating choices created instant disharmony. Beverley told Dawn to sit in back, she got comfortable in front. Al wanted his girlfriend beside him, but did not want to upset his apple cart. This served heightening Dawn's suspicion, regarding Al and her sister. He winked smile at Dawn, bit his tongue and swallowed spittle silently. Going in the cinema, there was clamour for box seating. Al told women to stand aside in lobby. Whilst he joined ticket queue, where he bought cheap tickets for "Fowl Roost" section. Loitered in lobby until strains of David Carroll's "Melody of love." Indicated, lights were about to be dimmed. On way to "Roost," Al told his party, box seats were sold out. Prices were generally low, but three pounds will not sustain four adults. Seeing two movies, and snacks each venue. In bathroom, Al checked eight shillings plus in his pockets. Slow cruise around bright spots would close out the evening's to-do list. Figured buying three shillings gas and get home with five shillings. Not bad, considering pleasure of evening with three lovely ladies. But alas, they were hungry, wanting snack. He drove into CB's kerb service. Waiter hurried out with show of pearly whites, to a car with four. Fertile source for good tipping. Ladies gave orders while Al said he was still undecided. Searching for ideas and coming up blank, he went in and called waiter. Begged him, come and say, stove broke down. They've run out of food, or something. As he had no money to pay for the fare. He stared at Al unbelieving, chuckled and asked. *"You sporting three woman same time and broke? You not have no money at all?"* Al said he had eight shillings, had to buy three shillings gas. Waiter thought for a minute then said. *"Okay, give me the five shillings, everything cool."* Surprised and relieved, Al now gave his order. Late night feast was on and CB's became favourite eating spot. For a time, until it closed. Waiter told Al of his next work venue, cautioned there would be no freebies. Doctor Bird Lounge, became Al and company's favourite chow spot. Caution please folks, being condemnatory on seeming debauchery and free spirited sexual mingling. This is good clean fun among like minded, consenting folks. Another script of revolving roles acted out by **"People at Play"**

Colleen G. Lowe

Parents differ... Children suffer-5

This rephrases adage. *'Doctors differ and patients die.'* It is an uncommon consensus among parents. Or later life stages, when they're grandparents. Children should be nourished, trained and groomed. As with hedging and trees. If they're to become adults, acceptable to basic societal standards. That way they can, nay should adeptly apply inherent and acquired talents. Pursuing self supporting, socially acceptable and fulfilled existence. For this expose` focus will be on parents, often adopting misguided mantra. Children should be allowed unreined freedom to pursue careers of choice and ultimate life path. A mitigating factor of "freedom for Stallion" mindset arises thus. Many yesterday's teens were desirous pursuing vocations of choice. Denied them by parents who insisted they pursue other fields. Carpenter's son carried on daddy's trade, although he was drawn to welding or brick laying. Midwife's daughter had to study for nursing. She was drawn to glory of being accountant, secretary or teacher. Helplessly distraught then, now as parents. They seek to spare their children, similar fate as they endured. Quite often, familial tensions began. When parent insisted, rigid training towards one vocation. Whilst other was about freedom for the Mare, sans blinkers. Arising from this, is common adage. "Good cop, bad cop." Let's examine real situation, see where it goes. Which is not to say. Similar situations would necessarily have tendency to trend likewise. What with there being exceptions to rules and so forth. Anthony was only male, among five Gillespie children. All had benefit of preparatory and high school education. Sisters heeded career guidance from uncles and aunts. As each attained appropriate age. They were admitted to institutions of higher learning. Opting for careers in fields of law, commerce, medicine and industry. Anthony lacked ability to focus, balked at academia. Opting instead for trades. Which is by itself, wise choice and got family support. At JAGAS he showed interest in, was encouraged to focus on teleferics. Such as cranes and hoists. Instructors counseled. Given, majority of students opting for motor vehicle repairs. He would find quicker, more lucrative opportunities in less crowded field. This required proficiency in many disciplines. Hydraulics, pneumatics and mechanical. His dedicated tutor, supported his yen for learning. Gave special attention, expressed surprise. Two years in of three. Anthony had grasped more than working knowledge in his field of pursuit. However, despite tutor's urge to fine tune his skills. Anthony wanted wealth at his disposal. Decided it was time to quit training and set up business. Basic common sense teaches, Anthony should finish training. Then get a job, honing skills. Doctors do not graduate medical school and hang shingle. They work alongside senior doctors. Learning unscripted arts and procedures, by observing real situations that weren't taught in school. Anthony's focus was getting wealthy before the moon changed phases. A friend told him, there were vast opportunities on the docks. Western Terminals' new fleet of Coventry forklifts, needed qualified service technicians. Anthony approached with proposal for contract. Western Terminals asked for diplomas. Offered, seven to three shift, six days week, one off. Like some cities, docks never sleeps. Notwithstanding this temporary setback, he failed to see disparity. His going for contract, offered payroll position instead, if credentials merited. Undaunted, he prompted parents to finance his setting up, motor vehicle repair shop. One thinks, technician semi-qualified in industrial equipment servicing. Could also be proficient in road vehicles repairs.

Excepting that, Anthony had not acquired reservoir of experience to do this. Certainly not in critical area of business management. Dad was against, Mom supported venture. Expressing anger and disappointment at her husband's refusal to support their son. She had faith he would succeed beyond expectations. Dad would not be swayed. Mom finagled spurious means, got seed funding by pledging assets and Anthony's shop became reality. Mom had business contacts with fleet owning entities, she could tap for support. For sure, mom's contacts told her. She could rely on their sending business her way. These things however, has a process, like links in a chain. Soon it became clear to mom and Anthony. Final approval was not in hands of mom's comrades. Something gets vetted and approved at one desk, lies bogged down at another desk. Meanwhile, Anthony gets patronage from friends and acquaintances. Which, therein lies the rub. Cash flow lags work delivered. Friends demands extended credit and buddy pricing. Customer's car was not ready as promised. Anthony lent his car. There was extensive damage from three vehicle collision. Made worse by sparse insurance coverage of two owners. Less than five months after opening, shop closes. Fleet business, yet to materialize. Anthony takes his "expertise" to established shop. Stays there for five months in silent understudy, then re-opens his shop. Fleet vehicles now coming in, he's happy for a while until he discovers. Technological design of these vehicles are beyond his training and expertise. He should know, there's need for refresher courses by way of manuals and online data. Now he must employ skilled technicians, at rates he can't afford. What's more, income trickles. Invoices again doing gauntlet of desks, managers and file thirteen. Not to mention, vehicles repaired. Comes back with original problem. There's growing dissatisfaction on both sides. One, citing incompetence. Other citing payment delays, vexing contributing factor. No surprise, Anthony closes shop again. Leaving parents saddled with enormous debts. Does not help, one of whom keeps echoing in partner's ear. ***"I knew it, I knew it!! It's not the Monkey that does the plumbing."*** Prompted and coerced by his sister, Anthony's uncle gives him a job to manage his business. Finds certain job aspects demeaning, he quits. All were mandated to sweep and clean up in rotation. Our lad declared. ***"I didn't go school to waltz with a f...ing broom."*** Stranded as it were, he knocks on generosity of mom, again. She obliges with airfare, on way to oil drilling site. Ten days later he is back with mom and dad. Siblings are pursuing their careers, started families and being responsible. He stays home with parents, has frequent squabbles with dad. Regarding chores such as, taking out garbage and mowing grass. Anthony justifies reluctance, saying. If he was not there, these things would yet get done. Dad counters, that's true. Food and utility bills would be lower. Mom cries shame on her husband, being mean to his own flesh and blood. There's contract work in foreign land. Anthony vows to repay sister's loan, for airfare and pocket money, soon as he's settled. He gets further loans from siblings, unknown to each. Promised, payable two weeks when his contract matures. Years go by and dad dies. Sisters sent airfare, he couldn't make presence at funeral. Berates siblings, having waited too long, before sending monies requested. It's their fault and will never be forgiven. Letting him miss opportunity to see his dad, one last time. Oh, how he grieves with a wounded heart. On this masquerade, he has mom's support. She chides daughters, for first taking counsel among husbands. Instead of rushing funds, with which they are overly blessed. To aid their brother's homecoming, on this once in lifetime occasion. Breaks her heart, to think her own daughters, whom she raised to be kind and generous. Especially to kith and kin. Could be guided by dictate of spouses, and not flash reach helping hand to struggling sibling. Deeply wounded, she died two years later. Anthony came home threadbare and broke. Demanding funds to outfit himself for funeral. Suggestion was, he check rental boutique. He balked wearing used clothes. Siblings, now free of mom's rebuke, stood their ground. He rummaged among dad's finery, was well dressed for mom's funeral. He could not accept there was no cash legacy as per the will. His sisters signed over their portion of parents real estate to him. He demanded, they make roof repairs, new windows, front door and repainting. Also loan to get new appliances. Present units, although miraculously functional. Had seen better times, now out of decor. Taking residence in marginal space, greater house area was tenanted. Yet. there were frequent utility disconnections and levy pending, for municipal taxes and interest. Tenant bought the property and subsequently had him evicted by court sanction. After he lived there one year and some, rent and utilities free. He tried rotating between siblings. Always lost favour, forced to move on. Took to vocally deriding them and partners for his ills. Cursed them, as selfish imbeciles and hate mongering to their children. When last he visited an acquaintance. Prefaced by request for money. He worked at a trucking company, living on site. I say to me, what a waste of opportunity. Young man born in privileged, middle class family, unlike many others. He was the baby mom did not allow to cry. Swathed him in woolen blankets, embraced in warmth of her cuddle, continuously. In childhood through teens, was allowed unfettered physical growth. Without parental direction towards a future, moulded to fit life's niche. Shielded from taking responsibility as adult.

Always being accommodated and deriding those who hesitated to. Anthony, even at this stage of life. Blames dad and siblings for his life's misfortune. His parting comment, poignant to his thoughts. *"My sisters never need all the money that was spent on them. University and those places, waste on woman. Because, from them born woman. Is a certainty, man going come take care of them in grand style, for life. Just because them born woman. You understand?"*

He asks, massaging his crotch and continues. *"Me on other hand, born man. Need all help I can get, because me have to take care of somebody. Before you know it, two becomes three and four. Maybe even five. So, they should have given me all help I needed, instead of wasting it on the girls. Look at my sister Lorris. You know she rent place to open her pharmacy? Yes! Not lie me telling. She soon pack her bag and leave CVM. That if she not resign already. September last year, her husband rent another space to expand him printery shop bigger. With only two and half ugly children. Why them need so much money? To do what with? All my sisters live larger than life. Top tier cars in them garage, spill out on driveway. Every minute they gone on trips to here, cruises to there. Would you believe, their top of the line grand kitchen and restaurant stove has never heated up once? Just there in the big grand house as showpiece. Maid come dust. Nanny look after pickneys and gardener look after flowers and hedging. Shiiiit"* He acknowledged, four children with three women and disputed fifth. Goes on spewing bile. Half child he callously refers to, has special needs from birth. Remember Hatlo's history and Henry Tremblechin? Had a byline. *"They'll do it every time."*

PE... Physical Education...Or?-6

Lending credence to suspicion, she called. Knowing his birthday was close. Taurus, Aries. Henry considered doing this numerous times, but never did. Searched internet sites, for a fee of course. At which point he would rethink and abandon. Truth is, there are many people Henry would want to know where they are. Talk to and reengage. It would take lottery cash win, making effort affordable. Another deterrent to such quest is. Although he often wondered about people, mostly women from the past. He knew, not all contact would be on cordial note. Women carry emotion for lifetime. Be it warm love, strident hatred or between. Hence the euphemism "Bag lady." So, there. Henry is curious, wants to talk. Meet and greet, even more pleasant. Will not apply a card in the process. Sometimes, as one man puts it. Dog turd gets sun baked. Loses stench, area pristine until. Idler comes along, kicks it and starts stink awaft again. He finds solace, averring on good inherent in most women. Without which, males would either be extinct or close to being. If their maternal instinct did not make women more accommodating and less retaliatory. Male of the specie would struggle for survival and possibly lose the battle. Mary exempted. We have to admit, grudgingly by those biased. Leery pushed her beyond human capacity to deflect and absorb aggression, both passive and assertive. This for her, was alien bombardment. Comfortable in kick butt confrontation. Devoid of defensive skills to counter passive aggression, she resorted to gabbing with anyone. Henry was quoted as having said. *"I don't doubt, over these past years. Having loved numerous women, there was reciprocation of emotion. Some fervently, and then there were only memories. Some brought warmth to a heart, others brought bile to One's throat."* They expostulated silently, eyes reflecting inner turmoil or petulant outbursts. *"I hope he rots in hell, that conniving Son-of-a-Bitch."* One such occasion arose when she had no amorous desires. Henry did unexpected and let her be. She had banked on his being persuasive, gently or otherwise. In pursuit of what objective? He silently pondered, but couldn't divine answer. However, he was in for long haul. Weeks turned months, turned years. She wanted to talk, so they did. Maybe, it was age related, onset of gender maladies, or? Both introduced probables, yet hydraulics were kaput. One can achieve what One embarks on, with deft concentration. Frannie is not only One so gifted. Soon becomes second nature and "Can't redo" flag goes up. Women, without doubt, are smarter than men. But there are times, woman gets careless. A man will lead her to outsmart herself. Truth is, this is emblematic of both sexes, but because woman wears wisdom crown. If and when the halo goes dim, there's instant awareness and ha ha.

An invitation to go camping was extended. **"Not me, can't venture behind thickets."** He said. Frannie happily savoured and reveled in monumental achievement of being in control. Months later, wife awoke. Tiptoeing to bathroom she glanced at peacefully resting partner. Saw tepee, recoiled in surprise. She was mentally non-plussed all day. Evening, she calmly asked. *"You don't think one partner should tell other. When there's progress, in situation affecting relationship?"* One fellow said. *"Hear me my yute. Me couldn't play that with Maxine. You must be mad. She would forget bathroom, grab centre pole and ask. What's this?! Meantime, she have it on rotation like joystick. And don't forget. That's after she already winged it downstairs and took custody of biggest knife. Ready to redo a Bobbett."* Frightening reality is, there are numerous Maxines at large. Which, had both come into same orbit. Could have led to his near or untimely demise. Both being endowed with mental temperament as they are. Television episodes brings solved and unsolved crime re-enactments, sometimes causes one to shudder. Close family member says. *"Hell hath no fury like a woman scorned."* Henry asks.**"Is there acknowledged rage in man scorned?"** Methinks he's mere denied, not scorned in true interpretation.

It began when Paddy called his office. Told Curves, his secretary. To remind him, there was urgency to unfinished business at the wharf. Curves called Zelma at Customs house, asking if she had seen Henry. If or when she does, please remind him Paddy called about unfinished business. A document was being used to clear shipments at two berths. Paddy, in act of trust, released one without notating the document. Henry raced off to Berth One. Came back to office and was given message from Paddy. Called and told Paddy, first thing next day he'd have the document. This being next day, advanced in hours. Hence Paddy's call to Curves. So far so good. He walked through a door, Paddy was saying to a vivacious young woman. *"Spoilt egg stank, does not make refrigerator "used." Yet, shipped in factory packaging."* We always think we are smart, when to an expert we are really dumb. Often makes situation worse by planting stink that upsets someone. To wit, this instance. Turning attention to door, Paddy greeted. *"Hey pardner! How's Specialist and weather today?"* Pleasantries exchanged, Paddy went on. *"Help this lady write up her bill of sight."* Both looked at each other then stared speechless, causing Paddy to break seance saying. *"Oh, you two know each other? All the better. Take good care of her."* They had never met before, could not explain mutual reaction. Henry was captivated by her graceful poise, youthful radiance and beauty. Brenda introduced herself. Both shook hands, hers, soft, warm and pulsing which Henry clung to, inordinately. She reacted, gave him a eyes head memo. Anyone ever paused to recognize and interpret. Encyclopedic language of eyes in particular, and face as a whole? Refrigerator and stove was gift of Brenda's mom. Agog anticipating, twenty-one year milestone. Planned celebrating with engagement party. Neighbours, all young men. Tripped each other, helping to carry appliances indoors. Refusing to accept money offered. Behind ajarred door, she told Henry. *"An envelope is on the dining table for you. If you like, you can call me at work. I am not feeling myself now."* Henry walked away with disappointed strides. Feet almost knotting for ankle stumble. Turned out "work" was training facility. Calls were limited to times and timed. Two weeks in, he was given house number. Chatting until he had to take sips. Six weeks later, she's going to New York. Hurrying to Air Jamaica's check in. Henry, winded in tow with bags. Heels glitched. Henry reached out, grateful for her near accident. Steadied her in an embrace. Stare was on again. She felt so, looked so, smelled so like, maybe he closed his eyes. Heard her soft soothing voice in a whisper. *"I don't want to miss my flight."* Later, relaxed with each other. She called and gabbed freely when met by Henry from her trip. Mom threw July 4th party, celebrating both birthdays. *"Would you believe? My dad turned up uninvited. Making the night so, just. You know what I mean?"* "Was it good or bad just?" He asked. Not wanting to assume. *"What?! It was good a hundred times over and guess what? He was on same flight, saw us at the airport. We were dancing and he just out and said."* *"Who is that old man I saw you with at the airport? I thought he was the taxi driver. But then, he was being overly supportive. If you know what I mean."* "So, what did you tell him?" *"Just what he expected to hear, nothing."* Henry, at mid forties, more than twice her age. Stung by, 'that old man' chose not to comment. She went on. *"Dad thought, Tyrone would have made the trip. I told him, he's saving for our grand engagement, birthday party of the century. Good thing he did not come though. He always feels intimidated by dad, without reason. Dad has a protective bark, meant to intimidate. But I can always heel him and he goes soft like a Pussy....Don't light up like that! Think feline. I might regard you as a possible menace or predator. If a simple word can get you hyperventilating, moreso at your age. How old are you?"* Henry responded with silence and a benign smile. She didn't press him further. He's thinking. *'I've got her going. See? She's hesitant to rile or offend.'* Exulting mentally, wasn't aware of his grin until she softly said. *"A mind is a terrible thing to waste. But a wonderful thing to invest in."* He asked, who said that. Now it was her turn to grin in silence. Tit for tat. Eve, August 6th, there was grand festivity everywhere. Another milestone on Jamaica's independence highway. For Henry, evening's thrill was their first kiss. Erotic, demanding and punishing to unyielding appendages. First lip lock, lasted twenty seconds before she broke free, softly saying. *"Stop. We should not be doing this. It is just not right."* Maintaining their embrace in silence. Lips came together again in tongue twisters for two minutes. Then again. *"Please, I am going home. This is getting out of hand. I feel bad about doing what we are doi..."* She lip locked again, tightening her embrace. Henry slipped two fingers and released her bra hook. She pressed upper body against him, denying path to pulsing nubbies against his chest. That was her castle's moat. Once those were breached, she knew it would be surrender with untold ecstasy. Still, the queen should never consort, much more capitulate to jester. She had foolproof deterrent to amorous excursions. Whenever she felt her grip slipping, she bit a tongue playfully hard. Which cooled Henry's passion for awhile. He being one to mentally diarize conquests. Was ecstatic at progress made in relative short time and silently exulted. Night of her big party, she was stunning in light pink. Her smile radiated aura, filling like angel's halo. They smiled at each other in hungered desire. Dad the scholar greeted, began probe. Henry, jinnal born, deftly parried and deflected. Both parted in good humour. In semi darkness of dimmed lights. Henry searched in vain for his heart's throb, without success. Until she walked over in light blue, asking if he and her dad got on okay. Simultaneously threatening. ***"Don't touch me or I will walk away."*** Henry obeyed her fiat with a grin, which she reciprocated. People do engage in such bull shit parodies at times, disgusting but having merit. We have to submit to dictates of good breeding and broughtupsy ever so often. She asked he come for her at work next day.

Playful and coyly teasing, she opted going his home before hers. Covered her head with a jacket as she raced between raindrops getting in the house. Seems, a woman won't mind drowning, so long as she keeps her hair dry. I know, I know. Maintenance cost is sky high. Hence a Do has to last as long as it can. Liberally damped here and there, she stepped out of her dress uninhibited, and handed it to Henry. Caught by surprise, he hung it on a hanger, asked. **"What about the slip?"** *"What about it?"* She asked with surprising ferocity. He calmly said. **"Nothing."** Striving to be at best behaviour. Not wanting to be taken as menace or predator, but gee. Woman's form shrouded in sparse rayon, excites and muddles man's mind. Guess she knows this, is bent teasing or punishing. She sat, admiring the room. Delicate lace gave shrouded glimpse of nubbies, cruel ecstasy. She chuckled and said. *"Your room is small and your refrigerator huge. Can't you see glaring disparity? I am sorry. You're starting a family soon, and buying to get ahead."* Henry asked if she wanted a Cydrax. She told him *"No! And neither do you. Come here."* See how she's calling shots? Comfortably at ease, in control of womanhood. Both were five minutes silent, he was tense. Fired up the music with Bert Kaempfert's "A Swinging Safari" on "Zenith Circle of Sound" *"Let's dance."* She said. They hugged, lips at nose level. He lost-in-a-dream satisfied with pulsating warmth of her embrace. Lightning flashed, thunder pealed and wind driven rain hit the roof with pebble like ferocity. Then she whispered. *"Say you will be unhurried and gentle. I will......"* Heads unbowed, lips met. Tongues tangled, evening became night and became dawn. Experience was so very beautiful, magical with fairy tale essence. Yet, question lingered in hallways of Henry's mind. He timidly broached. **"Can I ask you something personal?"** She guffawed. *"After everything we've done, you now want to ask something personal? Go ahead, I am dying to hear it."* As was his wont, he hand gestured more than verbalized. **"Well, I've never asked anyone this but I am kind of. You know? Okay. I get a feeling I am your first. Would that be right?"** She stroked and smoothed hair on his chest, whilst thinking how to respond. Maybe, if she should. You never know what's going on in that beautiful mind. Went to bathroom, returned. Still deep in thought, then she began. *"I never thought doing this, until there was Tyrone. Then I found out he has a problem with PE and it frustrates him. Sometimes he can't get started. Becomes sullen and angry, throws a tantrum. Then I get scared of him."* We can be smartest cookie and yet be dumb to certain things. So Henry asked. **"They force him to do PE at work, that's why him extra tired?"** To that point in life, only PE he knew, was that done in school. Physical education, shortened at times in high school to Phys. Ed. Or PE. His daughters had PE uniforms different from school uniforms. Henry had not slightest inkling what Brenda was referring to. She fixed him a glare, asked. *"What does workplace have to do with what I just said? I am going to bring you one of my course books. Remind me."* He never did. Ashamed to perpetuate idiocy, comfortable knowing. Tyrone's PE disadvantage worked to his advantage. Months later she said. Mom asked her to migrate, at end of her studies. She wanted to marry and have children but Tyrone could not sire. Mono track minded Henry jumped at the idea, saying he could. She cold stared him without response. He said, he was making a joke. *"You find too many serious situations damn funny, for an old man!"* Ooh, now she was twisting her dagger in anger, but only for a second. Instantly hugged him, saying. *"I am so confused and very sorry. Come on, kiss and make up."* Soon she was chiding. *"Hey! Kiss, is make up. No further action required. Jeez! Are you wired? I should say, programmed."* Henry was hurt most by, "For an old man" He never saw him as old, but recalled Elizabeth's candidly saying. *"Come, come now my dear knight. However else did you see yourself? We laugh, we touch. We go here, we go there, as friends do. I sometimes suffer a hug. Even when we are not dancing. You do behave in common with a pin. But you are old, first and foremost. I have always enjoyed company of an old friend."* Henry accepted, in eyes of youth, he was indeed old. Made mental note she had not answered his question directly. But of what significance would that be? He had tasted of the fruit and it was indescribably good. Granny's wisdom dictated. *"Bwoy, you come to drink milk. Don't stand up counting cow."* Now, we are back on her dilemma and what to do about Tyrone. Mom likes Tyrone and suggests she marries and brings him to the US. Very day after Embassy allows. There being treatment choices to overcome his PE. They could begin a family and life together. Seemed if mom had her way, she would keep Tyrone dusted and polished like treasured artifact. Mom's idea sounded promising, if things worked as expected. Might Henry confess, still in ignorance. What was malady of PE? Knew it was medical condition. Since it was in Brenda's text books. Now, relationship and emotional conundrum of sorts existed. Brenda's dad was fourteen years Henry's senior. Brenda and Henry were in love, unquestionably so. Her parents were divided on Tyrone, in that. Mom liked him, dad didn't care much. Thought the young man was not as manly as man should. Still seeing Henry around, told his daughter. He hoped, she was not thinking of having serious relationship with "The old taxi man." These opinions, related to Henry, went in one ear and out other. When emotions reached boiling point. They assuaged each other in wild abandon, until stars brought clash of seasons. What else could Henry be concerned about? Emotional stability, that's what. Wedding was being planned, creating changes. One warm night as they lay spooned and glued by erotic sweat. Brenda told Henry. After her marriage, there would not be 'them.' She had no intention finding another lover. Would adopt celibacy until Tyrone's cure. Sobbing at reality of, saw no other option. Dad introduced his wife at the wedding, asked Henry. *"What exactly do you do for living?"* **"I am licenced Customs broker, among other things."** *"Yes! Like what other things? If you don't mind my…"* **"Real estate and property management company.**

Electrical installation-maintenance company. Pace Auto Stores and agents for Hawker Siddeley of England." *"Impressive, very impressive, I do say. Inherited family businesses or?"* **"No, sir. Not at all. First hung my shingle, August 1971. Now replaced by a bill board. Thank God."** Cannot identify his business but it was definitely more impressive than Henry's. Still, it must have shaken him to find. Henry was not a taxi driver. A girlfriend recommended Henry to John LaRoshke. Both met, agreed, after discussions. To add first LaRoshkean office in Jamaica to his billboard. Brenda stayed aloof but chatted long and frequently by phone. Was steadfast in pre-marital vow on clandestine sexcapades. This she could only accomplish by staying afar. Admittedly, the aching was sometimes unbearable. However, she had to be firm in this endeavour. Henry got JBR to run promotion for LaRoshke. Francis and Nerda were talents, getting great listener response. Back in his triangle days. Beue promised to be at Farky Hall fete but never showed. Henry requested a song of Kingsley and danced with a young unknown woman. Disappointed he did not get his message across. Figured that song was apt for Brenda and he. Got approval for three minute spots. A Sunday, his friend did her show. Talent was all Henry's. **"Arthur Prysock on the Old Town label "Only a fool breaks his own heart" From you know who to an angel in blue."** Said at first, she listened out of disinterested curiosity. Refusing to believe he would go to such lengths. Next, she told herself it could not be as many repeats as he said it would be. That somehow, broke her tenuous resolve. They resumed impassioned existence, sensuous gallivanting until. Breakup was sudden for Henry and final for both. As is inevitable, love dies on the vine, memories fade and life goes on. Time does not stand still, neither does rivers runs dry. But, hope thrives. Sleep won't come, Henry went downstairs.

Turned late night news on. Flipping channels, infomercial caught his eyes. He flipped back to an eye opener. Men with PE and ED, encouraged to call 800 number for relief. He watched with jaw dropping attention until deciphering caption came on screen. Premature ejaculation and erectile dysfunction. Smacked his forehead in disbelief. How could he not know that? What we know, we know. And that which we don't, we don't. Oh, she never conceived, has long abandoned efforts. Tyrone is overwhelmed with happy, long as she's with him. Showers her with nauseating adulation, can't imagine life without her. I say, Tyrone is happy being selfish, not seeing Brenda's agony. She might as well join a convent and rub pot covers with an obliging sister. Maybe he feels that way, because he too is being denied. When man looks at woman Brenda's, absolute work of art, her form engrosses. Wondering what enthralling joy it would be to get with her. He fantasizes and at times, may self gratify. If he's been there and knows what he's missing. Fog horns and fire sirens goes off. Chapel bells peal in his head, driving him to near insanity. You understand Henry's pain.

Here they are for old times sake, having lunch at "Bahama Breeze." She avoids eye contact, tells him. *"Your signals are blocked, you can stop transmitting."* Henry suspected long ago, Brenda now confirmed. Being upset by her mom's molly coddling Tyrone. Had to once remind mom, therapy sessions are for couples, not family. She prattled on about horse having died, as a result the cow got fat. Henry did an eye movement, got her attention and whispered. **"Could we…. You know?"** *"Hell! No."* *"What are you? There's got to be invisible Puppeteer or a windup key in your back"*

Reflections of Solitude & Isolation-7

Henry laid abed thinking. Nigh impossible these days, hiding from average Joe or Jane, if you live in developed world. Third world isn't as closeted as used to be. Not with internet and most everyone having smart phone with camera to boot. But there is sanctity from face recognition scanning. Forte of big brother, who's always on alert, watching. Do crap and right away you get pounced on. Drawback being, while you were being watched your intentions could not be read. So you crapped and tried to flee. Give big brother a night's sleep. He'll come up with a system that identifies and prevents. Gonna go preemptive on your scheming psyche. So, in his thought train he is in the past. His bane would arise from philandering and there are women who felt cheated on, whilst they cheated. Like Sandra, who got her thing on with Barry. Although both her and his wife attended same church. Barry gets invited to Sandra's party, dances briefly and then takes off with next door neighbour, Viviene. Nearly two hours later, Barry comes back to the party alone. He is accosted by an irate Sandra, who asks. *"Why you look so dam happy, like the cat that ate the cream? I hope she told you, her man is police. Excuse me."* She is mad, really strung out and needs to be watched. Others won't walk with daggers or swords, most times keeping their angst secret. That part of their life they never want revealed. Guarantees there's no angry husbands, lovers, boyfriends or whoever. Those Sons-of-Bitches who are like Viviene's boyfriend, walks with keen edged swords. Be his joy to run a dude through. But what he doesn't know, won't hurt Henry. Self assurance is refreshing antidote, even if elation is temporary. Longevity brings experiences, also maladies denied the youthful. Having tinkled and going back to bed, looks at monitor in eight and single frame. There's always blanket of twining and cordage that obliterates everything else. More than once he went out, corn broom in hand. Swept the air and came back in. Looked at that frame with anticipation of achievement. Only to see blanket suspended where it's always been, undisturbed. Water crystals appear chain linked, large as mother pearls. He goes out again, determined winning battle. After all, he is human. That blanket is work of an arachnid. Who wants to be outsmarted by a minor animal? Considering, arachnids are of arthropods group, largest in animal kingdom. There could be some invincibility at work. Staring at monitor he marvels at stillness of everything. Leaves sag as if asleep, nothing stirs. It's 03:14 hours, he steps outdoors. Refreshing cool, swamps his face, bringing realization. Outdoors is cooler than indoors. Which felt quite comfortable before the contrast. He peers in dark of night, not expecting to see anything or anyone. Listens for night sounds. Owl's hoot, rustle of grass or bush, disturbed by nocturnal creature. There's pervasive hush. No barking dogs, moving vehicles or emergency siren. Strained ears now, zooming in turnpike traffic. It's always there during daytime, low rumbling waves on Richter. Nothing. Never knew this until presently. We thrive on noises and sounds. Henry got frightened by calm. Senses an uneasy, surreal feeling. Maybe he's in different place from everyone. There's sounds and movements where they are. Where then, can he be? The cat rubs against his leg. Startled, he kicks. Cat looks up at Henry and meows. *'What you done that for?'* Henry abruptly turns, hurries towards front door, lest it disappears. Someone said. ***"Thinking can be very dangerous. It is not something One should want to make a habit of."*** Ella Fitzgerald sang ***"Imagination is funny, it makes a cloudy day sunny."*** It can also make a dark night eerie. Now he's safely back in the house, where he will not be bothered by silence. Not in his house. If he believed in such things, he would say it's haunted. That "clunk" he knows, is water heater timer cycling. What are those sounds popping up so often?. *"Those are house settling sounds."* Said a coworker who has explanation for every event, no matter how trivial. *"Nothing ever just happens, it is caused. You might not know cause, but it's there. A house expands by heat of day and contracts by cool of night."* He confidently avers. Now our dilemma or mental fragility becomes obvious. Silence and solitude scares us, so does sounds we cannot identify. Solitary confinement is proven psychological punishment, intended to break mental resolve. Quote by this author reads. *"One never fully appreciates beauty and freedom of outdoors, until One gets forcefully confined indoors."* Henry's confinement was not solitary. There were sixteen souls with him. Cell was dark as night. Hearing traffic sounds gradually escalate, he knew night had turned day. Summoned outside, was astounded to find it was close to noon. Sent back to dungeoness confines, feasted eyes as long he could. Like crossing the desert and finding an oasis. Decides to drink stomach full and some, before moving on. We are creatures of comfort and takes this for granted. Not once do we pause to think. *'What if well runs dry?'* We establish convincingly, solitude and confinement are anathematic to our existence. Yet thrive to attain some level of objective isolation. In recent housing depreciation era, next-door-ers lost their home to foreclosure. Abandoned and vacant, bereft persons came and went. A capture was underway, by what neighbours deemed, undesirables. Police were notified, they came. For a week or two, things were normal, but itinerants' trek resumed. Police were called again, cycle went on. Henry's wife was nervous, comfort zone had disappeared. She wanted a gun. Henry said.

"I could get you a cat." *"A puss!"* She asked, befuddled. **"No, not just any puss. One that roars. You sic him on them one time. You don't need sic him twice. Trust me."** She ignored him and retorted, in tense fret. *"We have to relocate."* **"Market bad, we not going get what we owe. We are stuck. As a good, God fearing Christian, watch and pray."** He sought to calm her. Eventually a family of four moved in. They were buyers, not renters. Henry sighed with relief, greeted new neighbours. Life returned to normal. Wife's heart was once again rid of anxiety, until. Every month end, neighbours had karaoke session. Wife claimed she could not sleep. Henry replied. **"Doesn't bother me hon."** This was taking toll on her ability to function at her day job. *"We should call the police, let them turn the noise down."* So said wife who, not long ago. Avoided being home alone, day or night. Fearing invasion by fence jumpers, bent on raping and plundering. She shook Henry awake again. Demanded he call the police. Being only solution to the problem. He shared a memory. **"I recall, not long ago. You were scared about itinerants invading. Engaging in suspected, illegal activities next door. We called police numerous times. Family moved in and all is well. Now, you want to call police again. Because the family is having a get together? Not me sweetie. I won't be party to that complaint."** Position made crystal clear, he went back to sleep. Next morning, wife asked. *"You heard a woman who was singing? Sounded like cat in heat."* **"No, I did not hear."** Henry replied. *"You never hear anything. How can you sleep through all that?"* Henry, feeling peeved, calmly told his wife. **"We have ability to tune out misery, but first we have to want to."** Henry never heard anymore complaint or mention of next door karaoke sessions. We need each other, more than we allow ourselves to know. Like not missing water until well no longer springs. Usually, herd moves on. Relentlessly searching for next life saving oasis. Animals are instinct driven to know. For most specie, water and food is a must for sustaining life and existence. Last to succumb, watched each herd member weaken, fall and painfully expire.

Here's classic, self induced calamity of thinking. Twelve years old, she walked in the door. Hugged and kissed her daddy, then asked tough poser. You know that kid was exposed to eye opening scenarios in school's science class today. When she comes home, decides to try on newly acquired knowledge. ***"Daddy, what would you do if you suddenly realized, your next breath of oxygen had disappeared? It could happen you know. Sucked out of the atmosphere, just like that."*** Snaps two fingers. Without pausing, he said. **"Tumbleweed! Wouldn't matter to me, because I wouldn't be aware."** Now, she's standing there perplexed and thinking. He adds kicker, tells her. **"Neither would you, my Cherie."** Now that's what I call flawed intellect on teacher's part. If you are going to teach about catastrophic dearth, of life sustaining oxygen in atmosphere. Tell them truth, it really would not matter. They would not be able to experience the difference. A person who dies in their sleep might know they are slipping away, but certainly will not know they have. Their last thought will be, he or she went back to sleep. From which, it is not known. There will not be, customary awakening. We do death's dry run, each time we lay us down to sleep. Comes a time, there's no more dry run but that last one. Another journey begins....?

And yet..Our Virgin prayed-8

Late 1970's, Henry, the broker and Ralston, the hustler were clearing goods at NMIA. Ralston sometimes side manned for him, but went off engaging informal importers. Lending basic expertise, hopefully for monetary reward. He brought a woman to Henry, whose needs were beyond his expertise. She wanted PD (Passenger's declaration) extract to clear items shipped by her from the USA, from whence she had recently returned. She did have excess quantities of merchandise. Hastened to explain. Family and friends gave gifts, clothing, food, and appliances. By unsolicited goodwill. For extended family and household. Dire importance were, back-to-school items for her only daughter, whom she feared would miss school. Customs duty $870.00 had been levied, on what was deemed "commercial imports." She ardently pleaded inability to pay. Hence, Henry was being introduced by Ralston, as possible solution to dilemma. Not only were duties mitigated. Got PD and extract for barrels coming by ocean freight. That hurdle having been cleared, her next task was getting goods home. Granny Louise ever postulated on wisdom, not lending her horse. Borrower will ask for saddle. Neither her saucepans, as neighbour will ask for firewood or coal. Unawares, Henry had a truck making client deliveries, she asked. *"How much you think a van man would charge to drop them boxes at my house for me?"* Then quickly added.*"Although me might have to knock pan hold saucer, call neighbours to borrow from."* Henry told her he would and the charge would be affordable. This however would not be pronto, but later when close to her address. For immediate transport, he pointed her gaze South to parked trucks and vans. Companion, whom she later divulged was church sister.

Pulled her aside in whisper, to which she audibly responded. *"Stop it Missis. Him is big time government man. Him not going run way with them. Me trust him."* That settled, she asked ETA of number 24 bus. Added in guarded whisper, a la stage aside. *"Me work with one old Mulatto, have mercy. Him miserable like cow at pasture without tail. Next thing him take half day from me pay and it so small already."* Arriving at her home, Henry was greeted royally. Introduced to neighbours as. *"The nice gentleman I was talking bout. Look after everything for me. Never pay one red cent."* Her daughter came to fore and was introduced. Shy, attractive teenager about fifteen. Beaming with pride, mom told how she passed multiple exams. Was awarded scholarship to better high school, where she continued to excel. Result of mom's incessant oversight. She was busy in kitchen, preparing evening's meal. Creating aroma that caused salivating and hankering. Henry indicated not tarrying. Was prevailed on to stay for dinner. Sure sign, coffers were bare, and someone would be deprived full share. He graciously declined. Just then a young man came on scene. Whisked off to a nook by the woman. Both engaged in anxious whispered dialogue. Henry caught bits and pieces, learning. Young man was asked to pony up money. Towards settling delivery fee, that was not forthcoming. Fact is, Henry had not yet been asked or stated amount due. Confirmed by eavesdropping, there was no money to pay him. He assumed, jinnalship or trickery at work. Abandoned hopes of collecting. Wrote it off to doing a good deed, that would come back to him one day. Person and source unexpected. Some incidents are funny without anyone intending. Young man went inside. Henry was joined by woman on way to street. She volunteered an explanation, he regarded as "beating around the bush." Or, as Granny Louise would say."Flogging a dead horse." Futile exercise she stridently warned against. Lore dictated, the horse would come to life and kick it's tormentor. Having taken elbow in grasp, which Henry took as being pretentious. She began.*"You see the Mulatto man me work with? Me is him floorwalker, and only reason him give time off to go airpo…"* Here, teenager approached. **"Excuse me mam, Mr Barr…"** She was paused by mom, who indignantly told her. *"You don't see me talking?! No baby not in house to drop off bed. So whatever it is, it can wait."* Young lady stepped back, her face reflecting anxiety and annoyance. Mom went on. *"Yes, sir. As I was saying. The old Mulatto trying hard hard to look me. Him don't know. This is one potato hill, him hoe not going stir up. Now or never, ever."* Henry tittered lightly. Noticed, teen winced. Initially surprised, with wide stared eyes and chin to chest, possibly embarrassed. Mom went on, oblivious to teen's presence. *"Me is Christian, me have to go church and praise me Jesus."* Henry said, he had to go. Was asked cost of delivery. Told it was gratis, she was beside herself expressing gratitude for day's combined efforts. Redounding to her benefit and it being her rare, good fortune to meet him. When she was adrift without rudder. He had been godsend. One could think, she was testifying from a revival pulpit. Walked to truck, hugged him, too long, saying. *"Feel free to drop in when you in the area, or better yet. Put yourself in the area and come visit anytime you feel like. No man not here to bust you head. Is me and me daughter alone deh here. You always welcome."* Let's remove veil of anonymity. Mom, was Miss Doreen, to neighbours. Daughter, was Primrose. Shortly after, inevitably. Henry became frequent visitor. In course of one month, more or less, he was regarded as acting or quasi family member. Seems Primrose looked forward to, was overjoyed at his visits. Thus causing

Doreen to remark. *"Poor thing, she never had a father. Me try me best give her everything. Is the one I have. Me love her can't done, but she well want a father. That's why she cling to you so."* By unseen degrees, Henry was taking care of Primrose, financially. Insofar as schooling were concerned. Mom showed fervent gratitude, rewarding enthusiastically and oh so very frequent. Recalls a mom whose boy could not get into school. Got in after mom convinced principal? Young lad mimicked principal's breathless, raspy grunts. A good movie, superb acting. Despite sincere pronouncements to contrary. Guided Henry, hoeing her potato hill. No words were spoken or agreements made. Things came together, everyone understood their position and obligations in this triangle. Every situation has beginning. Primrose brought fund raising letter from school. Mom handed it to Henry, saying. *"You familiar with gibberish, as a businessman."* It was a note asking parental support for students to panhandle, supporting a project. With award for most successful student. Henry found this morally reprehensible, but did not voice aversion. His daughters attended high school. Where, when project funding was needed. This was introduced by principal at home school meetings and parents' support were requested. He chafed at idea, his daughter at any age. Going out with paint pan or red kettle to solicit funds. His company had a "community support" account. Made for respectable cheque be placed in the envelope. Both looked and eyes opened in surprised appreciation. Primrose grinned broadly. *"Thank you very much uncle Henry."* Accompanied by sincere, sustained hug. Mom cut the appreciation ceremony short, admonishing Primrose. *"Alright! Go easy. Make him breathe."* Primrose walked away dejectedly. One could see her prolonging her hug, as directed by sense of gratitude. Soon after, Mom asked Henry. *"You see list Primrose bring from school? I swear them think money grow on tree and I just shake it every time."* He scanned the list, handed over a cheque. From then it was understood. Notes from school on funding, got brought to his attention. Fearing risk of being disingenuous, he dared accept. This factored, in frequency and fervour of Mom's intimacy pursuits. But what did Henry know? Maybe it's just rant of an egotistic buffoon. Time marched on. Primrose went, or in truth. Was goaded by mom to enroll in business college, although she favoured nursing career. Term breaks, she went dockside with Henry, familiarizing with procedures. Her expressing an intense interest in ships. Although stipend was a given, he had to convey importance of earning keep. Instead of being supported, as manna fall. She was flower bud that bloomed, exuding radiance and charm. Had suitors going in circles. She confided having boyfriend, church member. Yet wanting to do "dirty things" with her. She rebuffed, telling him fornication is sin, very wrong. *"Pastor already warned. No way until, if or and when they were married."* During conversations, she divulged. Mr. Barry was her dad's cousin, whom she hated with a passion. Always trying to touch and cuddle her. Tried kissing her, day her complaining to mom in Henry's presence. Then, along came Mr. Alfred, like Jones.

How Doreen met this gentleman, was never explained to Henry. Possibly because, there was no need, and he made no effort at fact find. Knowing he was not there for long haul. Had to be a change going come, oh yes it will. Henry was introduced. *"A very dear and good friend, better than pocket money."* Now there was new man friend. Engagements of comfort between both became furtive and infrequent. This amused Primrose, who volunteered. Mr. Alfred asked. How long her mom and Henry had been "very dear and good friends." To which, she told him. *"I think you should ask my mom that question, sir."* She did not like him either. Always giving her intense, lusting stares that unnerved her. Henry and Alfred got into guarded discussion. Alfred asked after Henry's trade, but was not familiar with practice of Customs brokerage. He was a builder, quickly adding. *"But me don't build fence. Anything me build, have to have plan draw on paper. Bad mind people have it to say, is fowl coob me build. Make me tell you, that is a big lie. Them chat what them don't know, because them never see my work. Me mostly work in country.* (Rural areas) *Specialize in poultry farmer's chicken house, hog pen and dairy barn."* He would not have known, but Henry had already been briefed by Doreen. On full scope of his business pursuit and their plans. These were related to Henry for opinion. Soon a marriage was announced, between Alfred and Doreen. She cautiously stated to Henry. *"Alfred getting restless, although me already tell him from day one. We have to go before parson before anything gwone."* Realizing ambiguity of her statement, she laughed and said. *"You get way with murder. Because, you did already go before parson. You couldn't go back, without going to jail. But Alfred never go yet, so now is fa him time. Me have to stand firm on that."* Coming from liquor store with beers and sodas. Henry and Alfred met at home. Both unloaded the vehicle. That done, Henry made for a hasty retreat, Alfred asked he linger. Went to his truck, brought a packet labeled. **"Wilkinson"** Said to Henry, while handing it to him. *"These are made of white gold. Superior to anything you can buy anywhere. See them there two swords? After months of shaving, I still can use them for paring bunions and corns."* Thinking him presumptuous in extreme. Henry gave back the packet, saying. **"You notice? I man don't support shaving. I is beard man, plan staying that way."**

Alfred shoved packet back at Henry, saying. *"Keep them, you never know when you might need a good razor blade."* Deciding not to at first, Henry had second thoughts and warned. **"I would strongly advise. You find another method getting rid of bunions. Razor paring can be very dangerous."** He laughed loud and walked away. Still experiencing umbrage at Alfred's giving him razor blades, without his having asked. Henry tried to rationalize. What was inference here? Had Doreen not insisted he attend the soiree, Henry would have stayed away. It was an affair to remember, hard to forget. With foods of the earth to eat. Seemed Alfred's farmer clients, gave of their chickens, hogs and steers galore. Guests ate hearty, whilst slamming cook's culinary skills. Yet went back for seconds and thirds. Where freeness exists, it's folly to resist. Speech session over, it was on to next programmed item. An unfolding woman, like a stemmed rose. Invites awed male stares, way an eclipse or orbital phenomenon does. Especially, when robed in delicate swaths. Accentuating virgin rounded hips and rising rump. Those tender mounds, bulbous pubescence, subtly trenching to reveal cleavage that sirens. Ah! Subtle overpowering lure, that is female's form. So it was, with gilded Primrose. Who quite innocently, was pebble in a pond. Alfred, silenced celebratory din with raised palms. Orated good fortune, finding wife and daughter so late in life's years. Hope having a family of his own, had long ago waned. This as he grinned, ear to ear. Zealously embracing both women. I should make mention. This wedding reminded Henry of his, years before. Not one photograph was taken, moment was all committed to memory. Calling Mr. Music to please play. Alfred let go of his wife and stepped forward with Primrose in a hug. She stood ground. Stared at Alfred astounded, and tried wiggling free from his grasp. Old men found it hilarious, arched heads skyward. Jabbed walking canes to ground repeatedly, grinned toothless gums. Biddies knotted pious brows, gnashed dentures in muted rebuke. Cousin Barry raced forward, tried prying prize from Alfred's Boa wrap. Everyone in attendance instantly recognized, unexpected spectacle. Adult males, both openly sparring for this unsuspecting teenager's affection. Impasse intensified, there was almost exchange of fists. Ere hostilities were quashed by intervening guests. Apparently put out, Alfred danced with no One that evening. Can you imagine, Henry's feeling of euphoria, not having missed this? He never would have believed. There was someone who could out scoundrel him. His wife had convinced him, he was lowest life form when it came to women. You know, the "Jump on anything that moves" reputation. Do you also see spectre of jealousy, as cousin Barry races to her rescue? Mongrels snarling over choice steak. It would be funny, were it not pathetic. Budding virgin has no clue. She's temptress and source of all this imbroglio. Ah, innocence of childhood. Although there are others who would. Doreen sauntered over to Henry, having changed her dress. She asked. *"You think that frigger drunk?"* Henry replied. **"It could be. But on what? Not liquor."** Later it was announced. Parcel of land, on which a grand family home would shortly be built, had been acquired. Until then, Alfred moved into the two room bunk with wife and daughter. Doreen lambasted Alfred's reneging on plans, to rent family house with conveniences. *"Him tighter than hangman's noose. Everything I say to him, give me money to buy. He says we have to save to build the house. I should get by as I used to, before he came in picture."* This grievance and others. Doreen expressed to Henry in anger, shortly after the wedding, adding. *"Fish keep more longer before it begin to smell."* Primrose too was having angst with a changed environment. Alfred was always ogling her. Seized every chance arising, to brush against her. *"Him go out of him way to rub him frowsy self on me."* She complained to Henry. Had she discussed issues with mom? She said, repeatedly. Now disappointed with mom's dismissal. Quoting her. *"This is best chance me get in life. Me not going make anybody spoil it."* This from a woman who said of her daughter. *"She's my only child, and I love her without end."* But we know, she says one thing and does opposite. Told Alfred there could be no sexual intimacy, observing Christian conviction.Yet, did so engage with Henry. Alfred intensified harassment of Primrose, she again begged for mom's involvement and was told. *"Alfred don't mean nothing, but. Me will talk to and tell him, don't go into you room. And him must knock on the bathroom door, before him just bore in like that. Because is not him and me alone live here."* Things got testy around the house. By sparsity of money and Doreen being disgruntled. Primrose's boyfriend dropped in for Bible study. This irritated Alfred if he was present. There were dour faces all round. Folks in same house not talking to each other. Henry had by now, ceased intimate contacts with Doreen. Anniversary had passed and despite enquiries. Regarding construction of family's dream house. Her making sacrifices, going without what she considered basics. Doreen could not get guarantees from Alfred, as to when family's living condition would improve. Tension was troubling, but unknown to anyone, would gravitate from bad to worse. Methinks, women have seventh sense, when it comes to remote hint of skewed relationship. Long before seed is sown. It's like she can foretell, without crystal ball aid. What's about to happen, how and whom participants will be. All this, comes to fore with surprising, uncanny accuracy.

Primrose called Henry from phone booth. Uncontrollably in spasmed sobbing. Begged he come see her quickly. She was in dire straits. Had no One to relate. Pressed for synopsis of problem, she demurred. He came, saw eyes red, face flushed. She wanted to go out. Home environment was emotionally disturbing. Sobbing ebbed, but tears streamed. Driven to Roadrunner for favourite ice cream. She began tale of woe, as did sobbing in spasms. Getting ready for class. Alfred complained not feeling hale. Her mother gave him ginger tea and went to church. Telling him, Primrose would render any further aid, when she came home. Primrose was accompanied home by boyfriend, who hastily retreated. When told, Alfred was home. Alfred groaned rather loud, so she asked what she could do to ease suffering. Told her, he had severe gas pains, could she put a hot towel on his belly. Coming in with heated towel, she saw he had stripped down to his drawers and asked. ***"Why you take off your clothes, Mr. Alfred?"*** I know, relating what's next could be omitted. Because you know what's going to happen. He kept groaning, moaning louder. Signaled her to put the towel on his belly. I would think, there must have been something else to warn her. She had a dis-ease with his request, but. Mom having co-opted her as nursemaid. She had sense of duty bound and moved in warily to comply. Quicker than brown fox jumping over lazy dog. Alfred was out of bed, holding her in a Python embrace. She struggled, but he was strong as a Bull. Pressed hard of his erection onto her. His hands all over her. Breasts, buttocks and crotch. She writhed and struggled, asked what was wrong with him. He told her, he always loved her. Would give her all money saved towards building the new house. Or build the house for them both. She told him he was the devil and. ***"Get thee behind me Satan."*** His clammy hand slid down from her breast. Tugged impatiently at her underwear, massaged her vagina briefly. Next, he lifted and threw her on the bed. She gave up struggling, covered her face with both hands. Began crying and praying at same time. More she prayed, it seemed Alfred became emboldened, was soon on top of her. When he entered, she cut her prayer, screaming in agony. Alfred's beefy hand, clasped on her mouth muffling her scream. His thrusts were frenzied, she resumed praying. Begging God for deliverance from onslaught. Which to her dismay never came, shaking her belief in God. Being woman, has to be hell on earth. When the prize makes One vulnerable to this kind of violent invasion. Henry did not want to scold. Considering severity of her ordeal. Putting himself in her place, up against physical prowess of the man. He got mental picture of her being totally overwhelmed. Locked in his embrace, she must have felt futility of struggles. Still, he gently opined, instead of praying. Fighting and struggling could frustrate penetration. Women can move their extremes, like tic-tac-toe. I once had a swivel hipped girlfriend. Who would take gold, if this was an Olympic sport. Moving target can play havoc with most fervent stoker. But then, that comes with experience. Can also provoke and escalate bodily harm. Henry asked himself, how long she could have endured. Before being worn down and the inevitable. Sexual intercourse requires stamina. Whether trying to frustrate or participate, and at times. Leaves woman, weak as a field mouse. While male trampooses and stomps like donkey, emerging from Nettle field. He knows women who go fetal, using knees and hands to shove, roll, twist and eventually frustrate ardent assault. Such scenarios are usually, between boyfriend girlfriend, or husband wife. In absence of which he knows, some males will quickly apply violence. Then again he reasoned, being her first. Lack of experience, might work to her disadvantage. But, isn't this fighting reaction, maternal instinct, rather than experience? Maybe, like in movies. Mom or someone would come home or be visiting. She was swollen, in severe pain and still bleeding. Seemed her period had also set in. After his dastard act, Alfred left house before Doreen came home. Vowing Primrose to secrecy with a promise, things would be okay between them. For her part, she could not bring herself to relate events to her mother. Who, in aftermath of near fiasco at wedding. Asked Primrose in accusatory voice, tone and furied eyes. Was she willing participant, in waltzing Matilda escapade by Alfred at their wedding. Now afraid she would be seen as willing Hen. Possibly earning her mom's wrath. Who's blinkered focus was on ascension to that big house. Primrose expressed between sobs. Wish for father's presence. He would have ability to punish Alfred somehow. Whenever she asked mom about her father, she got angry. Told her she had no father. An obvious source of distress as she knew differently. After Alfred left, she decided on ruse to explain condition of mom's bed convincingly. Fall asleep there until mom came home. Not unusual when Alfred was away. Her period came unexpectedly whilst she slept. Henry insisted, she should find a way to tell mother her truth, but she resisted. Decided to share instead, a secret she never told anyone.

Ten years old, postman brought letter for her. A first, she was agog and excited with curiosity. It sat on window sill awaiting mom's return. Coming from foreign? Too much angst to contain. Anxiety on contents, fomented overbearing impulse to open the letter. Decided, mom would never know of it's arrival. It was from a man, whose photo was enclosed with a birthday card and US$5. Letter told of writer, being her father in America. Would come see her soon. From that day, she kept items wrapped tween covers of text books. When time came to exchange books, she unwrapped.

Checked condition. Kept wrapping and unwrapping until she put items in bottom of her grip.(suitcase) Gaiety fled the household, existence became tremulous. Each was silently distressed by their thoughts, unknown to the other. Alfred spent longer periods away, working in rural areas. Primrose was never herself after night of terror. Facial radiance dimmed to weather beaten features. She was most times mopey and depressed. Henry made efforts, show her life's positives. Gently reminding, had she fought whilst praying. Maybe, reprieve could come from unexpected source. ***"Lord helps those who help themselves."*** Alfred thwarted, had to know he dared not get violent with her. Outcome could not be hidden, nor silence coerced. She got miffed and said. Henry was insensitive to her suffering. But she understood, it came with being a man. Predisposed to thinking way they did, one tracked, hence her hating all men. Except her father, whom she was yet to meet in person. Lore dictates 'He who feels it, knows it.' Primrose could be correct, saying, a man cannot grasp magnitude of her suffering. Doreen asked Henry his opinion on Alfred's prolonged absence from home. Did Henry think he was living with another woman somewhere. Henry bit his tongue, remained stoically silent. She was going to have a talk with him, about promises and commitments made and not kept. Primarily, lack of financial support for his family and ongoing failure to begin building their home. She got cold feet when he came home, not wanting to hurt her chance at good things on horizon. Once again, as in recent home comings. He infuriated her by not showing interest in intimacy. About to leave, she stridently told him. Whichever day he next came from country, time would have to be made. Occasion had come and gone for them to engage in serious dialogue on festering issues. Proverbial straw that broke the camel's back, having been laid down. ***"It will be eggs or young ones."*** She declared, not knowing how prophetic her thoughts were. That was last face to face meeting. Alfred never came back to that house. Doreen had no clue where he might have gone, found shelter or what became of him. Bad already got worse, next stage is worst or worser? Some dare say, worserer and worserest. Dictionary says all are archaic. No longer in proper usage. Times Doreen was in angst regarding Alfred's no show. Primrose was at phone booth again, in tears. Henry went to see her, tried counseling and consoling. No way would she have a child out of wedlock. For a man she hated, and worst of all. Could never tell her child about it's father. Then wondered if similar fate had befallen her mother. Why she shielded Primrose from knowing her father. Getting very angry when questioned. She was determined to seek an abortion, whether or not Henry helped. Unpardonable sin according to religious teachings. Yet, she reasoned. If God didn't strike Alfred dead when raping her. He would forgive, her aborting result of. She was mad with God and the world. Got ambivalent with Henry, because he was man. He scratched that address from his itinerary and kept on keeping on. In surprise reunion, later years. Primrose migrated, her father lives with her. She studied and qualified in her career of choice. Has never married or pursued intimate relations with a man. Has never told her mother, events of night she fell asleep in her bed. And her period came without warning. Mom knows nothing about event that changed her daughter's life forever. It remains a secret, known only to herself, Alfred and Henry. As for Alfred, he would not know he made her pregnant. Nobody heard gun fire about him, since morning after the night before he left. In today's cyber managed world, he could not stay underground successfully and not get caught coming up for air. Primrose celebrated her forty-fifth birthday recently. Gabs with Henry on varied topics when she calls. Told her he would be writing a movie script based on their experience. Now as they snack at Panera Bread. She agrees with Henry, putting up determined fight. She could have cheated Alfred of his depraved pleasure. This from attending rape victim therapy classes and self defence sessions. Says emphatically, she's ready for another Alfred. Henry reminded her. Careful what you wish for, rape can be like gambling. You got to know when and whom to fight. When to give in and live another day. Then flew a kite with a chuckle for a tail. Saying, if she wanted to test her training, he was willing to role play. She studied his face and he hoped she was seriously thinking to take up his offer. He studied her eyes and features generally. Again the though. *"It really must be hard being born woman."* Reasoned in retrospect, man also has Achilles vulnerability, known to hasten demise. Similar circumstances, woman scarred, at least survives. When she spoke, it was like being in a trance. Soft voice and faraway look. She cautiously divulged another secret kept over years, with father's photo, $5 note and postcard. An eight page love letter she wrote, upon graduating high school. To the man she loved with all her being. Had to watch and listen in envy, as he and her mom caroused ever so frequently. Even more alarming, was her disclosure. Pastor's and her's stricture imposed on heart throb boyfriend. Would have been redundant and out of question. Ignored for this man she secretly hankered after. Henry was speechless. Told her it was a mere crush, going into what is called, puppy love. Born of her yearning for missing father figure in her life. Gratitude for him being there, giving financial support of her education. She slowly shook her head, said. ***"You never wondered how I felt those nights.***

Hearing, knowing you two were inches away, sweating in rapturous pleasure. Times you both let your emotions run wild. Forgetting the teenager laid abed, other side of partition. Know why I will never be intimate with another man? I feel soiled, dirty, as they say, unclean. I could never experience pleasure from sex." Tears slowly trickled down her cheeks, she ended. *"I deserved better in life, there's no excuse for this."* Of course she did and so did countless others. We are all of us in same world. Sometimes the good never encounter the bad or the ugly. Other times they do, with disappointing results. Says so much about people and emotions. Doreen visits ever so often but stayed home, although she could have migrated. She hasn't said it but it's certainty. She blames mom's indifference to her complaints about Alfred. As relates to his behaviour with her, for contributing to assault and rape. Reason enough her keeping incident from her mom, taking it to the grave. It is said in adage. *"Chip never falls far from the block."* Compare Primrose to her mom. There's unmistakable genetic similarity in their steadfast adherence to religious beliefs and devotion as Christians, to teachings of Holy Bible. Doreen will not engage intimately with her boss the old Mulatto. Because, she has to go church and faithfully praise her Jesus. Imputing, one act would contradict tenets of other. She begins an intimate relationship with Henry, whilst still going to church and praising her Jesus. To an extent, her daughter whom she loves without end. Gets raped whilst she prays, by a man. Whom feminine intuition or maternal instinct, must have alerted her. Had lusting eyes towards her teenaged daughter. Seed of doubt having been sown by his choice of dancing partner at her wedding. To extent, she harboured a not unheard of thought. The girl might have been in collusion with her husband. She might not have been convinced, but surely. Embryo of mistrust, incubated somewhere in recesses of her mind. Alfred enters and again is told, no intimacy until after marriage. This being against her religious principles. Hypocrisy blatant, she joked to Henry. He was already married, therefore their shenanigans were acceptable. Not wanting to cast boulder of reproach against her. Nevertheless, her behaviour has to be viewed through lineage. Primrose of similar persuasion, upholding Christian values and being chaste. Despite boyfriend's coaxing and sweet nothings. However, reveals secret lust for a man who would be her acting stepfather. To whom she wrote a letter revealing pent emotions. Granted, letter was never delivered. Although she has not said why. But she is now confessing, had it been. She hungered being receptive to that man. Slaking thirst for uninhibited sexual gratification to heart's content. Knowing the man Henry, as I'm certain I do. I visualize him sitting, listening to her confession of smothered desires. Going over in his mind, what she looked like back then, and even now. Beating himself senseless, ruing. *"Damn, how could I have missed those signals?"* Unsavoury as it sounds and actually is. This would not be Henry's first or only, mother daughter romp, he would've engaged in. Seems there is point at which, most fervent Christian. Finding themselves inundated with unfulfilled sexual desires. Will abandon faith and muse. *"F.... me without inhibition. Let me revel in pleasure of sexual bliss"* After all, isn't this what countless congregational leaders shamelessly indulge in. Some go further and commit murder in their quest to be so satisfied. Get caught, tried and languish in our prisons as you read this paragraph. "Meat eaten in secret is sweetest". Proverbs 9-17. Some indulge and pray forgiveness. Others, doesn't even give it a passing thought. Heaven help us all.

Paternity Issues-9

Back in chapter six, Henry sat with Brenda for first time in years. During which she carped on Tyrone's inadequacies. And her mother's coddling him, giving her attacks of nausea. Henry, always on hunt for "opening" Winked a suggestion to her which she dismissed with visible contempt. Job takes him countywide and an upside so far. Is that he runs into people from back home, he wouldn't otherwise have chance doing. As said before, ever in quest of "opening." Keeps connection with Brenda hoping, vulnerability can be exploited somehow. Possibly reestablish, clandestine song and dance. You know it's said. First cut is deepest. Women never forgets their first lover, not ever. They sometimes meet at Panera Bread, Bahama Breeze or P.F. Chang's. Henry gently nudges her in particular direction, that always rises her bile level. You also know, her dad plays very influential role in her life. Like every other occasion. Today's theme is all about, Tyrone's inability to get an erection. Brenda bites her lower lip and thinks for fifteen seconds then says. *"My husband has got to be only man, medical science cannot come up with cure for his ailment. After nearly thirty years, seeing "specialists." Trying different "latest FDA approved" techniques. Know what my dad said?"* She goes on, not giving him a guess at what dad said. Guess it wasn't really question question. *"Dad says, Tyrone conditions his mind. Weans himself mentally, from ever having sex. There's no therapy or snake oil that's going to reverse that mental block. But guess what?"* Again, no chance to take a gander at, before she goes on. *"He wants to have children, and my mom whines supporting him." "Well, you know Cinnybun, forget him for a minute. Focus on yourself. Every woman should experience motherhood. So do it for yourself, if not for him." "So I thought about it* *and said to me. For once, my mom says something that's worth serious consideration. I was not rushing this. Hell no! Got checked and artificial insemination was recommended, as best method for us and least complicated. You know I'm a private person, doctors aside. I didn't intend discussing this with close friends or acquaintances. Because, you know. You tell Mary, and she vows secrecy. But voila, you're being discussed at the water cooler. Every time Marie came to the office, I couldn't help thinking. She's got to be in her sixties and look at herrrr. You go, woman."* Henry cautiously raised finger. Brenda testily asks. *"What!?"* He says. **"Marie? Who is Marie?"** She glares him as if his ignorance is unforgivable. *"Marie, was on radio for years back home. I can't recall her last name. She was very popular then. Top cat and all that. Then she suddenly gave it up and migrated to Miami. I must be getting old, why I can't remember her name. But it will come when I'm not thinking about her. Let me tell you, if you saw that old woman. No, I shouldn't say, old. Women mature, men get old. If you saw that matured woman. You would think her age is still on home calendars. Between February and thirty day months. I swear. Know why she's preserved herself so well? Because, she never had children. So I'm thinking what my mom said, about motherhood and I'm looking at Marie and…"* Henry asks. **"So, Marie was motivation to not get pregnant when you could?"** Brenda stares off into the distance, then slowly begins. *"To an extent, Yes! But real kicker came from my dad. Went down, to help him celebrate his 75th. As usual, we got round to talking about mom and Tyrone. I told him, I had lunch with the old taximan recently. Should have seen his eyes pop and his jaw drop."* "What! You carrying cane and torch for that old man? Thought he was in nursing home by now." "I* *laughed and told him. Dad, his white hair is hereditary, not indication of age. You know how my dad is? He's just crazy about his little cinnamon bun."* Henry looks at her in deft anticipation. She blinks rapidly, and goes on. *"Told my dad about the procedure and my hesitance. Time was on my side, still on the calendar and all that. So my dad says, it's all up to me. Don't be goaded in either direction, follow my gut feeling. Because ultimately, it's my gut and no One else's. But he thinks, any male who calls himself 'Man.' And cannot give his woman, token pleasure of sex. Does not, should not, deserve joy of fatherhood. And? Here I am at point of no return, happy with myself."* Henry sees opportunity and says. **"Well, you've had more than token sexual pleasures. Genie is still outside the lamp. Didn't go back in, so there's no need to rub. But I agree with your daddy, about having children. Father's hood is important, especially if married. Hood is key."** Brenda began gathering phone and pocket book straps, as she stared at Henry and said. *"You are a hopeless dirtbag. Go to hell, and stay there."* Then walked away miffed. What did Henry say or do to merit such vitriol? We know there were times, they romped uninhibited in wild abandon. Her discarding resolve, to abstain doing so after her vows. So, what's new Pussycat? What's changed, for her to now see him as dirtbag? Henry accepts, he has always been that, without rancour. He's been told similar with different epithets by women, throughout his life. Only difference would be, he's now old dirtbag. Henry and Brenda have not met for sit down since. They keep in touch by phone. Exchange birthday greetings. She always initiates, and he always forgets. Recently she called and said. *"I know it's your birthday, but I'm not quite certain how old you are."* Henry told her he was seventy-five. *"Seventy-five!?"* She exclaimed. *"Seventy and five years old? Holy virgin*

Mary, mother of Jesus. Seventy-five. Where was my head, what was I thinking? Maybe I wasn't thinking, period. Seventy-five. I'm sorry, my dad is on other line, I got to go. Seventy-five?" Things we did one summer, brings unbridled joy to hearts. Now brings disdainful remorse, and stomach churning bile. Henry's age kept pace with hers, steadfastly separated by years as when first met. When she celebrated twenty first birthday. Henry was already mid forties, which she had no problem with. It does beggar the question. Why does she now find seventy-five so out of reality revolting? Her dad pointedly recognized and always referred to Henry as "The Old Taximan." To which she was both deaf and blind, until her discovery. Next lines are reality check on how much attention you paid to what you read. Did you get it. Her parents weren't married? Brenda was surprised when dad turned up at mom's birthday party. Remember? Also, at her wedding. Dad introduced "his wife" to Henry. Who was not her mom. Dad never ended intimate affair with her mother, while married to his wife, who was her aunt. Both women were top and bottom half sisters, living in same house, when.

There has always been an elephant in the room, house, city and state, that everyone ignores. That of paternity issues. We are more astute, accurately deciding. Whose Dog bred that Bitch. Than we can, between man and woman. Despite, male is participant in the process. When a woman gets pregnant, it is assumed, husband or boyfriend is father. Sometimes, this is far from truth. Risanne lived with boyfriend, Errol. In single room rented from Johnathon Gibbs. Whom she entertained often, for rebated rent. Derrick Gibbs was Errol's drinking buddy. He too, demanded sexual favours of Risanne. Failing which, he would tell her boyfriend about shenanigans, between her and his daddy. It is common among men, who dally with other man's woman, to not use contraception. It is what's called "A safe watering hole." Errol was a happy dad, when his daughter was born. So much so, Lying In staff had to enforce daily visiting hours, and threats to summon porter. Good citizens unanimously agreed, bouncing baby was a Gibbs. Question was, which One. Eventually, quandary was solved, citing adage. *"What drop off head, lands on shoulder."* See how issues are solved, before morphing into problems? Childhood sweethearts, Dezrine and Desmond. Got married at tender age of twenty-two. Convinced, 'D' in both names meant, destined for each other. Folks came and imbibed, whilst whispering reservations with the union. It was unanimous knowledge. Dezrine had been "around the block," few times. He was so naive, she would probably have to unzip his pants and point his penis. Fresh from secretarial college. Daring, dashing and vivacious, she got a job. Went on "working lunches" quite often, with her manager. Folks said, hers was an oops! pregnancy. Reinforced, when her fair haired and complexioned daughter was born. To Negroid parents, grand parents, as far back as lineage could be traced. Beset by malicious whispers, knowing stares and innuendo. Dezrine encouraged her husband to, and both relocated to another state. Happy in their new home. Friends gathered to celebrate their daughter's fourth birthday and house warming, with gifts and good wishes. She confided to a friend, she was again pregnant. Declared with a knowing wink. *"When this baby born, them will have to eat them words, and swallow them with wagging tongues."* In today's technologically advanced society. There are resources at our disposal, that did not exist five years ago. If we venture back twenty years, it appears those were dark ages. Thumbs up for brilliant minds that experimented. Bringing empowerment to our lives. We must concede, this is not always taken as positive, when it works to our disadvantage. But, this is world in which we live. We change things we can and accept those we can't. Do not knock your head against a wall, it only hurts more. It is taken as fact, man is more than likely to be unfaithful in a relationship. Let us not forget, he is ably aided and abetted in this despicable variance by woman. In some cases that comes to light, women too have compulsion to be unfaithful. Aided by man with similar proviso as relative to female. Toni was eldest child of the family, going on eighteen years old. Asked her father, why was she a virtual prisoner. Whilst her brothers at sixteen, fourteen and eleven. Roamed free as mongrels, in search of garbage cans. Dad told her, it was simple. *"Any trouble they make out there, they leave out there. Trouble you make out there, you going bring home to us here."* Figuratively, dad is talking about pregnancy. It would seem, he doesn't care what boys do out there. So long as it stays out there. Toni is very much different. She will be "discovered," by parents. Or come, in regretful tears. But, it's theirs to deal with as best they can. I was four years old. Playing "Ship Sail" with grandma. In between chomping crisp corn kernels and coconut. She tutored on life lessons. Do's, don'ts and things beyond my years, to grasp pros and cons of. She felt duty bound to protect women from men, including her grandson. Had she been once bitten? *"If the woman call you name, mind the belly. You can't smell of scallion, unless you go scallion bed."* My father's approach to this subject was. *"If she shake the hat and pick out you name, mind the child. It can either become, feather in your cap, or crown of thorns. Sometimes, the jacket we wear early in life. Keeps us warm, when days become cold, and at times lonely."* In Jamaican parlance, "jacket" in paternity issues. Is a child with marginal or no resemblance to. But a man accepts as his own, or is forced to. A "waistcoat" is child, having no resemblance to. Yet, man gladly accepts. Notable waistcoat situations are usually, child of fair complexion with straight hair. Eagerly embraced by Negroid male, everyone sees could not be his. Child's attributes, makes it bright, desirable feather in his cap. Which he wears with unbounded pride. On sole occasion I questioned paternity. I was goaded by my landlady, who was proven right. Given I was being threatened and coerced to do so. That big head boy, is now a fifty odd years old man. My mind goes back to post, Miss Candy's era. Perchance she could be impregnated by child, yet to see his twelfth birthday, or having just. Lord knows, she could not tell that to her man.

Simon began telling of a new family discovery and possible crisis brewing. *"My brother Jonas, bad like yaws from him eyes at him knees. My mother send him to relatives over "Bois Content." Bwoy go tie Jackass at pass, meets Pinny granddaughter, Beatrice. Them go same school, and before anybody know, things start. Every chance them get, is happy hour. One day, Miss Rebecca call him and ask, who him people be. Cut long story short, bwoy now drop fun on him half sister. Nobody did suspish anything, except Miss Rebecca. My daddy eat the sweet fruit, it set Jonas' teeth on edge. When it comes to sexing, most times. Anywhere you turn, prickles and burr thorns might stick you. Friend is foe, and stranger can be family."* Things used to be different, in a positive way, from my perspective. Then it was a world of give and take, where paternity of children were concerned. For every woman that dillied, there was a man who dallied. If by chance a child emerged, from this dilly dallying. In true spirit of give and take, child's future was somewhat secured. Man who went out to dilly. Accepted, he could have given his child to an unsuspecting man to raise. Hence, when time came for him to raise child of his own. He accepted possibility, he could be taking on another man's child as his own. Evidence of this can be seen, in some Jamaican families of blacks. Where a Chinese, Indian or Mulatto child, comes into a family by birth. Especially if mom also helps in the shop. Not to mention, children attending school. Having different surnames, yet are twin images of each other. Like two Leroys with different surnames, who were thought to be twins. Nobody fussed or went DNA testing. Not that it was available in them carefree days anyway. Aubrey and Corina, were wife and husband. She worked with Dubois', family of Mulattoes. She had twins, one white and one black. Talk about them, being talk of the town. Actually, this would be second of such event coming to light. Folks argue, there is a negativity to this kind of accepted behaviour. People often meet, and initiate intimate relationships with close kin, unawares. I had a sweetheart, who turned out to be wife's niece. Frighted to peeing, when her mom greeted, as we sat embraced on her verandah. Then calmly asked. *"How's Cynthia?"* Could also have been my child, of which I was unaware. Having started out procreating, quite early. Other peril cited, arises from folks needing medical tissue. Person who turns up, in belief they are parent. Sometimes, turns out to be unrelated. Hence, there is no lineage to rely on, for hereditary traits. This clean, easily rewarding lifestyle. Ended, with onset of HIV and AIDS. Or has it? I am to think not, because when folks are tempted to pursue ecstatic thrill of fornication. Temptation blinds senses to perils, real or imagined. As some say. *"In heat of moment."* Then thrill dissipates and sanity returns. Folks asking unanswered question. What if? Suppose? Trusting fate for positive outcome, trembling at thought of the worst. After years of marriage and cohabiting, she tested positive for STD. Can't be cured, can be controlled. She strongly suggests, it could be his philandering. He gets tested, proffers evidence of negative results. Repeats his test one year later, still negative. Silence is on, things aren't as they use to be. Why? Somebody done somebody wrong song, and they needs sing. But they ain't gonna, for sure. In long run, more aptly in very short time. Trust is broken and dies. Could possibly be mended by confession, but there's no yielding of position. For someone to take, someone's got to give. Not judge her by his standards, she rebuked. Truth is. Did he have a standard? If he did. What was his standard? That which dictated. He, was hypocritical, sanctimonious whore. Seeking to discourage competition by a woman. It is my stated inner conviction. Women should not be slut, engaging in extramarital affairs. As men are mongrels, similarly engaged. And demand chaste respect. I have concept of female, being virtuous, noble and circumspect. Standard of do good purity. After all, she mothers and nurtures children. Yes, men has role, fathering children. Also, a responsibility to be equally circumspect in behaviour. If only to be an example to scions sired. Men didn't start the fire. It's been always burning, since the world's been turning. Maybe it began in biblical era, but fact is. Women are held to higher standards than men, because of who they are.

A fervent "I love you"-10

A woman asked. ***"Why men find it hard to say, "I love you?"*** Ruminating her question, mind went back forty years to Cassandra. Talking points introduce misunderstandings that defeats original intent. Cassie said she wanted to talk, that evening. We sat, I sang, to dispel frown on her brow. ***"Here we are again happy as can be. All good friends and jolly*** *good company."* She scoffed and scowled, was now dour. *"You know?"* She began. *"From we've been together. You've never told me, you love me."* "Well, now that I think of it. I've never told anyone, I love them. I believe in lore of yore adage. *"Actions speaks louder than words."* Way I treat someone, should convince. I do love them. Don't you think?" *"That might be true, but I still want to hear you say it sometimes."* "What about Tuesday evening, when I came in? I hugged and kissed you. You paused the machine and we….." *"That's not saying, you love me. That's saying, you're horny and lusting. Way you always are. Anyhow, I am saying it again. I love you."* Silence is on. She asks. *"Well! What do you say? I just told you I love you."* "Oh! Me too." She leered, then was silent. I tried making light, to stanch rising anger. **"Don Tappin says."** *"Times I purify my lips with sacred fire to talk to you about love. But right words don't come. So I just play right groove to make you move. Can you dig it?"* **P334** She rose, resumed doing laundry. From infancy, I knew mother didn't like me. She hated my father for "tricking" her, and not giving sufficient financial support for my upkeep. Her reaction was rife among single mothers, raising children with little or no monetary input from child's father. Granny said. *"Bwoy, you mumma does use you puppa fat, so fry you."* Between floggings, Granny often hugged and expressed regret for severity of punishment inflicted. But emotions were never vocalized. I rarely told my children, I loved them. They knew it was not because I didn't. Saw me striving to make their lives far better than what I had. Laying foundations for their future. If that was not love, then what was it? Now adults, they often say. *"I love you, Dad."* I respond in like vein. Terms of endearment, were never feature of my early upbringing. Or among children who, like me. Had only single parent, focused on scrounging to keep hunger at bay. Our lives were daily repeat encounters, with misery and disadvantages. Truth be told, there were times. We were seen as obstacles to parents' progress. We learned to detect that stare of abhorrence. Making ourselves scarce, to avoid a whupping, for no reason. Other than to release mama's pent up frustrations with hard life, the world and daddy's wife. It is probably not recognized by people. Accustomed to hearing those three words. Majority of times, it is said quite flippantly without any real commitment. I think, for this expression to have meaning. I have to hold a woman in warm embrace.

Look intently through eyes, into her inner being. Kiss her tenderly and softly whisper **"I love you."** That way, she sees and feels my energy or vibe, aflowing and atingling. "I love you" is not to be bandied about. Way we do "Good morning, How you doing?" It loses potency and purpose. That's not to say, there's absence of emotional ties to persons we utter the line. But, that deep inspired conviction is not there. It's a fool's game. Let me elaborate and illustrate. We don't just holler "Help me" for sake of. It's expression, saying someone is in dire straits. So should "I love you" be provoked by intensity of desire and purpose. Two female coworkers at end of workday, on way out the door. One says. *"Enjoy your vacation. See you when you get back. Love you."* Other responds. *"Love you too, take care."* That's chitchat among two friends, without any deep emotional connect. Maybe that's just me anyhow. Actions speaks louder than words. I'm sticking to that mantra, make exceptions when situation calls for reciprocation. Otherwise, essence is absent and phony reigns. Remember now. "I love you too." Feel me?

Short train ride to adventure-11

Frank was a hard working, and hard smoking man. He had been with PE&G after graduating college. Happy in his job, until new company policy, prohibited smoking. Within certain perimeter of main building. Smokers had to go remote when urge arose. Trips to beyond, were part of employee's breaks and lunch periods combined. Hence, habits could not be indulged, without constraints. It was assumed, but never proven. Shortly after, company declared, smoke free campus. Retaliation, when smokers decided to buck management on first policy change. Coming swiftly as it did, less than two months after remote rule. Employees were given notice, latter change would be effected and enforced. Failure to comply, would incur disciplinary action, up to and including, the "T" word. Termination. Smokers were offered therapy and other cessation options. Based on seniority, they could transfer to facets of operations, where smoking was not fully banned. Those affected were in hushed discussion, on what was seen as arbitrary and...company wasn't done turning screws. Next salary negotiations, smokers and obese employees. Should expect increase in health plan salary deduction. Smokers now joined forces with obese, speaking as vocal majority. They took sick time and hollered at wayside, citing discrimination. Company quickly agreed, with unexpected twist. Yes, indeed. Current equality policy, discriminated against employees who observed healthy lifestyles. Yet, paid same salary deductions as those who didn't. Frank got transferred to Fleet Services, where smoking was prohibited. He volunteered counting, light poles, transformers and cable drums. Too often, he was warned by supervision. One would think, he had more than enough issues to confront. But, life can be very challenging and sometimes brutally punishing. He was diagnosed with esophagitis, that morphed to esophageal cancer. His West Palm Beach lawyer, encouraged him to join class action lawsuit against big tobacco. Treasure hunt was on, with as much fervour as cancer took over Frank's body. Sadly, cancer won, before treasure was found. Wife Irene, was consoled in grief by the lawyer. Who told her, a settlement was imminent. From which she could erect, mental or physical monument to Frank's memory. That was more than six years ago. We know, corporations will out wait victims. Until next, second or third generation, accepts paltry sum. She still visited lawyer's office, taking requested hospitalization documents from Frank's diagnosis and treatment regime. Seems, every time Irene jumped hurdles and provided paperwork. Others were demanded, which frustrated her. Assured by the lawyer, fruit was maturing on vine, almost ready to be plucked and enjoyed. She took comfort in and soldiered on.

Today, Irene was one tired woman. Tired waiting for good news from the lawyer, and now the overdue TriRail. This time of day, she knew there would not be vacant seats. Was delighted when a young man offered his. She plopped herself down hurriedly. Stared his face, expressing her gratitude. Went on to say. *"Oh, I thought your kind were all extinct. It's good you're one of the survivors. How good, you'll never know."* Ken smiled acknowledgment as the train sped up, then slowed, horns blaring on approach to crossings. One rider left the seat, Irene shuffled to the corner. Quickly touched Ken, patted space she vacated, for him to sit. He sat, Irene began. *"You're saviour, twice in a row. Hate sitting aisle. Passengers with backpacks, humongous bags and stuff. Swinging and swaying to and fro, as they race down aisle. They could take an ear off, and an eye out without knowing or caring."* Each introduced themselves and shook

130

hands. Ken told Irene he was medical trainee, attending symposium and looking forward to it's end. Not relishing, daily back and forth. Irene told Ken, reason for her travels. He expressed regrets at passing of her husband, kinship was formed. Irene began as they say, running off at the mouth. *"I've got one daughter, with writing degrees. Journalism, philosophy and God knows what else. Except how to find a good man, and give me adorable grandchildren. I detest the riffraff she hangs out with. Thank God, none of them have been taken seriously up to now. But, can you imagine. Young men with earrings? I told one of them, if I knew he was that destitute. I could find him something more decent in Frank's wardrobe. He laughed and left, then Karen told me. Jeans he wore, was bought like that, with knees and cuffs frayed, for over a hundred dollars. Can you believe that? Who pays more for old rags, than for new clothes?"* Train rattled on, Ken and Irene prattled on this and that. She demanded his phone number, gave him hers and address. Went on to tell him. *"I don't know if you're religious, and I am not caring, but we celebrate Easter. You are invited to our Palm Sunday family event. You can come as you are, don't bring a girlfriend. I want you to meet Karen. Give her a glimpse of the other side. You will come or else. I will make sure you face the firing squad."* Getting home that evening, Irene brought Karen up to date, on lack of progress at the lawyer's office. And having invited a young man, to their Palm Sunday family event. *"Put on clothes Karen, not threads, I beg."* Irene defiantly told Karen. Later confessing, she couldn't help loving Ken, moment she saw him. Had to bring him into her life, somehow. *"I just knew he was good boy, cut from fine enduring fabric."* As things turned out, one could say, she had good nose for winners. Karen and Ken dated, got married on anniversary of their first date. Irene barely concealed anxiety, to dote on grandchildren. When couple celebrated second anniversary, with Karen not getting pregnant. It is said, Irene confronted her. *"Listen to me, you have to live up to your wifely duties. Don't let your husband wander. Ken's mouth reached the door, before his hand touched the knob this morning. Husbands should leave home with satisfied smile of past night. And come home with grin of tonight's expectation."* As a couple, Ken and Karen rightly kept certain affairs to themselves. In that regard, Irene was not aware. Both had decided to put off having children, until they could acquire their own place. Miserly saving to achieve goals. Good family vibes notwithstanding, he was not keen, starting family in mother-in-law's house. At christening of their first child, Irene joked. Event reminded her of the great New York blackout. Which by coincidence exactly nine months after, there was unprecedented increase in births. This, it is said. Elicited an embarrassed eye roll from Karen. But what the heck? Irene was just being jovial, carefree and over happy. Setting stage for next carefree spoof. A new "Save-all-you-can" store, opened on Dixie Highway. Three adults and baby went grocery shopping, where Karen slowed checkout frequently. Consulting phone to compare shelf and register prices. She had come to know, quite often. Register prices exceeded shelf prices. This time she called a halt. *"No no no, that was.... Never mind. I am sorry."* Register price was few cents less than shelf price. Karen swore, this was like twice lightening strike in same place. It always happened to customer's disadvantage, never retailer's. Cashier was showing low keyed discontent. Ken decided to get creative, asked Irene. *"Does farts have lumps?"* Quick on uptake, she replied. **"Oh no they don't. Rainbows don't have black, and farts definitely don't have lumps."**

Cashier's head jerked at Ken and Irene. Karen's mouth hung wide. Ken continued. *"I must have shat then."* **"Oh, yes my friend, that you did. Mary's little lamb found a hole and burrowed through. You know what that means, when it comes to sheep? Rest of flock gonna come rushing out. That's nature of sheep for you my boy, can't be helped."** Irene ended. *"KEN!! MOMMM!! PLEASE!!"* Karen said, anguished. Quickly said to cashier. *"I am not with these people, they are not with me. I don't know them. Oh my God. Can't you see, these are horrible people?"* Cashier too was somewhat, one would say. Discombobulated? She too did not know what to say, but stuttered. Telling Karen her total, and asking if card was debit or credit. Karen was in stunned silence. There was lull during which Karen seemed distressed. Irene and Ken were punch pleased. This ends their story for that day. Their saga however, is just beginning. Suffice it to say, Karen continues to endure, her husband's prankish behaviour. Quite often, instigated by mom. But they enjoy each others' company. Irene, never failing to remind Karen. It was her who went out searching, brought home a good husband for her. What are your thoughts on the shopping escapade? I think it was cruel and went too far. That's not fun, embarrassing a person like that, especially a woman. Do it to a man. He usually doesn't care one way or another. We would think. Happy abides in this union, despite Irene's and Ken's poke at Karen. Alas, we would be wrong. Karen complained to lunch mate and very close, peas-in-a-pod confidante. *"I've always dreaded living with mother-in-law. Never in my wildest dreams, did I think that person would be my own mother. She sucks up to him at my discomfort, like you would never believe. I feel like a domestic/whore. When I am not being reminded, what Ken enjoys for dinner.*

I am reprimanded for not living up to wifely duties. Because Ken did not seem happy this morning. Just makes me want to give her details, ask if anything's missing." **"How does Ken react to all this?"** Lunch mate asks. *"Oh, him? He's one, two faced patronizing Son-of-a-Bitch. Trying to hide satisfaction and same time, walking around all smirky. Doesn't he observe his wife is tense. Ready to go rummage in the cutlery drawer? He comes to bed one night. Starts talking about how happy my dad must have been, having a wife who's sensitive to making a marriage harmonious. I told him, dad was never happy camper. When it came to their marriage, my father was reduced to two words. "Yes, dear." "Okay, dear." "Sure, dear." "Anything you say, dear." Does that sound like happy, contented man? Anyhow, next weekend we're going to see his mom. She's in hospital with fibroids, and opting for surgery. I am no authority on these things. But if I got to sixty-eight and...By the way, let me ask you this. Do fibroids, kill you, as a rule. Or just gives you permanent pregnant look? I ask, because. Mrs. Jenkins had fibroids, up to her forties. She said, doctor told her. They would start shrinking when menopause sets in, and it does seems that is happening."* Lunch mate ponders for a while, then says. **"I can't give opinion on that, because, so far. None of men or women on either side of our relatives, have had this health issue. But bear in mind, with surgery, it's going to be personal choice."** Karen continues. *"Where was I? Lost my tho... Oh yes, I was saying. Ken wants to take the baby along. I say, definitely not. He begins his pathetic whiny whiny. "Oh Karen, it's not fair to my mom. She hasn't seen Kenan since birth. Whilst your mom takes care of him, minutely. Enjoying his coo coos and such. He has two grandmas, you know?" Tells him straight up, without even a blink. My child has one mom, who got her* *surgery scar, bringing him in this world. She says he is not going to visit anyone in hospital, at this stage of his life. Exposed to microbes and viruses floating around. Everyone knows, hospital is most unhealthy place anyone can visit. It is not absolutely necessary, and grandma can see him, when she's out and home. Between us. You know why she's never seen her grandchild? Because, she's disappointed he wasn't born a girl. That's why. But suddenly, she wants to see him? Not if I can help it. And, this one? I can."* Lunch mate thinks, then suggests. **"Maybe, she fears not coming out of surgery, would like to. You know? Who knows, it could be her first and last chance. Seeing her grandchild, Karen. Maybe, you want rethink this."** Karen defiantly replies. *"All reason why. I wouldn't want her seeing him before she kicks out. Having his features fixed in her consciousness. She would be sure to come back and haunt him."* **"Karen! Don't tell me, you believe in superstitious crapola."** Karen sharply retorts. *"After you suffer morning sickness, cramps, untold discomfort and pain until that C section heals. You believe anything, trust me on this. I've been there done that, only once. Not again."* Lunch mate was silenced by Karen's stark, unyielding defiance. Irene was getting on in years, dreading West Palm Beach trips. Lawyer says, settlement awaits signatures of all parties. At which point, court will issue acceptance order. Allowing for funds being disbursed to aggrieved persons, or their assigned dependents. Her health was failing, house falling apart. Ken and Karen did band-aid fixes. Not wanting to make permanent repairs. Irene wanted the house preserved for her grandchild. She loved being in her house. Dared Karen to attempt selling it, before her eyes closed. Child's parents had no intention staying there much longer. Area was not conducive to raising Karen's boy. Life was good for Ken, as long as Irene was in the house. Karen embraced ability to save on rent, whilst living with and caring for mom. Money saved would go towards either her son's college fund, or down payment on their house. All told, with house's sale when mom passed. She should have good financial start on life's journey. She never mentioned insurance windfall, but we can look at that possibility. Which, if it came to fruition. Karen and family would be, as the saying goes. Set for life. Storm season came, blowing friends and lunch mates apart. Table consultations and whispers ended. Ken and Karen went house viewing, met a grandma. That's where someone said, "surprise." Mrs. Muir entered the picture again. Not her from relationship with the Ghost. This one was with Frank, when both were coworkers at PE&G. He often took Karen to take-your-child-to-work days at the company. Mrs. Muir went out of her way, overly doting on Karen. Who at twelve years old. Asked her father, if Mrs. Muir was his girlfriend. Her dad did not take the question kindly. Where Karen got assumption from, nobody knows. She entered puberty, into teenage. Believing, both her parents had workplace sweethearts. And it was natural social pastime. Mrs. Muir lives with her son and family, in this house they bought, less than two years ago. After developer's stops and starts, seemed it would never get built. Now, he's been offered a position, to head his company's division in another state. Hence, the house is up for sale. Mrs. Muir chirps. **"My my! How young people have changed in just over twenty years. And by golly. Who is that young man? Is that the little baby boy? By jove, it is. I am really getting old."** Karen begins loud whisper. *"Getting? You are old."* Ken goes into loud, dry coughing fit. Drowning her out, whilst fixing her a reprimanding stare. These days, Karen doesn't care one hoot what Ken thinks.

A ? of Abortion-12

Ever paused in the daily helter skelter of life and reflect on a blooming fruit tree? Some flower profusely. Were every bloom to become fruit. Branches would snap under enormous weight of. Agronomy teaches. Nature gives trees, wisdom shedding flowers and fruits during development, ensuring plant's structural survival. Nature does not always get it right. Half of my Ackee tree, crashed to ground one calm day. Unable to support it's load, when I was so fascinated with abundance, and looking forward to bumper crop. Ah well. Animals, including humans have natural ability to limit fetal development, during gestation from embryo to birth. Also true of incubating process, where some eggs fail viability. A bountiful harvest of most crops, is always welcomed. Given it brings monetary returns in some instances, also sustains human existence. Most animals enter food chain at birth, prey on others, until others prey on them. Quoting from article I read. *'When dawn breaks over the Serengeti. Lion knows, he must outrun an antelope, or starve to death. Similarly, antelope is aware. It must outrun that lion, if it wants to see another day.'* In essence, surplus animal and agricultural production serves a positive. In human situation however, starvation often decimates. Creating never ending need for relief that is always insufficient. It's been said, our world is over populated. Others counter, it is not. There are too many in places where resources are meagre, and few, where there's abundance and some. Used to be, my conscience got pricked when washing my car. Even worse when I saw fire hydrants opened, so children can play in precious, gushing water. There are millions whose lives would be so much better, having access to that, we flippantly lay to waste. But, we are where we are and they are where they are. Self tells me, there's nothing I can do. So, I wash my car and am thrilled with buffed after sheen. There are countries or societies that limit population growth, for supposedly constructive reasons. Recently, did fact find research on countries, having negative population growth. These are among industrially developed nations, purportedly because. Most these countries, close borders to immigration. Goes further, and where immigrants are allowed in. They never can qualify for citizenship. United States of America is one of few, more apt to be only country. That not only opens it's doors to immigrants. But confers citizenship on them, and children born within it's borders. Now we sing about, "The way it used to be." As of recently, there are efforts to selectively curtail this open door policy. In pursuit of limited entry, or exclusion. It is indisputable fact. In recent times, minority of those admitted. Attempted to, and succeeded. In misguided pursuit of wantonly destroying life and property. Clearly then, it cannot be "business as usual." Methinks, this country should maintain a system that has served purpose in years past. That is, would be immigrants, vetted at origin and approved or not. Allowing multitudes to clamour inside gates. Is a designed out-of-control situation.

Addressing topic. Growing up in 1950's city of Kingston, Jamaica. Literally, writing was on the wall, and zinc fences. Anywhere that could convey a message, was emblazoned with slogan. 'Birth Control. Plan to kill Black People.' This, in response to efforts by Elizabeth (Beth) Jacobs, Jamaican black woman. Pioneer of Family Planning programme outreach. In a semi-literate society, wall scrawl found fertile ground. Social workers came with sheaves of pamphlets. In vain effort to convince deeply skeptical women. Whose menfolk, kept them under threat of beatings and serious injury, if they dared follow birth control guidelines. Within this sector, women who could, and did take measures to prevent unwanted pregnancy. Were called "Mules" and socially ostracized by other women. Thrusts also came by newspaper and Rediffusion ads. Engaging people, who could not read or sometimes marginally so. Neither could they afford four shillings a month for radio rental. A brush and bucket of white lime wash, defeated message. This opposing mantra was aired for residents in certain sections of city. Where overcrowding, from over breeding, in ramshackle housing created. Lack of basic utilities, education, skills training, fostering. Dependent on woefully inadequate social and health services for survival. Despite years of different programmes being introduced, over breeding is obstacle to people development in many parts of our world. Having looked at the 'prevention' aspect of life. Let's look at the 'cure' scenario, for what it's worth and it's vagaries. Abortion subject, has always elicited fierce debate. Religious beliefs are introduced, and to some people, it's a cardinal sin. I find it very hypocritical of lawmakers, who support citizens. Making health choices in this pandemic, to their detriment. It's up to them, deciding to mask or not, vaccinate or not. Yet, pass legislation, denying women right to decide whether she should abort or not. The debate is alive and well, laws notwithstanding. Some see it as wanton murder, others say it should be woman's choice. In instances of incest and rape. Methinks, accepted norm favours abortion. It seems contradictory, some women expend small fortunes, try desperate measures to conceive, without success. Whilst others so blessed, make equally sustained efforts to abort. It is not recognized that women often gets bullied by man who impregnated. To either abort or bring pregnancy to maturity, as he decides. Usually, this comes about from a young man.

Said to be 'sowing wild oats.' Not wanting to defile his or family's image, with bastard child. Instances, his inheritance is at stake, should he fail taking action to preserve doyen's or doyenne's status quo. Hence, *"It's the woman's choice."* Is accepted, unchallenged fallacy. Let's not forget, there are women who open their fields, to thrill of wild oats sowing. Unwilling to take this crop to harvest. Lest she be seen as loose, shunned by society and courting by a resourceful desirable male. She too makes similar choice to abort.

Here's an amusing tale, with wry twist on this theme. McCurbins, Annabelle and Devoux. Had been married, going into fourth year. Devoux wanted children, but his wife could not conceive. This was her second marriage, first for him. Already in mid thirties, Devoux was anxious to get daddy party started, before she hit the big Four O. Despite her putting it off, Devoux insisted both seek fertility assistance. You know, I've always maintained that women are smarter than men. They really are. Where they often lose out, is in cleverness. 'Smart' is associated with book learning. Whilst 'cleverness' is that edge, city folk has, over suburban petty bourgeoisie. City folk faces survival challenges very early in life. They learn to be clever, from being, 'once bitten' and always 'shy.' Now remember, 'clever' is also 'smart.' So, he's doubly armoured for battle. You also know, insurance is not paying for these tests and procedures. Devoux spares no expense, they go and have preliminary tests done. Next visit, doctor confirms what Devoux already knew. Nothing wrong with him, he is viable to impregnate his wife. However, Annabelle should stop her oral contraceptives. Come back for further tests, forty-five days after. If she has not conceived. You expect there was cussing and fussing? There wasn't. Devoux introduced two children, from extra marital affairs. A third was on the way. Thanks to their housekeeper's niece.

They all came together as one family and lived ever after. Can't claim 'happy.' There was spectre of unresolved worm cans. One dared not open, and have their can exposed. So...?

Genevieve was full fledged woman at seventeen, when she came to tend Roache's three children. Her father brought her grip up the step. Mrs. Roache greeted, and introduced her family. Wise old man Ebenezer, took instant dislike to Mr. Roache, saying. *"Him look too dam happy seeing the child. Not take eye off her, showing him thirty-two."* Ralston Roache was accustomed staying out. Most nights, confronted by wife Jean as to his whereabouts. A fight ensued and he got worst of, being partially inebriated. She often took pots to his head. He retaliated with punches, slapping air. Genevieve smiled with Willy next door, he became boyfriend. Ralston began coming home "for lunch." A new routine for him. Genevieve complained to Willy. *"Mr. Rally trying to bother me when him lunchtime. Me want go back to country."* We know, Acorns of jealousy once sown. Becomes giant Oaks overnight. Friday evening, Genevieve told Jean, she's writing her father to come for her. Because of Ralston's lunchtime escapades. Saturday morning, after Friday night's shebang. Jean coercing Genevieve to stay. Ralston found two tires on his taxi flat. Angered blind, weekends being best earning days. Jean too was irate, although subdued. Questioned Genevieve on her possible complicity in, or knowledge of the who. She truthfully denied awareness of or aiding in vandalism act. Certain she had either a hand in, or knowledge of. Ralston saw Genevieve as an enemy. That, for intents and purposes, suited her. He fumed and bided. Ebenezer's wife having died at childbirth, he raised eleven children as single parent. Four boys and seven girls, of which Genevieve was last born. He was never told, Roaches were being processed for migrating to the USA.Wanting Genevieve to accompany them. Had to be adopted before she turned eighteen. When approached, he declined. Emphasized, being misled. Genevieve was in love with Willy, did not want to leave. Older siblings told papa, this was rare opportunity. Sister going to land of opportunity, opening doors for others. He should not deny her that chance of a lifetime that might never come again. Truth is, they were anticipating all good gifts and remittances. Also, perchance. Genevieve could one day be in position, to "file" for and bring them to the USA. Buoyed with expectations, stymied by papa's refusal to budge. Decided, there should be a grand family get together, upcoming holiday weekend. At which, fatted calf would be served. Oak barrels of fermented juices unplugged, and at end of it all. Having been prevailed upon by majority, Papa would be in frame of mind, to see things clearly and agree. Call it misunderstanding or deliberate trickery. Folks in rural enclave, greeting neighbour, Ebenezer. Congratulated him on big news of his youngest daughter going to the USA. He told first such person. *"Clean out you ears ma. Nutt'n not go so."* More he denied, good wishes kept pouring in. So he just smiled and nodded in resignation. First thing Ralston did, after landing in USA. Quarantined Genevieve's immigration papers. Reason and means never disclosed. Suffice to say, this could not be positive for her. He attained dominant household status. Browbeating and physically trampling his wife into submission. She was in no position to shield Genevieve. Although she knew her husband had designs on her. He, who with a broad smirk, once told the teen. *"You think, me pay plane fare, bring you to America. Turn round pay rent and feed you. For what? Sit down and look on you? You would have to be in frame, with glass in front you before that happen."* Jean took Genevieve to confirm her pregnancy. Told her, abortion was only option. No way, she could be in the house. Whilst other arrangements have to be made, tending Jean's three children. Her position was dictated by iota of jealousy and rancour. Told Genevieve, she never saw her making token resistance to Ralston. Maybe, she played along. He quarantined her papers. What could she do, without having them in hand? Yes, she had legal options, but she would not know where to start. And if she did, where then would she live? That would probably give her option returning home. But we know, woman to woman. Can be eyes and mind closed unfair, when jealousy taints the senses. Only empathy she felt, was for Self.

Mr. Otis: Man around town, who knew every woman. Most every woman knew about him. Some, driven by curiosity, got to know the man, and carried life long token of his affection. He worked two day jobs, as labourer on the docks, and at the Sugar Warehouse. Born in Mocho, Clarendon parish, came to Kingston at age 19. Leaving six children from four women. He set up house with a woman, who had two girls for him. She passed, giving birth to his third child by her. A relative came to help with those three. Born so close to each other, were dubbed step children by kind folks. Which they were, but folks meant. 'Step' as in stair, that is. This relative whilst caring for her step children. Began caring for her own and soon had her stair going. Wisely decided, there was need for added income, supporting the fast growing brood. She set up makeshift cold supper shop, under big tamarind tree. Cooked food was displayed in showcase and served to diners. Surprised by volume of patronage, she invited friend Ruby to help with the business. It rained buckets one night, Ruby slept over. Shortly after, she began making family. Right there in that house with Mr. Otis. It was talk of the town, folks were awed. House was small, living conditions were cramped. Unbelievable aspect of this saga was, both women lived in sweet harmony. Some said, convenience or politics, makes strange bedfellows. Both women reaped financial gains from the business. Obviously, one could not get by without other. Jealousy had to be dispensed with. Mr. Otis leased land and decrepit buildings. He refurbished and rented to single female tenants only. First time he became aware, a man was visiting his tenant. She was given verbal notice to quit forthwith. Enforced by unhinging front door, and threat to inflict harm by machete on male trespassers. This then was heyday of Otis Monteith's existence. His wife had an always pregnant figure. In later years, doctor told both, she had to stop having children. Her health endangered, from giving birth to fifteen children. Friend Ruby had had three. Mr. Otis now worked at the concrete plant, had been for years. His truck sideswiped a lane bollard, he denied responsibility. Until, telltale yellow paint from, was pointed out to him on the truck. After another similar incident, he was sent for eye exam. Found to have impaired vision from cataracts and borderline glaucoma. Was reassigned to crushing plant. On advice of a son, began smoking copious amounts of ganja daily. Inevitably he lost sight in both eyes. It is said, there were other eye diseases, brought on by undetected diabetes. At this late stage, could not be reversed. He did not take infirmity well, oh no. Became boisterous, vulgar and genuine curmudgeon. His power went with his sight. He could no longer monitor rental holdings or ogle young girls. He was, as is said. Like a fish out of water. It is worthy of mention, his sons were chips off old block. Procreating in wild abandon with women near and far. A daughter ran private school in nearby church. Folks joked, most students were of same family tree. Mr. Otis' grandchildren, played ring games at his house among themselves, until parents came for them after work. Other times they played with grandpa, who being blind. Relied on sense of touch, identifying who was who. We know, he knew children by voices, especially grands. If One stood aside and watched Mr. Otis, it was very revealing. Playing only with girls, he reached out, asking. *"Who this?"* Child would respond. **"Me, Daddy Otis."** He would take hold of that child, still probing by touch. There was no mistaking, where that child would be palm massaged. Lower torso and chest probe, does nought in recognition, except deviant gratification. He had keen hearing, often asked. *"Who that, just come there?"* This to ensure, there were no witnesses to his innocent, sight by touch activity. Of course, not all one on one took place outdoors. There were unseen liaisons, and children are sometimes coached to be wary of strangers. Leading them to assume, family members are okay. Methinks that's been changed. Instead of "any stranger," it is now "anyone." One of Otis' daughters had close friend, both worked at same profession. That daughter had thing going with friend's husband. Friend, being last to know, and would not dare to guess. Occasionally, visited her mom in Canada. Mom called, saying she's not doing well. Wanted to see daughter, lest. She dreaded going to Canada. Balked, *"My God, even in summer, the place is cold."* But, mom wanted her presence, so off she went. Asked her friend, to keep eyes on her girls during her absence. Just in case, they needed female attention. Unaware, how prophetic she was being, without substance. Her ten year old, prepubescent daughter became sick at school. Puking, lower stomach cramps and haemorrhaging. After urgent surgery and slow recovery, hushed prognosis was. Child's immune system, went into pregnancy rejection mode. Who would have thought? This is where story ends. In truth, this ending was indeed, beginning of unending episode. The foetus died, but hatred and ill will came to life, and lives on perpetually. Ever seen or heard of fights and swearing at graveside? Happened at Mr. Otis' wake and funeral. Some kin vehemently refused. *"Speaking any evil of the dead."* Someone swore intent to not leave the cemetery, without first pissing on the grave. Regrets he could not relieve himself one step further. And bear in mind good folks. All this rancour and bile were among family. This led to disunity, feelings of ill will towards and malice. There are those who found it hard to believe. Otis was guilty of this dastard act. Some say, child was of age to know, whatever was done to her was wrong. She should have spoken to parent about this. You have heard of "Blame the victim" scenario. Another faction speculated, quickly agreed. Old man Otis, had lost behavioural awareness of involuntary actions. Result of his mind, having regressed into senility. Them that put forward this lame excuse. Had never stood silently by, watching this old man at play. Even having such opportunity. It is conceivable, bent as they were, discrediting detractors. They would yet be witnesses who are blind. Because they will not see, and deaf because, they will not hear. When senses matter, will not, cannot. Creates more conflicts, than are solved. Whatever the cause, effect was tragic. This then, is where One's ability to forgive and forget, faces acid test. Goes without saying, Jubby will hate, never forget the departed. Will she forgive garmps? Only her heart has answers to. Answers we can guess, without confirmation.

The body: Is amazing machine. Rarely, does One recognize it's resiliency and self healing properties. We exacerbate natural function, when taking anti virus shots, patent medicines and antibiotics. If we abide healthy nutritional guidelines, avoid city smogs and industrial emissions. Our bodies would keep us free from most ailments. There are age and gene related maladies, which will onset and ravage. In absence of mentioned, shots, medicines and antibiotics. We have to admit, environment chokes with particulate pollutants. Monumental levels of health and life compromising, invisible debris. Hence, our need to keep taking slow poison, voluntary and otherwise. Ours is a no win existence, and it's not getting better. We are doomed "It" Bells pealed, heralding wedding close at hand. Bride to be, was youngest of nine women. Whose papa kept going back for a son. Three had had children. Lived with "baby fathers" in unwed union. Five others were married, after starting families. Expectation was, this last virgin would crown clan with prestige and legitimacy. Remove tainted common existence. Raise them to acceptable societal standards. This was to be most resplendent affair, outclassing governor's ball by every scope of comparison. Guest lists were scrolls, lengthened minutely. Boutiques were invited to arrange special viewing of trousseau collection. One socially aware sister, suggested "hope chest" or "glory box" as must have accessory. This aside, logistics were mind boggling and confusing. Agreed plans were constantly being changed. Making way, for overlooked or must have items. Banquet hall reservation had date availability issues. Family agreed on food preparation. Younger kin, whom we know, could not boil water and not ruin. Doubted perfection skills of those who fed them to survival. Ever experienced a deafening din, suddenly going silent? That's how, clamour surrounding this wedding. Died without rhyme or reason, upon entry of bride-to-be.Well, rhyme and reason was known, but only to few persons. All others were in dark, begged to hear why. Bride-to-be called postponement of plans, simply saying. She needed time to think. ***"What's there to think about?"*** They asked. ***"Does she not love Beau? Does Beau not love Belle?"*** It was most unsettling situation. When people don't know, they begin guessing and assuming worst. Once these gets whispered, among them that thirsts for truth. Thoughts takes wings, ogres and fairies are created. Simple truth is. Virgin bride-to-be was pregnant. Her close, very tight clique, knew this. Were on needles and pins, devising ways keeping it secret. Bear in mind, this wedding was more than two people being married. It was face saving, redemption of status for this family. How could she? How could they be so selfish? This was worse than treachery. Knowing she was saviour of the clan, even unto those yet unborn. How could this travesty be pursued, disregarding untiring efforts. Being feverishly volunteered, to make historically worthwhile and memorable event. Maybe, appropriate group chorus would be, Clara Ann Fowler's, hit song. "Go on with the wedding." Never heard of her? Professionally, she's Patti Page. Ensuing chaos was silenced, came germane proposal. Actively considered and agreed on by majority of family's inner circle. Question arose. Who would impart grand proposal to Belle and Beau. Before revealing agreed on plan, let's examine what's etched and scrawled. Disco Jock and banquet hall, had been reserved with non-refundable half cost. Six minibuses were reserved, lower deposit amounts asked. Anything else held in reserve, could keep. One thing becomes blatantly clear, which is. When people pursue selfish objectives. Sanity and common sense takes flight. So, what was this grand suggestion? They should abort pregnancy, allowing wedding to go forward as planned. She owed it to the family. Being last female having power, to break curse that attended siblings. None of whom were virgin brides. Fact did not dawn. Virginity is lost at copulation. Even if pregnancy did not result from. She would not be virgin bride. But, who would know, besides Beau and

Belle? Bride-to-be endured angst and disappointment being pregnant, for different reasons. She hankered for glory, three or more months after wedding, before getting pregnant. That way, could not be taken, as expected wedding night shebang. Managers at her office, adjusted rosters for new brides taking maternity leave, nine months after marriage. Women balked the practice and silently hollered for change. So how was this contentious affair, brought to amicable resolve? To this day, there are hard feelings. Seems, families keep flames of discord burning among them. Far longer than they do strangers. Possibly, prolonging feud with strangers, could get someone viciously undone. Most families just pay lip service to issues, or resort to malice. Belle and Beau went off quietly. Did registry marriage, long before her pregnancy was visible. Both were praised by some kin, condemned by others. Glitter and fireworks were held, for face saving anniversary repeat of vows and celebration.What a life....As young teenager.

Al was told by older teens, who knew what they were talking about. If a girl jumped up, stood erect after sex, and gulped down ice cold Pepsi. She could not get pregnant. Pepsi would drown sperm and flush it in urine. He firmly believed, after seeing Pepsi or Coke. Used to loosen rusted bolts. No kidding, ask anyone. Thirteen years old, Llorna Beswick, schoolmate. Invited Al for happy Sabbath. He came with a pip bottle of Pepsi. Herbs, such as Rat Ears, Leaf of Life, Guinea Hen Weed, Ramgoat Dashalong, Ramgoat Roses and many others. Were reputed to be excellent abortion aids. Concoction was more potent, when boiled and drank with added Lime juice, Garlic and green Papaw or Papaya. As long as humans continue to exist. There will always be reproduction issues. Question is. Avoid conception, or abort after?

Old man….Young woman & Child-13

Patience turned thirty, when she met Theodore. Twenty-eight years her senior. She would not have given him second glance. Except for fact, he resided in the USA. Costs nothing to smile and make him at ease. She told herself, then told him. *"If there's ever a time, I regret tying off my tubes. It is, since we've been married. I've always wanted a son. Was not keen it happening, by either of two worthless cruffs, I have called husband. You are so much, the man I dreamed being married to. I am willing to consult medical expertise. Regarding surgical reversal of, or anything that could make this possible."* As his Granny would say, in similar situation. Theo swallowed spittle. Which is to say, instead of spoiling a moment. Swallow a thought, hopefully, it will be forgotten. Untold truth is, this dovetailed perfectly. Coinciding with Theo's plan for them. Patience was not aware of that. Not satisfied, his lacking interest. In her commitment to make sacrifices for their happiness, Patience again broached the subject. At which time, Theo with deliberate nonchalance, asked. **"You meant, having another son? That would be so nice."** Rapid twist of her head, and bulging eyes stare. Told Theo he touched a nerve. She quickly recovered composure and asked. *"Another son? Why you say another?"* **"Oh, I seem to recall your saying, your first pregnancy was a… but. You know what? Forget it. Probably getting you confused with someone else."** Theo lied. *"Yes, you probably are. You have had so many women in your life. Now you're getting old, your head is bound to play tricks on you."* Patience said, with sighed relief. Even as she said that, her head was spinning like a top. Did she let slip, her first pregnancy? Is Theo going to think and realize she did so confess? Wily Theo, deliberately played ruse on her. There was no power of clairvoyance at work. It was simply, smart versus smart and clever. He considered himself a sleuth, who could study. Make people utter truths, they would otherwise keep in mental vaults. His thing was, focusing on the involuntary face and eye reaction. In split second, brain absorbs visual or oral incoming. Kind of, way detectives do at…. Maybe I should begin at the beginning. Only lying children and conniving adults, tells stories in reverse.

Theo at twenty-eight years her senior, and like his father before him. Had an inherent attraction for younger women. After their initial meeting, his interest piqued. Contrary to his normal behaviour, kept in touch often by phone. BellSouth gave installment options, paying his $2000+ bill. Suggested calling plan at reduced rates. One up for lowly consumers. WhatsApp, by and large, made that necessity redundant. Seen as miser by many who knew him. He decided it was cheaper to fly and see Patience, rather than pay to babble. Chances were, he could get into her head. And, who knows, maybe her bed. Vibes flowing, told him he might be able to pull this off, or set it up for next trip. He sent funds for hotel and taxi, plus. They eagerly embraced and kissed at airport, elevating his expectations and…In answer to Theo's question. No, she was not going home. Toddler was being cared for by her mother. She had been twice married to worthless men. Was hoping to find an ambitious man. Who could appreciate her ass-ets, as well as her intellect. Goaded Theo to reveal his data. Is he married? Who he lived with? House or apartment? Rented or owned? Could he walk freely? Or had to look over shoulders, for Border Patrol and Immigration Agents? She had heard stories, seems. Some people existed, running the gauntlet. Was he One such? He became evasive, pleaded exhaustion, suggested they retire. Seeing her in bra and panties, aroused the "don't-say-it." She stared open mouthed, so he told her a Seinfeld joke. *"These are not buoys."* As she came under the covers. Theo made subtle moves. Oh, she got righteously indignant and swore at him. What kind of man is he? What kind of woman, he thinks she is? Were it not so late, she would call a taxi and be off. How could he expect her being willing, to roll over and spread her wings to him. That's very insulting and demeaning, to say the least. Folks! Grown assed Theo, covered his face. Bawled like Tuco, in front of Blondie. Who's Tuco and Blondie? You ask. Never watched 1960's spaghetti westerns? Begged her forgiveness. Peering at her, through fan spread fingers. Face mirrored her thinking. *"If I can get this old coot to bawl and beg forgiveness, way he is doing. I can get him to do anything, he is smitten."* For his part, Theo pleaded. **"Don't leave me, please don't go. I am sorry, hfff. Did not mean to offend you, hfff. You know, I love you and, hfff, hfff."** Kept pulling air through his nostril. Snivelling at end of his cry. She could not see his grin in the dark. Was conciliatory, gently prodded. Told him, come to bed. Not done, Theo continued sniffling, told her. **"You gwone to bed, hfff. Me wi sleep on floor, hfff."** Still peering through fanned palm. He enjoyed her effort. Standing him erect, than he did, standing himself. Some things are damned easy, it's shameful. Both laid, sullen and quiet in bed with their thoughts. "Don't-say-it" "accidentally" brushed a thigh. He quickly massaged, a side of her behine, saying. **"Sorry, I didn't mean it to happen. But, you turned sudden."** She replied. *"It's okay, is my fault."* Soon, rabbit was in burrow. Oh, what a night it turned out to be. Proving without doubt, kind of man and woman they each were. Daybreak she asked with frivolity. *"Thought you wanted to sleep?"* Theo planned staying weekend. Changed itinerary to week of enjoying life.

Two year old toddler was taken to daycare. Older, eight year child, stayed with maternal grandma. Theo suggested instead, enrollment at pre-kindergarten environment. Where tot could be taught basic skills. Patience agreed, citing lack of financial support. Not only from child's father, also ex husbands. Theo volunteered taking on expense. Patience confirmed repeatedly, kind of woman. Theo knew, she was. Wordlessly expressing gratitude for generosity. Taking advantage of hard phallus, and soft heart. Sworn to as natural, stimulated body reaction, by a girlfriend. Patience had a debt list, causing her sleepless nights. Asking Theo's help in eliminating. He took care of, making her debt free. But alas. She pled. There was a debt overlooked, and could Theo please. He told her, the good ship Trust. Was now being battered by this new wave. However, agreed sending funds to erase. It was time she paid a visit, and so she came to see. Oohed and aahed about Theo's house, but could not understand. Why homes were surrounded by vast acreages of tomatoes, peppers, okras and strawberries. In her corner of the world, farmland is bush and wilderness. Homes are built in developed areas. This mixed environment, was hard to understand. Nevertheless, she liked what she saw. Was desirous doing whatever it took, to make life in this country. As is said in verse. Longest journey begins with single step. He again told her, his trust was shaken by that forgotten debt. Insisted she come clean, restoring level of confidence. She said, it was mother who put her up to it. And she reluctantly obeyed. Despite five pails, let's tug cow's teat some more. Reason why, cow often kicks pails over, it's not coincidence. Mom agreed to keep her children, while she tested water to find if Theo and herself shared compatibility. When she refused mom's request, tugging teat for another bucket. Mom reneged keeping children, and so she came, all three in a package. Had they been boys, there would not have been any chance of Theo attempting assimilation. Girls were easier to grow, less gum beating. Now, Patience was living stories she had heard. Jumping in her skin, each time she saw a State Trooper or Border Patrol vehicle. On way to and from her illegal day job, in Orange County. Theo once pointed to a bus and said. **"On it's way to Krome, with smugglers. Others attempting entry on false documents, and roster of crimes."** Children suffered separation anxiety, from friends and environment.Younger, cried daily. Older got into brawls, was disruptive and confrontational with students, unprovoked. Theo had excellent rapport with both children, and enjoined Patience to divine and address issues. Mistaking Theo's concern, for disgust. She declared. *"No child going spoil my chances of success in this country."* Older child was sent to grandpa. Younger was given up for adoption, by grandaunt in Nigeria. This hit snag with authorities. Wouldn't sanction, unless both parents consented. Patience told her aunt to say, father was deceased. Aunt said, documentary evidence of, was being requested. As if there was an option to bureaucratic red tape. Failing which, child had to be out of country by near date. Child was boarded with foster mom back home. Life went on, with occasional bumps and sways. Both children, in timely manner rejoined parents, having personal qualms. Which neither of either wanted to discuss with mom. Older child, once described mom. Snarling, teeth bared, fists clenched and head shook in a tremor. Wow. It is safe to say, mom was insecure. Older child was in love and acting out, missing boyfriend. Once more, she could not settle at school. Was as is quoted, a square peg in round hole. Schools and workplaces have one thing in common. If they want to get rid of you. They will find a way within regulated policies to do so, that cannot be called into question. Now out of school, she was restless. Something else was missing. Funny Theo, showed her weekly grocery flyer. Ten green plantains for $1. She told him, she was not that keen on plantains. He told her, she could keep them under her pillow. Take out a ripe one, as needed. She stared at him, quizzed for a moment, before gist hit. Both laughed out loud, as she wagged a finger at him and walked away. Young child asked Theo to a walk in the park. Where she related, foster home events in single digit years. Now weighing heavily on her mind, could jeopardize her future. Over grub at Steak 'n' Shake. Theo tried putting her mind at ease. Told her a simple probe she could do, when taking next shower. Minutes after coming home. She came to Theo, exulting. It was good to see pain drained from her face, and light in place. When both broached subject of boyfriends to Theo. Which they dared not discuss with Patience. He told them, straight up, no ifs, ands or buts. Only baby he wants disturbing his rest, is one for whom he is father. Having hung up his breeding boots. Means zero tolerance, for anyone who finds themselves pregnant. On very serious note, he reminded. Pregnancy was not worst that could happen, from unprotected sex. There could be an infection, for which there is no simple cure. Older child piped in. Celebrity ball player was living quite healthy, despite having been infected with HIV. Theo said, celebrity ball player had resources. Affording required drugs to inhibit or cure his infection. However, he wanted it known and made clear. He would not mortgage his house to treat anyone. Because, soon as money ran out, so would life. Told both, all he could promise.Was a beautiful white dress. Frilly pink bonnet, and hearty send home rendition of "Thee we adore" Or as folks back home say. Deewiadoor. Theo believes, girls are easier to raise. Less prone to be peer influenced, and are self confident. Not having to chest bump, fists pump and show boat. Adage warns, 'expect the unexpected.' Could not have been expected scenario forward. Foresight would've been anticipation, not expectation. Event climaxing this saga, set Theo searching for answers. Took him into new dimension of child rearing. Opening window of insight, that helped him to understand. How some men found themselves in dire, disgraceful situations. Aware of what they were doing, and where it could lead. Yet, went unheeding to infamy and incarceration. His theory is, girl who bonds with a male relative. Father, brother, uncle, cousin. Will sometimes develop, intense hero worship, or kinship innocence towards that male. Going into puberty and taking more than passing interest in boys. She unconsciously uses relative as behaviour template. Acting out fantasies, secure in belief. Relative will not overstep boundaries. There are others who are curious, willing to sate curiosity by going distance with kin, instead of street deity. He is that insulation, allowing her to play practice with fire and not get singed. We know there are occasions, both get singed. Each in his, her detrimental way. Life becomes, historical journey of haunting, unforgettable and unforgivable memories. Scribes, in rabid condemnation ask. How could he? Why did he? Villain stands isolated.

Coming home from school, she had ritual. Greeting Theo with cheek smack. One day, he trying to remount microwave. Swung his head, fumbling and ended up lip pecking. Next day it happened again. Theo began thinking, maybe yesterday was not innocent as thought, decided to pay attention. Few days later, she rushed past him to bathroom. Came out, held arms wide open, grinning in unbounded joy. Hugged him for their peck, as Theo thinks. *"Now, it will be proven, hit or miss."* Only, this time, he felt quick warm dart beyond his lips. He recoiled, looked askance at her. **"You learned a new trick?"** *"Not really. I just did it, because you are my daddy,*

and I love you." She replied. Caught between hurting feelings, but not wanting to make habit of this. He gently said. **"That's not how daughters and daddies greet."** Seeing her walk away, chin to chest. Hit with remorse, he reached out to her. She flounced slightly, saying she had homework. Went and locked herself in. She was sombre all week, greeting ritual abandoned. Mid next week she came to Theo and said. She did not want to greet, other than verbal, going forward. Theo said that was okay and hoped she was not hurt by his rebuke, days earlier. She just walked on by. Theo rued on, was frightened of what could have begun. Men are so strong, physically. Yet, emotionally weak at times. There's a line some blindly cross. Relationship returned normal and gaiety prevailed. Could have been weeks or months later. Theo was not keeping tabs. House was three bedrooms, with bath for two, and shower for master suite. Patience forbade girls, using master shower. Theo didn't mind, so they splashed when mom was out. Bathroom door was 180 North of the bed on which Theo laid. Looking at television 90 North West of bathroom door. She came to have her shower, but opened up a conversation. As to how she should protect herself, from a rape assault. Engrossed in, unwilling to divide attention. He told her. Sometimes, it could be life saving. If rape victim appeased attacker. Always the possibility, she could become violent when resisted and resort to injuring or killing victim. Which was not really her objective in the beginning. Think she caught gender anomaly back there? Gave him that leery stare, he goes on. If victim can attract attention by passersby. Then holler, kick and scream like hell. When One comes under attack, One never knows intent of villain. Hence, no sure do's and don't rules. Next, she asks, if she got pregnant from such an attack. Would Theo still throw her out. He told her, suffer it not to be. But, so far as he knew. Rape victims are usually medicated after an event, to forestall pregnancy. Every answer to every question. Brought another, "what if" scenario from her. Theo asked, if she planned going for a walk through the Black Forest. If so, she should ask Mr. Horst Jankowski to accompany her. This really was another bit of inanity, based on Jankowski's orchestra, way before her time. Possibly, detecting fallacy. She retreated in bathroom, softly closed the door. Theo breathed relief and focused on the boob tube. It did occur to him once, there was stoned silence. No water running or splashing. Maybe, she was in discovery and auditing. Observation quickly vapourized.

Fifteen or twenty minutes went by. Her voice came to him distinctly clear. Instead of behind ajarred door, as had been in first instance. Head turned, eyes saw her standing, framed in open doorway, fully nude. ***"You know? I just want to have experience of being penetrated. Because, I've been.. and.. it's not."*** Theo was stunned speechless. She just stood there looking at him. Was there anticipation in her stare? She remained unmoved. He laid on the bed. Television forgotten, mouth agape. How long, he could not say. It might have seemed long, when in reality it was seconds. He softly said. **"Go have your bath and come back."** She retreated and closed the door. He thought, mocking her. *"Why close it now, you already shown me all there is to see."* He didn't want to chastise and alienate. She was vulnerable and going for broke. He went to kitchen for pot with good round handle. She came out the bathroom. He told her. **"Go put your nightie on."** She walked off, draped in terry towel, he asked himself. *"Wonder what's going on in that beautiful mind of hers?"* He patted bed beside him, she hopped up. Watch closely now. Taking condom from secret stock, lesson began. **"Tell him, show you the packet. Make certain it is sealed. When he** opens it, let him puff air in. Like this. See how the nipple extends and stays, until air is released? Watch him put it on. See how it glides over the handle? Your future, and maybe your life. Might depend on this simple latex boots. Don't let him tell you, he will withdraw at right time. We cannot! Trust me! I am certain, you have been told in your science class, or whatever they call them these days. Sperm can begin swimming down, long before ejaculation erupts."** She was silent for a minute or more. Then asked him. *"Why you showing me this, and all this?"* **"Because, from that day you checked yourself in the bathroom, and was giddy happy. I have always talked to you about, staying as sweet as you are. Until you're mature enough to protect yourself. Want me to play that Nat King Cole song again? However, after tonight. I think you want to experiment. It might be with older male. I want you to take precautions. Know why? Because I love you."** She hugged Theo. Buried her face in his chest and sobbed silently. He held her close, she began laughing amid sobs. Told Theo. *"Would you believe, if I told you. I don't know why I did that? Maybe, because you were really ignoring me, while pretending to listen. So I just... You know what I'm saying?"* He told her. **"I don't know what you're saying, but, I understand."** She is now an unattached adult, still hasn't experimented. Made a promise to Theo, which, he told her. Did not come out right, but again. He understands what she's saying. *"Whenever I decide, it's time to experiment. I promise, you'll be first to know."* Theo tells himself. Maybe, in her heart she's still a child. Not grasping what her words truly means to a listener. Just as she did not fully understand, import of her actions, night of her shower. Final note. She experienced puberty miracle, aged nine. Theo will not frighten anyone by

159

revealing her age. That night she stood in bathroom doorway. Can you imagine her, years later saying to querying boyfriend or husband. Because, they always want to know who was first. Even when they are. ***"One night, I went for my shower and my stepfather raped me."*** That's if by then, he's not doing time, as convicted sex offender. We also know, she's not going to tell total string of events. Not that it matters anyway. Men, read, be warned. Don't go for every nugget that glitters. Adage teaches. All that glitters is not gold. Could very well turn out, Fool's gold. Know who's the Fool?

Oh what a tangled web-14

In Puss kingdom, when Tabby is away. Tom might find mice appealing, develop appetite for and play with them. After nine years wishing and waiting, Rebecca finally got approved for USA immigrant visa. This at behest of brother Benjamin, who migrated in early years. Endured excruciating hardship as farm labourer. Benjie had simmering discontent with his parents. They favoured Rebecca, in both siblings' pursuit of academic excellence. Not mincing words, father, Julius reminded Benjie. Had he beaten paths to school and be studious as his sister. Instead of running board horse races in the gully. Stoning mango trees and gambling for marbles. He could have attained an education, allowing him to make forward strides in life. Julius never denied spending more, giving Rebecca private lessons, and whatever it took for her to attain scholastic excellence. Not intending to *"Waste powder on Blackbird."* This is old folk's adage, meaning. What One shows themselves to be by inherent nature. Will not change, despite cosmetic adorning. Despite simmering and often feeling cantankerous towards. Benjie recognized there was tangible bond he cherished. Between himself and only sibling. Willing to help his sister, whom he loved dearly, in any way he possibly could. She needed only to ask. I say, kudos. Two raised fists for Benjamin, who had handicap he could not escape. Benjie was a clever lad. Illustrating mindset of someone academically dunce, yet smart in a clever way. A school's fun day, Benjie won four of six races in Egg and Spoon event. Start of fifth race, a teacher took and examined Benjie's egg. As she suspected, it had been tapped just enough to squat flat. He was disqualified, earning nickname. "Crack egg Benjie." Mid eighties, fame, if not substance of crack cocaine was well known. Symbolized by deportees, easy living, no work philosophy and attitudes. Someone looked at our Benjie, an underachiever and referred to him as "Crack head Benjie." Although, mere syntax slip, diction error. Benjie could not shake the monicker. Attempts to join police cadet force and army recruit, was stymied by Justice of the Peace refusing to recommend him. Frustrated, he reverse migrated to rural area. Eventually was selected for farm work programme in the US. Political nepotism playing role.

Rebecca was manager of financial support business. Disliked by some female employees. Given her rapid ascension into top positions. Bypassing others with more experience and seniority of tenure. Her successfully, self employed husband, Fredrick. Told his wife, he could not see necessity her migrating. At a time their financial security, was not remotely a concern. Home in suburban Armour Heights, St. Andrew parish. Vehicles and healthy bank balances. Not to mention, their small children.Who would be deprived of mother's care and guidance, without iota of tangible justification. She told him, she feared politicians of the day, were bent pursuing communism. Quoted scriptures. *"I go to prepare a place, that where I be. There we all may be also."* Resigning himself to circumstances beyond control, as she made plans. He asked how long she'd be staying. She replied, having accumulated fifteen weeks vacation and sick time, give or take. Before leaving, her Aunt Sophie joined the household as children's nursemaid. One of whom had just started nursery school. Farewells said, before echo died. Aunt Sophie made it known to Fredrick. His late homecoming hours was not in best interest of. 'These poor, orphaned children.' He needed to be home, longer evening hours. So they would not suffer mental anguish, from absence of both parents. To say he took umbrage, would put it extremely lightly. His response was loud, profanity laced tirade. Of course, this was embellished and told Rebecca. Who responded in like vein, vehemently condemning her "no good" husband. Name calling of low life, and other demeaning epithets. Some would say "the gloves were off" Yet asked. How could state of affairs, come about so quickly. There was no concealing, figurative bad blood flowed between Fredrick and Aunt Sophie. Indeed, on previous occasion. There was almost letting of blood and pistol whipping. Averted when Aunt Sophie, hastily hied to neighbour's house and called police. Lawmen turned up, evening of next day. Station's Land Rover being out of service. Cops listened as both related. One cop asked Aunt Sophie, just before slamming vehicle's door and driving off, visibly annoyed. ***"Then you did expect to come into the man house and rule him. Like him is one of the children? But see here woman, you not easy."*** See why, in the islands we always say? "No problem" "Be happy" America would put Fredrick in jail. His kids in foster care, and hang a restraining order on his neck. Preventing him from going near his own house. Next phase would be trial and conviction. Third World existence has privileges. Aunt Sophie was forthwith relieved of duties by Fredrick. Sent kicking and screaming back to her dungeonlike rural abode. Fredrick opted earlier homecoming, after delegating functions to employees. New nursemaid, Samantha, came on board. Much as she was younger than Aunt Sophie, and naturally, less draconian. Children quickly accepted her embrace, and there was harmony in house. When children got tucked in bed, Samantha embraced Fredrick. They slept peacefully, and harmony became ecstasy. Who said "Life could be a dream?" The Crew Cuts, that's who. For Fredrick, it was dream come through. Rebecca goaded Aunt Sophie, making surprised visits. Checking children's welfare and reporting to her. A year since she migrated, Frederick expressed anxiety, her job might not be open on her return. **"If they can do without you for a day. They can do without you, period."** Was his wisdom on the situation. He eventually heard from a whisperer. Rebecca had been given generous severance purse by bosses, at retirement. Asked to confirm. Rebecca admitted truth, and told Fredrick. Benjie offered a managerial position, in his trucking business. Plus free basement housing, until she could afford otherwise. Somebody said "Oops," twin boys were born to Samantha and Fredrick. One and half years later, another twin birth occurred. Girl and boy. There were now seven children in their home. Oldest being eight years old. Now, if we pause and look at this saga. One is bound to ask. What are odds, smooth sailing and happy landing? There are headwinds, crosswinds and tailwinds, gusting around this family. Not to mention, slippery when wet, surfaces. Situation seems to be yawing out of control. Think this can be brought in for a safe, but turbulent landing? We see people going about their business, and never give them second glance. Because, we don't know their story. Even if we did, probably would not care. Why? Because we are focused on our situations.

Samantha feels overwhelmed, caring for seven small children. This was not how she saw future taking shape. Paused studies, pursuing certification in her accounting/auditing career. She brooded being mother of four, fathered by a married man. Having discussed her fears and despondency with Fredrick. He empathized and comforted her, saying. **"Don't worry Sam. I'll get somebody to help with the children."** Oh, she exploded. *"F..k the children Fredrick! And f..k you too! What about me!? What about us!? I am a late child for my aged parents, without career or job training. What am I going to do with four children, at this stage of my life? I can't bundle and dump them on my parents. They need, I need, we need stability in our lives. I can't go on like this. You told me, when I first got pregnant. Your wife had left you and filed for divorce. What's taking it so long?"* If Samantha had a gun nearby, she would have shot Fredrick. He, thoughtlessly said to Samantha.**"I never would expect to hear f..k, coming from your mouth. If anyone told me you uttered such a word. I would swear they were lying."** Frustrated or out of depth, she yelled as tears streamed down her cheeks. *"Believe your ears, cause you going hear it a f..kin' lot. F..k you in hell, with the Devil. Where you belong too, Fredrick!!"* Her face reflecting deep angst. Aunt Sophie soothingly asked, source of Samantha's misery. In need of someone to understand her female situation and empathize. Samantha opened up to motherly, caring Aunt Sophie. Totally unaware, older woman's interest in her affairs. Was to milk her of intimate details, and relay back to her niece. I consider this, back stabbing betrayal, at it's worst. One human being to another, experiencing despair.You encourage them to. Lean on me. Older and wiser, I may be able to point you towards the light. Truth yet, motives are selfish. Seeking only to add to her distress. That's our world. Deceit and treachery teems. Gertrude's daughter migrated to England. Leaving daughter Desiree in grandma's care. Desiree's cousin, Phillip, worked at Fredrick's company. Her at fifteen, in high school. Having been awarded place by common entrance exam. She struggled to maintain satisfactory grades, although being recognized as gifted child. Home was at Mavis Bank, in rural St. Andrew parish. Her daily commute, had her leaving and returning home in hours of darkness. She was sleep deprived, physically tired and despite her best efforts. Grades lagged, to point. Were it not for homeroom teacher's intervention. Would have been asked to discontinue tenure. Extenuating circumstances known to Principal. Were understood for what they were. However, there was no such policy in place, accommodating abject failure. Adding further. Once a door is opened for One. Precedence is established for others, which then can't be denied. And therein, seed of discrimination is sown. Given Desiree's situation seemed permanent, with no foreseeable hope of redemption. It is said *"A drowning man will grab at a straw, or tip of a sword."*

So it was, Desiree came to live at Fredrick's house and help with house duties. One more plum on forbidden tree. Not yet ripe. But, given time. Most things mature with age, like fine wine and young women. As told, she went home to grandma, Fridays after school. Guiding her to church in observance of holy Sabbath. Trekking back to Fredrick by Sunday evening. Samantha was now, woman-of-the-house. Jealousy reared it's ugly head, when Fredrick was seen making subtle advances on Desiree. Which, to her credit, she emphatically rebuffed. Notably, she constantly told him. Name is pronounced, Des-i-ray. Not, Desire. Fredrick laughed this off, calling her, way he felt. Soon Rebecca and Samantha established affinity.

Demonizing Fredrick, which to some, was hypocritical in extreme, given factual knowledge. Rebecca had obviously given up on her husband long ago. Samantha lives with him and their children. Indulging him wifely favours when nature calls. If there is one trait that could be redeeming for Fredrick. It would be, all his children went to private school. Reliable taxi owners were contracted, to pick them up from respective school, and bring them home. His enterprise thrived, he spared no resource to benefit his children. Question arises. What would be fate of those children, were he not so blessed. Absence of wealth, would not have reined his inherent, promiscuous nature. But let us not give him more than his fair share, fetching water by wicker bucket. Rebecca yearns to see her children. Hell no, she doesn't want to see Fredrick. She coaxes and bribes Samantha, doing honour of chaperone. She says yes, but am reluctant to leave her four. *"With whom?"* She asks a meek Fredrick.*"Not your teenage concubine."* Fredrick denies, but it's said, women always know. Aunt Sophie, now on verge of being crippled by arthritis, agrees to sit the four. So her niece can be rewarded, seeing her three. Prior to take off, bureaucratic turbulence was introduced. Reluctance, allowing children in company of stranger to enplane and or disembark. It is not made clear, if this source of conflict was generated in Jamaica or the USA. Suffice it to say, affidavits were attested to byh parents. Allowing aims to be met. Don't raise eyebrows, neither should you laugh out loud. It's abrewing. Samantha arrives with Rebecca's three, and finds her with two of her own. Fathered by her live-in male friend, who promptly tells Samantha. He can get paid suitor to marry. Get her, green card status in just over two years. During which time, both would have live as man and wife. In addition to her paying dowry. Take note, two US born kids. Should also have Fredrick recorded, as their father.

To whom their mother is still married? Rebecca encouraged Samantha, seize opportunity. To which she enthusiastically agreed. Until she returned to Jamaica, three days after landing in USA and openly declared Rebecca, insane. To think, she would leave her children to grow themselves. Whilst clutching at straw of US green card. Now hear this. Rebecca assured her husband, children would return to Jamaica. In company of a friend, who would be travelling at that time. She did not tell anyone, shortly after arriving in the US. She fell out of grace with brother, Benjie. Could not find employment in field of expertise. Refusing what she considered, paltry reward that came with job offers. Her boyfriend was in a lucrative field. Allowing the family to live comfortably. Aunt Sophie succumbed to old age. Benjie came, bearing all good gifts. To provide memorable farewell and celebrate her life's journey. As well as updated status of his sister and her new Beau. Now, chickens came to roost. Facts that were hidden, now bared, revealed.

There was federal roundup of men. Including Samantha's suitor and matchmaker. Assets were confiscated. Rebecca's boyfriend abandoned her. Opting instead, getting to know forty-eight mainland states. Comfortably on the run, he was involved in fender bender. Other driver quickly accepted liability. Told him to bring relevant papers to his office. Exchanging information and check for vehicle damages. Almost fainted from surprise when handcuffed. Given long sentence in federal prison. He was paroled, after government ran out of boarding money, and deported to country of origin. Rebecca, now existing in turmoil. Beset on all fronts, without escape plan. Questioned numerous times by federal agents. Regarding her role in boyfriend's enterprise. House had been searched, papers seized. But she was not taken in, as feared. Possibly for lack of evidence, or presence of children in her care. She was told to not change residence, without notifying authorities. Be available for interviews as necessary. Fleeing, or attempting to, would make her, criminally suspect. Other side of coin, are those shortchanged by boyfriend. They too keeps tabs on her. Some, in friend mode. Hoping to recoup lost assets or information on location of. That is, by any stretch of imagination. Nerve wracking existence for a woman. Fraught with consequences too dire to contemplate, and yet cannot be dismissed.. When events showed initial signs of and began unfolding. Benjie offered his sister, she agreed. He providing financial shelter for five nieces and nephews. Fredrick visits children often, despite Rebecca's insistence, no contact be allowed. What kind of shrew dictates, children be denied contact of another parent? Especially given, negative existential aura she allows to surround them. Grandma Gertrude lived to ripe old age over a hundred. Desiree and her two children, flew from England to pay their respects. Surprised? Oh! You weren't aware, she had had children? Oh yes, she did. You see, although she rebuffed Fredrick's advances initially. He eroded her resolve, way constant water drips wears away limestone. She slowly thawed to subtle acts of kindness, and smooth soothe talk. Disillusioned and spiritually broken. Samantha endured mechanical existence in the home. Not having anywhere else to go. Or anyone who could be financially supportive of her and two twins. Despite her being caught in quicksand existence. Spirit attained buoyancy, by academic brilliance of her children. Eventual attainment of success, in respective fields of endeavour. Two of whom joined and carried on father's business. As did two of Rebecca's three. His having retired from day to day involvement. Focusing, once again on

Desiree. Preoccupied as Samantha was, in her uncertain future. She saw but did not care or dare. Try dousing, glowing flames between Fredrick and young Desiree. She let them be, finally telling herself. Fredrick was not worth her angst. Even after learning that Rebecca had left him. Uncertain rumour being, she divorced him and Samantha doubting this could happen, without papers served for his attention. She recognized, he made no effort to improve their emotional situation. She was there, he came and went. Civility gave way to a chuckle, but theirs was essentially, civil roommate's existence. Between people sharing same space and accepting, other had right to be there. He couldn't ask her to leave with his four children. Since he had financial resources to do so. He took care of them, and that was that. She was probably desirous getting more, but could have been hesitant to rock the boat. Lest it capsizes and worsens her predicament. Disappointed in first love, she made no effort to seek or indulge intimate male companionship. Although there were them who came courting overtly. Others subtly, to which she showed no interest. In any event, no matter their attempts at secrecy. In time it became evident. Fredrick had moved on with Desiree. She dropped all initial resistance, or sham of. There is no timeline, as to when things happened with Desiree and Fredrick. Suffice it to say, this had to come about. Between her leaving high school. Eventually going to her mom in England, at age twenty-two. She had to quickly realize that, unlike a fish in the ocean. Guaranteed abundance of life saving water. She really was trapped in a net with others, the crowd was stifling. She had to get out to open waters. If she were to bask and really be at peace with her surroundings. What better then, than flee to mom. Who no doubt, being told of situation. Encouraged repatriation, anxious to see her grandchildren. Mom knew, if Desiree was naive and didn't. She would just stay on Fredrick's farm. Increasing their brood together, with no future to her life, other than. So, come to mom in motherland. Whilst still favoured by youth. See how things come together, and each gets some satisfaction. From what at times, appears so dire and hopeless. Desiree was accompanied by her two children. Bringing Fredrick's tally to nine at home, possibly eleven. What with Rebecca having two more in his name and our world keeps turning. A big merry-go-round.

Parents and children-15

Let us look at relationships between parents and children. There are different scenarios arising, having equally different solutions. What solves one situation, at times muddles others. Because, no two persons have same life script. Not even best regulated of families. There's talk on dysfunctional families and would hasten to think. Some we encounter and observe, fill that classification. It could be, someone assessing our behaviour. Thinks similarly about us. Let's drop in on the Drummonds and their children. Fay sat at her desk, flogging new IBM correcting Selectric II typewriter, to break in speed. She was that good. Her skills proved burdensome at workplace. Tasks requiring speed and accuracy, somehow always segued to her "In" trays. Contracts, briefs and this multi-paged deposition, her boss had asked. She ensure be ready for court submission on Monday. Unlike other times, when similar requests were made. In this instance, there was incentive of monetary reward. It was past office hours. She passed time waiting for husband, Walter. Samuel McDougall, building's custodian. Walked by and reminded her, as per policy. Central air systems had been turned off at 17:00 hours. Although not yet evident, except by equipment silence.

Temperature would gradually rise, and in any event. Building had to be armed and vacated by 21:00 hours, after cleaners left. She told him, she was working for as long as it took her husband to come for her. This would happen, long before temperature rising or cleaners leaving. Deal or steal? Walter was at that time, having excited verbal exchange with Jacko. Fleet services supervisor at their employer. Walter asked Jacko to get new battery at discount. Some mornings, his car hesitated starting, he dreaded being stranded. Even as Jacko assured, this was no problem. Walter emphasized importance, buying from outside source. Knowing, suspecting rather. Jacko would try purloining from company inventory. Jacko assured Walter, he had brethren at Tropical Battery. Who could get a brand new for $100. ***"Don't worry man. Keep the tar on top you head little bit longer. Snow can fall later."*** Jacko tried convincing, dubious Walter. Keys going from hand to hand, like the silver dollar. Jacko again echoed promise, everything would be okay. Evening, Walter tested the starter, and kicked that engine like a steed. Opened bonnet, was elated seeing new battery in cradle. Elation quickly morphed to surprised anger. Word "EXIDE" jumped at him. He began sweating involuntarily at this betrayal by Jacko. Walter had been told, car would be taken off site during lunch. To a shop where batteries could be exchanged. Brand Exide was exclusive imported brand, used by company in their units. Self adhesive decal, with serial number and other data. Could easily be peeled and discarded. Word "EXIDE" was moulded in silver letters, both sides of casing. Walter was out of his mind with worry. What if someone witnessed theft and installation? He did not want to lose his job. Couldn't stand shame and indignity that comes with. Worse of all, his paycheck loss. When prospective employers finds out, you were fired for dishonesty. It's curtains, you're done. Lucky if you can get yard work to chop grass. You stood better chances on incompetence, tardiness and insubordination. He was having regrets and should haves. He should have shut eyes tight and bought a battery on the up and up. Money would come from somewhere, somehow. Jacko listened with contented smirk as Walter moaned. *"You done sweat up youself and agonize?"* He asked Walter, then told him. *"Step back, make me add finishing touches."* Roll of Cellotape, sheet of thick paper, and two bright yellow black peel off labels. Finishing touches all done. Battery sides were covered with labels that read. TROPICAL. Now beaming, Jacko asked Walter. *"You did think is idiot you have working for you?"* His anxiety level came down a notch. He yet asked Jacko. **"How you sure, right now, nobody not watching we?"** Ever confident, Jacko replied. *"Man like you, you own heart attack you, and kill you stiff stone dead."*

It was close on 18:00 hours. Walter finally stopped at Fay's workplace and honked the horn. As she told him to do, whenever she worked late. He honked and waited. Honked again, waited again. Being Friday, they would stop at Hi-Lo for groceries. Earlier, Mr. McDougall had come to Fay. His face mirrored a peeve. First, he reminded her. Mr. Blades would not appreciate her giving out. Conference room private phone number, for anyone to call in. Normally, he would simply tell caller, they had reached a wrong number and hang up. Only reason he came down to give her the message. Was because her daughter was calling, from a phone booth with urgency. As he turned pompously on his heels. She tried telling him, she had not…..He was already gone. She detested that old police sergeant's, uppity condescending attitude to others. At loss, figuring what urgency could have arisen with Venice. She hurriedly got to the phone, but there was no One.

Knowing a call box could not be monopolized by a person. Whilst others waited anxiously, brows knitted and tension rising. She sat and waited. Hoping Venice got another call. Now she fretted, what if Walter came. Whilst she's waiting for Venice to call back? Mr. McDougall would find her. She hated being at his benevolence. His having displayed intemperance, bringing Venice's message. Making no effort to disguise, what she saw as veiled attack. That was second place in her mind. Not knowing what dilemma her daughter was in. Girl could have sung Barbara Lynn's "Letter to mommy and daddy." It would not convey gravity of situation. She had, she told her mother. Finished a months long essay project. Had reviewed and made corrections. Intended leaving it somewhere, for parent's attention. Hoping both, especially her dad would find it to his liking. Levels of antagonistic tension existed, between father and daughter. Maybe, before going further, some family background is required.

Venice was middle of three children, born to Drummonds. Only girl, after Walter Junior, and before Stephen. Walter Snr. was a funny uncaring guy, who said things without thinking. Or, if he did. Then he didn't much care, what others found objectionable. He just fired from the hip. For instance. Once, Fay told four year old Venice go rock the bed. In effort to comfort, nattering, year and half old Stephen. Walter balked, said he knew she hated her brother. Recalling how she diabolically hollered non-stop at nights. In vain effort to stop him getting Stephen "in the oven." **But I got that dough in, came back many times. Stuffing it with superior ingredients. Now look at that loaf. See dimples in his jaw? Where you think those came from? Pencil tip where good lead came through wood."** He said "wood" suggestively, leaving no room for misunderstanding. Fay cautioned, he not underestimate. Infant's ability to perceive and understand. **"All the better."** He replied. Everyone should know history where they're coming from. Cited that as gospel, according to Bob Marley. **"You know Fay. Biggest idiot you can find anywhere on the planet. Once him take few puffs from the pipe, him get wiser than Solomon."** Growing up, boys were contented souls. Truth is, Walter showed caring for them and loathing for his daughter. She was an egotistic, demanding and impossible child. Fay spent numerous lunch periods at school's office. In conference with teachers and principals. Trying to explain, Venice's refusal to accept and follow rules. Taken to behavourial professionals was not helpful, as the child remained mute. It didn't help, once when on way home, Walter said to Fay. **"Make me tell you from now. If she turn woman and find a man. I won't be there to give her away. Because, in few month's time. That man would be looking to shoot me. I just want you understand that from now. So that if and when time comes. Can't say you never did know."** In a pout, Venice shouted. *"Shut your face daddy. You're always talking, and not making sense."* Fay rebuked both, husband and child. He told his wife. **"Leave her alone, make she ease her mind. Till she have to take food through straw. But, see how you get her to talk? You have to mash her corn."** Walter Jnr. got scholarship to high school, travelled early morning by bus. When Venice was equally successful, she fussed. Back then, bus operators by law. Had to carry school children at reduced fares. Forbade them to sit, whilst full fare paying adults stood. Venice carped endlessly, adult men rubbed their frowsy selves on her bottom. Her brother was told to make certain, he stood behind his sister. First day this went into effect. She complained, her brother was no better than others. He asked, what was he to do. When other passengers braced down on him. Passengers stood two in the row, back to back. Relief almost came Venice's way, that would have been to her detriment. School principal requested presence of both parents. They turned up. Fay greeted and preempted, saying. She knew, Venice had attention deficit issues. But with patience and under…Sister stopped her there. Quite rightly so, that's display of bad manners and poor breeding, to jump in like that. You are summoned to meeting, you listen. Do not preempt. We know, sister took very dim view of this. Quite likely said to herself. She had just gotten insight into child's angst. Told both parents. School has rules, and they will be obeyed by all students. If their daughter has handicap, there are special schools for her. This high school does not have special needs teachers on staff. Both parents are being warned. Next time Venice's behaviour comes to her attention. They will be summoned to take their child. It will not be a suspension. She will be expelled. *"Do I make myself clear?"* Sister sought parent's confirmation. **"Oh! I know quite well what you saying sister. Because, like how you don't have a good hairdresser and…."** Fay kicked her husband's foot. Expressed thanks to sister, hurried both out the office. *"Jesus! Have mercy, Walter. What kind of thing you're saying to the woman? No wonder Venice is who she is. She is your child through and through. You need to see the dam shrink, more than her. Lord, will you please help me."* Fay moaned, lifting both arms to sky. Allow me to explain. In inner city culture. "Hairdresser" at times, refers to "dressing" pubic hairs with "natural oil." Having nothing to do with head coif. In offbeat chat, meaning is determined by facial expression following usage. Kind of face that says. *"You know what I mean?"* Let's say, a woman seems down in the dumps.

Clique of women or men, will look at her and comment. "Her hairdresser get a better job." Or. "She want good perm." Walter meant. Nun being celibate, wouldn't be heartless, if she had a man. Parents are grocery shopping, actually. Fay is grocery shopping. They both walked in. Walter, directly to liquor display. Took bottles Bailey's Irish Cream to checkout. Signaled and mouthed, or lip synched to Fay. *"Waiting in the car. "*Believe it or not. He's addicted to the stuff, and will tip sip until Fay raps on the window. Children present, she often codes him to get out of the driver seat. Later that night, she hauls him over the coals. He says it won't happen again. Until next month end, that is. She couldn't get a grip on shopping. Curious about this essay Venice wrote. Why couldn't it await their arrival home. It was not making sense. Walter Jnr. and Stephen, were let off at maternal grandmother, most evenings after school. Grandma quietly told Fay. She'd rather Venice came visiting with her. To prevent Venice ransacking her place, like Hen seeking worms for chickens. Parents stopped, gave grandma items bought. Then left with the boys, calling out. *"Tomorrow."* Reaching home, Fay took mail, dropped them on a side table, declaring. ***"I'm done looking at bills for this month. Not looking at another one until next month."*** Letters slipped apart on polished surface as Fay turned to walk away. Saw from corner of her eyes, one envelope without stamp. Before noticing that envelope, she had called out. ***"Neecy, we are home. Where are you?"*** She picked up the envelope, saw it was unsealed. Again called out, louder. ***"Neecy! I brought your favourite. Doughnuts."*** This is where mind begins to confuse. And we often get to a point in our lives, where we reflect and say. If I had only followed my mind. Other times it is. It's a good thing I didn't follow my mind. Whilst we are caught in this mental imbroglio, we don't know which path to follow. In this state of confusion, whatever we opt doing. Eventually, will be an unconscious selection. Fay, not hearing Venice respond. Was minded to postpone attention, her having identified hand writing. Told herself, child might be asleep. On second thought, she unfolded note sized sheets of paper. Scanned briefly, before exclaiming repeatedly. *"Oh, my God! Walter. It's Neecy. Where is she? My God!! Are we too late? Oh, God! Oh, God! Oh, God!! Don't let us be too late."* When they found her, limp and unresponsive in the bathroom. Walter sent Walter scurrying, to the crime scene photographer for help. The policeman ran to, Justice of the Peace's home to call 119. In this tropical paradise, 119 did not bring paramedics. Equipped for emergencies and resuscitation. It brought police. If station's Land Rover was not out of service, awaiting repairs. After tense nail biting minutes, trying to resuscitate. Two cars set off on race to University Hospital. Child took cocktail of pain killers. Cold medicines and mother's contraceptives. Evidenced by packaging at crime scene. Slowly recovering in hospital, her family visited a Sunday. Venice was rolled out onto breezeway, in wheelchair by a porter. Family left to themselves. Mom smoothed daughter's hair. Asked how she felt and why she did what she did. Would she promise to not do anything like this again. *"Oh, my God. Child. Few more minutes, and you would be dead."* Next up was Walter's turn. Fay dreaded his input and tried forestalling.*"All right Walter, let's hold off chastising and condemning until we can sit down. Talk quietly and calm about this."* Walter insisted having his say. **"What, I can't say word of encouragement to my child? You think I have dagger under my cloak. Give her encouragement to do herself in, soon as we leave?"** With that, Fay relented and Walter drew closer. I hope you're visualizing this. Took

177

daughter's limp hand in his and began. **"You know, Neecy, I unde...."** Venice angrily snatched her hand away. Turned her head opposite side, away from him. He seemed to ponder if he should go on or go. Appeared to have decided but changed his mind, resettled his rump. Again raising Fay's angst level. I would love to see this in a movie. He went on."**As I was saying, I understand how you feel, and did what you did. I feel like doing same thing plenty times. When I think, if we going find money for school fees and books. Oonu win scholarships. We still have to pay bundle for this, that and Devil knows what. When school give Oonu letter bring home. Is not Christmas or birthday card. Is money them asking for. And we better send it, or else. Food, the car, light bill and of all things, rent. Every six months Grubb raise it. Sometimes you mother and me sit and wonder, if a day will ever come. When we stop live in rent house. Pay down on little coob to call we own. So don't think I don't feel where you coming from."** Fay relaxed her anxiety, as she listened to her husband empathize with their daughter. Still, she knew her husband, as no One else did. Was nervous by deflection of anger, she heard in his voice. He went on. **"That is why me keep Mr. Bailey close. A tat with two ice cube, sometime a raw sip. And me reason out things. For past umpteen years, it's how me survive. Not that me telling you to start thief out me liquor, when me not looking. At any rate, you too young to drink, and you is girl child. Start drink from now, you grow up turn bumper and worst of all, bar fly. But, is one thing me can't understand. From then to now, all the try me try. If you really did want do it. Why you put the letter, where you know we bound to find it as we come home?"** Fay sprang, grabbed chair handles, unaware brakes were engaged. Whilst she fumbled with, Walter raced monologue in raised voice. **"You shoulda did put it on top of the box, make breeze blow it way. Or somebody passing and think money in there and just…"** Fay pushed, dragged chair down corridor out of earshot as Walter's voice tapered. Walter Jnr. said to his father. *"Neecy is sick dad. She needs understanding, support, and love."* Walter asked his son. **"You think she reach almost nineteen, without all what you talking bout? You sister's problem is, she don't know when enough is enough."** Walter was tongue in cheek making the point. This child did not have any problems, her parents faced daily. She lived carefree, insulated existence, where everything came to her. What was there that made life so unlivable? Granny would say. Venice suffered from being too live well. She was idle dog, who would go out and worry sheep. From being bored and cussed. Should instead go pasture and tell cows howdy or count their pats. George Bernard Shaw wrote. *"The secret of being miserable, is to have leisure time to bother about whether you are happy or not."* Methinks it fair comment to say. Venice's inherent nature, demanded more than her fair share of attention. As her father said. Enough was never enough. Walter Snr. migrated to the USA. Landed good paying job, aided by vast fleet management experience. He and Fay bought more than a coob of their own and are now retired. Boys have done well, raising families.What about adult Venice?

Married and divorced twice, lost count of vocations tried and abandoned. Now, does tax preparation. One client describes her thus. *"Good at what she does, but lacking home training."* Getting set to give examples. I introduced myself as friend. She thought I was prospective client. Sought to warn me, but now clammed up tight. Venice and I went to

Jamaica Kitchen for lunch. I asked about Wilmot, the intellectual. I enjoyed talking with him. She divorced him out of her life a year ago. **"Divorced?! You two were married? I know about florist and then, there was the doctor from Baptist. I never knew you were married a third time."** She guffawed, haughtily replied. *"First, Damian was not doctor. He was an intern, trying to be doctor and failed miserably. Actor with self made script"* **"I knew you and Wilmot were boyfriend girlfriend. I didn't know you two got married. So why was such a quickie? Quick getting married, quick getting divorced?"** I asked and she related with amused aplomb. *"He knew I did not want children. I tell them all, before we get into anything. If you want to scatter your seed, this is not going to be fertile ground. Woke out of my sleep one night. Found the Son-of-a-Bitch trying to breed me. I kicked him off the bed and hired a U-haul at daylight. It was his mother's townhouse. So, I was the One leaving and that was that."* Life goes on, but let's look at this thing, as best we can in an impartial and objective manner. Venice is one spoiled rotten, grown brat. Would it be fair comment. After eighteen plus years, growing up with a father. Whose attention she could not get, in a positive way. She decided to, show him? It would be easier to answer that and many questions, if essay contents were known. Any truth in Fay's assertion, Venice is Walter's clone? How does a parent, begin implying to a nun. If she had a man in her life to get her groove on. She would not be unyielding and draconian? Maybe, he banked. Her suburban social realm, would not make her aware of the innuendo. We have to ask. Did the thought not occur to him. She might take intense umbrage and react to his child's detriment? We know for sure, Venice hates her father. And, by extension, it seems, men. She strives for companionship on her terms. No give and take, no compromise. Walter asked his daughter, at her sweet sixteen party. How come she passed the evening whooping it up with girls and not once dancing with a boy. Then told her, before she replied. Or maybe, did not intend to. **"Two pot cover can't steam cabbage. Every cover needs a pot, to be useful."** He probably figured, at sixteen that went over her head. Maybe it did, and maybe she retained and deciphered later. Family structures are made up of members striving to maintain positive equilibrium. As well as bad and evil people, contributing to toxic relations. Bad children, mothers, fathers, grandparents and close relatives. Such as cousins and in-laws, who impart known lies for truth. Assumptions and history that changes and distorts facts from person to person, generation to generation. *"No, your grandfather did not fall from a tree. Aunt Liz says, he hanged himself."* Maybe, he hung himself and someone decided. It would be less traumatic on a child, if he fell from a tree. Accidental demises are easier to accept than suicides. One is final, other leads to. *"Why did he hang himself?"* I have seen parents, making strenuous efforts, to limit grandparent's influence on children. It is not by accident, why some move far away and make excuses for not visiting more often. Most times they tell blatant lies. *"John just got promoted. We had to scrub our planned vacation."* Or some other nonsense rigmarole.

Here's a family, teetering on edge. Soft spoken wife, hollered for her husband. Which was quite uncharacteristic of her usual whispers. He ran to see if there was an accident or fall. Barely able to control her ire, told him. *"David! Tell David Snr. Not to teach my seven year old child, profanity. Or, so help me God. I will lay him out stone cold."* **"You sure of that Peg? I think, I heard him teaching David Jamaican.**

Dad wouldn't teac...." *"My child has a penis. He does not have a Dick. What is next lesson. Where on a girl to put it?"* David called his son, saying it was time for lunch. Then sat and had quiet talk with David Snr. Who thought there was no need for what he considered, over reaction to harmless pun which everyone knew. Margaret called the airline, seeking earlier departure date. Could not get flight to her mom in Bermuda, without extended layover. She had to getaway for a spell. Sight of father-in-law rankled her to near insanity.

A father's admiration-16

Paolo was European, with **"Good Fellows"** Paulie-esqueness aura and attitude about him. Complete with huge cigar he held between lips. Chomped on and constantly talked around. True to form, everyone called him Paulie, he had no quarrel with. A rotund jolly fellow, he told colourful stories of his youth in Italy with grandparents. Usually, he lapsed into dialect but hands and face conveyed gist. He and his girlfriend were past mid forties. So he married her much younger cousin, and she had their first child. A cherub, folks are wont to describe as "bouncing." Full bodied and chubby. Tomcat's kitten, One might say. Do not dare think there was falling out of persons. Oh no, there was genuine cordiality among cousins. This clan was intact. Max's girlfriend and himself, attended a function ensuing Italian ritual. Maybe it was equivalent to christening. I really cannot state for fact, what it was. This was era of Polaroid camera, that took photos and ejected them. To develop slowly, as you watched images appear. There were about sixteen snapshots being passed around, between group of ten. Rotating to daddy's safekeeping. Quite pleased, he beamed occasionally. *"Just look at her. See how she raises them feet high? Ready to* *kick ass. She's a fighting gyal alright. Youse better watch out for them fists."* One photo was spared stares, passed quickly to daddy. He stared at it, grinned broadly and said. *"Ah, this one, I like most. Look at the little pussy. Eh Eduardo? Fica!"* Eduardo stared. He too smiled and nodded. **"Ah! Fighetta."** He continued speaking in dialect, which Max cannot decipher. Gave photo to daddy, who took it back. Stared adoringly again, then turned to Eduardo. *"Actually, this is lot of pussy, on a baby."* Eduardo said something in dialect. Made a chin point to the group. Paolo retorted in dialect, both laughed loud. Max, only other male there, looked askance at Eduardo. Mumbled briefly in dialect, then did dismissive hand wave. Women's faces mirrored indignant surprise, but lips remained mute. It's not something, Max put significance to or was perturbed by. Coming to expect, any and every kind of behaviour from this guy. Barely getting seat belts on, Max's girlfriend began chewing him out. **"What did I do, you didn't?"** He asked. **"We ate, drank, admired baby photos and are on our way home. I barely glanced at the photo, before passing it on. You, of all persons. Know I never get chance to revel in sight of nudity, baby or adult. On rare occasion I get in the playhouse. I have to play piano in the dark. So come on, give me a break here. Don't try taking water in your palms. It's an exercise in futility."** She remained quiet, not saying a word in rebuttal. He likes that. Next day, called Vanessa at the bank. Told her, he's coming by with an urgent matter. Invited into her office, she motioned him to a seat. Then unexpectedly began. *"Can you believe that man? Having fixation with a baby's vagina, not even keeping it to himself. Did you see Barbara smiling, in embarrassment? Poor girl, poor baby."* With a finger to his lips, pointed to note attached at top of bill of lading. Having expected to have it brought to her by counter staff. *"Lack of shipper's endorsement guaranteed. Release cargo authorized."* All he wanted, was for her to authenticate with the bank's stamp and her signature. She went on. *"You men have no shame. Lusting at new born babe. You're all worst than animals."* He thought without uttering. *"We are all animals, we cannot be worse than."* That child is now an adult. Did anyone tell her, daddy salivated at her nudity when she was months old? Why do some women daub all men with paintbrush of indignity. Simply because one, stands out by his inherent variegated colours? Paolo could have admired photo, without vocalizing. But then, his long stare and facial excitement, would have betrayed, revealing inner thoughts. I do not believe, an adult male should take interest or find pleasure, admiring a child's vagina. Such behaviour reeks of perversity. Having said that, I seriously don't think. Paolo's utterances and actions were dictated by lust or deviant intrigue. He and others with similar affinity, are persons who laughs at whatever they finds funny or interesting. Totally unaware of civil norms, probably living era of upbringing. Where men enjoy scenes of bawdy and uncultured expressions. But then, we can't change the world. Now can we.? Let it be, let it be.

A tidbit....call the Police?

Jean and Juan were Janet's and James' back to back neighbours. Jean was very friendly and outgoing. Always had questions about island life, gabbed frequently with James at their fence. Which, soon after, would bring, normally reclusive Juan out to the fence also. Jean sent Janet and James a Christmas card, from her and Juan. This led to his pointing out, at a 'thank you' fence gab. They lived in different zip codes. *"Imagine that!"* Jean chirped. *"We talk across our fences, and yet we are in different zip codes. Just goes to show, segregation is still alive and well."* Both had a good laugh and went their way. A morning, as James spread lawn fertilizer, that kills weed as it feeds grass. Let me ask you. Have you noticed, after applying these blends. New, never before seen weeds appear? Or is it just my lawn? Anyhow, Jean came outside, looking physically spent. Dishevelled and adripping with sweat. Greeted James and told him, they are house remodeling. She was taking breather from dust and chaos, would talk to him later. About 16:00 hours, Juan called, asking James to meet fence side, said. *"We overestimated, and mixed too much concrete. You want some? I hate to just let it go to waste and dump it. I was wondering, if you have any little project going that would…you know?"* James snapped fingers and told Juan. **"Dam! You a day late. I already burned the body. Come to think of it, digging is hard work, which I am not fond of. I would have passed on your offer anyway."** One could see Juan, mentally recoil before he recovered, laughing out loud and saying to James. *"I got to go, catch you later."* So, what did he go in the house and say to his wife? James went in and said to Janet. **"Jean just asked for you, with some degree of urgency. I know you're busy, but would suggest you go holler to her at the fence."** This, to preempt their thought process. Sort of confuse them a bit more. Kind of like. If Janet is alive, who the hell did he murder? Janet had a better idea, she called Jean. They gabbed for five minutes and each went back to their task. James watched the monitor, but there wasn't any unmarked car stopping. Cops never came by to investigate. Juan would not have hesitated, reporting the chat with his neighbour to the police. Jean must have talked him out of it, telling him. ***"You know he's always making outlandish jokes. I just spoke to Janet. We didn't see no smoke, didn't smell no bacon. Stop being stupid."*** I am here to tell you folks. Next time your neighbour tells you something similar. Do not take it as a prank. He might not be joking.

Who might our neighbours be?-17.

07:53 read display on my HTC1 cellphone. I normally slept until nine down or up ten. Today, I was victim of mind control. Back in high school, I looked forward to Thespian role. Chance at portraying different roles, based on English literature. From Oliver Twist to Julius Caesar. Soothsayer role appealed most. Endowed, with unconscious awareness and mystery of the Ides. Throughout life. I counseled those in my circle. To be wary of the Ides. Not just March but any month. It can be averred. I developed chronic superstition, relative to the 15th. Out of fear, I took extra precautions in pursuit of daily routine. Before falling asleep, previous night. I was aware, if I woke and saw daylight, it would be the Ides of July. I think that caused my mind to rouse me earlier than usual. I would normally get out of bed at 05:00 hours. Hie back roads and be present in bookie room by 07:00 hours, for start of daily safety meeting. My wife had to be up at that time, but she preferred multi-laned turnpike, and safety-in-numbers route to Broward by 08:00 hours. That changed when I retired. Given age differences. She would not be eligible for luxury of retirement any time soon. She promised to be quiet as a mouse, getting dressed for work, so as not to disturb. Let me say, here and now. Mice being quiet, is one great myth. As youth, in still of night. Granny and myself could hear mice gnawing the cupboard door. Once we stirred, they stopped. Only to begin anew when all was still. At daybreak, there would be gnawed wood chips as evidence.

She feathered the pantry with kerosene, which acted as deterrent, for a while. So there, one more myth made redundant. My not yet adjusted to sleeping in. Despite her being quiet, I would still awake. Not wanting her to feel guilt, I fake snored and watched her. Sometimes I got a visual that primed senses for later. It's called, The games people play. You wanna hear a rhapsodic rendition of song so titled? King Curtis Ousley on saxophone. Duane Allman on guitar, backed by The Kingpins. It permeates and excites your receptive cranny as nothing else can. It bothered, I didn't hear her astir this morning. She went through routine and left without my knowing. I was mildly troubled this should happen. today of all days. Thoughts took wings. For my entire life. I had gone through a third, in state of being dead. Granny always said *"Take sleep, mark death."* Dramatizing similarities between both. Dreams I had, places I went. Is that how it is in death? I sat on the settee reflecting on my day ahead. Elaine asked me to check her car battery. This was going to be rare occasion, I hesitated being in female company. You see, she used to be my girlfriend, before I married my second wife. It was always same ole song with same meaning. Every time we met or chatted on the phone. Cusses me out for having traded her in for a newer model, then rubs salt in her wound. Saying, I ought to be ashamed. Living with a woman who is younger than my children. Usually I shut her up, telling her. I live with a woman, whom my family has met. Unlike her brother, who lives with a man as his wife. Visited ye olde country, twice and makes excuses why Jaime can't come with him. Maybe, someone ought to whisper. Jaime is really James, and let fireworks go off. A recent habit of his, old folks would disown him like Peter did Christ. Woe if this becomes open secret back in ye olde country. Despite misgivings, I'm wanting to go see her. If only because, she flirts. Old Jamaican proverb. *"Old fire stick easy to catch."* Just might prove true. You never know luck of a lousy cat. Amid reverie the doorbell jarred me into fright. It was on things-to-do list. Dismantle and put padding to muffle resonance. My twelve year old genius scolded. *"Daddy, bell was designed so it can be heard, wherever in the house people are. Padding will defeat it's purpose."* See?. I've always told you women are smarter than men. When they attain double digit age. They begin flexing and honing skills for next stage, teen. Then they are not only masters of their fate, but also of yours. Watch out parents, you've been there. I told her about my elementary school bell, that boys were given honour ringing. Big heavy brass bell with steel clapper attached to chain that hung from centre. Both hands were used to swing it up and down. Doorway was nigh Miss Fuller's desk, and the bell obviously upset her. She brought one of those bedside ting-a-lings. Tinkled on Monday and Tuesday. School yard wasn't big, hence it served it's purpose. Headmaster tied newspaper turban to the clapper and Wednesday morning. The brass bell was back in service. Instead of pealing, clang-a-clang-a-clang. It went thuck-a-thuck-a-thuck. She found story funny.

Jarred back into hubbub of sixteen waking hours, I asked me. *"Who the hell can that be?"* The bell rang again. I decided to dramatize the event. Since someone was bold enough to ring my bell this early. I'm going to show how unprepared I am for invasion. Loudly asked, then said **"Hudat?! Breakfast not ready, come back one hour."** Voice replied, urgently. *"It's me, your good buddy, Karl. Open up, I just wanna ask yo…."* As I yanked the door open, he paused, stared open mouthed and went on…*"Jesus mon! I will wait out here while you dress."* Told him. **"This is it pal, so step on in and let me close the door. Keep gnats and lower life forms** out. Come on Karl, quit staring and step in or talk from outside the door. Do something, before something do you." He timidly steps in and declares. *"I have to tell you. I feel bit queasy. Home alone with my friend, whose only garment is his drawers."* "I just got up half hour ago, and haven't selected which tux I'll be wearing today." *"So where's the pajamas?"* "I only used those when I was in Baptist, recuperating." *"So, you sleep at nights, in just a pair of drawers?"* "Yep! When tingling starts, less bandage on cast. Sometimes, I go bowiebat under the tepee." He appears baffled, so I tells him. "You know, one of them Indian tents you see in cowboy shows? I still haven't figured, if it's same thing they call wigwam." He nods his head vigorously and says. *"Hey mon, I know it's early, but can I borrow your plumb bob kit?"* I try telling him, again. "Lawrence, it's not mon or mun. It's just "man." Why do some Americans think Jamaicans talk like that?" *"Well, be it so or not. In my book, thems not fighting words. So keep your drawers on. No need to get riled. Because I have to ask another favour. Kind of bigger, like. Next time you going the Lowe's or the Ace. I'll be needing a ride, please and thanks. If you don't plan going in a hurry. Just remember, your buddy and neighbour, needs to. Okay?"* So ended Karl Lawrence. My good neighbour, four doors removed. I told him. "Okay, I'll run you to Lowe's later." He responds. *"I know I'm asking a favour, but jeezaloo. You leave me no options. Why later, and not now? Why, Lowe's, and not the Ace?"* "Why, Lowe's? I'll tell you why, Lowe's. We could walk to Lowe's on Pine Island. Or make short hop to one on Veterans. Why later? Because, contractors and handymen swarming stores now. Our time, is ten thirty onwards.

Why not Ace? I can't recall seeing Ace sign near here. Maybe, we'd have to go Fort Myers." *"You make it sound you must swim Caloosahatchee. There's a bridges you know."* "I know there are bridges. Cost $2 to get you home." *"Not me, you doing something wrong. Let's go Ace. I show you how to get home free by the Trail."* "What Trail you talking about?" *"The Tampa Miami Trail. Never heard of Tamiami Trail? It's Cleveland Avenue, going North."* "Oh, so I am going to burn, extra $2.89 gas to get around $2 toll. Never thought of it, but that's huge savings, Karl." *"I hate it when you go sarcasm."* "You mean, sarcastic?" *"That's other hate, when you correct. You are British schooled. I am American. Tomato, tomawto is same..... thing. See? I knew you was gonna jump on fruit or vegetable thing. Caught myself in time. You said your piece on Lowe's. Now let me say my piece on the Ace. All that stuff, I used in hobby kits way back when, I can sometimes find at the Ace. Sometimes it be at the Lowe's, but with slight difference. And boy, do they make you pay for it."* "Ace doesn't? Lets you walk out with stuff, scot free? They all make you pay. Call cops if you go out the door and not pay." Karl thinks, silently before asking. *"What did I say that brought that on? Of course, they make you pay. Know what I think you should do? Stop and scratch your head before you talk. That way...I am done. If I need that ride, and lord knows I do. My probation has ways to go, but it's not a life sentence. I will get licence again, and life will be worth living. Meantime, be nice to your friends. Not tell them how they can be better people. How's that, sounds good? Come here. You know I love you? We would get along better, if we could sit in my backyard in the gazebo, and sip few cold ones. But you won't drink. I'll tell you. I never met island man who didn't drink, and I am talking about hardcore stuff. You guys brew that sugar rum, squeeze them bottles dry. How come you not take a beer? I think you just a sissy. Although I know gyals drink best there is, right under the table. What? What's that look for?"* "You really calling me, a sissy? You, of all men, whose pair is yet to grow, or been shrunk? Don't get me started. We might get to fisticuffing." Karl says. *"I'm gone, but before I go. I am begging. Not just asking. Ride to Ace today. Please sir. Jah will bless you."* "What you know bout Jah? Jah won't bless me, I am not Rastafarian." *"See what I talking about? Always the correction. Peace out mon. Mann."* Later I honk at his gate, he scurries out. I roll the window down and says. **"Whoa, take screwdriver or tool from your pocket to puncture my seat."** *"Whoa mon, why you think I have any....you have bonic eye?"* "No, I don't have bionic eyes. It happened before, under similar circumstance." He enters and sits, looks around. *"This is nice, I like this. But honest to God, I prefer the old…What you used to call it?"* "You mean, The Green Machine?" *"Yes! That truck was a beast. When you select fifth speed and let her go. Torque of 4.9 straight six, tingles your ass. Mon, mann what a rush. Where we going?"* "Pine Island Lowe's." *"You not take me to the Ace?"* "Where, is the Ace?" *"I don't know, but you can put it in your screen thing there and find it. Can't you?"* "Seat belt Bro." *"Why? We just going up the road."* "I don't want you slamming into me. At any speed, that's gonna be quite a crush. You got to be, at least 230 pounds." *"You are wrong, it's 268. And it takes that there bus, to budge me from where I sit."* "Don't change my radio. You are not girl or co-pilot." *"You island guys are all same. Walk on your heads for pound of flesh. I was not going for your radio. What you got.*

Serus?" "You crazy? Why would I listen to pay radio?" *"Yes, yes. Anyhow, I was trying to turn on the ac. You know it's kinda warm in here?"* "Karl, do not turn on, adjust. Or in any way interfere with anything. Just sit, make yourself comfortable. It's mind over matter. Tell yourself you're comfy and you will be." *"I'm telling you, I feel like bacon on grille. Swear to you, my drawers stuck to my ass."* "Look at that screen, it's 72 degrees." *"We keep our house at 64 degrees."* "Ours is set at 78, that's where Trane goes choo choo and starts running." *"78?! 78? You guys. No offence intended, but. Born in the tropics, I can understand. It's kind of. What's the word? Climatisating or something. Me? You looking at New England born and bred kid on the block. I gots to be chilled, or lose my cool real easy."* We at the Lowe's, Karl exits and asks. *"You coming in?"* "No, I don't need anything at the hardware store." *"You could get weed killer or fertilizer for the lawn. I see Arab desert creeping in, little by little."* "I am waiting a sale, to get what I need." *"Now that we parked. Why not ask the truck where's nearest Ace. My wife drives a Ford Fusion. She asks directions to places and gets answers."* "I'm sure she does Karl, but in my case. It's not the fiddle, it's the Fiddler." He returns empty handed, sits and says to me. *"You ever have signifying Monkey on your back?"* "What the hell is signifying Monkey?" *"Funny, you African American and ask that."* "Karl, I am not African American. Don't even know what it means." *"How you identify yourself, ethnicity?"* "Black or Negro, full stop." Karl begins. *"I want to tell you something."* Then lapses into silence. I start the truck, he says. *"Hold on a little time out. I want to give my side of this thing. Two years and change leave, on this probation shit. I bound to go crazy, before it comes to end. So, I want you hear my side. That way… I started driving at fourteen, and now in my sixties. I am grounded like a f...in kid. That judge screwed me, simply because I spoke up for me. Claims I did not show remorseful. I tell you, between us, here and now. I still don't feel any kind of remorseful...ity. Remorsefullness. Idiot, jaywalking to prove to the girl, how macho he is. She hauled ass to sidewalk. He stopped, smack dab in front the truck. He's lucky, only got tiny sideswipe. I'd a gotten him flush and square, he'd a launch like weather balloon. But nobody wants to hear, or look at truth. Not cop, not his family either and not the judge."* "Karl, let's look at facts. Orange Blossom Trail, Orlando, 15:25 hours, peak traffic. What prompted your fleeing the scene? You must have seen eyewitnesses, hollering at you, STOP. Must have figured, someone was going to or already calling 911. Giving make and tag of your vehicle. Ever heard saying. You may run but you can't hide?" *"My friend, those questions I ask many times. Jail snitch asked me too, so I told him. I was on my way to job for the mob, and if I didn't get it done. Would suffer slow excruciate death."* "Think he took you serious?" *"Oh yes! Shit, between jail and prison. I did near six years. No One ever looked at me, and not smile. One of my homeys from Hoboken came to visit, and I tell you now. Just his demanner and talk, caused their faces sag, and their eyes pop wide. Told them he was, Capo Generalisimo. Flew from Sicily with message from top. To tell me, everything settled with local boys. My position was there, with promotion, soon as I get out. I been meaning to ask. You get freaky in here sometimes? What's with surgical gloves there?"* "When I do re-fuel, I put on my hand to input data and hold pump nozzle." *"Why emergency room stuff? You ever see anybody else doing that? You ever see them staring at you, funny like? I'll tell you now, Bro. I look at you. Especially last year, when we went to pick up my son, and we went rest stop. Andre and me went straight to an urinal. You went to basin and washed hands, before taking a piss. Then zipped up and walked out. Most guys wash hands after. You wash before, and then that's it."* "I use a glove, because. I don't want to transfer cache of germs, from pump to steering and hands. Left by hundreds of nasty hands. I touch my skin, grab a snack or whatever. As to bathroom protocol, it's just me. I got to have a clean dipstick. In case I meet someone, whose oil needs checking. That way, they don't call me three days later. Demanding money to go see a "Gist" I'll do an "after" wash, if I tinkle my hand. Before is a must. After, not necessarily." *"Ain't gist got something to do with how a person talk or? I'm not sure what you said but…"* "I'm doing abbreviation Karl, for professionals whose jobs end "gist." Like Gynaecologist, Ophthalmologist and…" *"I get it, I got it. Let me tell you something you don't know about us humans. We are built to indestructive, and live thousands of years. Just like old guys in Bible times. It's called, immunitive system. We all born with it. More shit we absorb and expose to. Better immunitive develops ability to protect. When you start wear gloves and wash before. You rob the…"* "Sorry to interrupt, Karl. But, it's "immune." *"Know, you right. It did sound kind of long, but.. You rob immune of things to do. Like everything humans have, if we don't use it we lose it. Being idle, it gets very lazy. Falls asleep and goes into coma. Along comes simple thing, like flu virus and Mr. Clean get knock over. Me? My boys kick ass, send flu hell bent out of town. I know what I am talking about."* We get to Karl's house, he gets out. *"Come in and look at my project. Next time I ask for a ride to the Ace. You will think it worth the extra mile."* He shouts. *"We are back."* She emerges. I greet from threshold. **"Morning Phoebe."** *"Morning? The privileged are siting down to dinner. Where you boys been so long, doing what? Caused you lose track of time."* She hollers to him….and me. *"Karl, Petri and your son are both in heat. You know, you need to keep close eye on him. Or take him with you, when you go out. The judge gave you custody, pending. Now I think, I might have to take the dog to ASPCA for examination. And it's not cheap. I'm taking the car to Firestone for oil change and brake check. I might have to call you, depending on what they say. So please Karl. Do not go astray."* Karl had not uttered one syllable, since walking in the house. Now that Phoebe left, he still seemed awestruck. I turned and said I was leaving. In a trance, he said.*"Just give me five minutes. I'm going in Andre's room to talk to him."* I told him. **"Karl, I got places to go and people to piss off. I'll catch up with you."** He yet pleaded. *"I want to ask you an important question."* **"Answer is still, No. We've been over this already. I can't keep Andre. Remember? You broached it very day we went for him? Answer remains same as it was that day. No is no, and don't ask, why."** He stares at me. Just then the phone rings, he tells me. *"Answer that for me, maybe it's Phoebe. If it's a bill collector. Tell him to take a number and join the f…in' line."* It was Phoebe. *"Karl left you to babysit Andre?"* **"No, he went in the room to talk with Andre."** *"That boy does not need a talking with, he needs a talking to. Tell Karl, listen for dryer chime, and fold clothes before they're cold. Looks like I'll be here a while.. I've put it off so many times, I have to get it done today."* I made note, her talking without greeting, and ending without a bye. Karl came out, I gave him the message. Still wearing that perplexed stare, he said. *"I asked Andre what he was doing. But he's not saying much, other than, 'nothing.' Says Phoebe told him to take a shower."* "Cold one?" I asked, with a grin. Karl chided. *"Don't laugh mon, it's not funny. If you look at that dog, you just might get ideas. But you would think you'd know better. You know what I am saying?"* **"I know what you saying. But it's common thing back home, man and animal get together. Man with goat, hog, Bitch. Guardie took on Jenny donkey, making news. Yours truly, brushed Mother Hen, and then she couldn't stand. Folks thought she was sick. Decided to kill her, before she died. We had nice pot of curried chicken stew that night. With that my friend, I must go. Remember, Phoebe says to listen for the chime."** I knew he had questions. His face depicted intense curiosity. He was a victim of temporary speech paralysis. I too had a question, but it could wait. Things have ways, dropping in your lap. It angered me, Phoebe did not seem to care for Andre, her only child. It was Thanksgiving, and at Phoebe's request. I was doing jerked chicken for her guests. They had heard about, wanted to taste. Marinating overnight, Phoebe worried. Plagues, known and unknown. Would infect the food and sicken her guests. Aroma wafting on the smoke, had everyone looking forward to sampling this new entree. Karl said he wanted to get hang, by observing. He really wanted to chat, so we did, quietly. I asked.**"Does Phoebe have other children, besides Andre, or he's an only?"** *"What you talking about? Phoebe never give birth and she never will. You think I should have him fixed? You know, thing they do at adopt place? I think it's neutral, or spray. Don't know, which is which. But one is for Ram cat and one for Bulldog."* **"Karl, it's neuter, not neutral. Don't make jokes like that. Your son is human. If he has a problem.**

He should be helped professionally, not cutting out his balls." *"Then, did you really f… the Hen. Or just trying to minimize Andre's? You know? Not look so bad?"* "Say what? Minimizing Andre's? Let me tell you something. Very early in my youth. Granny taught me to stick finger up Hen's rump. And feel the egg, to know when it would be laid. Some made nests away from home, had to be locked up in the coob. Sticking fingers in a warm moist orifice. Gave me a thrill. Rest, I already told you. So, what's up with Andre and Phoebe. Who, at one time was her son, now no longer is?" *"Well, she's been pissed ever since the judge said we had to accept custody of Andre. Because his grandma could no longer care for him. And he would have to be sent out of county, if taken into state care."* "There's a lot you not telling me. If you don't want to, that's okay by me. But I do recall your telling me, Phoebe was his mom. He'd been staying with his grandma, her mom. And yadda yadda. I'm gonna cut up some taste bits. Where are the toothpicks?" After putting out taste bits, I learned something about male female behaviour.

Most males were eager to go at the bits, even before platter hit the table. One, voiced standard comment. *"This tastes like good shit."* Women showed little interest, if at all. Agreed, odour of preparation was not appetizing. When full platter was served, they gingerly came forward. Soon were hogging the jerk, as men smilingly yielded to them. Phoebe introduced me as "Chef par excellence" to a woman, with two pieces on a sani-plate. Asked me to give a recipe, that she would fine tune and try out at her place. **"There's no recipe to speak of."** I told her. *"There has to be."* She rejoined with emphatic aplomb. *"Every facet of preparing food, must be guided by* *formula. Creating that acceptable taste experience. Moreso when it's being made, to court public acceptance."* I tried telling her, traditional method of Jamaican cooking. **"With us, it's know how, learned from observing older heads. We season pot and taste from a condensed can^. Adding tot of this, dash of that and sprinkle of secret ingredient. That's basics of how it's done."** *"That's all well and good for a family fare. But you can't prepare food for the public, and lapping the pot as you mind. That would be so disgusting."* She ended and walked away. Karl joined me and said. *"Mon, if you take this recipe to Pollo, they go for it big time. They already have tropical theme going."* **"Karl, hold down your Pollo Tropical intro. What I did, comes nowhere close to real Jamaican jerk. A Yawdie wouldn't touch it, if offered free. Would most likely scrape it to Rover, who'd probably sniff and walk away. You know, dogs will eat anything. Well, maybe not American dogs. Jamaican dogs not partial to anything. They'll raid garbage cans and eat any shit, but not third rate jerk. Anyhow, just so you know. Some Publix and most Jamaican shops, sell the bottled stuff. Look for "Jerk Seasoning." Many brands out there. I think "Walker's Wood" tops others. I wouldn't volunteer that to Miss Highbrow, she's too It. What she does? Runs business, flophouse maybe."** Normally, he would laugh or react in some way. He was deep in thought. Glancing about me, everyone being festive. Enjoying themselves and each other. Andre was one of three boys, circling a young girl, who spoke animatedly. Gesticulating to each boy as they laughed, engaging her and each other. I unconsciously uttered my thoughts and said. **"Three young Roosters against one Pullet? Her comb gonna get mangled and torn before she can sneeze."** *"You can't forget that Hen, eh?"* Now, he laughed out loud. I did not tell him what I had been muttering about. We at times hesitate, exposing people to our base, depraved instincts. Without prompting, Karl began. *"You know, sometimes life has so many twists and turns. You can't figure out where you came from or going. Then by time you get it figured out, it's time for you be leaving this life. Shoot, some folks get taken away, before they even get figured out. You a man who's hooked on wonderfullness of woman. See? Just that mention, brings smile to your face. Would you believe, if I told you. Aside from my mom. Every woman I share close encounter with, ended in misery? When Lyndsay came into our home. I thought she was my father's outside child. Nobody talked about anything, she was just there."* I raised finger, bent on asking. "Who is Lyndsay?" Recognizing the finger, Karl said. *"I am on a roll here. Don't pause me now, I won't restart."* He   continued. *"She had a daughter at seventeen, then, ran away with the boy. They lived up state New York a while. She kept in touch with us when she ran into money crunch, and needed help. She said, her dad went to Nam and never came back. He was never declared prisoner of war. Missing in action, or awol. It was as if he never existed. Her mother had no answer to her questions, but took and raised her daughter. She is now young lady. I don't know what 9-11 had to do with the situation. But she left her man and stayed with me for a time. Fearing he would track her down, we moved to Trenton. She got pregnant. She's not just good in bed, she's fantastic mon. Ever ran till you're breathless, and still force yourself to keep running till you drop? Girl makes you sweat and love it. I tell you. We planned to get married, after Andre was born. She kept putting it off, and then. One day, she was gone. Now, I had a one year child to care for. Phoebe and I hooked up, we moved to Paterson. But she was always on the move. So I took Andre to Lyndsay's mom in Secaucus. For a time, things were on the level. Phoebe got into her dark age. Oh yes! You wouldn't know it, but that lady. She has her own dark, deep existence, she takes pains to conceal. She will kill to keep it that way. I don't know half of it. But what I do know, you won't hear from me. Not ever, even at gunpoint. So let my execution begin, and be over and done with. After Phoebe's sabbatical ended."* He guffaws and continues. *"We moved to Florida and got married. Just as we settling down. Out of the blue, Lyndsay hollered for help. I could not do anything, without talking to Phoebe. Seeing, we were living on her dime. Her boyfriend was caught in a sting, selling yeh yoh. He rolled over on Lyndsay, taking her down with him. That was one version, other version said. It's her who rolled over on him. I pray that's not truth, or else, when he gets out. She best already migrated, behind the iron curtain. Either way, both feared. If other was left out, roaming freedom trail. They'd hook up with a partner and live high on the loot. I heard, there's lots of it on ice, just waiting. I know if Lyndsay got the chance, she'd grab the stash and dash with another fella. She gots to have a fella in her corner, just like prize fighter. She needs encouragement to go after prize. Her mom went childcare, or whoever. Said she getting old and unable to cope with Andre. Truth is, it started with incident at school, in house cop took matters in hand. I don't know full story, and as usual, Andre won't talk much. By time they searched through papers. I barely seen natural sunlight, three months. They came knocking on my door. Scared crap outta me. I was back before a judge. She said, as natural father. She giving custody to Phoebe and me. What pissed Phoebe was, she did not have say in anything. Had to accept what judge said, no leeway. I tell you, she don't go for that shit. She make her own rules, and break em when she feels like. So that has her in a bind with him. Other thing is. Her math to put me with Lyndsay, when I was with her. Not coming out in her favour. So she wants to tweak the wall paper a little bit. Make a year, seven months, and make some months, fifty days. You know what I mean? Bullshit, if you ask me, but nobody ask. God's truth is, I ain't up for saying anything. Andre is my child, I don't have problem with whatever. Phoebe is different. I silently think, hope she should understand. Especially given her own thing. But right now, I'm in dog house, and you know how that goes."* He signaled end to his ranting oration. I said. **"No Karl, I don't know how that goes. We don't have dog houses, where I come from. Dogs stay outside to guard yard and house. If he inside, he can't serve purpose. Begin barking when invaders approach. However, I know what you talking bout, from a figurative standpoint. No Jamaican woman, puts her man in dog house. Because she done know. Every puss house gonna open door, invite him for pampered shelter."** *"So, you telling me. Andrea never…?"* **"Karl, you hearing but you not listening. What me just say to you? You want me repeat?"** *"No! no need to. I hear you alright. Y'all guys sure lucky."* **"Luck has nothing to do with it. It's tradition, way back from slavery. It somehow got steeped into our makeup and into our DNA. Slave owners, having a strong sturdy male. Used him as stud to breed female slaves. That way, they got children with robust stamina, and tolerance for hard work from early age. Adult males were dusted and polished, not put outdoors like rusty machete. In our corner of world, women outnumber men. Some are killed in criminal** activity, political violence, drug wars, and very often by law enforcement. Others are in prison. Man on loose is precious as gold nugget, to down and out prospector. Dawg house? Wha name so?" Silence was alive for two minutes, slain by Karl, who said. *"I have a problem I want to run by you, and hear what you have to say. Me start support Andre before him born. I have a dollar, I give Lyndsay 25c. I make ten dollar, I give her four. She go court, say not enough. They raise it and take out my job. Well, Orlando thing happen and they put me away. When I get out and begin straight out my life…..What!? Me say a word wrong, why you start smile?"* "Don't worry you head Karl. Ignore me and talk you talk. Me suffer from same disease, malapropism. Girlfriend correct me all time."

Karl grinned in satisfaction, saying. *"Yes?! For real?! And me think you did know more than me?"* He laughed, then resumed, after a pause. *"Yeah, they say I owe back money for time they put me away. I ask the judge. How can I owe, when I wasn't working? They forget, I was doing sentence? Can you believe that crap? In same time frame, judge did custody thing, because Lyndsay gone up the river. So, I ask judge to cancel the garnish thing. They not going give her money, while she in prison. I think she was giving money to her mother, to look after him. When we went for him. You could see he was well eating, clean skin and. You know what I'm saying? So now, they taking garnish. What the hell, and doing what with it? Meanwhile, on top of that. He has to go school, books, shoes. Money for this, that and devil knows what. Know what judge tells me? That there is another matter for another court, another time. I been figuring, court and judge was justice."* "Karl, I'll tell you how I deal with certain issues, that arise on my life's journey. I'm telling you, because it works for me. Court will continue garnishing, whether you like it or not. You told the judge how you felt. Judge said, it's not within her power to rescind order. Forget it, keep that load off you head. Maybe, one day in play of things. It will happen, way you want it to. Let it be a pleasant surprise. For now, treat it as a loss and move on. One less worry, one more hour of peaceful sleep. Change what you can, accept what you can't." *"I hear you, it's good advice. If you can muscle willpower to do. Maybe, you be like my doctor. Tells me, give up this, don't eat much pizza. His magic repeat word is, motheration. Anything else, is murderation. He laughs, and his gut bob and weave like sparring partner, because he's funny. That advice coming from chubby, 400 lbs sweat hog. Is contradict his advice and profession. I want ask you a favour, but you not make it easy. When you refuse money for gas and such. So let's get a Uberish thing going. That way, if I want go the Ace. Ace is where we go."* "You don't need me to achieve your goals. Just call Uber or next outfit. You'll get where you want to go, when you want to go. I am retired, doing things at my own leisure. When I want, because I want. Not because I have to. Not in all respects, as things are. I have to get checkups. Would rather not be stuck with a needle. I have to file and pay taxes, or go jail. So you see Karl, I'm just trying to cut down on must do's. I make exception for my children, because I hope. When time comes, they'll make exception for papa." *"I hear you my friend. Anyhow, next Thursday 15th. I asking you take me courts office. Drake promised, but he's not reliable. If I miss the date, no tell what they do to my ass. So you're my backup plan. Here's a real kicker for you to figure out. Drake never refuses money when I offer. Asks for it at times, like this once.* "Smell the fumes Karl?

When you stop smelling, we stop moving. Where you going buy gas?" Still, he's unreliable. Time I wanted to go Gainesville. Forty dollar he says. Buy gas today, we leave early morning next day. F...er went hiding for months. Surprise him at Flea Market. Say he was in hospital. Was gonna send him back in, Phoebe gave her look. Whilst you on other hand...On Uber thing? Phoebe has that under wraps for herself only. Her and the guy might have thing going. You never know." "It's same driver all time?" "Don't think so. See about four other guys. Remember, she is woman. They're very resource, same drop honey catch many. Like way back when we hang flypaper in the barn." I attempt a response, think better and clam up. Not before he notices and prods.*"What? No. No, say it man. I likes hear island man wisdom on things like this. Come on mon, don't go shy on me."* **"I hesitate, because I shouldn't comment on your relationship. Don't want anything I say taken wrong. But if I felt way you just expressed about your wife, or any woman sharing my space. We would not be together. Mark you now, don't go divorce her and say idea came from me."** He stared, upper body recoiled. *"You see Phoebe, but you don't know Phoebe. No man divorce Phoebe, unless she tell him. Phoebe is business by herself. Not corner store, big stock thing. See ya."*

Wending way home, in melancholy mindset, thought. *"Phoebe is really big business by herself. Sounds like he giving that woman too much credit."* Being reliable, not being compensated. I rang the doorbell three times. It's my formula for contacting people, by phone or at door. After three rings, figure. Person either busy, unaware or ignoring. With doorbell, I count thirty seconds between rings, before abandoning effort. Hearing sounds, I hung around beyond. Phoebe opened the door a crack, standing behind closed half.

She said. *"Oh, it's you. Come on in."* Head was wrapped in a towel. I didn't know if she was aware, her robe had parted. However, her question, taking me off balance, told me. She either knew, or didn't much care. Them who knows me, will aver. Question must have been, sonic boom to my consciousness. Being figuratively a hunter, when prey steps out of the brush and asks. *"You want some tail? Fresh from the shower. So fresh, it tingles. Nice aroma too."* It's intimidating and creates fluster. **"I, hmmm, I wouldn't know what to do with it."** I calmly replied. She looked me over. *"You too? Young man in prime of life, standing there and….You know that's a freakin' insult? Come have some coffee. Caffeine might give you a lift."* **"I don't do coffee."** *"Is there anything you do, like normal people?"* **"I have high blood pressure, coffee makes it worse."** *"Oh, me too. But I got to have my jamoke. So, I ignore the doctor. Caffeine gives me kick that keeps me sane. Prevents me going bazooka on lots of people."* I recalled *"Phoebe is big business by herself."* but replied. **"I am a tea person. But again, it would have to be caffeine free. So, I regretfully have to decline your hospitality. What is jamoke?"** She ignores me and goes on. *"Karl's buddy came for him, early too, and waited. Son-of-a-Bitch. They went girl watching. Just kidding, he went on serious business. Relax, make yourself at home. We can get happy, if you're up to it. Why you looking at me like I stepped out of a dome, with antennae on my head? I will light your Joe and put it out, if and when I decide to. Not simple as I appear. Travelled highways, back roads and animal tracks. I'm restless, not cut out for this existence. I'm like beards of yore, who set sail uncharted oceans. Discover and plunder for good measure. To victors go spoils and…."* **"What? You got** thieving psyche, bottled in that perfectly round head? You're Bonny looking for Clyde? Sheriffs these days are better equipped. They track your car by VIN." Ignoring my comment, she speaks as if I hadn't spoken. *"I've got to run few errands and pick up Andre from school. That child has been through too much in his young life. I know, it's just not right. I shouldn't go without having something. I'm gonna make eggs. You want some? Or you have thing against eggs?"* **"I'll have some eggs, thank you. Was he really having a go at Petri?"** *"What, you think I was lying on a child? He can't help it though. It's part of his DNA, it's in his makeup. You know his mother was pro?"* **"Pro what? Wrestler, baller wha...?"** I've got to ask, it's bad jumping to conclusions. Phoebe stares at me, says. *"Pro, as in first syllable of ten letter word. Four vowels, six consonants. Don't you watch game shows? She was pro dog catcher. Yes! That's fitting. All men are dogs anyway. And your friend? He was her manager. Same net she used to catch strays? Took it home to catch Karl."* I thought a minute, then replied. **"In fairness to both, she only has one net. I am sure, it's used with cover or muzzle on strays. When she comes home, as they say. The gloves are off. That's usual way isolating chiefs from Indians."** *"Never mind all that. He still doesn't know for sure, Andre is his, and he doesn't want to. You're being warned. Open your mouth about anything said here today. I'll tell Karl, you made unexpected grab for my crotch. He can be a mean mother. Bet you didn't know, he has Mafia connections. Come on, we leaving now. Want a ride home?"* **"No, I walk for my exercise thing."** *"Yes, I know how you exercise. With your eyes, ogling women. I saw you in action at the party. In your day you were probably a pervert. Worse than Andre, no doubt. Back there among them island gardens.*

No wonder it's called paradise. Y'all got this slogan "No problem" I been there and met…." "In my day, you would not dare. Flaunt tun tun in front me, walk away unscathed. Joegrine and Dicky, work you over. Punishing and unforgettable, like Nat King Cole song. Later." *"Whoa! Hold up cowboy. Don't run off like this, come here. You can't leave me hanging. Ride with me, tell me little about fellows Joe Grind and Dicky."* "It's not Grind, it's Grine. He's guy who tugs strings and works Dicky." *"Hold on, let me toss some of this junk in the back. This car has so much crap, and. If you search through it, you wouldn't find a dollar to save your life. So, who is this Grind?"* "Phoebe, Grine. Joegrine, rhymes with wine. Got it now?" *"Not yet, go slow. Joe Doe I know, and Joe Blow. Tell me about Joe Grine, the grine part."* "Sex, in smooth intensity that brings out agony and ecstasy." *"You talking about rough sex?"* "No, nothing is rough. This is prolonged duration with seemingly dispirited, sensuous intensity." *"What's dispirited, sensuous intensity? You sure, you know what you saying? Cause, I don't. When you say, prolonged duration. How long a duration? With some men, sex loses fizz real quick."* "You ever heard on radio and TV. Ad for solution to ED and PE issues. Promoter says, this great supplement has men lasting. Upwards of thirty, sixty, ninety minutes or more, easy peasy? *"You sure they not promoting, threesomes or gang rape?"* "No, that's standard for a woman who comes from her father side of family. Then she sings gibberish, like French girl in Rod Stewart's song. "Tonight's the night." Man like that, famous in community and beyond. As "Bedroom Ninja." *"I know that Rod Stewart song, there's no gibberish at end."* "There is, in official Utube video. He's playing a guitar, there's a flame. It's 3:46 of hmph. After he exults, whooo. She begins the supie supie mi amor. You can hear her voice softly erupting, with satisfaction of sated pleasure. I tell you now. I would pause a sex bout, listen that music to it's ending. I probably wouldn't go back to what I was doing. That's how fulfilled with rapture I would be. Or maybe, I would be tranquilized. Go the three hour non-stop gig. That would certainly make her sit over a pail with hot water and epsom salts, steaming her jewel. As steam rises, she does clench exercises to keep that tight fit. No woman wants too much space between door and frame. Some opt to pay for surgery that brings back the virginal fit." *"I hope to God you not talking about my vagina. Pail? Hot water? Bedroom Ninja? That's fight. Sounds like rape, or very close."* "You don't understand. Some women demand, hardcore action. No bag-o-mouth. When bwoy can't reach expectations. She tell everybody, him is saps. So, to keep fame intact. Him must perform, to not just meet. But also, sometimes, exceed expectations. But me can tell you, Cherry always happy. When it comes to steaming, some home have bidet. Make things simpler. Others have proven methods, but it's all in getting shrinkage. Shrinkage is good for women, bad for men. Woman can't let shrinkage get out of hand. She have to keep it under wraps, as they say. Once she lose focus and drop asleep, by she wake up next morning. Done it done. You wouldn't know this. I've seen men at rest stops. Feeling around for ding-a-ling and only finds it. By a warm stream fouling hand. That tells how long it took him to find it. I'm not talking about senior citizens. These are late forties, early fifties. It's cause for embarrassment, I tell you. Now they, have to wash after. If not before and after." Turns her face upward and laughs hilariously, thumping the steering with both hands. **"Phoebe, the signal changed."** *"So now Mr. Joe Grine. I suppose you're going to tell me. In your day, you pulled all nighters, just like that? What you call it, just now? Easy cheesy without pleasey."* **"No, I never went for dusk to dawn thing. Had to catch last bus or walk home. One night, I actually began twenty-four mile walk, not sure how it would end."** *"You go twenty-four miles to get some? What was so special about that one?"* **"In 80's, was building a house in rural area. Young woman came round. She flirted and asked for monetary favours. I asked for taste of honey, in return. She promised, this night. Soon as her parents fell asleep, she would come. I had doubts, because she was a Christian and deacon visited often. They ran mom and pop grocery store. More than once, her dad told how. He slept lightly, armed with a machete to thwart robbers. I waited until 01:00 hours. Set out to main road. Nothing in public transportation went by, either direction. Not even a generic taxi. I feared sleeping in the house overnight, it not being secure. If looters found me there, they would probably kill me in my sleep. Before I could use my gun. So, I began my foolhardy walk. Didn't really have viable option, other than. Guess, disappointment made me stupid. You know, pent emotions? About a mile out, I saw headlights and flagged. It was an out of service bus. Crew said, at first they thought I was a ghost. When told, I was going to Kingston. Driver asked, if I was seriously going to walk that distance. Said, I was lucky. The bus broke down, and mechanics came from Kingston. Made repairs, and they were on way back."** *"I'll tell you, respect your dedication, but that sounds like addiction. So come here, my worthy tramp. Tell me about your duration skills."* **"I did a** three hour stint, although wasn't non-stop. Things weren't planned that way, it just happened. We began working about nine-ish, and went till about eleven-ish. Got thirsty and went downstairs for water. Mitsubishi was still on. Searched for remote, without success. However, show was interesting. Sat and watched it to end. Went upstairs and took up where I left off. She had fallen asleep, surprised I was still going at it. Said she thought I had finished. I said "No" I only went to drink water. She tried insisting, time lapse seemed greater. I did not prolong discussion. Got on pony, going to town again." *"Don't tell me. She was your girlfriend. I know a wife would not tolerate that crap. Not after she has security and power of that gold band on her finger."* "You're partially right, she was neither my girlfriend or my wife. She was my housekeeper." *"Your what?! I didn't hear you. I'm sure. Your housekeeper?! Your freakin' maid! For crying out loud. Your maid?! You, do, your, MAID?! She works for you. Cleans your freakin' house. Does your nasty laundry. In this day and age. Housemaster stays away from the dam charwoman. What kind of lowlife are you? Now I can see why you and Karl are buddy buddy."* "You done cussing me out and name calling? It's no different from secretary, brushed by board chairman. Jerry Seinfeld brushed his maid and everyone found it funny." *"She's, your MAID! Your MAID! Your MAID! How low can you go? Seinfeld thing was comedy from script, making sitcom. It wasn't real, don't dare make comparisons."* "Whoa, whoa. Let's do female lineup here. Starting with my maid, next up is secretary, doctor, senator and a first lady. Strip them all, it's same oasis tween them thighs. If they're healthy, they have similar issues and capabilities." *"So what? She works for you, she is your MAID. How low, can, you, go?"*

"Phoebe, pums is pums. So long as it's not Petri's. And you're conveniently overlooking women, who give it up to their gardeners and chauffeurs. Even he man handyman." *"I don't know now. If you go twenty-four miles to get laid. Maybe, a Petri would keep you from making the trip. I can tell you though. I would not put up with, your drink water and come back crap. You would have to screw yourself, or go open and close the door."* "That tells me you're not brave as you thought you were. You're scared of a good workout. That's why you opened up to me this morning. Old man, on his way out. You probably thought I couldn't rise to the occasion. Bet you would not dare do that with a young Buck. Trotting round the block on three legs. You'd know meaning of "Ring of fire." *"I'll bet you didn't know, you left Cape Coral a long time ago? A walk from here, is much more than exercise."* "You have to go for Andre, har-di-har." *"I can have him picked up and head over to Naples, har-di- har-har."* "If Andre is dropped off and can't go inside. You will be on six-o-clock news, wearing regulation togs. Har-di-har-har-har-har." *"You have the answers eh? You got lucky this time."* "Not just this time. I am not called "The Lucky Bastard" for nothing." *"Now you going away, with what in your mind? I am teaser of old men. Whom I suspect, can't make the grade. Go up the hill?"* "Not really, I figured you wanted a hit, and there I was." *"A hit? You mean like, dope fiend, drug head?"* "It's happened before, I am certain, quite often. It's just that women aren't burdened, by obvious display of sexual arousal, desires and lust. They enjoy many throbs, spasms and squirts. Without anyone being aware. A girlfriend confided. She sat at her desk and masturbated, mentally. Always wore panty shield, and had her sweater as backup. Before heading to bathroom, to check extent of exposure, or not. Men, on other hand, stand out and. Sometimes go to war with their senses, in an effort to stymie and detract. But alas, the mind is a powerful thing. Relief does not come easy. Someone stares, points and whispers, both laugh. Cat is out the bag. Time to tie me Kangaroo down." *"Hold that thought, while I pop in there. Eggs passed through my stomach, I am hungry. Come on, my treat. You don't have to get pizza. Try their wings, it's delish."* We sit and she makes two circles with her index finger. *"The cat was out the bag and?"* I said.

"I am going to tell you an unforgettable experience, with very conflicting emotions. In my twenties, Betty was my girlfriend. She got a job as live in maid with family DeCordova. In hilly suburbs of Saint Andrew parish. City bus did not go up the hill. She had to walk four miles, from bus stop to her workplace. She came home biweekly. I went with her, both directions, assisting with personal effects. At interview, housemaster agreed. Taking her to and from the bus stop. Drive her home with luggage and stuff. First Sunday, she waited in vain. Coaxed robot taxi owner to take her. Promising to pay three shillings fare, when she got paid. Master said, he was there. Waited five minutes, then left. End of first fortnight, he volunteered taking her down. Ever so often, as he told how pleased, family was with her work. His hand, came resting on and inching up her thigh. It was then she told him. Her boyfriend will come for her next time. We tried, but could never get space in only taxi plying the steep, serpentine route, when it wasn't broken down. Betty hesitantly confided, she sat on a man's lap that Sunday. Walking in labour of love, there was no stress. We chatted, laughed and next thing. We were at the portals. Until a weekend, it rained and drenched us to the bone. Lady of the house was concerned for my health." *"Oh! You poor man, How can you ever think keeping those on. You'll get yourself a proper round of pneumonia, be in the sanatorium. Come on in, let Betty see to you."* "See? Maternal instinct, trumps aristocracy. Phillip, the gardener. Lent change of clothes, whilst mine was being hurry dried with iron. Lady, conveyed need for urgency to Betty. Lest master should come and find me there. She was beside herself with anxiety, maybe even reconsidering her act of charity. Too late. All was well that ended well. Betty conveyed regards of Lady, who said I seemed a nice young man. And so it was, I got invited to Christmas party. Master reservedly told Betty. *"Missus thinks, it will lift spirits if your man friend came. But bear in mind, you will be working. I will ask our accountant Mr. VanWhervin. To give him lift to a street lamp, when all is said and done."* You know, in my mind. Would have been nice to sleep over. Naive to protocol of masters, servants, mores and customs. Very wise when it came to my emotional deprivation. Here was I amid jubilant crowd. My woman in servant's uniform. Traipsed back and forth with trays and permanent smile. Every now and then she flashed me a grin. Danielle, their top half daughter. Surprised me with sudden appearance and question. *"Do you want to dance?"* I quickly stuttered, Yes. Furtively glanced about for Betty, Master and Lady. *"Well come on then, you can't do it seated."* She said, with officious air. That song ended, we stayed embraced. Next record began. Brass Ring "Dis-Advantages of you." It's kind of melody that plays over and over in your head, long after you've heard it. You can find it on YouTube. A truly rhapsodic, lilting melody of strings, keyboards and percussion with serenading female voices. *"What's your name?"* She asked. Jerry Lewis. I replied. She snuggled closer, then kissed me long, with deep passion. Taken by surprise, and awed. I thought. *"Lord, what is this?"* I felt a head rise and frightfully wondered. Is anyone seeing this? Betty, Danielle's dad, her stepmother? I shuddered in a panic as emotions collided. Pain of discovery, and infinite pleasure of most heavenly, life moment. Her, mulatto and pretty, enhanced her allure. Soaring my spirit to seventh heaven. You have to understand, although this was 60's. My being with mulatto woman, was socially unacceptable. Rare to non-existent. These weren't middle class people. They were movers and shakers. Felt elated, like cat tasting cream. Never, had any woman, kissed and so inflamed my passions. Later, I realized. That was essence of my having elevated her to goddess status. As the music neared ending, she whispered. *"Follow me."* I did, into the bird house. She hugged and drew me to her warmth, as I nervously said. Me did think all birds went to sleep at nights. That kiss was on again with intensity. I was not engrossed in this. Mind raced, asking, what ifs. Her father found us here. Would Betty think, if she suspected. After five minutes, we were off again. My hand, firmly grasped by hers. Into the house by way of a rear patio, with large fish tanks and more birds. We entered a room, obviously hers, by wall decorations and furnishings. Turning her back to me, she said. *"Undo my zip."* It went down to top her rising rump. Shaking hands free, dress fell in crumpled heap at her feet. In made brassiere cups, pointed upward like urns to be filled. Flopping on a chaise, she held out her hands. *"Come here Jerry, lick my breasts."* They were like small pink stalagmites, rising from grotto floor. Nipples were cherry red. Phoebe, believe me. I went silently delirious. Part of me hungered to ravishingly exploit this unexpected opportunity of sexual gratification. Other part cautioned." *"Suppose parents came charging in. Her dad especially. He might shoot you and then say he thought you were burglar. You know how these rich folks have pull with police. They could even tell the girl to say it was rape. Shoot, she would probably say it was, without parental coercion. Not wanting to bear shame, consorting with my kind."* "Nell", I began. It's not that I don't love you. But, here is not place for us to share our love. I don't want to guzzle and belch like drunkard. I want to sip and savour. Let's arrange to do this one weekend. At my place, where we don't have to worry about anyone barging in." I'll tell you Phoebe, I was shaking in angst. Even as my mouth said that. I wanted to choke on those tits. Get a rabbit hump going. She rolled on her stomach, I stared. Not getting response, decided to make my exit. Whispered as I tiptoed. "I will go to phone booth, call you one evening when I think you reach home. Okay? I really and truly love you. Mi gone." Girl never grunted, ahem. Walked out front, where Phillip was upset. Heeled guests, disregarding parking instructions. Yet to understand, rich folks were adept at enforcing orders. Had problem taking them. Especially, from uniformed servants. Know what's funny about human psyche, Phoebe? Now safely out of danger. Secure, my fears of discovery, not being realized. I began having regrets, not going for the prize. Tsking and berating myself, letting this easy apple slip through my grasp. How major stupid could I be? Other surprise was, I never stirred to an erection. Too nervous to get my mojo working. As I assisted drivers out of tight spaces, that was where my Betty found me. Bringing Phillip a plate, she pounced accusingly." *"Where were you all this time? Know how long I'm looking for to give you something to eat? You were out here all this time?"* "I hugged her and walked away. Not wanting to lie, and be at Phillip's mercy to back me up." *"Who and you was dancing? You stink of expensive perfume."* "I came clean and said. "Oh, me and the daughter was dancing. Betty guffawed and said." *"Oh! Her? She would dance with a donkey. If she could get him to stand on his two back foot."* Phoebe found it hilarious, told me. *"That did not say much for you my friend. You got into your head about love, when the girl was horny crazy. She would find joy, squatting on cactus."* "If I stopped to pick it apart, I guess it wouldn't. But when you're in love, you take everything your sweetheart says. As compliment, coming from the heart. As to Danielle, I expressed emotion felt from our encounter. You see what I'm saying Phoebe?" *"I guess. What happened after? How did it all end or did it?"* "Well, as things wound down. I sought VanWhervin about lift down to flat. He said there was no room in the car, he brought guest. I couldn't understand what he meant. There were himself, his wife and his guest. Surely, there was space for at least two more in back seat. Then again, us plebes never fully understand thought process of upper classes. Starting out tired, close to 03:00 hours. Hied four miles plus downhill, hiding from duppies. Downhill always easier walk than uphill. Reached Papine Square after 05:00 hours. Went into Henny's cold supper shop and had breakfast. Took a bus home and slept all Boxing day. That's what we call, second holiday after Christmas day. Anxious to ride that pony. First time I called, it was my Betty who answered. *"House of DeCordova, good afternoon."* I hung up. Got an idea, went to Calvin's house. Got back and waited our turn. Told

Calvin, ask for Danielle when someone answered. Standing beside him, I heard Master yelling at him before he hung up. Told me, a man answered. Yelled at him, not to call back. Or he'll get the police to track him down and put him in jail. Who the hell is he. How did he come by this number anyway? All good things that could have been, ended. For a long time, I regretted having passed up opportunity. To her dying day. She would remember, "Peasant Jerry." Who planted flagpole on her hill." *"Don't be disappointed my friend. Believe me, walking away is never bad. Because you never know, what tragedy you avoided. True, it could be bliss and memorable pleasure. But there will be other times, more pleasurable moments. A tragedy can end it. You neither have regret or reminiscing. And, using your own words."Pums is pums, no matter how you hype yourself thinking, Danielle's was one of a kind."*

Her phone rings. She answers, then says. *"Your buddy is stranded, let's go pick him up."* She espies him from afar and says to me. *"Watch this."* Pulls to a stop, says to Karl. *"Mind driving sweetie? My shoulder aches."* Karl replies. **"Okay."** Moves around to driver's side. Waits for her to exit the car. Phoebe asks him. *"Do you really want to get away from me that bad. You would rather go to jail?"* Import of the question hits him, he hissed teeth. **"I wasn't even thinking straight what you..."** I got out the car at City Hall, as both protested. Phoebe was going to take me home. I reminded her. I was yet to get my exercise, with a knowing look. She says to Karl. *"You know, your friend is a trip? Trip shows no sign coming to an end."* I waved and walked away.Week later, Karl tells me they are going on a cruise. I ask if it will be Caribbean cruise. *"No, it's a tour of Italy on Ferrillo* *thing."* I wished them bon voyage, will see them when they return. For a month, their house was quiet. Now it's occupied. Renters, I assume. That means Phoebe and Karl is touring longer than planned. Or is there another explanation? However, it's no skin off my teeth and is quickly dismissed. Into third month, I went by to ask after them. Was told to ask next door neighbour. I did so and he said. Karl left a lawn spreader for me, but a wheel fell off. He's been trying to get one at a yard sale. Failing that, he'll buy a new one and drop it off at my house. Now remember, I am only four doors removed. Yet to see him or the spreader. A bigger question nags at my mind. They must have known. Comes time on horizon, they were getting out of Dodge. As folks are wont to say, sooner or later. So, when Karl was persistently asking I keep Andre. Was it their intention to leave me holding him indefinitely? They would not do that. Or would they? I know very little about them. Have heard even less since, from them. Then again, maybe I have and didn't recognize. See? You never know, who might your neighbours be. *"You want some tail? Fresh from the shower, so fresh it tingles. Nice aroma too."* I relive this minute every time Karl or Phoebe comes to mind. Expect the unexpected is sage advice, but Wow. ^Page 198-condensed milk can, generic sippy cup

Friend, Couple & Sweetheart-18

Elaine and Al had been close friends since '94. She was wife of, his then girlfriend's brother. Were their house guests for months, while getting loose ends tied. She effervesced with Al from day one, it could be said, they clicked. Counting cents, he went to barber school for haircut and came home with a scissor nick. That boy was overly gay, jiving to reggae and snip snipping to rhythm. She dressed and tended, as her husband and sister-in-law watched with broad smiles of approval. End of, she declared. ***"Better you did ask me to cut you hair. At least you wouldn't lose blood."*** And just like that, she became Al's groomer, as need arose. Girlfriend and Al visited often. Elaine would. ***"Look at you head. You try to grow dreadlocks?"*** In the garage they'd go, let the grooming begin. During which, they gabbed about people and places. Husband and Al were tighter than yarn in a shawl. Went places, did men things and shared secrets. Mainly about unknown female trysts and pleasures from. He once asked. ***"How you woulda feel fah win lotto and couldn't go claim it."*** Al told him. **"I have resignation psyche about me. If it's out of reach, for whatever reason. I accept situation, cleanse my mind and move on."** They kept chatting, he said. ***"Remember Peego over Lehigh? She have baby last month. Sweet little girl, me tell you. The blind can see is my pickney. Athline agrees, but automatically, her husband is the father. I want tell you, she right now fretting him might see me, and draft up the resemblance. Man, you don't know how it burns me. Because is long time me want have a girl, with my five bwoys. Me not comfortable with so much balls surround me. That's gang right there, and them will plot against the old bwoy. Me remember when me was bwoy. We used to plan and thief the car, when the old man drunk and drop asleep. Say something man, you just quiet with that smile. If was you, I would encourage you one way or other."*** **"My Granny Laura, always say.** *"What gone bad morning, can't come good evening."* **You had pleasure sowing the seed. Now, stand back, let next gardener take care and nurture it to pretty evergreen bloom. Remember now, neither you or Athie can say for sure. Let it go, and take comfort watching Susie grow."** ***"Susie, who hell is Susie?"*** **"Girl's name for Scotty."** He guffaws. ***"Your brain really*** *resign."* Months later he drops off his car at Triple A Auto. Asks Al, come take him home, until called. Sees him hugging very adorable young woman, who has a cute toddler with her. He stoops and hugs the child, kisses her forehead then makes introductions. Her hand is soft and delicate, perfume wafts and allures. Enjoying the moment, he anxiously says to Al as jealousy pricks. *"We haffi get outta Dodge quick. Husband gone over Home Depot. Don't want him come back and see me. Next thing him put one and one together."* As Al drives out, he asks. *"You see the little girl? Talk truth. You see me, you see she. Is lie me telling?"* Al asked. **"That's a girl? Thought was a bwoy. There's no plumage, she's bald as it is. To tell you the truth, I was more kinda taken with big girl...so."** He stares at Al, jaw dropped then says. *"That's true bout the dry head. She take after Athline. She have dry head too. Don't make the shoulder length fool you. Whole heap of horse braying for them hair. Or maybe, it's weave thing. Me see you though."* Both have a good laugh, are content with each others emotional out of reach.

Came time, girlfriend at brother's and sister-in-law's house. First step in Christmas baking ritual, marinating fruits. Husband at work, wife loading laundry whilst de-stemming and dicing fruits. Girlfriend is watching "Days of our lives." Al would rather be watching "Bonanza" rerun, so he's bored. Elaine comes in, all frustrated and out of sorts. Machine fills but will not start wash cycle, despite. Girlfriend tells Al. *"You are Jack of all trades. Go look and work your magic."* Elaine and Al goes in wash room. He's looking at this, pushing that, checking wall plug, looks at circuit breaker. Stands in deep thought, hand on cheek. Lifts lid, looks into machine. Closes lid and begins. **"I really don't...."** In that instant, machine makes a sound, goes silent. Al focuses on the lid. Open and close again with a bit of force. Machine makes another sound. He holds lid down with a hand. Voila, machine begins cycle. Elaine is agog with excitement. Al asks for Cellotape. Puts three slivers across plunger's nib and closes lid. Machine works without hand pressure. Girlfriend calls out from living room. *"Told you, Jack could work magic. What was problem?"* Told both women, plunger pushes tab to make contact and get machine working. Either contact is worn, or hinge is strained. Hence, tape closes gap and all's well. Girlfriend goes back to her show. Al stays with Elaine as she sorts. Second and third loads, coarse, delicate and fine. Asks about his youngest daughter. *"She still with you or she gone back to Virginia? Of all your daughters, I don't know why I like her so much. Although, I don't know any of your other daughters. Only going by how you talk about them with so much pride. You don't have any boys at all?"* "Yes, got one with ex-wife, and ex-girlfriend says her son is mine. But, she have to keep it hush hush. Because, she married at the time, and still is." *"How many girls in all you have?"* "Come on Lainie, we're friends. Don't ask embarrassing questions." *"Sorry, Sir. Never mean to step on your bunion."* Elaine says with a laugh, pauses, looks off into the distance. Goes on softly. *"You know, I always wanted to have a little girl. Comb her hair, dress her pretty, like my mom did. But it hasn't happened. I planned having three children, at most. Now we are up to five. Don't get me wrong, I love my boys. But little girl or two would be so much fun, and I miss out on that part of life."* "Well, you're only mid thirties. You have lots of time to jump in the ring and make another shot at the prize." Astoop, Al fell back on his rump, when she asked. *"You going be the father? You seem to have, all girl genes."* Led by inherent nature, his mouth opened, to gleefully retort.

"Yeah, man." But tongue froze. Al swallowed spittle and looked at her. Imagined their heads in perplexed anticipation, of pleasured roll in hay. Not going for debauchery. Bighead chastised. *"A friend's wife? Your woman's sister-in-law?"* Littlehead retorted. *"She brought the prize and dropped it in your lap, bwoy."* After minute's tense silence, he said. **"I'm gonna go.."** Pointing, not ending the sentence. Girlfriend praised Al's skills with washing machine fix. Went back to her show. I know, women are asking. What's wrong with this guy? Why is he even obsessing about this woman's gaffe? Al sat and rued on possible scenarios. Thought. *"Shoulda strike when iron was still hot. Having allowed things to cool. I can't go back and say. That baby thing you was talking bout. How, when, where, we going set it up?"* She would likely look at him and cry shame. ***"I was only running a joke with you, as a friend. How could you take it so seriously?"*** You know it could go like that, after she thinks it over and asks herself. *"Is what came into my head, make me say a thing like that? Hope him don't take me serious."* Now mistrust creeps in, preemption in tow. Al was determined to toes test waters, when opportunity presented itself. Worse that could happen, is her laughing him to ridicule for taking her serious. That would be their private joke. Seemed, she thought. Al would discuss with girlfriend. Who would of course, say to her brother. Wife decided to, flew wash room gaffe by husband for a reaction. Getting herself mired deeper in???. He was livid. They argued part night. He reposed in their guest room until daybreak. ***"What kind of joke is that to run with a man? My sister wouldn't run a joke like that with me. Puss come into kitchen watching you. Soon as you rub butter on him mouth. Him going lick it off and stare on butter dish. Way how society set up things. Man can't afford to sidestep something like that. Because, next thing you know. Word***

get out, him is chi chi man. Given choice, me prefer wearing Joegrine hat. Any day, instead homo jacket. All if temperature drop near freeze." She made spark that smoldered briefly, and would have died. Had she not fanned it, by casual disclosure to her husband. He had long suspected there was something afoot, prior to wife making offer. How else could she have come with that question from left field. Friendship chilled between husband and Al. Tension arose and last straw was. Girlfriend and Al went separate ways.

He and Elaine maintained distance friendship. Often gabbing by phone. In period when this saga began, to present 2018. Al got married and divorced. Circled girlfriend and said. **"You know, we could do this better, second time around."** Disco hit from 80's by Shalamar. Played extended version for her. She laughed at him, but they are close friends. Girlfriend and her sister-in-law maintain civility, without being friends. As often happens in marriages, year ago. Husband said it was over, kaput, done. Elaine leaned on Al in a kind of, father figure for moral support. And male guidance on things beyond her knowledge. Not raised to be worldly and in step to recognize. She often puts situations arising for comment. Which, if Al suspected had to do with family circle. He most times plead ignorance. She tends to follow specific routes to and from. If route becomes impassable, temporary or otherwise. She will go round in circles until totally lost. One incurable idiosyncrasy, is uncanny fixation with peripheral signage. Indicating parallel or highway connection, instead of that she's on. Gets laned into "can't undo" exits when she shouldn't, and gets lost. Having relocated to Tampa, she would once in a blue moon come to town. During which, she found roads realigned. Ramps, where none existed before.

Hopelessly lost, she calls Al. He guides her to a ramp, from which she can only go where she wants to. She calls again, it's dusk and she's… He'd find and escort her home. She did not expect being lonely in separation, and yearns for close male companionship. Now they spend time together, enjoying each other's company. She once ventured, saying to Al. *"After my divorce, me not getting involved with a man my age. Or, God forbid, younger than. No way. Him have to be an older man, like you."* Fifteen years her senior, Al thought she was kite flying. Stored it with guarded expectation. Recalled washroom episode, years ago. Gave this comment time to brew and simmer. Weeks later he cautiously asked, if she thought they could be more than good friends. Had to tippy toe on this, not wanting to be laughed at. You know, fear of rejection and that. She replied emphatically. *"Of course. Why not?"* He told her, it could be seen, by some in in-law circle. They had been carrying on, whilst she was supposedly happily married. For certain that thought would cross, soon-to-be ex-husband's mind. If it had not already been fixed with him. She discounted this as being of no concern to her. *"That's fah him business if him want think that way."* Al was uneasy, not as dismissive. She went visiting mom in Nevis. Called long distance frequently to ask if he was okay, and did he miss her. Told her he did and wished she was here. Phone was passed to her mom. Came on line, lambasting son-in-law. She knew he was no good from day one. Daughter should never have taken up with him. When good man as Al, was there for taking. He did not point out, her daughter had been married over forty years. So, he was not ever there for her taking, until now. But let her rant and give vent. Al figured however, mom's assertions. Could only arise, as daughter discussed possibilities and expectations. Confirming this was serious endeavour and worthy of pursuit. He felt energized. Elaine came back, bringing all good gifts. They began close mingling, hugging, smooching and all that. No hesitancy now, Al was on right track. Divorced since 2015, Al told Elaine, his last intimate excursion was just under a year ago. She said, hers was going eleven years. He smiled and said. **"Woman, you maduro."** She got testy and asked. *"I am what?"* He told her, that's word hung on street vendor's avocado display. English meaning is "ripe" *"So, if I'm ripe, what that means?"* **"You are ready to be picked and enjoyed."** Al replied with a laugh. She let it pass without further comment. Funny thing here folks. Maduro is also name of current or de-facto Venezuelan president. In our changing world, might not be, when this comes off press. She wanted time off her job, for them to spend a weekend. So they did, frolicking and gabbing. Al took steps to bases without resistance. Dormant emotions suddenly rekindled. Next, she made plans taking off two weeks, month after next. One, taking part in her brother's wedding. Other, she would spend with Al at his pad. ***"Think of it, one whole week of us together."*** She beamed, as he cruised the Alley, taking her home a Sunday. She planned pleasant things they could do. Al was alive, couldn't wait to be kickin.' Tuesday she called, saying the week's rendezvous was too far away. ***"Let's do this again soon, whilst magic lingers."*** She wanted to spend that weekend, if she could get someone to work for her. Called Wednesday, it's a go. She found a substitute. Wanted Al to cook beef kidneys and boiled bananas, again. As done on previous weekend. Everyone who has ever prepared and cooked kidneys, knows it's labour of love. First it's chilled to rigidity, ligaments, chambers, arteries all have to be trimmed. If a piece is missed, it is not chewable and spoils the dish. Al went for and brought her home, cooked, and they enjoyed the fare. Enhanced with crisp, diced, par-cooked sweet onions. And bowl of Makoto, honey, ginger salad. Sated, they teased and led into a romp. She let on, not wearing underwear, sometimes. Suggested, present might be a such time. *"It's for me to know and for you to find out."* She teased. Taking cue, he sprang and. **"Let me see."** Toyed with milk jugs, confessed not being weaned from infancy. Gravitated to breasts every chance he got. Dusk came early at 17:00 hours, it was now going on 21:00 hours. Al, ever "saying it with music." Told her he was going to play a song on his cellphone. After which he would turn it off and she should do same. She asked why. He told her, just listen and follow cues of song. YouTube got Rod Stewart's "Tonight's the night"

You know the song. On first note, he guided her to master suite. She said she's tired, has to take five in guest room. All fired up and raring to go, he yielded and told her. When she's rested, come make Dick Whittington make her happy.*"Who is, Mr. Whittington?"* She asked. **"Oh, a Charles Dickens character from same named novel."** *"Dick Whittington?"* She echoed, not making connection. But not everyone perused English literature, way Al did and still does. Every now and then he rereads, D.H. Lawrence's once banned novel. "Lady Chatterly's Lover" It made Jeopardy's quiz appearance recently. Al napped, woke in anticipation. Looked down the passageway, saw room door firmly closed. Not a ray of light visible, dark prevailed. Seethed and stayed awake till morning. Told her, now was good time as any to get it on. She looked at him in surprise. *"You was serious about what you said last night?"* **"Of course. Wasn't that your reason, craving this weekend. Instead of waiting two months, coming back from your trip?"** He asked her. *"Oh no, you got that wrong. You move too quick. I don't jump into bed so fast. If you think I am lying, ask my husband. Know how* *long him sweat, before him could get anything?"* She replied, taken aback in disbelief. So, they had a big tete-a-tete, during which Al called her a "Dick teaser" Well, that's the way that one went. Both are now enemies, after twenty-six years. Well, not enemies, in true sense of the word. Her mother passed. Al expressed sympathy and condolences. Told her, mom died from disappointment, not having him in the circle. She says, he's funny. Women who usually chastise Al being a player, agrees. He did nothing wrong in this instance. So, having read the story. You should get inside view of "People at Play" Shenanigans they sometimes get up to.

Years ago, I was friend of a couple. They shacked up twelve years, during which they had three children. PTA friends, dubbed her Mrs. So she quietly got married, and in two years they became separated in same house. They would not file for divorce, as neither wanted the home sold. Or could buy out the other. It was an eye opener. Visiting and observing those two, existing in malice. To the point it was no longer funny. Each insisted having equal access to areas of the dwelling. Wife tuned her television to sole broadcasting station. He mounted a dish and received foreign transmissions. Both sets going, simultaneously. I suggested, both could take turns viewing in their bedroom. Cooking arrangements were ridiculous, but wait. When refrigerator broke, man bought one and kept it in his bedroom. I wished the gas stove would go next, wanting to see how that would go. It's happening again and both are close to their biblical limit. Ah well...

First floor or ground-19

Condo owners were notified of special board meeting. Main agenda item, special assessment for new elevators. Chairman decided to update owners on another matter, before going into slated business. Board had approved design for new signage, both sides of vehicles entrance. As everyone was aware, artistic hand lettering.**"Park View Condominiums"** Which graced both sides entryway, for past twenty years. Had been vandalized by spray paint and now reads "Park View Condoms" New signage would be, oblong framework with wrought iron lettering, vines and leaves. Replica was passed around among those present. Everyone cheered, relieved vexing eyesore was being given long overdue attention. Some were certain, vandalism had resulted in calamitous erosion of their property's value. It could hardly be coincidental. But seemed, neighbourhood was beset by someone with deviant mindset. Half mile North. A power transmission tank had decal that read. "Cant Hole" Decal was defaced with. Let's say, whiskers. "A" in "Cant" exchanged for another vowel. Word made, not a coin. Could have commonality with condoms. How creative of some bright artist. Maybe, I should explain and clear air. Large, fifty feet and higher poles, with transmission power lines installed. Are called tanks, in the industry. Usually made of concrete fibre, they are not poles. Built with a straight thru hole. After tank is stood in place, a bar is inserted through the hole. To manually cant or rotate the tank. Until desired, face street alignment, and line tandem position is attained. So much for connection, between condom and cant or variation of. Here's something else, not many people know. What's called reel or spool, on which wires or cable comes coiled, is really a drum. Names don't always describe items. Go figure. Cost of elevator project and each unit's share having been outlined. Chair, Charley Dunn, asked if there were questions or comments. Mrs. Rutherford said, amount was burden on monthly resources. Venturing to add, she spoke for most, if not all owners. Chair said, another option was to seek a loan. However, that would inflate cost of project. Board was open to suggestions. Would adopt what was voted by majority. Sergio stood, addressed the meeting in usual halting intemperate English. *"This chit not no fair."* Before he got further, Chair pounded gavel. **"There's no using common, vulgar innuendo. We can discuss among ourselves, without brothel language."** Sergio resumed. *"What's a matter this guy? He see me, brothel? If he see me at the brothel, he was come out and I go in. No? Anyhow, I say this is no fair. You and you, and you, you too."* He paused, searching faces around the room, then went on. *"Some not here with me, but we never use alavator. No need alavator. We live right here."* He stomped floor for effect. *"We get out the car, walk in, and go our house. We not go up, we not go down. So why we pay for alavator? Let who go up and down pay, but not me. And all who live here like me. Agreed? Make very much sense?"* There was minute's silence. Mrs. Bentley said. *"Mr. Valentino has a point. We live on ground floor, we don't use…."* She was interrupted by Mr. Steer. *"You, live first floor, madam. There is no ground floor. There's basement, first floor and second, third, fourth, fifth."* Mrs. Bentley angrily averred. *"When I walk from street to front door. I enter at ground level, and go to my apartment, without using elevator."* Turning attention to, she called out. *"Sergio, you are very much right. Let's fight this, tooth and nail. I wasn't going to say more than in passing. But, I hate being told. I don't know difference of ground floor and first floor, as if I stupid."* Chair said, elevator served all floors from basement up, it not matter what it's called. Mrs. Evans asked permission to "talk sense" into debate. She was duly recognized by Chair. ***"Basement is all management, nothing down there.. Not one of us has access there. It's meter rooms, machines, many golf carts, maintenance and storage. Now let us say, perchance elevator broke down, or there was a power failure. Us on first or ground floor, whatever you want to call it. Would never know difference. Because we would come and go, just as we normally do. So, yes is true. We really do not need elevator. It's not to our convenience and we should not be putting money towards this. I say we should take the matter to court."*** Mr. Dennison replied. ***"Court not going hear the matter. Judge lazy. Will force parties to mediate and we already know how that end. Big mop on end a stick going down your throat."*** Chair said, matter must be voted on. As always, majority would prevail. Then he did a con job, by explaining to all. Voting to exclude first floor owners. Would inevitably result in much higher cost to other owners. He would caution, whilst being fair to your neighbour. Careful being unfair to yourself. Sergio became unhinged, jumped up with clenched fist held high. Other pointing at Chair as he yelled. ***"That mother f...er just sat there and sold us out with crazy chit talk about..."*** Needless to say, pandemonium broke out. Chair tried vainly restoring order, whilst censuring Sergio. Having failed, Chair called security, to expel Sergio from the meeting. He reacted, grabbing the chair on which he sat. Raced blindly towards Chair, threatening and yelling. ***"Throw me out, you piece o chit?. Watch they carry you out."*** Despite his rabid display of ire. Sergio allowed himself to be restrained by old women. Most others, having vacated the room. Next meeting was attended by attorney who told residents. It made no difference what floor they resided on. If they used or didn't use elevator. Equipment was part of and relative to entire building. Like it or not, everyone paid. Only thing to be voted. Should there be a loan with incremental repayments, or one time. Sergio refused demands for an apology. Told Chair instead. *"What for I say sorry? Only words, I not mean. And you? Not change for you nothing. You still what I say you be. So, no make sense pology. What you do? I stay here and stay until I go."* Against attorney's advice, Board yielded. Allowing residents to pay assessment in three tranches. First tranche for agreed deposit, second midway and final at inspection and certification.

End of the meeting, Sergio made verbal assault on Chair, telling him. *"Fix they do to sign and read giant condom, that be you. I think you change first. That how your son get more contract to fix. That's a what I think, but that's a not what I know. So you can go crrrazy if you like. Scream loud for pology. I not care. I love think, what I think."* Chair said, Sergio's comments were recorded in the minutes. He should expect, facing punitive retaliation for baseless accusations. I think Sergio nullified that, by making the point. His utterances were not factual, but merely his thoughts. Don't you think? It's secret knowledge. Some condo and HOA boards, awards service contracts to family members, friends and allies. For doing work at inflated costs, putting owners at financial disadvantage. Acid on sore is law which gives boards, right to levy on property for disputed or unpaid dues. We live amongst evil, greedy persons. Focused padding their nests, conscience doesn't stand a chance reigning them in.

What's in the Red Pouch:-20

Cindy promised Clarence, she would take him shopping at BJ's Wholesale Club, her next visit. His response lacked enthusiasm, so she asked if he already bought what he needed. He told her, no he hadn't and yes. Holler at him when next she's going. Truth between us, he was having second thoughts. Regarding benefits, shopping on her card. She always picked items and refuse to separate them at register. First time it was $22, next time it was $18. He feared, what it could be next trip. She pressed him for reason, his apparent reluctance, and he lied. His credit card is close to being maxed. Bulk buying saves, but he spends more at one go. Then it hurts, paying 14-21% interest on groceries in pantry. Sooner or later, he forgets. When he does recall, best by date has passed. She said she understood part of what he was saying, but not part about "best by" dates. She saw him fixing three years old "Festival" mix. Cringed when she watched him chomping and enjoying, after saying *"No thanks, I had lunch."* to that given her. Antibiotic cream he applies, has pharmacy tag of 2015. Five years ago. But, it's up to him. If he didn't want to go then, he could tell her when, and she would oblige. He rebutted her comments, she reiterated. ***"Clarence, juice was two weeks stale, and instead of pouring it down the sink. You sniffed and sipped, until it was all done. People like you, are reason for bathroom extractor fans."*** She laughed up a storm. He didn't see the joke. Clearly tiffed, he hurried out on his way home. Then called her saying, she should call him when ready to do next foray. It was an I scratch your back, you scratch mine scenario. Cindy did not drive. She benefited from use of his car, as he did from her card. Monday, she called. ***"Is Thursday a good day?"*** She asked. He said, yes. **"Okay"** She told him. Come around ten, they'll do shopping and if he has nothing else worth doing. They can hang out at her place. Play Wordle till she's ready for work. He walks in the door. She did not expect him so early. He points out, it is now 10:20 hours. There's a show on TV she wants to watch. Second glances admiringly, at his red, hand sack and says. *"Is that your fanny pouch?"* **"No, this ain't no fanny pouch. Don't you see, it's in my hand? This is my opportunity kit."** He replies. She looks at him kinda off kilter and asks. *"Opportunity kit? What the hell kind of kit is that? I never heard of an…What you really have in there, to make it an opportunity kit?"* He laughs and says.**"You know? In case of fire, break glass, situation? Think along those lines. Your story! You missing the action."** He says with urgency while pointing at TV. Trying to diminish interest in his sack. *"I can watch it later, with Sidoney."* She tells him, eyes still focused on the pouch. *"Hold it, let me see what's. "Fursillo Lada."* She reads, then asks.*"Where you got it?"* He says. **"In the mail. Company sells water sports equipment."** If you're a man you know, once some women latches on to something. She never stops until she gets bottom of, and frankly. This was a matter of no importance. It wasn't usual. *"Where you been? Who is girl keeps calling here and hang up when I answer?"* They weren't, boyfriend girlfriend. Which made it hard for him to understand her pique. Read on, see how this develops. She stares him down and walks away, he sighs relief. She calls from somewhere in the nether areas. *"You want a slice of pizza?"* He hollers back. **"I am good, thanks. Had breakfast."** He laughs in memory. She comes out, brush and foam in mouth. *"Oou un dt pch."* She tries to talk, quickly holds a palm under her mouth. Catches dripping foam before it hits floor. Hurries back to nether. Having offloaded, she comes back and asks quite coherently.*"What* *could you possibly have in that red pouch, that makes for an opportunity? I am really and truly puzzled."* They argued back and forth. **"Oh, you know, knicks knacks."** *"What the hell is knicks knacks?"* **"You remember, knick knack padawack gave a dog a bone. This old man came rolling home?"** *"You're too old to be reciting nursery rhymes. What's in the kit? That's what I want know."* Like a Shure, caught in groove. She's not getting past this. He decides to talk off cuff. You know for certain, it's going to be tactless and possibly abrasive, but with a grin. He often gets into that, don't give a dam frame of mind. Throws his head back, roars a hearty laugh, then says. **"It's my opportunity kit, in case something drops in my lap. I need taking quick advantage, before it rolls to floor."** *"Oh yeah? You better be careful, in dropping, it don't crush anything you might need later on."* Great comeback, give her that round. See how island people full of comedy? **"That's never ever going to happen. I play only middle weight division. Stay far from Gorilla class. Whapp'n, you fegat what kill puss? Not going bathe and go where we going?"** He asks. *"I want you tell me what you have in that pouch."* He unzips and begins itemizing.

"Toothbrush, wet wipes, Biscotti, medication, mouthwash, lens towel, condoms and Vagisil." *"So, you is man. What you doing with Vagisil? Condoms, I understand. Isn't that an itch relief salve?"* **"No, this is moisturizing gel, says it right there."** Pointing the tube, and goes on. **"Like butter for toast. Makes for comfortable and smooth swallow. Dry toast chaps lips, scours gums and tongue. Lordy, lordy, lordy, take it from me. I've had my share of eating rock hard stale bread. Surpassing quality of well done toast. It's sheer abrasion to mouth and tissues. As woman, you should know. After a certain age. Before she can get involved. It might be necessary to prime the keyhole. So**

key moves free, without squeaking or grating. Skin to skin is no different from metal to metal. If there's one virtue I have. It is being considerate of others, especially my fairer sex. I'll take a bet, if you stopped ten men. Who have fanny pouches, or kit like mine. You wouldn't find a pack of Vagisil or better, quick lube preparation." She's been stony silent all this while, just staring at him. Finally, she begins. ***"Let me get this straight, see if I understand you correctly. You leave your house, coming to my house. Expecting me to drop into you lap. So you can lube me up and….But see here Negro, you not easy. Me look like bird with broken wing. Looking for limb to perch on. Or lap to fall into?"*** Silence is on again. Her face is all twisted, like a candy wrapper. He says. **"Let's do the BJ's another time, if you ever feel like doing it. But right now"**….He leaves rest unsaid and is already half way through the door.

Waves a goodbye hand, closes it softly. It's been seven months since and she hasn't called. He's not really experiencing any regrets. Cost saving convenience sought was not being realized so far. Being inquisitive sometimes brings unpleasant outcomes. That red pouch goes where Clarence goes, always in his blue bag. He exits the vehicle and takes it along. One never knows when a need might arise to clean glasses. Chomp on a Biscotti, or ? Life is darned funny. Some people makes it worth living. Women are so ultra inquisitive, they always have to know. Curiosity infects them and they paw themselves in misery like a flea infested dog. Most times, they not going to be happy with the revelation, but they just gots to know. Here's a well kept secret. Some men are worse. Shhh.

Bathroom celibacy?-21

Claudette came home from her night nurse's job, totally weary and out of Self. Stepping from the shower, she called Clarence. To ask, he stop by her house, next time he was in Kendall. She had a light meal and climbed into bed, when her doorbell rang. It was Clarence, with a big grin standing at her doorstep. Squeezed past her in fireman's rush, saying. **"Hold on little bit, gotta take a leak, so as not to make a flood."** By which time he was already in the bathroom and continued. **"I'm on this Doxycline thing and have to keep flushing my kidneys. But, you know? What goes in, must come out."** She sauntered down corridor. Said, hinting discord. *"There's reason, bathrooms have doors."* He said. **"Mi done."** Attempted to exit between limited space, created by her standing in his path. *"What happen! You not washing you hands?"* With a quizzed stare, he told her. **"Me never leak or drip on me hand. It was a synced event, like stage presentation. Mi just lean forward and let it rip."** *"Well, I didn't care for symphony assaulting my ears. Why do men refuse to sit and pee? Nobody needs to know what you're doing in there, please wash your hands. There's hand soap, scented, unscented. And there, hand towels."* He sat, briskly rubbed palms for a minute. During which, she stared at him in silence. Ending his palm massage, he slapped them loud and said. **"Yeah, that was that. Where were we?"** *"You don't use paper towels?"* She asked. **"Nuh really."** He said resignedly, then added. As if a bulb went off inside his head. **"Doing my part to save rainforest, but seriously. You see, like when you bathe. If you allow you skin to air dry. You be surprised, how supple and tenderly soft to the caress it would be. You could enhance pleasure. Having a slow, feather touch massage by hands like these."** Holding both palms out, he stared at them, and softly said. **"These hands have been trained to exude pleasure. Unlike those of prettiest boxing Champ, which brought pain and punishment."** She began. *"You know! My late Nana, God rest her soul. Every student that passed through her guidance. Remembers her for using one word, to describe unsavoury behaviour. "Niggardly" It's a word that would be frowned upon today, as marginalizing black people. But, I honestly think. Sound of urine stream, echoing off water in toilet bowl. Is niggardly. You shouldn't find amusement in that kind of base behaviour."* He thought on this for brief seconds, then laughed. **"When I was a bwoy, and draw out my Nana's pisspot, night time. I would hold it up and get the stream going. Then move it up and down, enjoying rhythm of pee against enamelled steel. And changes as more liquid collected. Then came finale, with prrrrp, tip tip tip tip. Prip, prip. And quite often, I tightened lower belly muscles to squeeze the bladder, for a "chrrrp" And then, final "tip" After that, I went back to bed and fell soundly asleep. Lulled by interlude of pisspot harmony. I will tell you something, a lot of people have not discovered. Hold a soda bottle under a tap, and listen to sound of water rising to a crescendo, as it displaces air and fills up. Let me tell you something, very seriously now. Wherever there's water, there's rhythm. Gurgling stream, babbling brook, pounding surf, pitta patta raindrops, cascading waterfalls and pisspot harmony. Now, if we could get those sounds on a board and synchronize them. What a melody that would be. Back in the 60s, Cascades sang about "Rhythm of the rain." Sure it's on YouTube."** She sighed, softly said. *"You know you need help? Quicker the better. I saw Elaine, your favourite actress. Once asking*

George. *"Shouldn't you be out on a ledge somewhere?"* **At risk of being mean, I think you should really be out on a ledge somewhere. That's why I'm telling you, get help, save yourself. I was not going to ask, but am curious to hear. Why was your pants, all way down to your knees? There's no "fly" as with normal pants. Or that too, is a project? With you, everything is. So please, kind sir. Promise, I won't breathe a word to a soul."** He guffawed and said. **"Who!? You!? A woman?! Me know you talk bout me to you girl group, incognito. Usually, start off with. "Listen, I know this guy." And then comes the girly shrieks and giggles at the end. But, is awright. As long as you not point me out. But, I want tell you now. Me think, if me ever come here and any of you friend them here. Soon as me leave, you gwine tell them. "That's the guy I telling you bout. But, no problem."** She slowly replied. *"Clarence, if you came here when a girlfriend was visiting. Once you started talking, I wouldn't have to identify you. They would be asking. "Who's that guy?" Your idiosyncrasy is your meme."*

He looked at her, asked. **"Meme!? Whadat?"** She told him. *"It's one of those words or phrases. Created by internet and social media users. Meaning, a person's style, behaviour or image that represents just that person. Like, if you sat down to eat a chocolate bar, using knife and fork. It would be circulated on social media and there, your meme. I think. Not quite up on, it's more a teen, twenty-ish thing. Come on, the pants down thing."* She urged, and he began after a good laugh. **"Going tell you something bout me me from school days. Teacher would give literature homework, and do oral exam next morning. We the dunces, use to clap we fingers and say. Me teacher, me, me. That way, teacher would bypass we and ask student who not so enthusiastic. Rawtid, teacher soon learn the trick and point on a finger** slapping dunce. Him tell her some fart, she give him two whacks over him back with her cane." *"Are you talking about finger snapping, like when you're keeping tempo with a song?"* "No, this was different kind of…let me show you. What you talking bout, you put thumb against ring finger and go like this. What me talking bout is. You put thumb and ring finger together. Then you slap both with index finger, like so. Hear difference between this, woman in birth labour. and this? Happy it's over. One is slappin', other is snappin.'" After a long stare, she asked. *"Which school you went to?"* He told her. "You have to ask me, which school I didn't go. My name in plenty register." She tells him. *"I'm getting picture of, you sound like one of those impish, mischievous neighbourhood kids, parents didn't want their kids hanging out with. I think you would be seen as roguish fellow. Just listening to your….anyhow. Don't distract, the pants down project."* He laughs, goes conspiratorial, begins."Now, you're not built for this. So, you might find it hard to wrap your head around. A guy shouldn't just unzip and drag out the serpent. Leaving peripheral gear suspended. Over time, this results in serious limping. Not limping, in sense of sprained ankle or…I mean limping, as like a sag. Succumbing to gravity. A good example, are breasts. Did you know! Before invention of brassieres. Tits used to reach women's waists? That's why they used to band them flat against the chest, from day one. To get a smooth, streamlined, head to toe profile. It's same thing with men. Without support, entire package soon sags to the knees. Indeed, there are a few, back in ye olde country like that. Folks call it a "boson." So, you unzip and get the trouser out the way. Reach in and gently take entire blessing, cradled in both palms.

Whilst providing bong support with one hand, other grasps Boa and aims. That's why men can give urine samples, without tinkling on hands. Women?..... I been meaning to ask a woman this. So, tell me. How do you tame "Niagara" into that cup?" She stood, took two steps, then turned to him. *"Do you really believe the things you say. Or you're just making funny, hoping someone laughs?"* "No Cleedy. What you talking bout? This thing goes back to and is based on Early Childhood Education. In some families, there's sometimes father, but always a mother. Mom teaches little girls, from half day, not waiting for one to dawn. How to take care of genitals. Like wiping and not taint fountain with cesspool remnants. Dads who know advantage of circumcision, gets this done to his son in that same day half period. Here's where boys and men are at a disadvantage. Every girl and woman is fully up on the wiping protocol. Far less boys and men are circumcised. And only a dismal few, know about the anti-sagging process I described." *"So, your dad taught you all that crap about to sag or not sag?"* "Well, not really. It was necessity making an invention. Don't eye me that way. You're not equipped to be dubious on this, so pay attention. About age seventeen I noticed, even was outpacing odd. Catching up as it were. You know, as kids we sang. 'Hey ho the derry ho, the Chief stands alone.' You never played 'The farmer in the Dell?' Anyhow, I decided, this could not be allowed to event. Next thing I'd have to be sitting on doughnut cushions as I got older. That's when I applied inventive genius and the rest, as they say, is history." She stares at him, wordlessly. He does two quick head to shoulder dips. She says. *"I'm feeling peckish. Come see if there's anything in the fridge that grabs your fancy."* Both, stand in front of the fridge. She begins. *"There's half a pizza, some mack and cheese. And there's bbq wings."* He opts for wings, she takes a pizza slice. Warmed in the microwave, both sit and begins chomping. She continues the dialogue.*"Where were you when I called? I just got home, showered and was climbing into bed when you rang the doorbell."* Quite glibly, he said. **"Impeccable timing, like Jimmy Jones. Let's go back to bed. I can soothe you into a deep invigorating sleep, and refreshed awakening later."** *"Don't you get tired being silly funny?"* She asked, steering him to the settee. *"You still haven't answered me as to where you…."* "I was lazing at home." *"You mean "home" as in Homestead?"* He confirmed and went on. **"On a Sunday, no Speedway event. Turnpike to 88 is a breeze. Would you believe? Homestead on ramp to Kendall Drive exit. Is less congested, than driving from the exit to here? Other thing I've noticed. When we got here mid nineties, it was North Kendall Drive. "North" disappeared from signage, leaving Kendall Drive. Big mystery remains. Where is, South Kendall Drive?"** She gave him that look, as if he's not right in the head. Matter of fact, numerous are times she has told him just that. He went on. **"You know it's your natural, but coming out or going into the shower. You always look like a fresh vegetable. Never mind you not Tony Rebel. Him still singing?"** She ignores his comment and begins. *"It's my bathroom again. The shower is back to slow draining. I hate standing in pool of waste."* He responds. **"You know, it's that shedding you're doing. Women your age, who not sexually active in long times. Get tostes tesorone imbalance. Testonstorone. I never can get that word right. Lemme see, I can do this. No prompting from audience, please."** Both are quiet, her with an amused smile. He's trying to Google something. Now showing her the phone dial and says. **"See? Testosterone. I was right. It's not widely known, but when women avoids sexual intercourse. Your thing there level, rises. This is fertilizer for hair follicles. They sprout like prairie wheat on Savannah. If you allowed yourself to be coaxed, having fair share orgasms in harmonious blend of sex. That would syphon reservoir and we both could be hap……"** She did a visual interrupt, by fingertip to her mouth corner. **"Wha?"** He asked. Slightly annoyed at not getting to his point. She again swiped lightly at her mouth. Seeing he was not reading her. She told him. *"Wipe off your mouth dear."* He did, checked hand for chicken remnant. Looked askance at her, by eyes language. *"No, not quite. Hold still, let me help you."* Took a Kleenex towel, dabbed both mouth corners, then said. *"There, it's all clean now."* He asked. **"What was it? I don't see anything on the towel."** *"Oh, I don't know dear. It was whatever you were talking. But gee, it looked very disgusting. Anyhow, not to validate your spurious argument. Testosterone is male hormone. In women, it is estrogen. Do go on. Your theory, though self serving. Gives a look inside that beautiful, mature mind of yours. Who would dare believe?"* Undeterred, Clarence went on.

"As I was saying. There's cause and effect at work. Let's start by treating cause, with a vigorous bout of happy sexual reunion. It's been a while, for both of us." *"You're right about that, twenty-five years and counting."* Claudette agrees. He thinks on that then tells her. **"Can't be that long. We were together up to 199?"** He pauses, stares then concedes. **"You know you're right. Who knows, if we had stayed together. We could be proud grandparents in our own rights."** She retorts. *"For one, I was not going to get pregnant. Out of wedlock, for a married man. And for two, it would be risky. Getting pregnant at my age, back then.*

I've seen on television news and society pages. Women, fifty and over giving birth. But we know, those are not ordinary pregnancies and births. I assure you. Can you imagine me, at mid sixties. With rebellious teenager on my hand? Girl or boy, single parent or both. That's more than challenging, in this country. Where parents cannot inflict discipline, as we do back home." Strung on intercourse and happy ever after, Clarence coaxed. **"I'll do a bit of snipping. Mow grass, so it fits perfectly with hedge."** She stares at him with that half smile. He presses on. **"Come on. Why the big deal? It's not as if I haven't been there. Right now, I could close eyes and my fingers would take us to paradise."** She broke her amused silence and said. *"I've been celibate over twenty-five years. You think I am going to break that. For twenty-five minutes, of you pleasuring yourself? That's if you can go that long. Next thing, you pass out or die. Heaven forbid, and I get arrested. For accessory to a crime, before and after the fact. Lord, are you listening to this crazy man?"* Now she really belts out a hearty laugh. Pauses, stares at him and laughs some more. He begins. **"What you talking bout being celibate, you have three adult children. Who have given you grandchildren?"** She wags a finger, scolding. *"Clarence, I never said I was a virgin. I said celibate. Consult your usual sources, see the difference. Then admit you are wrong. In all seriousness though. I will tell you this, because as you say. We are adults. You have been in my corner and I in yours. There are times, I do get urges. But am stymied by my next Obgyn visit. He would know I have been sexually active. And fact is, for a woman my age, that is embarrassing. No woman, especially at my age. Wants her doctor to find evidence of romping, in playpen. Worse yet, if there's snack crumbs and foreign matters left lying* *around. Why you think I haven't changed my health care providers? For fear I will also have to change my doctors, and lord knows the thought frightens me."* He tells her. **"Listen to me, life is uncertain. Let's live for the now, tomorrow is promised to no One. I'm glad to hear you get urges. Now let's sate ourselves and be happy as drunk sots. By time your next visit comes around. Your Obgyn could have died and you will have to find a new One anyway. Or, suffer it not to be so. Either or both of us could have died too. So there, let's repair to your edenic boudoir. Where we'll indulge our heart's desires. Till spirits take wings, soaring like eagles. Giving us contentment that defies words. Making today, enriched, first day of rest of our lives. You don't have to be Joyce Pennant, although I wouldn't relish you being Linda O'Gilvie either. But there's got to be women with middle of the road tolerance. Which embraces and acquiesces man's emotional uplift. That's an integral part of existence."** *"What is?"* She asks, mockingly. **"Assuaging the uplift."** He replies, then goes on.

"Although, there have been occasions where this was done grudgingly. Malice, covertly spread words that dripped sensuous encouragement. Beguiling and bewitching, to near demise. There are women, who having turned fifty or thereabouts. Adopts celibate existence, moreso when there's no partner in her life. One perfect example, Joyce Pennant. Then, there are others, like Linda O'Gilvie. A woman who's now in mid sixties. Constantly harangues husband, Roderick. Whom, although early fifties, is not fulfilling her sexual expectations. Seeking moral support, from brother-in-law Solomon. She told him. *"Listen Sal. I will take your brother and hang him up on a big nail or tree limb. If him can't give me what I want, as much and as often as I want."* **Coached by his younger brother,**

244

Roderick tried new tack on Linda. She sat on his face and stifled him within a nick of his life. Poor fellow is still on life support. But prognosis is positive plus. See what I'm saying, how love so right, turned out to be so wrong? What do you say, seriously? Hows about you just toss inhibitions and we get insanely jiggedy? Bust a sweat for your beauty nap, as it were." She rose and headed to the…Clarence could not believe his luck. How he luxuriated in renewed anticipation. His loins stirred as soon as the joy hit his brain cells. Claudette stopped by kitchen and opened the refrigerator. Took out and handed him a pip sized bottle of water. *"Here, soothe blisters on your tongue and lips. You've done more talking than a county fair auctioneer."* As she said this she right about turned, going way she had just come. Opposite direction away from where he thought, hoped she was headed.. He stared at her, eyes pleading. His face a quizzed frown, still hoping. She smiled and told him. *"Don't look so non-plussed, go on. Let me bolt the door. I'm going back to sleep, if I can. Just might lie there laughing at all the crap I've heard from you. I know you don't believe half the things you say. Know something? You should write a book and get it published. Who knows, you could probably have best seller and not know it."*

Now that she mentioned it, he just might do that. You think he should think about it seriously? Think it would be a best seller? That would surprise her. Would it not? If only we could tell before we jumped in. Just when women are seeing Clarence as a crotch crazed coot. He upped and decided to create a surprise. Went shopping at Lowe's for lye solutions. Bought a plunger too, and went back to Claudette's house. Her shower now drains faster than a whirlpool. See? Clarence is not crotch crazy. He is driven by conviction, he can get things done by rationalizing to other person. Ever seen sport Angler having multiple baited rods in fish hole at same time? One has got to get caught on his barb. As he told a pal once, who asserted he had balls. It's not balls that does it, it's heart. Peggy Lee said it. *"You can be a hero, when your luck is battin' zero. You can open any door. There's nothing to it but to do it. You just gotta have heart. Miles and miles of heart."*

Happy Family & Twins-22

Melissa and Vanessa Myers, never got along in infancy through adolescence, and now as adults. It all started when mom, Audrey. Joked to relatives and close friends, that at birth. Melissa kicked Vanessa out womb's warmth, minute's after contractions began. Then hung around enjoying comfort of, for nearly two hours. Before doctors successfully coaxed her out, and into this world. So vexed the infant was. She uttered not a sound, until prodded with spick to the rump. Mom told that story so often, to so many people, in so many places. She was once reminded by Father, and took righteous umbrage, when he said. **"Yes, Mrs. Myers. You told me before, and before that before, and...."** She abruptly walked away, whilst giving a bit of advice. ***"Look out for Mrs. Pinnock's mongrel. That animal needs to be put down, so citizens can walk in peace."*** Adding insult to injury, from day one. Radcliffe Myers nicknamed Melissa. "Runt" Lifting her high, playfully saying. **"Come here Runty. Mama hiding titties from you? Oooh, Runty also stinky. Audrey! Runty crying for another load. Just drop one from this morning."** Final blow to Melissa's persona, was Vanessa's repeat reminder. She was older of the two, and demanding big sister privileges. As infants in same playpen, Vanessa used toys and pummeled her sister, often yanked her hair. Of which she had none, being born almost bald. It's as if, she knew what she was doing. But everyone argued, an impossibility at that age. Didn't change as both grew older. Melissa gleefully migrated to grandparents' home, where Grampus showered her with TLC. No one knew, she had unease with her pet name, until eight years old. She asked Grampus. Why he didn't call her by pet name, as her dad did. He asked, if she knew what "Runt" meant. She said, no, she didn't, then asked him. What did it. He took time, before telling her, it meant, little and cute. Like the small, brown, floppy eared puppy, among bigger ones. She countered, the puppy was not cute. It was skinnier than rest of the lot. Didn't run and play happy, as others. Then she asked him. If she was cute, why did mom, often tell her father. *"Do not call my child a Runt or I will make you One."* Grampus laughed so hard, whilst hugging Melissa. She laughed too, although not knowing source of humour. Maybe, Grampus walked into verbal minefield. Laid out by a child, and didn't know how to get out. Myers family coexisted, with usual foibles and unresolved tension between sisters. Melissa selected different high school, but was awarded place at same chosen by Vanessa. Seems she could never shake her twin from her circle. She needed breathing space. Twelve years old, Melissa said to her father. *"Dad, please stop calling me your little Runt. It is negative and demeaning. The funny stage ended long ago. Should not even have started."* Cause for pause, he looked at her in surprise. Trying to figure what to say, or how he should respond. Got the feeling he shouldn't, at least not right then. But, he overrode and asked. **"What that you just say?"** She calmly told him. *"I know you heard and understood, please stop it."* Then she added knockout punch. *"Dad, don't let me detest you. It might grow into something,* *neither of us would be happy with. So, please. I love you, goodnight.*" He sat in stunned silence, thinking.*"Me could think such a thing, much more say it to daddy or mammy?"* Was getting ready to be parentally rambunctious. She had let wind out of his sail. He walked away in deep concentration, thinking. *"Did Audrey have anything to do with his daughter being forward?"* If he tried that crap with his parents. They would banish him from the home, to sleep with farm animals. After losing teeth initially. This new generation thing not right at all. Now, he had unrelated situation at work. Which, unbeknownst to him, would come home. He couldn't find, hesitated reporting, loss of company's gas card. When swiped at pumps, there was prompt to enter mileage. Which, if out of range. Fuel would not be dispensed. For that reason, he wasn't overly concerned. But, if successfully used, during time it went unreported as being lost. He could have to answer questions. So it was kinda nagging at his head. Twins now going fifteen, stopped for math tutoring four evenings, at Mrs. Aguilera's house. Whose only child, Daemon. Was seventeen years old, and had a crush on Melissa. She ignored his subtle wooing, and once threatened. To have her dad talk to his mom, if he touched her again. One evening, the lad confidently hailed Melissa with exaggerated flourish. Handed her, what she thought was credit card, telling her. **"I found this in mom's room, two days ago, and did not know what to do with it. Your father must have dropped it, when they were talking about what's focus for your break sessions."** He took few steps, before swiveling sideways and adding. **"They had a long, long talk, till way into the night."** Then he did girly runway strut, with body gyrations, head cocked side shoulder. To which, Melissa mumbled. *"Little Sprite, bwoy toy."* She got home and later when her father did. Greeted him with a hug and perpetual smile, that grew when eyes met. He repaired to the den with favourite magazine and a newspaper. Called. **"Lissa, come here before starting assignments."** See?. She's now Lissa, on equal status with Nessa. A little frank discussion between parent and child, can make for happy coexistence. He began. **"Whapp'n, is you eat the cream? Tell me how it taste. Never had it, although me grow on a farm."** *"What cream, dad?"* She teased, whilst slowly taking a plastic card from her pocket. *"You looking for this, dad?"* She asked. **"Yes! How you, when you... Where you find it?"** She calmly replied. *"Daemon Aguilera gave it to me. Saying he found it in his mom's room days ago, and didn't know what to do with it. Bye."* You know that gay "bye" with finger dance and sly ogle. He called her. **"Hold up now, before anyone else want know why you so happy. Come here. You know, that bwoy real name, is Demon? That's what on his driver's licence. I saw it, when he filled out a form last year, for summer job at the plant. But forget him, give me a hug."** Kissing her forehead, he went on. **"Lissa, ask me not the question. I will tell you no lie. But that would probably make things worse. So I am asking you to keep this between us, and next thing. I never did tell you sorry, for calling you a Runt. It was a joke to me, until that evening you asked me to stop. I sat down and thought about it. Never told you I am sorry. I am telling you now."** This soon to be woman, does not hesitate speaking her mind respectfully, when need arose. Tells her dad. *"Dad, I hear and appreciate what you're saying. But, truthfully now. Although you felt remorse over the years, after I asked you to stop. Don't you think, I am going to doubt your motive and….. Seeing as how, you're only expressing it. Whilst asking me, to keep your indiscretion secret? You didn't have* *to ask. I would not have shared this with anyone, for any reason whatsoever. I just found, mental visual of you and her...so amusing. I mean...okay, dad I'm done. And give you benefit of doubt. Thanks for not only feeling remorse, but expressing it so timely and sincerely."* Caught with his pants down and off. Seems Daemon was indeed christened Demon, as days later he told Vanessa. **"Your father dropped a credit card in mom's bedroom. I found and gave it to your sister last week. Ask him if she gave it to him."** There is a quote by English Poet, William Blake. "A truth that's told with bad intent, beats all the lies One can invent." Vanessa asked Melissa, who very nonchalantly told her sister. *"Of course I gave it to him. What else could I, would I do with it?"* At their eighteenth birthday party.

Melissa's dad, proudly announced her engagement to Master Cromwell Gaylord. Intern with law firm, Gaylord, Powell, LaTouche, Erickson. After congratulatory hand kisses, hugs and speeches. Frivolities continued amid wining and dining. After which, floor was cleared for dancing. Melissa asked Beau to yield, as she walked to and took her dad on the floor. He whispered in her ear. **"Lissa, you gleaming just like you 24 carrots ring."** She tittered and asked. *"You mean karats, Dad. Like my ring?"* He replied. **"Carrot, karat, you know what me mean."** And she retorted. *"To think, I started out a Runt."* Dad quickly told her. **"Me forget bout that long time. Why you have to bring it up again? Anyhow, remember now. This is only engagement, so tonight is not the night. When other ring go pon top of this one, then him can go pon top o...."** She pinched him into silence, told him. *"Mom and I were going through papers from the hospital. She showed me our birth umbillicals, in two powder boxes. That's how I saw, Vanessa was almost two pounds heavier than I was at birth. That really makes me*

Runt, I can frankly say. So long as no one else does." "Big sister" Vanessa was hamming it up with girlfriends. Kind of free spirited and gay, on champagne, called "little sister"over. **"Show Antoinette your ring and stone."** They all closed in and gawked, expressing oohs and aahs. Vanessa said. **"It looks like real gold."** Melissa flashed her sister angry leer, asking. *"What you mean by that? Dad says it's 24 karat, and I am certain, he should know real gold."* Vanessa said to Melissa, among her friends right there. **"Well, even if that's true. If I were you, I wouldn't go for 24 karat ring. Next thing, your finger strip and fall off. You know how we have sensitive skin. And at any rate, 24 karat too soft. Better you get it changed for 22 or 18. Which is what most people go with."** Next day, Vanessa asked her sister. **"Was I rotten, last night?** Melissa said. *"You were you."* Vanessa went on. **"Think I was, and now feel bad. Hug sis."** Midst of their embrace, Vanessa began. **"I hope this fella doesn't break little sister's heart. When he goes off to law school. On the road and meeting people. Begin rubbing shoulders with his kind and forget about you."** Melissa ended the embrace and walked away. Suppressing anger, without saying another word. Can you see sibling jealousy at play folks? Didn't enhance Melissa's comfort, when dad invited her. To join him in a hammock, under the June Plum tree, and began. **"Lissa, I know you head in clouds, and head over heels with this lawyer want to be. But remember this, and take it from me. Him only want dive, and swim in the triangle. Then boast to his crowd, what a grand time he had. That bwoy spoon fed, from him birth until now. And will continue for rest of him life. Them don't know loyalty to anything or anyone. Other than them own cause and survival. That is why anytime him come here. I give him a**

man handshake. Make him know, if him form fool. It can wrap round him neck and squeeze even harder. One last thing I have to say to you. Be a lady, don't be a whore." Wowee, that is strong dialogue, coming from father to daughter. Don't you think?. Let's tune in on the retort. *"Dad! Why you have to be so crass? I was listening for your favourite pronoun, that begins with 'mother.' Mom talks to us about life as we mature, dad. And we learn a lot about your early lives together. Some of which, you are now being very contradictory or hypocritical. Hearing your present stance on certain things. For instance, mom was virginal at sixteen, but not at seventeen. Why? Because "Cliff" was basking in her triangle. She came to live with you, in the studio apartment on Bird Road, when she was twenty-two. Had her twin girls at twenty-three. Question of marriage, did not cross your mind. Until, faced with possible huge hospital bills, if mom went into surgery. You agreed to marry her, weeks before her due date. So she could be added to your workshop insurance. So dad, tell me honestly. When you two got married, what was mom's status in society. Lady or….?"* Dad pounced verbally, cutting her off. **"Watch you mouth child. Don't be talking shit about your mother. She was, still am and will always be, a lady."** Silence, described as awkward, ensued until Radcliffe stood to leave and had last word. **"All me telling you, me never raise you as fool. Don't play One for anybody. Nice little talk Lissa, we must do this more often."** Vanessa made a comment, that nagged at Melissa. She called out. *"Dad, come here one minute. Why would an intern, be going on the road?"* **"What you mean, when you say "Going on the road?"** He asked, with a frown. Lissa went on. *"Vanessa was bad mouthing him, and said. When he goes on the road and meet other lawyers and…"* Radcliffe thought for a minute, then a bulb lit. He laughed and said. **"You sister never get the full rumour. The boy get, or is being considered for a Rhodes scholarship. Is a white man it name after. Nobody not going on road to meet nobody. But see here."** With that, he walked away still laughing. Whilst Vanessa's comments could be taken as sibling jealousy. Dad, Radcliffe had different axe to grind. He was focused on what this wedding would cost him. His predicament would have been less severe. Had the wedding been planned for storm season. In calm weather, overtime trough was bare. Supervision tried keeping it that way, in obedience to dictates of management. Failing which, they were out. He sat in his truck, fourth in line to the slow running diesel pump. Thoughts took wings and. *"If I could get twenty hours per pay period, that would. Well, would need twenty-five. So I could take home twenty. Thirty would be nice, but then, uncle would grab eight. Now, forty would be bitter sweet as uncle grabs twelve."* He creeps forward to second place and he's now chagrined at. *"Imagine me busting my hump for that lazy mother f...er and her two boys who live rent free. Get free electric, gas, water and groceries. Us working stiffs are f...ed by ambition. I need to swallow a pill before my head goes poof."* Seething at a stay-at-home woman, with three adult girls and five children. They all live on public assistance, in a four bedroom house, on street across from him. Frequent parties and late model cars they all drive, grates his last nerve. His wife tells him, ignore what he can't change. Nevertheless, he's chagrined. Pulls up to the pump and swipes his card, there's no activation. "See Administrator" message flashes. He's now swearing at Munoz, who's behind him in line. After suggesting to Munoz, it would speed things up, if he allowed him to use his card. Munoz asked him. ***"How do I explen hundred gas at one*** *time?"* Now irate, he tells Munoz. **"Now you wait, mother f..er."** He walks over to Automotive, mumbling. As Munoz yells Spanish cuss epithets at him. He could, should have driven the truck off stand. Allowing others to access pumps. But, today he's he. At Automotive, Simms was working on a boom and didn't want to leave. Now had to, because. As shop steward, he was only person with clearance, other than shop manager. Walking to the pump, he said to Radcliffe. *"Park your truck on service line, when your shift ends. It's overdue for PMS. Need four Monday Friday for Saturday."* Radcliffe says. **"Count mine out, I'm working Saturday."** Simms retorts. *"Use a spare."* Radcliffe asks. **"You crazy. Know how long it takes to move shit from one truck to another? It's guaranteed, I'm gonna be on job site, find there's something I need, and don't have."** Simms tells him. *"I'm going slap a "grounded" tag on it this minute. Deal with it."* Radcliffe smiles and says. **"Selective elective, absence mechanical failure? You cannot ground truck for PMS. What's more it's already memoed in. Go check."**

See what's happening here folks? One has ticket to the trough, and other trying to justify presence at. Content with winning, Radcliffe awaits tree trimmers at job site. Depending on when tree trimmers arrive and leave. He could probably make this an eight hour job, by time he gets back to the yard. That would be a stretch, considering it's just a one pot change out. Hand held crackles into life, it's supervision. Accident over at. Truck took out a pole, that serves intersection overhead signal. He's to get over there and assist crew en route. He smiles inwardly, at prospect making sixteen with meals. One minute ago, he was anxious about making eight. Now he thinks beyond today, and decides to come in Monday for safety meeting. If there were questions after the session, he would fail miserably. As everything discussed, went over his head.

Figures, after meeting he could house keep, restock his truck. Taking him to 15:00 hours, start of normal shift. He struts round to Automotive. Simms tells him. *"Your truck needs a sensor, but it will be ready on time."* He stands in silence. Hours at time and half, slips through his fingers. Simms says to Radcliffe. *"Hold on, let me check."* Hollers. *"Perkins! Rectum been here since today?"* Unseen voice replies. **"Nope"** Radcliffe is confused, asks Simms. **"Did you say, Rectum as in assho..?"** Simms says. *"Mention the Devil and he appears."* A box truck had just pulled up. Radcliffe studied trademark on side of vehicle. He got Recht, but couldn't get "tum" of what was left. Seeing his glow, Simms popped his glad bag. *"Don't look so sappy happy. We not going drop everything, to work on your truck. When you shift not starting till later. See yah pal."* Resigned thoughts to adage. We win some, we lose some. As life sailed on by, on seemingly calm waters. There was an undercurrent roiling below the surface. At twenty two years old, Mom chastised Melissa in strident language. Not having chosen sister Vanessa to be her bridesmaid. Choosing one of her friends instead. Melissa told her parents. Vanessa had so voluntarily, taken on every aspect of the wedding. She spared her, burdensome bridesmaid task. Fearing she gets overwhelmed. *"I am getting married, and Vanessa does not make suggestions and get feedback. She tells me what's going to happen. And who is going to do what. Only way I can get her to check herself, is to scream a few of dad's choice words."* Melissa ended as Radcliffe and Audrey Myers told their daughter. *"If you want a good cut ass, before your wedding night. Go ahead and utter one of them words, in our hearing."* Radcliffe added. **"Or make anybody tell we, them hear you."** Melissa stared at her parents slack jawed, until dad was done admonishing. She began. *"Dad, Mom! We grew, from our ears were transmitting to our brains. And heard you two, describing anyone you thought weren't in your corners, as fu..ers. Sometimes mother was added, or they were just fu..ing lowlifes. Y'all expressed yourselves, giving vent to feelings. Without considering two little girls who were....You know, in grade nine. Vanessa told....Never mind. I should only talk about me and so far. I have not found it necessary, to echo any of my parents' disturbed sentiments. But it's early days yet. Who knows what lies ahead."* They laughed and did emotional trio hug. Two years later, Vanessa married Ainsworth Dillon from a clan of eight boys and nine girls. Of this lot, three girls were sired by Mr. Dillon, unknown to his wife. Until women brought and unloaded infants at doorstep. Unable to care for them, lacking financial support by Mr. Dillon. Compounding family potpourri, Mrs. Dillon had three girls, before marrying Mr. Dillon, who brought his two boys with him. So from the get go, there were step children and step siblings. When they began having children. There were first, second and third cousins, aunts, uncles, nephews and nieces. Who in time began having children, and kin didn't know what to call their relative. They would give it a shot, explaining to someone. Then end up saying. *"But, we related somehow."* Now folks, I have to tell you if you have not already guessed. Within this extended clan, were good, bad and ugly. From hard working, successful professionals in legal, commerce, medicine and industry. Hourly paid artisans in every trade, to petty criminals and ne'er do wells. But they were family, with mixed fortunes. An example. Melissa's mother's first cousin, had two daughters who were interns in a law firm. Melissa trembled when going to functions or kin get together, where sister's tribe. Who by extension, were her in-laws, would also be in attendance. Her family thread is short and tight. Father-in-law is head partner in law firm that bears his name. It could be said, they are seen as aristocrats. We know there is no safer place, where white collar criminals and miscreants are given silent asylum from prosecution. But public perception puts them atop society's citadel. Maybe, this is fact not worthwhile mentioning. Because Melissa's in-laws, on husband's side, has never graced whooping sessions with their presence. Always, it's Melissa, boy Cromwell and baby makes three. Twin sisters agreed. Thanksgiving would be celebrated to include, Christmas and New Year's events. This to control expenses, that always fell disproportionately on the few. Whilst them that delved, and consumed most voracious. Had very little, or nothing to contribute. For some, that's a purposed career. Years past when it was Melissa's turn to host, she rented club house of her apartment complex. Having moved into their new home, with spacious areas. Three car garage, front and rear, manicured lawns. It was time to bring festivities home. We know, wherever a function is being planned. Vanessa takes reins and begins managing. Oblivious to anyone else's input. Serving tables were set up in the Lanai. Tables and chairs for eating, were arranged on rear lawn, among trees and ornamental foliage. Vanessa said, there should be ground cover. Tarp or plywood, because of insects and vermin in the grass. Melissa softly countered. Lawn was mowed and critters would not hang around, where there was human hubbub. Less than an hour into the affair, was Vanessa again. Hollering for everyone's attention. **"Listen up. Rain is forecast coming this way, sometime next hour. So we have to start moving y'all inside."** Melissa, caught by surprise, hurried to her sister. *"What you talking about, what rain? Can't have that inside the house. There isn't* *enough hard area to support food, drinks and foot traffic. Somebody is going to spill stuff. Nessa, carpet cleaning is not cheap."* Vanessa tells her sister. **"My dear, you should have decorated your house, livable. Who in right mind, installs cream coloured carpet in a house?"** Melissa gawked at her sister. *"I don't believe am hearing this crap. Listen, we decor our house to suit our tastes. This is not a fast food joint or strip club. I refuse to have you or anyone dictate to….You know what? This masquerade is over, right now."* With that, she moves to. Slides back glass doors and hollers. *"Listen everybody, weather has changed everything, the fun is done. Everyone can take their food and drink "to go." Get your stuff, walk round the house and drive home safe."* Still in charge, Vanessa took to soapbox. **"Tell you what. Everybody, continue as you are. Soon as rain starts,, just grab and run to your car, before it begins to pour. Keep on doing what you doing. Watch sky for black clouds shifting over your heads."** Turns to Melissa and says.

"We have to do better, organizing this once-a-year get together. Maybe you can talk to, and reserve the club house, as in previous years. But this house is not people friendly. Sorry, sister dear. I call it how I see it." Melissa in an almost whisper said. *"Only residents have option renting clubhouse for functions. I have never seen outsiders being rented the facility. Even if they would consider renting, it would have to be slow season, when it's gonna be idle. With holidays, weddings, engagements and birthdays. That place is always being used. Nevertheless, will call Racquel and ask."* Heeding Vanessa's edict, guests began stacking plates with food, grabbing sodas and headed to their cars. But alas they made a Bee line and came back to resate bellies. Like squirrels, they had merely stashed Acorns for winter and was back at the Oak tree. Vanessa called sister

Melissa's attention to. **"Cousin Gert dishing food, as if it's the last supper. My God. Soon there'll be nothing left. Open up this thing, let me borrow few Pyrex to take home some…."** She pauses, seeing sister staring at her slack jawed and goes on. **"What!? You expect me to walk out with food in paper plates. Like homeless Helga, coming from the soup kitchen?"** Let me bring you up to date on what's going down. "Thing" Vanessa wanted opened. Was free standing, Mahogany curio cabinet. About five by six, by two feet deep. Floor anchored on recessed platform, to guard against accidental tipping. Custom built by rural, cottage industry craftsmen. Who were awarded job, panelling law firm's conference suite. Also, making five oversized, tri-pedestal tables. Thirty upholstered, leather, Mahogany, captain's swivel chairs. Project was almost three years in making. Tempest tween these two siblings, are brewing to a storm, as Melissa says. *"There's no liquor here. You must have stopped and got drunk elsewhere. These are our prized, priceless, Pyrex Corning collection you're looking at. Those are "Spice of Life" Beside, are our "Country Festival" and "Wildflower" pieces. And you expect me to let you take your pick, to cart home food? Come on."* Vanessa, now angry, retorts. **"Gamma gave you some, because you were first to get married. Pffft. And you've got single pieces that are not in sets. I really don't see what's the big deal. They are just things. Possessions that can't reach out a hand to you, if you're slipping. Cromwell got you living this fantasy world of big house, carpeted in deep pile cream. Birthday Navigator, this and that…Trip around the globe to here, trip to there, trip to almost everywhere…and. But let me tell you Lissa. Blood thicker than mud. Don't you ever say no to family, especially siblings. Cause when ball ends and**

chariot turns into pumpkin. You're gonna need a long ride back to reality." Truth told, when Gamma gifted Melissa the Corning sets. She had them in everyday use, until one day her son's Cuban nursemaid, said to her. **"Miss Mel. You not scare these fall to floor and can't take up? These very prize. Make one time and then no more. So, they old and prize."** Melissa was skeptical at first, but asked round her circle and got rave feed backs. She went EBay, Amazon and other online markets. Acquiring pieces, sets and an education. About value of some Pyrex Corning ware. Soon, this endeavour became joint hobby with her husband, and they began collecting. Just as Vanessa ended her quiet rant to Melissa, or maybe she saw him coming. Cromwell walked into the house from work. Where he had been tying loose ends, and called for attention. Read three licence plates data, asked owners to remove them. **"We have to leave section of driveway, clear and accessible to emergency vehicles, such as paramedics. In case some of us gets too enthusiastic and chokes."** Last three words he barely got out audibly, as he began chuckling. Seems, visual of someone stuffing their face and being choked was overly funny. Ask yourself folks. What else could be so funny, he could hardly finish his sentence. Turned to his wife, saw her looking tense and out of sorts. Asked her. **"You okay, Mel? There's a log on your shoulder. Talk to me."** She spoke ever so softly, he knew that was a bad sign. Told his cronies once. **"When my Mel lowers her voice and forces you to listen. Someone is about to be undone. Believe me when I tell you this, and take it as gospel. It's as if she's conserving energy to make the strike.** Told him in slow count. *"It all went down before you got here. But, it's just people as usual. And my sister, being herself. Micro managing everything, to distress of others. Not giving a dam what…..Look at that woman* *overloading that plate. Can't she understand. It's called paper, because that's what it's made…..See that shit? That's what I'm talking about. Freakin' plate bent, dumped everything on the floor. She could at least doubled it. Or held plate flat in her palm instead. Fu..in' two left handed, retard imbecile."* "**Mel!**" A startled Cromwell exclaimed, mouth wide, staring."**Come with me.**" He said, walking her away from the scene. Asked. **"Should I call Dr Wellington's nurse for an emergency. What's got into you over you? When did you start fu..in?"** Again, last question ignited his funny candle, he laughed until heads turned their direction.

These then are everyday people, living everyday lives. In situations, some of us navigate, having different experiences. Getting on each others' nerves. In their way, or enhancing their joy. See how we wheel and deal to secure our and ours' position. Screw other guy if he's not as equipped. It's healthy existence in what's called. A dog eat dog world. So long as no One gets riled, they take down a sword or shotgun. Truth is, these days it takes very little to bring out weaponry, creating mass destruction and gloom. Bad as this might seem, this was among family, relatives, close, far and distant. To where they couldn't be classified. Someone gave up trying and just said. Somehow, we are related. What about when we come across strangers. Recently, I am stopped in right lane, white line of two, straight ahead lanes. Driver behind begins honking non-stop. I look in the mirror. He wants to make a turn on red, if traffic allows. I am going straight across. What am I to do? Can see he's irate, his door opens with force. I turn right, makes Bee line through corner gas station and comes back to join traffic. He's moved up to where I was, but can't turn. Traffic flow is non-stop. Pray for serenity.

Family foibles and Lifelong Scars

Languages and Intent-23

Fabiola was in mid fifties, son Fabio was late thirties.
Husband, Benjamin was late seventies, head honcho of
family's handyman business. His early years recalled.
Created unanswered questions in my mind. For instance,
Canadian born. He relates mining lumber and bleeding
Maples for sap. Yet spoke fluent Castilian Spanish. He didn't
say which US state he was a trooper. His car wore a disabled
veteran tag. In my book, I tagged them "White." So much for
ambiguity and confusion. Fabiola was business manager.
Took calls and monitored emails for quotes. Benjamin priced
jobs and gave his wife, who gave it to her son. He then
adjusted quotes upward, unknown to Benjamin. One could
say there was chicanery going on. But what the heck? It's a
family affair. Benjamin whispered to me. *"The boy going
Texas for couple months. Got subcontract on great wall."*
Then hurricane Maria, September 2017, laid waste to Puerto
Rico. Fabio took off for US territory. Shortly after, Fabiola
went, for a few weeks. Benjamin does not have clue, what
Fabiola's input in the business entails. He makes light of it,
says to me. *"I look at jub, tell the guy. You buy at Lowe's all
stuff here. You pay me $300. I do jub very good. I needa haf
I begin. And one more haf when I end. See, whatsa so hard
in that?"* It would be reasonable to assume. Pickings in
Puerto Rico, are not as slim as one would think. After all, ruin
does create fervour of rebuilding. It's been over a year since
mother and son left, her for few weeks. He, passing up
contract on the wall. Benjamin gets invited to Isabella's
house for dinner, but has spurned repeats. She looks too
pretty and smells too good. *"The hands got fingers out to
here. And all with the paint on tup, and the paint under.
That there my friend is mucho dinero, ooh la la. I use to buy*

hand paint in Canada, "Cutex" You got in Jamaique the "Cutex"? For Angelique, she love Benjamin. I do for her the fingers and toes too. She love me more. No more at the farmacia, "Cutex." Isabella goes to shoppe with more women. Sits in comfy chair, with big bowl on tup. And there do the everything. She comes out, I jump back as how I got the fright. Is no same person went in, person come out. But I soon see all is well so I take her home." He extends an arm, lifts the cuff and tells me to look. *"What you see my friend?"* **"Your arm in thicket of hair. What am I supposed to see?"** I ask, he says. *"Paciencia mi amigo, paciencia."* In isolation, some Spanish words have no meaning. In context I can quickly grasp. From sixties spaghetti westerns I knew, amigo is friend. Now, wagging index finger and paciencia tells me, patience. Venturing into alien culture can be minefield scary, where silence is akin to standing still.

Lourdes was my new girlfriend, visiting her friend, who recently gave birth and doing a party thing. She cued me outside the door. *"Remember now, you're supposed to smile and admire the baby. It would be nice, if you remarked how pretty it is. But do not give speech."* In this scenario, I would be "A man of few words." We went in, girlfriend greeted mom and they did their habla. She head gestured my way, which I took as silent introduction. I was only black person in crowd of whites and fair skinned, all gabbing in unknown language. Decided right then, maybe I should wait outside or...Mom took my hand. *"Ah, so good you came, habla habla habla."* I replied. **"Gracias!"** Tongue frozen between Senora or Senorita. Gave it up, and ended. **"Mucho pretty bambino."** Her smile contorted instantly. *"No! no, no pappy. No bambino, pappy. Bambina, pappy, bambina I tell you. I* *show you? No? Yes? And you believe bambina?"* She spoke softly to One's ear. Voice, eyes and demeanour however, conveyed Arctic chilled terror. Girlfriend quickly intervened and sought soothing her, in the habla. They spoke, gesturing to me, the baby. Then mom walked away, still muttering. We went out the door to my truck. *"Are you out of your freaking mind? It's a girl, not a boy."* Girlfriend ranted. I said I thought, babies were bambino, in Spanish. She said I was lucky child's father was absent. Things could have gotten worse. **"For what!? These people are too damned thin skinned."** Said I. Oh, that was another war got started. Girlfriend exclaimed. *"These people!! My God! What's that supposed to mean? Haven't you noticed, I too am one of those people?"* I raised both palms in surrender. Our journey ended that evening. A disappointment for me. I had bent over to nurture and cultivate this relationship. To prove or dispel certain intimacy rumours that came to me as fact. You know?

But, lest I digress, as is my wont. Let's grab horse's rein and get back to theme of the minute. Benjamin invited patience, wait and see. He pointed to Lena who lived with Leopold further down his street. Both Black or Negroid. Leopold was a Vet but did not sport a tag on his car to indicate. Whilst Leopold went on his daily away from home, Lena Gypsy roamed the community. She would probably be taken for homeless, were it not for her being recognized as living at. She seemed mentally unbalanced but was clean and well put together. Roaming at will, stopping to pluck leaves and buds, that overhung hedges and fences. She sometimes accosted passerby, asking. *"What is name of this leaf, do you know?"* Mostly, a person gave her that wary eye, said no and kept going. Benjamin, on other hand, watches and waits to seize opportunity. He's convinced he can lure her into an embrace. Which, although she seems unbalanced, has resisted with a benign grin. He thinks it took more than money to keep his wife in Puerto Rico. Wonders what she's going to say when she comes home. I thought saying to him. *"If she comes home."* But again, bit my tongue. In aftermath of senorita and myself, having our little dust up. I sat with, asked Francisco to explain bambino, bambina, blunder. He told me. ***"Pappy, it not make difference. Bambino is all baby, boy, girl. Some people want hear Bambina. It is not the Spanish pappy, it is the Italiano. You see? Your friend you go see. I say, she not, eh. How do you say? Aah, the suff, delicato, pappy. She not delicate woman, she pendejos. Old puta."*** Now the day of my imbroglio has arrived, and I exchange places with my children. As they grew older and asked certain questions, I would have answered. My wife however, quickly intervened and dared me not to. Because, she claimed. I always gave more information than necessary. So I would tell them a brief response, to which they would ask, why or why not. I would be forced to say. **"Because there are more questions than answers. And the more you find out the less you know."** I set out wanting to get this bambino, bambina thing straight. And in the process, comes new words "puta, pendejos." Way it was said with derisive contempt. Tells me it was not supporting a virtue. In due course, learned. "Puta" in English, means "whore." "Pendejos" has similar but varied meaning. Ever so often, I meet folks who get excited, hearing my Jamaican accent. Wanting to familiarize with underground language, especially those ending in cloth. "Clawt" really. Caucasian males are eager to get gist of tun tun, pum pum and punaany. African American and Latinos, seem to grasp intent of and often spice vocabulary with these words. Now, I am similarly mesmerized, wanting to learn Spanish and Italian underground quotes. French, and oui oui, sounds like something a baby says, when being potty trained. But "puta" has succinct appeal, that gratifies and enflames inner bawdy traits. Way Francisco said it, was like spitting in utter disgust. I visited an old man, who greeted at front gate. Directed me to second gate, other side of his house, and quickly explained. *"El perro malo pappy mucho caca."* Last word resonated with me in a profound way because, as a child. If I erred and giving Granny an excuse, to forestall a whipping. She often said. *"Bwoy, stop chat caca in me ears."* We did not as a rule, speak Spanish. Our languages were English and its broken derivative, patois. Carried down from plantation slavery era. I've got an ace in the hole from boyhood. I can talk Gypsy language. Wanna see sample? Here goes. *I've otga an ace in eedi oleh umfra oyhoodbo. I anca alkta Ipsygy angwichla. Annawa eesi amplesa?*

Telling truthful lies-24

Lying is a chink in every person's armour. What has always amazed me. Are, those that prosecute others for lying. Closing eyes to their guilt, in this facet of human existence. Everyone lies, some more than others. Some lie selectively, others lie every time they say something. It's a disease within, they just cannot speak truth without adding a lie. Take this novel for one. Litany of lies, tagged "fiction." Bible swearing is a redundant exercise, that should be discontinued. There being nothing to guarantee, swearer telling truth. We know and accept, people swear and lie, barefaced without blinking. Bible swearing would be relevant, if a time in recorded history. People fell dead whilst lying after being sworn. That would make others refuse to swear. Which many do, citing religious beliefs. But if there's no tangible distress from swearing and lying. We will continue to swear and lie. And lie without swearing. I was raised by Granny, she hated lying.

Was convinced, every liar will become thief. Every thief will in time, become murderer. Was therefore important, I be deterred from lying. Three years old, she told me. If I wanted my rump covered. I should learn to "hold needle and thread." Failing which, woman will take off her drawers and beat me over the head. Essence of that warning means. A man who relies on woman to meet his needs domestically. He's so handicapped, she assumes unprecedented liberties. I feared sewing day, one of reconciliation. Trembling when we sat across from each other. She used a two inches, brass tipped needle, mine was much shorter. She would fold and tack, tell me watch her and sew the seam. Then she would ask. *"Bwoy, you won't stop thief the sugar?"* I would immediately deny, in a voice that quivered. **"Me don't thief out any, since the last time, Granny."** She would tell me, stick out my lying tongue. For to be pricked. Also, hand I used open the bottle and steal. A needle, although small. Is a frightening tool when coming at you. Crying in fear, I stuck tongue out then pulled it in when needle neared. Never mattered, I still got two pricks on a hand, thigh or anywhere. Did punishment deter me from being evil? Nary a chance. I'll tell you though. To this day, I dread going for doctor' blood work. Let's look at Granny's role in my lying. Her two room house was built on a large leased plot. She farmed the land extensively, sold crops to neighbours. She had a conviction, not to credit food items. Because, after it is eaten, it sickens stomach to look at. She departed this rule, gave credit to our neighbour who lived farther up lane. Debt went unpaid for a long time. Working our garden, weeding and picking peppers. Granny heard telltale drag of woman's slippers nearing. Hid behind the house, said to me. *"If is Miss Cooley, and she ask fah me, tell her me not here. But if she bring the money, she can* *give it to you."* You can guess what happened. The woman wasn't stopping at our gate. If anything, she tried sidling by in evasive mode. As she moved on down the lane, I called out. **"Miss Cooley, mi Granny say to tell you she not here. If is the money you bring. You can give it to me."** Miss Cooley replied. *"Tell you Granny, she don't have to hide from me. If me did have the money, me woulda did pay her long time."* I gave Granny the message. With brows furrowed, she asked, what I told the woman. I repeated verbatim. Was slapped hard across the face, in near topple that stung, ere my narration ended. *"I'm going teach you sense, hear bwoy. Dyam idiot."* In other words, she's going to teach me art of lying. She forgot, or wasn't aware "Children live what they learn." I have found, to lie convincingly. It should be kept basic and simple. Less details, better chance of success. Lies are harder to remember than truth. Loading lie with too many components, is recipe for failure. I lied more in pre-adult years, than I have since. It had to do with being a man and recognizing. I should be able to say my say, without fear. If I had to rely on a lie to get my way. Then I was still a boy, cowering at someone's needle or mercy. Since then, I lie only if absolutely necessary. Here's a tip. Don't lie to police, unless certain you have covered all possible loop holes. Invariably, you will overlook a minute detail. And, therein lies your Waterloo. Police are trained to detect lies. In some instances, they know something you don't. He asks you to tell what you know. You say, you heard a sound. Went to open your door, in fear decided not to. As interview develops, he compliments your jacket, car or fine leather shoe. Takes you into a game, asks if you are Heat's fan. Then, he says. *"When you heard the sound, and looked outside the door. Was the man running, or had already gone out of sight?* If you are truthing, you will respond. *"I never opened the door."* If you

Colleen G. Lowe

are lying.You pause to think, and that's all he needs. You are thinking. *"Did I say, I opened the door? I never told...."* Makes it worse, if you now stutter when talking, but spoke coherently prior. Cops begin psychological profiling, moment they lay eyes on you. Sense sniff for violent threat, unstable posture and lying, among other negatives. Never mind the smile, that's facade to keep you inert until he makes reasonable assessment. Some lies are so believable.....

Robert brought older children, to "Take your child to work day." Co-workers expressed surprise, the girl was only ten. She could pass for fourteen, they averred. She began staying at school after classes. Hanging out with male athletic students. Much older than she was. Robert decided to put his feet down. Repeatedly told her to come home after school. Do homework, chores and computer assignments, or else. She put up resistance. As folks are wont to say, rebelled. At thirteen, she confronted Robert, saying. *"First of all, you're not even my daddy. If you don't stop bugging. I'm going tell, you're molesting me."* **"When did I ever molest..?"** He began a denial, to which she said. *"See who they will believe, you or me."* Jauntily sauntering off, she flashed a winning smirk. We have to admit, brazen as that lie is, will make a man tremble in his sleep. That kind of thing keeps him awake. He's thinking. *"Would she really do that, after all I've done for her?"* As if contending with dread of being lied on, was not enough to create angst and disconcert. He could not get over this sword of Damocles, that impinged his working safely. In vocation fraught with unforgiving perils. Sought advice from friends in law enforcement, got assurance. If situation ever arose, methods are in place to establish veracity or otherwise. When depositions are taken from complainants, moreso children. With that reassurance, he breathed easier and child was left to her own devises, whatever behaviour she chose to pursue. Likely detrimental to her future. Sad indeed.

Carol confronted, husband Louis. *"You know you should not eat, just before bed, late as you came in last night?"* He told her. **"You're still dreaming. I didn't eat anything last night."** She rebutted.*"You probably made sandwich, three slices ham are missing, from our go with ham and eggs breakfast."* He insisted. **"Must have been kids hon, or Wilmot. We know he's ever hungry because of hookworms."** She decided to end the charade right then. *"No Louis, none of our children, or my brother. Slept in our bed last night and breathing through their mouth. Another thing. If you snack at night, please remember to brush before you come to bed. If I had to tell any of our kids that. I would do so with slap for good measure. How you want your eggs, fried or scrambled?"* He rambled out, muttering incoherently, without answering. Ashamed being caught as is said, pants down. Carol shouted at him. *"You shouldn't lie on your children. They'll beat you with briars and brambles when you're old."* Lowered her voice. *"If you live that long. F…in' moron, lying on your kids."* Barbara broke hush at our lunch table. *"I think that's what they call compulsive lying, just like gambling. Those people just cannot help themselves."* Richard chuckled and said. *"Homeboy needs help, he best make appointment. Go talk to them at LFO."* Why do people lie? A famous line by Al Pacino, goes. *"I always tell the truth, even when I lie."* Sometimes we are lied on. But it never comes to our attention. Usually, when a liar sets out to do his deed, he first cautions. *"Remember now, you cannot repeat this, ever."* Or. *"Anyhow you repeat this. I'll say you're lying. I never told you anything of the sort."* Thus challenged, the lie takes a bit longer doing rounds before getting to your ears. Sometimes, it never does. People giving you disdainful looks and you wonder what's that all about. Maybe, you're like me. Flat out refuse to be concerned. I have come across constructive lying. That's taken as opposite of destructive lying. I am still pondering that. My usually reliable source **"Google"** Is not making it simple enough for me to grasp. In previous vocation. Imported goods, left on the docks, beyond certain period. Had to be moved to government facility, called the "Queen's Warehouse" Goods that could not be so moved, were legally. Constructively warehoused where landed. Subjected to fees, as if actually stored in government's warehouse. Based on that, I take it. Constructive lying is not necessarily an uttered lie, but one created by assumption. Let's say. Two women are discussing a third. One asks. "Her husband beats her?" Other, doesn't say, yea or nay. Asks instead. "You really have to ask that?" Methinks, that's constructive lying, in open minded ambit. Following incident, methinks. Dovetails constructive lying model perfectly. It could uphold truth test, prima facie

Archibald was in sixties and seen as a curmudgeon. Living in ye olde Dickensian era. He declared, no One rang his doorbell or phone after 20:00 hours. Relatives had until 21:00 hours, and better have a damn good reason for disturbing peace and tranquility, abounding. His roost, his rule and life went on. Until, stepdaughter Phylicia joined the family. On way from MIA, he told her. **"When you find a man, don't tell him where you live. Mek him drop you off on the avenue. Don't mek him bring you to our door."** Take note, teen was only seventeen. He didn't say, "If." Certain, she would find a man, or man find her. She cautiously asked. *"Suppose it raining, uncle Archie?"* He testily replied. **"You**

271

can get 99c umbrella at dollar store. One more thing. Don't give me house number to anyone, unless is job. In any event, you can't work. So, that solves that." Wife Veronica, Phylicia's mom. Tried soothing and nudging him in bed, cut the teen some slack. Give her bit more flexibility, as she was stressed. He told his wife, teen had no reason. She eats, listens to music, watches television. Sleeps on designer mattress under a roof, protected from elements. She is really going to experience thrill of being stressed, having to rent her own place. That's not too far off, seeing her attitude and disrespectful demeanour. Typical seventeen year old, we can accept presence of. What aviators call, clear air turbulence in force. She got hustling job doing dishes, waiting tables and peeling onions at nearby restaurant. Said, it was first in life, she cried without being flogged. Archie told her to soak onions in water before stripping. It eased her discomfort briefly until Chef asked what she was doing, why. Told her, go back to former mode. Phylicia was on six months visitor's visa. Being employed, was illegal act by her and employer. Underaged and underpaid, under table. Tony, her married boss. Figured he could get under her skirt. This is thing where island folks will say. "One good "Under" deserves another." She was royally pissed to the nines, with all and sundry. Tony asked her out on party shindig, after closing shop, coming Saturday night. She declined his request. Saying, stepfather locked the door 22:30 hours, without fail. Asked if she did not have her own key, she told him. Uncle Archie says, she can get her own key. And her own door, in which to turn it. Tony ruminated a bit then persisted, that's no problem. He could find them a spot to bunk down for the night. She asked if "spot" would always be there, because after first night. Spot would have to be permanent home. No way, she could get back in Archie's house. Tony thought about this and lusted. Brushed against her at the sink, longing for close encounters of satisfying kind. So close and yet so far. Damn that old uncle Archie. Frustrated, he told Phylicia, as both sat sipping hot cock soup..*"That's how every stepfather behave. When them dying to draw down you drawers, and you put up resistance."* Phylicia did not respond, kept silent. Tony took his assumption as fact. Archie frequented the joint for festival and jerk, chicken or pork. Spreading word to co-workers, who patronized the chow spot. One such visit, Tony pointed out Archie to kitchen staff, telling them. *"The old man is Phylicia's stepfather. Can you believe, any day now. He's going lock her out of their house? Poor child gonna be homeless, because she won't give him punaany."* Not familiar with punaany? Check Admiral Bailey-Gimme punaany-UTube. Alarmed by this news, Chef asked.*"But, don't him and her mother married?"* Tony replied. *"That never stop them kind of man, when them tail start slap them legs. Want ride both Mare and Pony."* Now, to show how mischief can create eddy, that becomes whirlpool and storm. Before long, tidal wave makes way to shore. Wreaking havoc, when it makes landfall. Cashier Aisha, and Archie had a thing going on. You know, like Billy and Mrs. Jones. Got stolid and monosyllabic, when talking to him. After one or two probes to find reasons for. He abandoned effort and cut romantic ties. Time cured her ills, and after months passed. They resumed chatting and yukking as people do. He was customer, she was cashier. Ignoring each other was not a do, unless Archie stopped coming to the shop. Archie never relit or took up torch between them anew, that was over and done with. Said to him, she heard Phylicia getting married, and is he going to give her away. Then she snickered and said. *"That's a funny thought."* He replied. Not being on roster, giving anyone away, but wanted to know. **"What's funny, about woman getting married?"** *"Oh, funny is not with marriage. It's with give away."* Archibald did not see the humour. So he left it at that, without probing. He's most times, not in a mood to pursue riddles. Will ignore effort on your part to get one going. Months later, Aisha asks him a favour. Her man is in Jackson and she's asking for a ride, taking things for him, he agrees. She gets in the truck. Says she has been itching to ask him something for longest time. Hope he doesn't get riled, but is there any truth to. First she tells him, what she was told by Phylicia. Of Tony's efforts to seduce her, when she first began at the shop. Then next, what Tony told everyone in the kitchen about Archibald. He replied, there's not much he can say on the matter. Asked why not, he told Aisha. If she did not believe what Tony said, there was nothing to resolve. If she believed, nothing he could say. Would convince her or anyone otherwise. She made for debating the matter. He stopped her by raised palm, went on to say. **"If we exchanged positions or personalities. I wouldn't take denial as truth. Tony's story is believable. You might as well savour and digest."** Archibald fumed inside, couldn't wait to get home. Break this consent by silence deed to Veronica. She insisted, Phylicia hadn't done anything wrong. Archibald averred, she should've corrected Tony's assumption when uttered. Say to him. *"No, he's not that kind of stepfather. Give him his due. He's never made any move on me."* Instead, she was happy to remain silent. Knowing full well, it could not redound positively to his character. To as it is said, rub salt into a wound. Veronica told her husband. Given his nature. Phylicia's reaction or absence of. Seems coincidental to how he would behave, in similar situation. Then went on. *"Maybe she has observed and learned a lot from you. In the short time she lived with us."*

Archibald, self admitted it was gospel. Brought to her attention, Phylicia refuses to apologize. Says it can't be her fault, Tony misinterpreted her silence. Rancour now exists among Archibald, Veronica and Phylicia. Archibald yet goes to the restaurant. Tony greets effusively and everyone smiles There was an inside joke, as it is called. Regarding Archibald. Employees had to wear PPE's, including hardhat. Putting aside his trademark apple cap. Archibald was noted for doffing one, and donning other, in swift movement. And only, either in privacy of his work truck, or bathroom. Someone once said to him. ***"Give scalp chance to breathe, Archie. It will look like last week's avocado, if you don't."*** Well, no One knows who started rumour. But co-workers began asking. ***"Is Archie-bald?"*** Punning his name. Methinks Phylicia felt inundated and helpless under Archie's power. Tony's assumption gave opportunity at silent retaliation, she gladly embraced. Sounds a natural human thing to do. Us endowed with inherent retaliatory psyche, to always get even. Experts argue, subject to debate. Not volunteering information is not lying. Sometimes I lie in reverse, not very often. Us liars always justify to ourselves, reason for. Convinced there was no viable alternative. If needs be we would probably do same thing again, possibly with fine tuning. In a lie post-mortem, we always come up with. ***"Dam, I shoulda told them that."*** Or ***"I coulda used my cousin's name instead. He ain't never been in trouble. I forgot to tell Sharon, I was going downtown. She would know what to tell them, in case they called."*** Lou Rawls reminded. Coulda, shoulda, woulda is always too late. We now come to ask ourselves the question. Is lying wrong? Or is it a way of life, we should have to accept and recognize we all do it. Let's not seek escape by adjectivising our lies into little, bold faced and white. We owe it to our children. Accept responsibility for this perpetual state of lying, and make effort to desist. Born innocent, learning from parents and each other. As they develop and are coached into becoming liars. First victims are usually, us trainers. Given a meal she hates, that mommy says is good for her. What does little Nancy do? She feigns stomach or headache, gets reprieved. Having succeeded, she passes this proven ruse on in kindergarten. There you have it folks. A budding generation of liars, focused on developing their art, as nature and time dictates. Don't give up just yet. Changes can come about, starting with adults. It is said. 'Where there's a will, there's a way.' We need only be consciously aware, our action ever comes under scrutiny, and are often aped by our children. Hence, be mindful of actions and utterances.

Forgive and forget?-25.

Forget it, not gonna happen. Neither in this life or next. We are not built to accommodate, that worthiest of traits. Bear in mind also, we at times forgive, but rarely forget. Both occupy same room in our brain. "Forget" holds key that decides when, if ever and how much. The door opens, allowing "forgive" to dominate. Just when things seem to be going okay. "Forget" is jolted by replay of an event, and closes door, stranding "forgive" outside. Human psyche can only achieve this perfect melding, in one of two situations. Irrespective of how egregious an act may be. If intended victim does not, or cannot absorb it in that light. Then there's no harm done. No foul cried, and nothing to remember, forget or forgive. In early teens, smitten with female classmate, who hated my shadow. Pursuing her relentlessly, she would sometimes angrily confront. *"What's matter with you. You take insult for invitation?"* If the insult was recognized for what it was. There would be ill will from me to her. Blinded by lust, her intended insult was taken as compliment. Under my intense ogling, she eyed me cross swirl as she stepped out of the pool. Slipped on peel and fell in the pool. Lucky for non-swimmer me, it was shallow end. That I didn't pause to consider, before jumping in to rescue. Holding that girl in wet embrace, was a feeling I could never find words to adequately describe. But there we were. Her in happy fright, forgetting dislike of hero, in sodden khakis. Her in already wet bathing suit. If pursuit gets rewarded with affection. Memory recalls insults, as happy crumbs leading to the castle. In essence, we need hurt or harm by someone. Vowing to never let our inner being be pierced anew. Fixating instinct of self preservation, neither forgetting or forgiving. We have been told, forgetting makes us prone to repeat deed, or facilitate same. This happens when we can control faculties. To extent it's recognized, we not always are. Hence we at times, listen to friend, family member, sibling or co-worker. Relate an experience, in which they took an action, leading us to ask. *"What made you do that?" "How could you say such a thing?" "Why didn't you say, no?"* You might not know it, but that person is asking selfsame questions. Sometimes, inner thoughts gets verbalized. *"How could I be so stupid?"* Know what's the answer? We pride ourselves, being smart and sensible on life's subjects. Truth is, we exist on edge, between sanity and insanity. Every now and then, we make a slip, venture over insanity side. A friend often remarked, middle ground is sliver of perfect space between good and bad, right and wrong. To extent we at times, close our minds in thought. And opens it on neutral side. When we return, if we do. That's when we beat heads against a wall in disbelief. And friends ask. *"How could you?"* Even while you are berating and making out. You would never be caught dead, doing something similar. You lie and not know it. Aaron Neville sings. *"Everybody plays the fool sometimes. No exception to the rule."* When our mental state gets visited by insanity, be it temporary or permanent. And, let us earnestly pray, worse does not morph to worst. Bringing feared companion, senility. Ability to forget and forgive, no longer resides within us. Would it be fair then to say, nay admit. Forgiving and forgetting, is involuntary element of our meme? I am not convinced humans are engineered to forgive and forget. Except by onset of mental illness or old age. Humans, being highest form of animal species. Puts spotlight on lesser animal lifeforms. Contrary to stated belief, dogs do hold grudges. Want to see dog holding grudge and get vicious? Visitor comes calling. Bruno lies quietly, head atop paws, pretending to be asleep. But really listening in on what's what. So he can spread word later. They discuss us you know, sure do. Visitor stinks atmosphere. Homeboy knows, friend lifted his tail. What does he do? Chases Bruno. ***"Git out, dam dog."*** Bruno slinks, pauses on the lawn. Looks back with a scowl. Homeboy tosses missile at. He ambles away. Gabfest and hilarity resumes, as visitor now clenches his, you know what. Unable to clear the air again. I guarantee you, when visitor gets ready to leave. Bruno is going to sneak out of hiding, and grab one of his ankles. I've seen it too many times. Rover did and so did Pronto. Can't be taken as coincidence.

The Urologist-26

I am certain you knew, I didn't. Washing machines are rough on clothes. Seems they beat up on small garments, more than they do on larger ones. If you're like Clarence and I'm told there are millions. Who will not throw away a pair of threadbare drawers. There's this umbilical knot, if you will. That's hard to mentally disconnect and they become trophied.

A second wife, when she was girlfriend. Came on extended visit, for us to feel each other out. Although, another girlfriend deemed such exercises, waltzing to futile flute, eyes closed because. Everyone shows their better traits during those periods. She tried making closet space for stuff. Woman rounded up my best historical drawers, stuffed them in shopping bag. I met her at the door, on way to the big green cart. Told her, for every of my drawers in that bag. I'm gonna get three of hers and make unisex garbage. That was our first fight, she wanted to end us before we began. I wouldn't budge, she called truce and let my drawers be. Weekend we were going to visit her brother. She looked at me and begged. ***"Please, don't put that one on. I'll do anything you ask, if you do that for me."*** Watched me pull it up and said. ***"You ever consider, if you took sick on the road and had to go to hospital?"*** We divorced after fifteen years and an ex-girlfriend, close to my age, took hold the baton. After doing laundry, she sat with needle and thread. Made tucks in stretched waistband, giving drawers extended service. Young women don't even know how to use thimble, much more needle and thread. Remember now, older folks are from era of mending and darning clothes. Hence it's not a chore, sewing drawers waists. Hold them up and admire handiwork, glow with inner satisfaction. Ours, was not a "throw away" age. Shoot, some of our clothes had more darns and patches, than original fabric. That's how "Patches" from Alabama got his name. See? So, Clarence shared with his son, discussing washing machine aggression towards small clothes. Son says, when they come out like that he just tosses them and forget it. Clarence replies with emphasis. ***"No, no can do."*** I intend making this a talking point. Will wear a pair today, on my Urologist visit. Junior laughs and tells dad, keep him posted on how it goes. *"Leave nothing out, put nothing in."* Clarence arrives at UM Medical Centre, 10:26 hours for 11:00 hours appointment. Got called, vital signs taken and put in a closed door room. Nurse enters and asks, why he's sitting in the dark. He tells her, lights went off after about ten minutes. She tells him. *"That's because you sat still. You have to move around. Shift a hand, foot or something. I am going to do a bladder scan. Please loosen your pant and pull down your…..Oh! What's….You got bit much going here."* He says. **"That's how it came from washing machine."** She replies. *"Oh! I see. I'm sure it's got more wear, than tear left in it."* She scans and tells him on her way out. *"I've had men come in bare, but you're my first partial. If lights go off, just wave a hand, it'll come back on."* Later, doctor came in and asked if he's napping in the dark. Clarence tells him he did wave, just as nurse advised. Lights never came on, till he opened the door. Doctor says with a guarded smile. *"My nurse tells me, you pulled caper on her. What's the story?"* Clarence spreads both hands and repeats.**"That's how it came out washing machine. Figured it was appropriate for your examination and. You know? When you did the biopsy intrusion and clipped snipped the kernel. You went through the muzzle up to the chamber."** He laughs, says. *"Actually, it's easier to do my examination of the chamber by going through the butt. As you will see right now. Hop on up here and let's play ball. Hmm, that's good prostate there. Was kind of easy, you prepared the area in…?* **"Not really, but."** Clarence reveals love of Scotch Bonnet peppers with meals. Aftermath makes dab of Neosporin necessary. Doctor gives him that wary amused stare and says. *"Hmmm."* Pauses, then. *"You know? When we talk I get such a…anyhow. So, how's the family?"* "Oh, **the young wife bailed"** *"Sorry to hear that."* **"Ours was a**

May, December thing. I knew it would lose steam before long." *"How long were you married?"* "Twelve years, more or less." *"Well, you got a long honeymoon. So you have a girlfriend?"* "Kind of sort of, but it's been about a year since any scoring." *"You know, if you not having sex you have to try masturbation. That's one way flushing the prostate."* "NO! Where I come from, we don't get involved in that kind of behaviour. We frown on "backing the fist." *"Backing the fish?"* "The fist, fist." Clarence makes loose fist and demonstrates back and forth action. **"You get into habit of self gratification thing. Before long, you hesitate to greet people. If you do, you keep hands in your pockets."** *"Why would you hesitate? It's a closed door…"* **"After awhile, your palms sprout hair and tickles other person in a handshake. Worst case scenario, person gets a jolt. You know, like static electric discharge. People don't take these things lightly, they talk. Then the cat is out the bag and everyone knows you're self indulging. But maybe, most revealing of all. Is that tell tale half closed fist, the palm naturally deforms to. At first glance, people think you had a stroke. Only other time a man gets that curved palm. Is if he's an addicted rum head, ever at the saloon, always holding a tumbler."** He stares unbelieving, mouth ajar. Recovers and says. *"I think you should get used to the idea. It's really healthiest way flushing prostate. It's just another form of therapy, like exercising. Come back and see me in a year. If you get any more ready made examination boxers. Turn the opening around to the…..I'll tell you though. I'm glad I woke this morning. Would have missed this, if I didn't"* Making his exit, Clarence called. **"You know Doc, I think you know about the static charge. Having experienced it from some of your patients. Last** time I was here, you gave an elbow bump just before you left, instead of a handshake." He laughs, turns his elbow and again. Bumped Clarence's like a fist bump. Clarence says, he never knew that kind of social interaction existed. Until he shared experience with a dude, who told him. *"Ohhh, yeah. I do that all time. Usually when someone is sick."* Clarence, as promised. Called his son, gave replay of the visit. Ending with a hearty laugh and. **"Told you the drassy would be a talking point."** *"I don't know dad. All depends if it's a good talking point, or bad one. Here's the thing. When nurse tells it among her crowd. If you were within earshot you would likely hear. "If he was my husband, I would divorce him." Women never see funny in situations like that. They think your crap reflects on them, more negatively than it does on you. Doctor will tell his golfing buddies. They'll have a good chuckle. One or two might admit. Having a few drawers from their med school days around, that they loathe to let go of. Yet, dare not be so bold as to put them on. Not even when coming to bed. Dad, you are a man among men. Remember where that came from?"* **"How can you ask, when it was I who introduced you to that movie? Great performance by great actors."** Son laughs loud and says. *"Nobody's Fool. Paul Newman, Bruce Willis and Melanie Griffith. Ah, Melanie. Gave me glimpse of hidden treasures. At seventeen, that brief expose' stays in my head."*

Promises hard and soft-27

Whilst we are on this near subject. Brings to mind, one of my favourite girlfriends. She has this most interesting theory regarding male anatomy. How man's brain reacts in certain situations. Brooks no questioning her adamant resolve on the issue. Having spent considerable time putting it to test. On various members of the specie, leaving no doubt. Regarding authenticity of her findings. Her research has proven beyond doubt. There is a mental and physical connection that takes place. When men gets lusting and wants to be sated. The heart, she maintains, loses rigidity and relaxes it's muscles. After having pumped, to create an erection. Now we have the phenomenon she calls, hard Dick, soft heart. This push and pull, in and of itself, would not be noticed. Were it not for it's intrusion on male's mental state. Sometimes, unwittingly and to his detriment. You see dear hearts and gentle people. She has established, when the heart is soft. Male makes generous promises, of lavish gifts and accommodation he normally would not. This endears the female to react by giving herself without inhibition. Allowing him to exploit at will, in pursuit of utter contentment. Never mind there are times. Some level of discomfort, might be experienced, during and after. She inwardly grins and bears intrusion that brings her, very little, if any, pleasure. Times, might even be numbed to. Because mental focus is on what has been promised, and halo of joy, anticipation brings. But alas, therein lies Acorn sown. That will grow into mighty Oak of disappointment. Creating ill will and vexed accusation of deception, this act of treachery motivates. Sword of retaliation is unsheathed. Male now sated, lies with soft Dick and hard heart in after rapture. Female, gently reminds him of promises made. Asks when, how can they proceed to fulfillment. Sometimes, he stares at the woman in disbelief. Adds insult to injury by asking. *"What you talking about?"* Girlfriend thinks, woman is to be blamed, literally taken for a ride. Sums up what should be, woman's modus operandi in every such situation. Man crawls in from desert. Ogles oasis with yearning, offers gold in pouch, for having his fill. She takes his pouch, counts nuggets then lets him slake his thirst. Any other way, he will drink his fill, then say water was brackish. Not worth the sand he crawled in from. With her, it's pay then pump, as at a gas station. Whatever he will promise after, let him bring to table before. One organ is soft, other will be hard. Maybe, I did not make it clear. She's talking about, boyfriend girlfriend situation. Where promises of birthday gifts, rent, utility bills assist and shopping in general. I will tell you, she is One of her kind, an intimidating woman. Ready to bruise any man who crosses her path, without yielding to her rules and respecting her edicts. But I love her without reservation. I have done for her and not to her. One of my nearest and dearest female friends, without there being a reason. *Want to read more about her?. Book three "The Lucky Bastard." A Customs Officer, a Cop and Me.*

Lure of America-28

Neil Diamond sings about it. People from every corner of the globe. Coming to America. It's centuries old lure that promises a good life. Free from poverty, persecution, repression and untold ills of our world. There are them that's got devious motives to pillage, maim and destroy.Wreak havoc and mayhem on our society. They misguidedly see as source of their tribulations and woes. I will focus on them, that come in peace with good intent. Quite often we are informed of disasters at sea, through various media outlets. Would be immigrants, risking safety. Clamber aboard overloaded vessels and end up stranded at sea. Worse yet at times, numerous lives are lost. We see stragglers, barely making it to land. Other than that, it's facet of life in passing. I firmly believe, no matter level of hardship, persecution or inhumane suffering someone is subjected to. There should be a process to seeking and granting asylum. Failing which, how then do we identify and separate wolves in sheep's clothing?

It's like going to ball game. After paying hundreds, rumour says it's sometimes more, for a ticket. Patrons are searched and sometimes. Denied entry, outside the arena instead of inside. Let's have barriers declaring, Buck stops here. Sonny Matthews had such sign in his home, for attention of teen male visitors. *"The Buck stops here, Doe goes upstairs alone."* Meant to educate daughters' friends, without acerbic language, for which he was infamous. Having thrown in my two cents on that vexing debate. I would like to bring to fore, existence of an underground crime spree. Extent of and wealth generated is unknown. As are victims of, because some get demised. Those who don't, will not talk either. Focused instead on hope, there is a way to fit in. These are they who come and enter legally, but eventually stay, illegally. Janet in mid forties, was housekeeper to Sanchez family. When fourteen year old Sanchez deciphered and accessed daddy's porn channel. Boy took liberties with her. Provoked beyond tolerance, she called him, little pissing tailed puppy, not yet ready to mount a Bitch. Even if he was, that Bitch would not be her. She did not come to America with sanded feet. Unwisely, alluding without evidence. His parents being Cubans, likely did. Having said her piece, told Sanchez Snr. She was leaving his employ and gave reason why. Sanchez smacked Sanchez, begged Janet stay. Took on role as Shadshan, found her a match. Marriage ran it's course. She filed for three children, bought a house and was honourably adopted by Sanchez family. She cared for pissing tailed puppy's children and those of his siblings, in turn. Now all's well that ends well, paradise gained. I will aver, this is not isolated, happy ending tale. There are numerous stories with similar ending, they are guarded secrets.Cheers. If only this could be rule, rather than fortunate exception.

Racquel, at fifteen, was an adorably elegant and pretty child. Sunday school were taking those who could afford, on Florida theme park trip. Long before Racquel was born, mom Giselle and Justin were high school sweethearts. He joined parents in England, they migrated to the US. Where he ended up doing a stretch in prison. Now on supervised release, he told schoolmate and former sweetheart. Her daughter could spend time with him and his wife. He would arrange taking her to see her father, upstate. Giselle's siblings and parents did not approve of this plan. Neither Racquel or Justin knew each other. Never met, were complete strangers.What with Justin having served time. No one knew what character he had developed, since early teen when he migrated to England. In all this, it was conveniently forgotten. Racquel's father, once bright and upcoming army officer, was in US prison, after caught trafficking. Oh, lure was on. Racquel saw herself all aglow in land of opportunity. Had silently vowed, not to return from her trip. If only she could find a perch. Giselle read her daughter's thoughts. Sat her down and reminded her. If she went awol, action would bring embarrassment and shame to mom. Her being, church deacon. We know, most people are selfish and Racquel was no different from you or I. Soon she was in house in Maryland, but not at home. She says, Justin was trying to get with her. But would not make too loud a noise about it. Having been told, she would be detained in juvenile hall and sent home, pronto. Maybe, she could survive like a candle in the wind. Year later, an uncle visited a woman. Whom he was paying, large dowry to marry. Giselle asked her brother to check on his niece, see how Racquel was getting on. She had been sending money to mom frequently. Said she had found steady employment and doing well, financially. Uncle was going to New York and in any event. His suitor did not want any visitor coming to her home.

Man, woman child, otherwise. She was in very cantankerous mood, as uncle came up short with agreed dowry funds. She wanted that money, to facilitate house down payment. His coming up short was unacceptable. Having his own troubles, he could not pay attention to his niece's. What with her being in another state. His not having means getting to her. We come now, to holy conundrum and tragedy surrounding these individuals. Caught up in chase of "Coming to America" lure. Uncle goes home, to beg, steal, or borrow. Trying to keep his wedding date. His woman, citing urgency of situation. Finds and marries another dude, without money issues. Tells uncle to cool his heels, but does not refund. In seven years, she will be able to make him the One. Racquel went to see her father. Only to find, he had been transferred to another facility in another state. Boyfriend did not understand need to, or meaning of marriage. Was comfortable, having trophy sweetheart by his side. Took her places, was energized by adulation and envious stares of other men. How he adored and fawned on her. She was living life on edge. Yearned for legitimacy, marriage brings. Met another young man. Who wanted to marry and take her to his parents in California. They owned large orchards acreage. Took her supermarket shopping. Urged, she sample fruits of the vine. When she did and showed satisfaction. Then did he grin and tell her. *"Grapes from daddy's vineyards."* You know folks, if it weren't tragic, it would be hilarious. Games people play on others and they succumb. But when you look to the lure, the lore will get to you. It's been said, but not confirmed. Justin was in some cahoots with Racquel's boyfriend. Week of her eighteenth birthday arrived, she began packing personal items. This was conveyed to boyfriend. Who then asked Racquel reason for, and she denied the activity. She was still on board with their planned celebration, but suspicion had been aroused. Early night before he arrived, she put effects in a taxi and left for destination unknown. Was followed to rendezvous where she transferred to another vehicle. Obviously waiting for someone. Probably ye whose elders, grew fruits in vineyards afar. There was confrontation, baseball bats were swung and when hurt proved unbearable. Someone decided to end misery. A gun was introduced. We know, when this happens. It's time for fight or flight. Both options having their own peril. Flight ended in vehicle's crash, and participant's hospitalization. Uncertainty arose in murky aftermath. Some say, Racquel was at some point. Victim of gunshot wound, in addition to injuries suffered in crash. She was only One of conflicted trio. Put on life support. Seems if you are illegal alien, without resourceful person taking responsibility for your keep and care? There's no confirmation, but inference is rife. Exposes the lie *"All you need is love."*Next, we look at Lettie Burroughs.

Century Investment's head office executive. She was being groomed to manage next branch office. Silently ran informal higglering, specializing in computer and data processing equipment. Had access to buyers in finance and banking industry. Built exclusivity, supplying software and hardware components, relative to their operational requirements. On inside track, made huge profits and dressed ostentatiously. Threw lavish parties for clients, was a name on who's who list. Within her circle, of course. If and when, promised promotion managing new branch became reality. She would be elevated to another circle. Society is like that, ever limiting One's ascendancy. Sometimes you top one circle, yet not count for rat dung in next circle. Why is that so? You now can understand why. I am happy, being my own circle. Usually, there's got to be leaks, on things about to happen.

But again, this might not reach your ears. Depends on which circle you are in. Not only did new branch not open. Existing and head office, were closed by government regulators. Citing, management's malfeasance. Some said, it was political reprisal gone amok. You might be tempted to grin, but please don't. CID personnel pored over paperwork and records. Anxious taking managers in custody. Oh, CID? That's Criminal Investigation Division. Later it became CIB, changed from Division to Branch. When you're part of a circle. Thoughts of going to jail brings acute attack of ague, loose bowels and high fever, all at once. Remember, I went to jail? Never experienced any of these maladies, because I am my own circle. The very thought of Lettie's name being seen in newspapers, or read on airwaves. Propelled her to act without delay, fleeing to the US. She had a bank account with Barnett. There were uncollected monies due from corporate clients. Her apartment and artistic furnishings, wardrobe and motor car, all left behind. She stayed at Day's Inn, US441. Such rapid life transformation would drive less fortified person crazy. Not Lettie, she was bulwark facing adversity. Monitored events back home, by rumours and telephone. Spent more on phone cards daily, than she did for rent. Notice how WhatsApp chat made those redundant? For once, consumers got unexpected relief. Soon, Lettie met up with Dalton. His father ran driving school, where she learned to drive stick. Told her, he was Miami Herald, and Sun Sentinel delivery contractor. From whom vendors got newspapers. He could bring her aboard, but she had to have a car. Unable to take a route, she donned trousers at midnight. Went with Dalton, loading box truck with newspapers. Dropping off to vendors before daylight. Bet you never knew, there are people who sweat dripping, in cool of night. But as sometimes happens, there's a reward. Trust you figured, she's now living with Dalton. In case you didn't, she is. He introduced her to a young man. Willing to do business marriage for $20,000. Seeing she was friend of Dalton, he would do $19,500. They agreed on $500 a month. Total would have to be paid, before walking the aisle. I'm sure you can smell rat here, because that's over three years paying. If all goes well, getting married is one small step. Being considered and approved for green card is major hurdle. She lives with Dalton as sweetheart, but his friend wants in on intimacy action. A feud begins, relationships are strained. She chooses side, goes with he who holds key to her future. Years go by, during which they do get married. More years go by, nothing happens with immigration. At loss, trying to understand why no effort has been made, seeing a lawyer. Finds someone, who can check status of her application. Search comes up empty. She is encouraged to snoop, try finding his SSN. Months later, the terrible truth. *"He cannot file for you, he only has a green card. Does not have citizenship."* She stared in disbelief for a long time, before weeping eyes dry. Confronting her husband with truth. Said he would return his half of money. Soon as he got tax refund next filing season. Other half, she would have to get from Dalton. It goes without being said, she is a strong woman in many ways. Picks herself up, dusts herself off and gets ready to start all over again. Guess, One cannot rise unless they first fall. Bounce, meaning so much. How she came to know Fernando, remains a mystery. Oddity here is, she doesn't speak Spanish, nor he, English. He has three children. Eldest is a boy ten years old, liaises between adults. Very interesting state of affairs for certain. Two girls, eight and seven, completes his family which Lettie is brought in to care for. Fernando is a short haul trucker, occasionally away from home overnight. It is safe to assume, ten year old played no role in his dad's and Lettie's relationship, taking on intimacy. Shortly after, Fernando declared willingness to marry her. She sang hallelujah, not knowing it was premature. It is not known, if this was love infused or to facilitate status change. Once more, she's in comfortable place, looking at happy future. Kinfolk descended as locust on mature crops. No way they're going to let strange woman. (Some weren't averse to shouting,Nigga) Just march on in, take everything Fernando's wife left for her children. He called them in council, explained having spoken to attorney on the matter. Was advised to draft agreement, excluding her from access to assets held, prior to marriage. Some relented opposition, haters' chorus drowned dialogue. One in-law demanded housekeeping position, at inflated stipend, and her opposition would end. Fernando, having eaten of the apple and savoured it's flavour. Was loath, all good feast should come to an end. Very quickly, it did. Lettie is once again on the move. Spirit broken, much slower and careful than before. These pages might not reflect, but lots of years has passed between first effort to qualify for permanent residency and present. Anyone can tell she is drained, physically and mentally. I said earlier, she is one strong woman. There are men and women who, subjected to kind of ordeal she has been. Would go insane, abandon hope and go under the overpass. But not our Lettie. She seeks solace in church. A mature woman who takes care of, preens herself and appearance. Pastor suggests, she brings husband or life partner to worship. He can see she needs strong emotional support. Oh! them wily parsons, their antennae picks up distress. Like sharks picks up drop of blood in an ocean. Lettie confirms, what he done suspects.There is no husband and no life partner. What she has, are stripes around her shoulders and emotional chains around her feet. Parson tells her, church will not cause her to fall. With prayer and faith, he will help her on her feet. Every now and then, might accrue to her advantage if she got on her back. We know parson is married, but sister Lettie has salaried position with church. There's not anything that can be said about parson's wife. There's limit to fiction. Suffice it to say, Lettie is now a happy woman. Having found her blue haven in church. Hopefully, on way to heaven. She travels quite frequently with parson, on church business in the US. Next time you see a person. Or maybe a co-worker, whom you can identify was not born in the USA as you were. Think on whether or not, they have a survival story and what it would be. Reflect on how many, have been duped by their own people, fleeced of moneys. Yet, none sought help of law enforcement. Some paid that ultimate sacrifice, there was no investigation. Because authorities would not know where to begin. They exist in shadows, between light and dark. Kind of what Rod Serling calls "The Twilight Zone" When they fade into darkness, no One misses them. Therefore no One searches for them. Someone, somewhere, grieves not knowing their fate. It is essence of lure's irresistible magnetic pull, and promise of a better life. Alas, tradewinds of our times, are blowing changes o'er this land of immigrants. Some good, others not....but? We have heard tales of One that got away. I'll tell you about One that didn't make it.

Twin Figueroa boys, Rory and Cory were friends of Nick Dennis. All three attending same all-age school, players on cricket team. They also traded expertise, breeding doves, pigeons, rabbits, Guinea Pigs and tropical fish that they sold. Between them, there was thriving cottage industry going. Truth whispered, Dennis and Figueroa tribes had historic unsavoury reputations in their village. Of which, folks feared discussing among themselves. Three purposed, inseparable boys. Folks dubbed, "Three Musketeers" Others, grudgingly claimed. Dennis' boy was Barabbas reincarnated. Twins were infamous biblical thieves, crucified beside Christ. Minor neighbourhood crimes and reprisal vandalism unfolding, was covertly ascribed to Barabbas and two thieves in whispers. Care taken to not make unfounded accusation and start an ado. If the DC came interviewing any of the trio, regarding neighbour's report. Window panes got pelted with pebbles, dog's legs got broken and kids were sometimes intimidated. Twins' mother gave up waiting on their father, who migrated years earlier, then abruptly ceased communicating.There was in the wings, secret suitor Joel Collins, whom she married. Creating buzz among guests, some of whom weren't invited. ***"Me did know bout them long time. Who them think them fooling?"*** Good citizens averred, first daughter Cindy, was born of too short gestation period. Hence, was rumour of dilly dallying confirmed. She went on having two more daughters, and in time, Nick took shine to Cindy. You see folks, Dennis senior reared goats and hogs. On slaughter weekends it was Cindy, like Tzeitel. Who was sent to collect mom's purchases. Both their ages made thirty years, and Nick was four years older. Saturdays when stepbrothers went cricket practice, she trudged along. Just to be close to Nick, both denied fact of. Imagine an open dusty field. Teenaged boys of shapes and sizes, egging team members on. Yelling game strategy, and among this furor is thirteen year old Cindy, wishing she had more hands. Gathers skirt folds and tucks firmly between thighs. Then quickly tries restraining hair, billowing on gusty wind floes. Whilst shielding eyes from airborne dust sand particles. When wind wins battle with skirt, hoisting it aloft momentarily. Brief glimpse brings wide grins and sharp exchange of pleasured glances. Unspoken question is. *"You see that?."* Some argue, this was deliberate distracting ruse, redounding to brother's excelling at game. Others quickly discounted this, saying, neither were that smart. Although romantic liaison was denied by both. At sixteen, Cindy gave birth and went to live with Nick's parent. Mrs. Collins having decreed. Cindy was sheep finding hole, other daughters were bound to follow. Dennis' shelter was only temporary. Man of the house, did not embrace invitation by his woman. Teen parents and baby moved to their own love nest. Nick made it known, to those who kept asking about their wedding. He would, when Cindy gave him son. Despite initial stridency, Ma Collins did take custody of first grandchild. Cindy could resume school. Hopefully pass exams and be equipped to face life. After child three, she sought preacher's advice, who told her. She was enabling slackness, Bible speaks unto these things as unworthy Christian behaviour. Dennis' again came to rescue, taking in fourth and fifth girl, born to Cindy and Nick. Didn't want any Dennis seed, boxing bout on street like dry grass on wind. Threatened his son. ***"Take it from me, as God make Moses. If that girl breed again. I going find way castarate*** (castrate) ***and turn you into Barrow."*** (castrated male swine). Now watch things quickly go bad to worse. Cindy and Nick are now in early and mid thirties. Both have steady jobs at nearby WalMart, life is good. First daughter Averil, is now living with parents. Schoolmate Ouida Jones, comes home with her some evenings, collaborating on projects. Unknown to anyone, except Ouida and father Marcus, who is lividly irate, she's pregnant. He begins shifting wardrobe and probing behind. She knows what's kept behind and flees to Averil's house. Her parents are yet to come home. Cindy stopped at her mother to see her daughters. Nick's at his dad for similar reason. Routine every weekend by rote. Not wanting girls to forget who're their parents. Nick nears his gate, scanning area as is his wont. Sees someone lurking deceptively, between concrete pole and fence. He sits tight for five minutes, decides making a circle. Senses aura of discomfort. As he begins accelerating, man steps out in his path, causing him to brake. Man comes up to his window. Signals him to roll the window down. Nick takes in, hands hidden behind man's back. Whom he now recognizes and greets. ***"Rawtid! Pa Jones. Is you that playing Hawaii Five-O stakeout?"*** Pa Jones replies. **"Yes is me, wind down the window little more. Me want talk to you."** Nick smells vitriol exuding, sees blazing hate in widely staring eyes. Cautiously begins window roll. Then, hand held in back comes round and Nick glimpses object. He accelerates, object smashes into and shatters car's rear windshield. He U-turns into side street and calls 119, describing the incident. Having clear view of Marcus Jones. Tells despatcher. he's headed to Racetrack station with something in his hand. Patrol cars converge on scene. Service station clerk tells cops, someone is hiding in dumpster. Marcus and his machete are taken off to jail and as story unfolds. Nick is sex offender, hiding from law and citizens, riled in disbelief. How could a grown man breed his daughter's schoolmate, who is practically same age as her. Marcus gets bailed and fervently prays he ends up in prison with Nick. So he can do to him what he done to his daughter, before slowly killing him. After that he will run like Jackrabbit to the chair or whatever method, state decides to demise him by. Well, Ouida did have Nick's son, he desperately tried for. Now he's awol. No One who knows, will say where. Life plays games such as these. This tale now segues into chapter's theme. Cindy, Rory and Cory went to embassy for visitor's visa. One was granted, others denied, but this was not a problem. Being in era before scientific biometric authentication. Both young men travelled on same passport. One went up cliff side, passed rope back down for other. You see folks, rope is sent down by courier and, for a fee is certified "landed" So it can again go up the cliff face. See? As Buddy Clark sang on RCA Victor records, backed by Wayne King's orchestra "Time was" when things were done that can't be done today. To avoid scrutiny, one brother favoured Idlewild. Other, Newark International. Giving timeline of events. By whatever means available, both brothers are now US citizens. Living good life in these United States. Barrels of goodies and Western Union remittances, bolster life's pleasures back home. Sister Cindy, would love to experience what she's seen on television, and heard stepbrothers rave about. New furniture, trappings of good life. Photos of cars on driveway, and in garage of fabulous home. Comes with pennies down, rest on credit and eternity to pay. Numerous attempts, she just can't land a visa. Despite going lengths, borrowing to bolster her bank balance. Interviewer asked if she won monies, as statement entries did not indicate timely savings. Plan was hatched and set in motion. Essence of which was, her adopting someone elses identity. It's been said, no One can claim absolute sanity, because the mind was not designed to support such a state. Reason being, we look at things arising and conclude. Based on mental dictates, that do not always meet basic parameters of sanity. To illustrate. We have at times, questioned decisions or utterances made. With the rider. "What was I thinking." Someone else would reply. "You weren't" So now, Cindy's mental fortitude is being put to test. Extent of which, she is not aware. She flies to Canada and settles in with friends, awaiting Rory's arrival. Who is going to take her traipsing cross border. To taste good existence that is the United States of America. It's a long drive, he asks Jack Poe and Herbie Dean to come with him. Taking turns at the wheel. These two know only, Rory is going to see his sister. They are not aware she is coming back with them, and asks no questions. Time and money is of essence, so three men book into a motel. Rory gives Cindy identity papers, she needs to study and be fluent with. Tells her ***"Me going call you when you in deepest sleep. You haffi recite everything without hitch, or else me just go back and leave you."*** She confidently assured, she would be ready and up to the task. Pshaw, this is no big deal. Cindy doesn't know, how fickle a brain can be. Moreso, when suddenly taken down unfamiliar paths. It sometimes gets befuddled and self destructs, in order to protect itself. Turtles and Possums have similar brain reflexes when alarmed. One recedes into it's shell, other rolls over, plays dead. Makes sense? No? Deceptive art, comes with practice and rehearsal. I'll tell you experience at seventeen. Went for driver's exam certification. Test comprised, identifying numerous road signs. Vehicle parts and functions. Reciting random road codes, and firing orders of four, six and eight cylinder internal combustion engines. Next came yard and road tests. Yard test was, parallel parking by reverse on driver's and blind sides. Don't get white wash on your tires, that's a fail. Next came dreaded, hill start. There was a steep two sided ramp. Driver stopped at foot of. Started vehicle, drove halfway up ramp and stopped. Switched off vehicle, applied hand brake and awaited examiner's instructions. He would tell you, start and go forward without rolling back, fraction of an inch. You drove and stopped end of other side. Then reversed half way up. Stop, start again and reverse over ramp crest to starting point. It was all about ability to effectively manipulate the clutch. Times, examiner showed you Benrus watch, and told you.

He's putting it behind the wheel. If you ran it over, you will not only be failed. But also have to pay, and you believed. Anxiety levels heightened with fear of crushing expensive timepiece, you knew you could not pay for. Unfair. Test finished, tension went. Breathed relief and went inside, relaxed to await road test. Examiner left for the day, unknown to me. Name was called by another examiner. Told him I already done yard test. He said there was no notation to support. Let's do this or lose your turn. Second time around, I aced parking but failed hill starts. Unable to control feet ague. Brain was not cooperating repeat stress in such quick time spans. Cindy left no doubt, she was mentally ready to successfully carry out this escapade. They went to a fair, had fun to dismiss tensions, before setting out for border post. Next in line, Rory made one last probe. *"Wha you name?"* **"Loretta Jackson."** Cindy confidently shot back as they rolled up, and was cordially greeted by border personnel.

You know these people are trained to kill with nice. While probing, with searching eyes. Ears that listen for tension in your voice, as you hesitate or lie. And oh, that relentless stare.Young man, about twenty-six with vivid blue eyes and broad smile. Took papers or cards inside, soon came back grinning. *"It is my pleasure, welcoming you back to the United States. Mr.?"* He stares askance, waits to hear a name, before handing over identification. Repeats to three men, and now it's Cindy's turn. He goes on. *"Hope you enjoyed your stay. Special welcome to you also. Miss? I am sorry. Is it Miss or Mrs.?"* Cindy is silent, he asks. *"Maam, please tell me your name and if it's, Miss or…?"* Cindy is silent, as she covers her face with both hands and ponders. He is gently hammering. *"What's your name, mam, and are you…?"* She throws in the towel, abjectly defeated. **"Me name, Miss Cindy Collins."** *"Is that so. Then who put you up to this?"*

She had no problem throwing Rory under the proverbial bus as she blurted. **"Is him sir, me brother."** All four were detained and questioned. When it was all said and done….. Yes folks, that's it. Says it right there. It was all said and done. Remember now, this is fiction and there are limits before fiction takes on cloak of fact.

Chow line kerfuffle-29

Back in the day, when sweepstake promotion was conducted at Knutsford Park. Advertising slogan, went. *"If you haven't got a ticket you haven't got a chance."* We know stark truth is, even holding numerous tickets. We still don't have a chance. I mean, look at the odds. But let's stay with the ticket scenario and One's chances, see where it leads. Who knows, horror of horrors. One could end up in the hoosegow. I decided to take a gander at a bit of rib for a change. What with cholesterol fears and all that. Had been a while since I had me a bit of pig. Seasoned and jerked in underground pit, but will settle for lesser fare. Getting to the door, there's lad of about seventeen. Peering through the glass, yet not attempting entry. You've heard of one eyed cat, peeping in seafood store? Misery, is sometimes of our own making. Lad yields to me, I open the door and beckons him proceed ahead. Let's call him, Willy. He deserves an alias. Willy enters and heads to condiment stand. Pumping sauce into cups, getting diced onions and all that. Tell myself there's someone ordering. He's waiting to hook up with that person. It's not as if I'm sold on watching him, or anything like that. But, the guy walks in. I expect him to be ahead of me in line. Hence, my interest in his……You understand what I'm saying? I order and step aside. He's standing aside, man in waiting among other men, ladies too. Although there was no "Lady In Waiting" present. Child bearing isn't as prevalent as it used to be. Now, you know how staff are hustling. Comes to counter, calls a number twice, moves on to another meal. Two dudes ordered before I walked in, are now standing aside, chatting. You know those guys, whose arms fill out their short shirt's sleeves and then some? Both got big irons on their hips. There's no uniform to identify them. I am almost certain they are LEO's. You do know that means law enforcement officer. I'm telling y'all, I needs start walking with camera team to capture certain unfolding events. From beginning, to thrilling finish. In old country, it was called "Man in the street" English, or should I say, British? Broadcaster went street roaming on weekdays. Randomly interviewing citizens on hot topics of the day or choice. Skatalites celebrated the team with tune similarly titled. Server calls number, let's say 586. There's no immediate response. She again calls 586 then does a Spanish call also. Two things happen within seconds of each other. Willy the kid, steps forward in response to second call for 586. As he is being handed one bag, another bag and it seems there's something else, server is reaching for. LEO1 steps up and asks server. *"You called 586?"* She says. *"Yes, but it's not for you. It's for him. You sure you have 586?"* LEO1 rummages here and there. Shows her his ticket, then says to Willy with a smile. *"Excuse me, can I see your ticket?"* Here's chink in this honour system. When number is called, food is given to anyone claiming. There's no attempt to verify, that person actually has a ticket. I would think, food should be exchanged for ticket. Willy studied and decided to exploit. He fumbles and tries handing what food he already collected to LEO1. Server huddles with cashier, trying to resolve situation. Totally unaware of interaction tween Willy and LEO1. They're likely trying to see if they messed up somehow. From where I am standing, it looks like we are going to need a bucket and mop. Willy the kid is sweating bullets. Thinking real ones could be headed his way. Any second now, there's gonna be a puddle on floor. Or heaven forbid, a mound. Well, we hope not. If he's as empty as he appears hungry. The drama is underway. Willy is now surrounded by LEO's 1 and 2. Both browbeat stares at Willy with bone chilling intensity. LEO1 asks him again, sans the smile. *"Sir, can I see your ticket."* Willy manages a quivering mouse's squeak. **"It's okay."** Tries sidling away. LEO1 says. *"What? You're really taking someone's order, without having an order of your own? Come here."* Marches him outside, stands him against the wall. Everyone can see, there's hard interrogation going on. Meantime, LEO2 collects all food and joins his partner. Willy the kid gyrates his head, pointing all directions. Like Aye-Aye in it's legendary death pointing. Customers inside are wondering what happened. Those nearby with dibs on first hand knowledge, like myself, are whispering eyewitness facts to those who will listen.

You know when all is said and done, everyone will leave with different version of events. After five minutes, all three comes back in. LEOs are no doubt angry, but for sure they are also hungry. This can only redound to Willy the kid's salvation. LEO1 tells Willy. *"Go on, stand right there behind that customer."* Customer looks around, steps aside, yields to Willy. Two more customers also yield. Willy is at counter, seems lost and frightened. LEO1 tells him. *"Go ahead, order what you want."* Willy, still shaking and out of composure. Looks nervously at LEO1, who repeats. *"Go ahead!! Whatever you want up there. Get it."* Willy orders, cashier asks him. *"That's it?"* He looks at LEO1, who tells him. *"Get yourself a drink also! Come on! There's people waiting behind you."* Can you imagine kindness being spoken in such a way, it sounds threatening? LEO2 steps forward, pays and turns to walk away. Says to Willy before leaving. *"You remember what I told you? Believe me, I wasn't kidding."* Now you see people overwhelmed by curiosity. They walk in the door, catches tail end of events. They stare at faces, asking unspoken question. *"What's going on."* You see, they want to know. If something is in progress, where they should run for their lives or? Eventually they figure, if everyone's waiting for food. Fire already doused, or holdup man long gone. Can you hear them relating to family or friend? *"I don't know what it is, but something was going on at the Nyam and Scram this afternoon."* Then that person rejoins. *"Maybe we'll see it on the news later."* And they settle in and await the revelation. Willy the kid did not have a ticket. But he got a chance not going to jail. I guarantee, if LEOs weren't hungry. They'd have made certain, Willy the kid got to Turner Guilford Knight Centre. In time to join day's chow line. Willy got reprieved, went home with a full gut and whatever was LEOs charge to him. This was reinforced by reminding Willy, he was not kidding. More you assess the incident, you have to ask yourself. What got into Willy's head, why he thought he could successfully pull off the stunt? Had he successfully done this before? Could it be hunger pangs unbearable and making him lose touch with reality? Did he watch them order and go outside or was he just stupid? See what I'm talking about folks? People at play, games they get up to. Unaware of, ignoring perils. Simplest mind will bring to One's attention, which we ignore and press on. Because we are smarter than sixth sense, or don't care. It's part of our daily survival.

Two Gun Kid saga-30

Now I know, your curiosity done been piqued about Jessica and me. So I have to tell entire event. Mulgravie was front room tenant of old lady Irene Detective of police, specialized in crime scene investigations and relevant photography. Back then we didn't say "crime scene photographer." Landlady's niece was getting married. She knew there was a thing going on between young woman and myself. Might even have hoped, I would be prospective groom. Treating me as family friend and all that. Did covertly call me into her quarters once and scared hell out of me. Retrieved and handed me an old, ugly, heavy revolver. It was her husband's service revolver. After his death, more than twenty years prior. Authorities never came in quest of weapon, or anything. She just had it in her wardrobe among his clothes, that she never discarded either. They smelled musty, as if he was in there too. Took the gun, drove to our police station. Went in and told officer on duty, I found a gun. Would he come and get it from the car. He said I should go for and bring it, which I told him. **"Oh no, sir. Someone come get it, or else I throw it away."** You know this story could have been written differently or not at all. After back and forth dialogue, he came and took hold of the gun. Then I had to give statement as to where I found it. You recall my thing about lying. Fearing I would trap myself if I began fabricating, upped and told him truth. Earnestly added, he could come interview old lady Irene at his convenience. She's always home. No One ever came. Old lady Irene corralled me under Bombay mango tree. Sought my help, stick picking fruits which she then sold me. Fruit trees, she explained. Was means paying property taxes and dared tenants to reap. Usually I washed and chilled mangoes.

Took out seed and filled space with ice cream. Yummy delight. Discussing things as they are set to be. She said, niece's Beau not working, never has. Always been walkabout, unskilled idler. She's at loss to understand, how and why they're getting married. Began itemizing wedding expenses for this and that, including photographer. I dared suggest, they tap Mulgravie for services. She looked at me with fierce eyes. *"Say what?! You know, is dead people him photo?"* She recoiled in indignation. **"No, not really. Him take car accident, house fire and so on."** I replied. *"Only car accident and fire, what have dead people. If nobody don't dead, what him would need do photo for? But you right after all. Because them getting married, is worse than accident. Maybe, you know what you talking bout. Them not coming here to live, hope him best know that. Mash up you little dolly house, eh? Maybe not. If anybody can walla in rain and still dry like duck, is you. Massa you too nuff."*(plenty) I told you, them old folks see a lot.

We come to Sunday June 8th, 1969 and Jessica from down the road. Young, buxom, attractive woman about nineteen. Type, Jamaicans call "Browning" Seen her talking to Mulgravie at the fence, few times once before. Saw that? Paid no significance to. This was a bleak night, after ten and soon a light drizzle began. Simultaneous with low rumbling thunder, a determined rattling of the iron gate. I looked out, saw a person standing. Went out, and Jessica asked if Mulgravie was home. Told her, if the Anglia was not round the side. Then, he was clearly not home. She hesitated, then asked if she could come in, from fast intensifying rain. I gladly said **"Sure, hurry."** Hugged her, we came in. My one room, was cramped. Groceries were kept on my new Zenith stereogram. She looked at and asked. *"What you doing with so much milk?"* I did not reply. Asked another question. *"Why you* *smiling and rubbing you hands. Like how cockroach rub him feelers? Don't get no fancy ideas."* Gave her a Cham. Babycham, that is. We began talking as she sipped. Brought her another one, seeing her draining the first. She declined, gave me a wary stare and said. *"No, you can have that one. You look like you up to something. If rain never come down, I would gone to mi yawd long time."* One thing led to another. We got a little, free-for-all shebang going, after which we fell asleep. Awoke to eerie quiet, rain having stopped. Shook her awake, told her she had to go home. She said, it was too late. Her sister probably locked their door. Promised I would walk with her, she had to go before my girlfriend got home. Scowling, she reluctantly slid off the bed. Mouth in a pout, lips tightly pursed and eyes squinted in anger. She got dressed in semidarkness. I did too, and sat waiting. She walked by me, paused at the door. Turned and said. *"Since me can't stay with you. You haffi pay me for my pussy."* I laughed, whilst reaching for the pull cord. Turned black light bulb on. Her face looked evil in purple, as I said. **"You must be mad. You think is so pay for play co.."** I stopped cold and stared, slack jawed. In less than an eye's wink, she made a slight stoop and came up. I was staring at, two long, thin, stiletto type knives. We called them, "Toothpicks" **"How much?"** I quickly asked. She named her price. *"Two pound."* A brief pause. *"And I want two tin of you condensed milk too."* I cannot put into words, many emotions including fear that engulfed me briefly, then recurred. Had me disbelieving every moment of this night, except sword play. Opened a sash window, yelled **"Two gun kid"** Making for better ending. Next, we come to little Jeanie, not yet seventeen. If you could ever read, smidgen of what's not been said about Jeanie. It would pale to nothingness, compared to what's being said. Actually, it has been said. You just can't make connection, and nobody wants it made. Jeanie and I, had a secret open, no secrets relationship. She would tell me, for instance. Next Tuesday after secretarial college. She's going to matinee at Ward Theatre, with this fellow she met. I would tell her, okay. Once, she even told me. Guy she met, invited her to day on the beach. Asked, I buy appropriate bathing suit and cap. *"I know you don't want me wearing in public, skimpy two piece I have. That's for when we at our private beach."* She teased. Now, mutual trust is funny. I looked at my girlfriend and knew. She would never get into an intimate situation with another man. Told myself, it just was not her. In that regard, I never showed jealous curiosity, or questioned her, about what went on, when she went out with anyone. Even in absence of my saying I was going anywhere, she grilled me on what I did. Where I went and with whom. I always had to ask. Why can't she reciprocate my trust. Give me benefit I gave. Her response was. *"Because, you name, man."* So there we were, happy together in trust and mistrust. There are things, some men don't pay attention to, and it again shows. Profound, inherent female skills, when compared to males. Not by training or experience, just darned INHERENCY.

Weekend after my stiletto experience, Jeanie is in the house lolling about. Fan oscillates, blowing hot air. So, we both get comfortable in skivvies, that suits me fine. I'm singing that Otis Redding song "Look at that Girl" Grateful, nature creates shortcut to paradise. I lie across the bed, gently massaging, cooing sweet somethings, anticipating. She seems distracted, but we are softly gabbing. Suddenly props herself on an elbow, stares at me with knitted brows and says. *"You bed smell of woman and is not me. Who she?"* Second time the week, I dare say to a woman. **"You must be mad. What**

you talking bout smelling woman in the bed?" Young woman went viral. *"Don't!! Ever, tell me, I am mad. I will show you mad. And you'll never forget."* I hugged and tried to calm her. She shoved me hard, told me. *"I want to hear bout the woman that was in this bed, or else we through."* **"It's not what you thinking."** I lamely said. *"Okay, if it's not what I am thinking. Then tell me what it is. First of all. Where were you, when she was in the bed?"* Notice how she already brought me admitting a woman was in the bed? Can't back pedal on that one. I stared at her, not saying anything. Henry told his son. *"Think fast and talk slow, when in situations such as this."* His exact words were. *"When stopped by police at dead of night. If you can think fast and talk slow, you might not go to jail."* When you love a woman and she's about to walk out of your life. Because she caught you with your pants down. Brain deserts you, and takes flight. Mocks you with exit script. *"You on you own, bwoy."* Thinking becomes redundant. So what do you do? You know you have to come clean. Makes last ditch try with a bit of subterfuge. Began. **"Jeanie, you know we love each other and I…."** *"You love the woman who was in you bed too?"* She's verbally stabbing, relentless with furied eyes. Resolve bleeds, you hesitate, hoping to contain haemorrhage. What's the biggest, boldfaced lie a woman will tell a man? *"Tell me the truth, don't leave out anything. Promise, I won't hold it against you. But it better be the truth."* Said my Jeanie and I spilled the beans. She listened in silence. *"You used protection?"* Was all she asked. Seeing her getting dressed, grooming hair and preparing to leave. I said, I thought she came for weekend. Going home Sundays, as accustomed. *"I didn't tell Nana I was going to stay out. And if you think, I was going to ever lie on that bed again. I don't have to ask* *the question. I can tell you without a doubt. You are dam mad."* Ends with cackling laugh.The rest you know. Having come in on the end before going to start. When a man loves a woman, it's never easy to accept the end, just like that. He tells himself. *"Give her a few days and try soft soaping her. Invite her to a movie. Get a mutual friend to intercede."* After numerous approaches and countless rejections. It begins to sink in, there's no redemption. Especially if she flaunts another suitor. Granny had an adage. *"Johncrow see dead dawg and well want go down. Little wind puff pass, him say that's what throw him down."* Some women go through this charade, solely to inflict punishment. Intending to bury the hatchet soon, and take up where they left off. Usually with a warning. Anything like this happens again, she's through for good. This change of heart, would not work with me, once I've been put through the wringer. There are two options open, and known to me only. First is to say, thanks but no thanks. I am cured and inured. Or I can say, yes. And go along for selfish reasons. Then calls it quits, when she's in deep, and tells her. "Payback" So, you say that's cruel? It's risk One takes in game of love. Man or woman, boy or girl when playing in love relationship, dating league. Humans are endowed with latent schism, which promotes retaliation against each other. Justifying phrase "Cutting off nose to spite face." We suffer in narcissistic solace, knowing other person endures misery at our making, possibly more intense.

Here's something else you probably did not know. I knew most of but not the name manipulation. Before British Airways, there were two major British airlines. BEA and BOAC. British European Airways and British Overseas Airways Corporation. Those two merged, to become today's BA. What I did not know, was that when British Aerospace built the Vickers VC10. A four, aft engined jet aircraft. It was intended to compete with Boeing's 707. VC 10 had advanced features over 707. Yet, major British airlines, were lukewarm supporting British built aircraft. Opting instead to purchases of and flying Boeing's 707. To extent, only fifty VC10s were sold. Boeing meanwhile, built and sold over eight hundred 707s. Disappointment in British aviation hierarchy, led to BOAC being renamed. **B**oeing **O**nly **A**ircraft **C**ompany. Kinda brings focus on present day competition, between Boeing and Airbus. Both striving to develop design superiority, with fuel conservation and flight control automation. In effort to convince would be customers, theirs is the better product. Doesn't it? Me? I am a Boeing fan. That's not to say, I am going to ask what type, then cancel my flight if it's not. I will do as I did, first time I had to board a DC10. Said a silent prayer, boarded and relaxed my head. One of my smoothest flights ever.

The Christmas Party-31

Delano and Dorothe' are an odd couple. It is not a happy union. Delano is an older, laid back guy. Whilst his much younger wife, wants to live it up. He doesn't mind, her going here and there with friends on weekends. Or whenever the urge kicks in. He insists however, when she comes home, usually in wee morning hours. She sleeps in guest bedroom until daylight. He can't be certain, invaders won't piggy back in with her. Who knows what can happen, if demands for assets are not satisfied. Devout Christian, she attends church sporadically, when not physically spent. Accepts obligation to give offering, but balks at fixed share of income. Doing so brings her grief. She rather gives what she can, cheerfully. Earning love of the lord, as written in Bible verses. Delano says, he recognizes blessings in his life, but was not a churchgoer. Until a Sunday, their daughter Patrice, pressed him to attend. Dorothe' seriously joked about their daughter's ability, getting Delano to do anything she asked. Went on to cite numerous times she invited him, with negative results. Joke lost hilarity, when Delano volunteered attending church, consecutive Sundays and every other, for a period. Needless to say, this confounded Dorothe' She proceeded to nag Delano on this. He told her she should rejoice, her prayers had been answered. Take it as redemption dictated from above. Truth told good folks. Delano had roving eyes, was enamoured of young choir leader. Came a Sunday, he told Patrice to standby two minutes, as he walked down to choir conductor. She greeted him with courteous smile, that quickly upended into a frown. Accompanied by stare of incredulity. Before excusing herself and walking away with purposed strides. Patrice loved her dad, was concerned. Went on to caution. ***"Dad, I hope you didn't say anything to Miss Parsons that's going to get you in trouble. I saw her walk away from you with purpose. What did you say to her that was so vexing?*** Abruptly as he began, Delano stopped going to church. Of course, now Dorothe' wanted to know why. There's the adage. Happy wife happy life. But this kinda blatantly shows, how hard it can be to make some wives happy. I might be wrong, but methinks it's a woman thing. If a man queries his wife, why she's going to church often and she stops. I think he's happy, and takes it, he has power heeling her. Hence he would not be wanting to find out why she stopped. But what do I know about women's psyche. Delano braced for pending storm, that did not come. Breath of fresh breeze did. Dorothe' came home from church a Sunday, said to her husband. ***"Miss Parsons asked for you, after church today. Funny, she thought you were my dad.***

Apologized ten times, when I told her you are my husband. Told her not to worry, I am getting used to it by now." Delano kept ears wide open for what should be coming next. Seemed Miss Parsons decided to let peace reign, as a good Christian should. As most stupid men would, he now experienced embodiment and mounted his steed once more. Now watch what happens next, good people. Delano decided he would go to church, a Sunday his wife was usually too tired. Make another stab at Miss Parsons. Got a better idea. Saturday at dusk, he went for Patrice. She had recently began practicing with the choir. Again, Patrice watched from a distance. As Miss Parsons scolded her dad, index finger raised for emphasis. Suffice it to say, Patrice was not privy to what was being said by both, on occasions of their brief chat. She knew it was not all hunky dory and do come again. Once more, Delano braced for a storm, that did not come and all was well that ended well. He came home one evening, saw a strange car in their driveway. His wife in painted on short shorts, yukking it up in living room. Seated Siamese close to young man. Dorothe' introduced him as coworker, who brought her home. Her car failing to start. Prognosis indicates discharged battery, and as Delano knows. All her credit cards are kaput, so she's waiting to borrow one of his. He tells her, she could have called him. He would stop at one of many auto stores. Bought and brought a battery to her. She rebuts, young man has method changing batteries. Without erasing car's data memory. Near 16:00 hours he gave her a card and both left. Dorothe' came home, when Seinfeld in second episode, about 23:40 hours. Madder than proverbial wet Hen, cursing and swearing at security guard. Who could not be found, to allow campus access. Having missed dinner at home. She supped at Olive Garden. Treated coworker too, explaining. He was not charging for services. Clearly, this union is a wagon missing a bonded team to move it smoothly along. Charlotte is CFO and board member at company both works. Dorothe' is her assistant, very unhappy in the job. She has vast experience in finance, information storage systems and human resources. Handles every facet of operations, with unsurpassed expertise. When Charlotte went on vacation and cruise. It was Dorothe' who handled that portfolio seamlessly. She grumbled, unlike her boss, Charlotte. Who had two masters degrees under her belt, earning six figures salary. Company car, generous perks and living expenses to boot. If Charlotte left, as she had whispered to Dorothe, was her intent. She would not be allowed graduation into the position. Would instead be kept in place, steering ship until another lettered person was found to take over. Assuredly, in interim, she would not be given perks and salary, acting in position. Charlotte now enjoys. If and when that day dawned. It would be source of her unbounded joy, to take a walk. Instead of guiding new hire, through peculiarities. Of the maze, that was company's operation. It irked Dorothe', to seeing green circles. She was never invited to board meetings. Had to wait for issues to surface. Which time, Charlotte brought her up to speed on policy changes agreed on. And then, only those things deemed, she needed to know. She was as is said, a very unhappy camper. Way Delano saw it, his wife was in a better place than numerous others. Living and working in then era of Miami-Dade. Salary, near $40 hourly. Better than police, paramedics or firefighters. Who were committed to enter burning buildings. Engaging armed criminals, often with injuries or fatal results. But then, his thoughts were his own and he dared not utter. This was as Christine remarked, after she bit into jerked chicken. ***"Yes, this is beyond ordinary. It just doesn't get any better."*** Myopic self assessment can mislead. Christmas holidays on horizon. Company made plans for annual party and awards function. Venue was one of many posh, storied facilities on Miami River. Charlotte and husband were there, naturally. Honour, reading names of deserving persons, who met and surpassed goals. For appreciation checks and certificates, was given to Dorothe' Everyone in attendance, were having fun, as free to indulge. Dorothe' was at work. Delano told his wife, he did not see honour, but she should smile for candid camera. Don't they usually hire MC for that kind of thing? Both were seated at a table among all women, young and Hispanic. Delano later learned, employees were not given invitation for spouses or partners, it was strictly for workers. By coincidence, some workers had their secret thing going. Here it all came to light, so all was not lost as couples go. Dorothe' says to Delano.

"Let's go dancing, before I am called to stage." He got up with veiled melancholy. Simultaneously, dude walked up. Greeted Dorothe' with cheek kiss. She made introductions, and both men kept hands in pockets, grunting a response. Midway second dance, Dorothe' was called into service. Delano headed to their table. Lupe' called him. *"Delango, come here. Let's go outside, and see da chips on da river."* He hesitates, she urges. *"Delango, you not get nothing. I not get nothing. Nobody call us name, let's go see da boots."* Both walked out on the balcony. Stood a while staring. Downtown skyline, skyscrapers brilliantly aglow in different hues amid myriad neon signs. Freighter is being guided upstream by tug. Lupe' says. *"You know him, Delango?"* **"Who, Lupe'?"** *"Delango! You wife just you and he, hello."* **"Oh, him. No, I don't know him."** Silence lingers for two minutes, then Lupe' says. *"Your wife, she know him."*

Delano says. **"Yeah?"** Silence is on again as Delano looks at Lupe' in mind's eyes. Before he can mentalize possibilities, Lupe' goes on. *"He, her friend."* Delano, again says. **"Yeah?"** Then Lupe' continues. *"Come see her at work sometime."* And all Delano says, is. **"Yeah?"** As he concentrates on her youth and Latino features in silence. Visualizing a fly kite approach. Lupe' comes to stand in front Delano. Stares him in the face, says. *"They do loonch, Delango, long loonch sometime. Miss Charlotte not say anything. We, she give small letter one time. Next time, stay home two days."* **"You serious?"** Delano responds and silence is on until he says. **"You like, we do lunch sometime?"** Lupe' says. *"Delango, I like you okcent."* Delano replies. **"Lupe', I like yours, also you too."** She seems briefly bewildered, asks him. *"You do?"* Then goes on. *"I say maybe, you not much understand. Because you say every time. Yeah!"* Now, he tells her slowly. **"Lupe', I understand everything you say. They are friends. He comes and takes her for long lunch. Miss Charlotte not reprimand her. Others, get memo and suspension if they late from lunch. Right?"** *"Oh! So, maybe you not like talking then. We go back inside now."* Delano tells her. **"No, Lupe'. Let's stay longer and talk. It's nicer outside. I like being with you, and you haven't answered about doing lunch."** Lupe' insists they go in. *"No loonch, Delango. Your wife soon stop call names and maybe, look for you. I is Timp, Delango. Hope soon, be no more Timp. So, we go in."* **"How long have you been a Temp, Lupe'?"** Delano asks, she says. *"Too long, Delango. More long than they say would be. Very much like you, but no loonch. Much sorry, Delango."* Both walks in. Delano heads to his chair. Sees previously introduced dude seated there. Delano scans the room and sees a vacant chair nearby. Reaches across table for his glass. That in afterthought, he really shouldn't. Given he is not going to drink whatever it was. Ice having melted is now tasteless water. But, in reaching across, Delano says. **"Excuse me."** Dude adopts confrontational stance, says in very loud voice. *"What?"* Delano says. **"I was sitting here. See? That drink, it's mine but never…."** Dude sprang to his feet. Arms flailing, eyes wildly staring. declared. ***"Well! I am sitting here now. What you planning doing about that, eh motherfu..er?"*** Women were startled, faces sagged in jaw dropping disbelief. Delano taken aback, by this unprovoked explosion of wrath. Laughed and said to dude. **"Hey man! Just between us. That's one sure way becoming daddy. You gots to let loose on mama. So if you ain't doing it, you better get your saddle ready, prepare to mount up."** Everyone laughed out loud. Caught off guard by Delano's reaction, dude says. *"Do you believe this guy. Is he something, or what?"* Lupe' calls Delano. *"Delango, come sit down here."* He did and that was that for the minute.

Lupe' caressed back of his hand in what can only be seen as unconscious empathy. Reality hit, she quickly let go the hand. In same instant, bolt of surprised ecstasy zzzzed in and over Delano's being. What a tingle…But there was still angst heavy in the air. When dude walked away, not bothering to stay put in the seat. Everyone chorused, asking Delano if he fussed earlier with dude. He told them, no. His wife introduced them. That was extent of their exchange. Women exchanged knowing glances but made no further comment. Women and their silent language. Eyebrows chacha, mouth corner twitch, eyelids jiggle. Where do they acquire these nuances? A thirty seconds furniture ad on TV, titled "The dance Lesson" Tells a most enthralling interaction between persons. It's all set to portray her as "Beauty" and he a slap dash fellow. Paradigm is exposed in final seconds, when he tells where he bought furniture. She makes sentence with subtle eyes and head tics. He responds likewise. Artistic beauty, rehearsed and captured to infinite perfection. Our story continues. Awards segment ended, Dorothe' strode to Delano. Eager getting her soulful strut going. Atmosphere still reeked of tension, Delano wanted to go home. Dorothe' calmly told him not to worry, she will get drive home. Cheek smooched him with a parting *"Drive safely now."* They parted for the evening. Delano had put the incident out of his mind, until mid following week. Dorothe' asks what kind of run in he had with the dude. He told his wife, verbatim, how what happened. Then she told him, dude is knob with federal branch of law enforcement. Close to top. Second to director or deputy. He's steering her through process. Getting a job in his department. Delano nearly soiled his brief when she said. He always has his gun with him. It was to Delano's fortune, tiff did not escalate and get physical. Now, Delano began thinking and putting two and two together. How did cop get invite to the function? By her of course. Only executive staff members were given privilege bringing someone as guest. So, Dorothe' finagled for her husband and her lunch date. Maybe, he insisted getting to know. Husband of woman he was having long lunch dates with. You know, see what sucker looks like. What kind of opposition, or challenge he could mount. Did he try provoking an altercation so he could have excuse to? As Delano tells it, more thought he gave about possibilities. He felt onset of slow headache, that intensified with passing minutes. He will not say if that was first, but that incident was definitely brad in their marriage coffin. Delano could not shake belief. Maybe, if dude was street cop. He would find reason to provoke, take Delano out in a confrontation, so he could take over. As they say, first the uproar, then the downpour. Delano takes comfort in dude quickly being surprised to find. Dorothe' is all he would be getting, if and when Delano was demised. Everything else was already signed sealed and delivered. Case closed as Archie Bunker was famed saying. Delano and Dorothe' parted amicably by uncontested divorce and Patrice having voted, was not into consideration for proceedings. They lived happily ever after, her in her small corner, he in his. Happy endings are beautiful life experiences. Rare but embraced and cherished, when they come to be without rancour. Everyone deserves happy ending to life's foibles. Don't they? Of course they do. There's got to be an alternative to drudgery and meaningless existence. Like the yo-yo, enslaved to it's string. Delano is unsettled by possibilities of dire events, especially watching TV crime shows. Came a time he had vehicle registration issues. County mailed new decals, he didn't receive. He goes downtown and walks stairs for exercise. Shout comes from escalator. ***"Delango, here, see me. I wait for you."*** Lupe' is happy to see him and runs off motor mouthed. About leaving Timp jub for best jub, and best pay and. Best thing she said in her frenzied chatter. ***"You want do loonch now Delango? Yes?"*** Lunch and more was on Delano's mind. He too had been severed from previous position. Maybe, just maybe, this could prove fortuitous and prompt Delano in song. "Oh, happy day."

Family Feud-32

Began much later in their lives, but let's retrace a bit. Madeline was only child born to parents, Joseph and Barbara Pinnock. His daddy had fourteen children by three women.

Joseph was hell bent surpassing daddy's record, but alas. Fate took a hand and he did not come back from Vietnam. I should say, far as his wife and kin accepts. They maintain skepticism, because coffin was sealed. So, no One knows, who or what was in that box. Just when Barbara began making peace with loss of her husband. Joseph's brother, Bertram moved into her house. As shadow, to show she was not widow alone. Averting exposure to possible disadvantages. He was self described, man for and of all seasons. Having been here and there, knowing ins and outs of many things. Sat sister-in-law down. Told her facts, unknown to Tom, Dick and Harry, about soldier's remains coming home from yon battlefields. Poignant element of his oration was. Sometimes, only limbs and parts of warrior can be identified and brought home. *"Don't be fooled by military pallbearers, straining with that coffin as it's brought into church. They are trained to carry coffin with feathers, and make it look like an elephant is inside. In some cases, the coffin is ballasted to equal weight of deceased. Hence it's often sealed, and will not be opened."* He ended with a stare and three sharp nods, reinforcing his tale. Needless to say now, Barbara's angst was revived tenfold. Misery etched in her eyes. She began making more frequent cemetery trips. Asked questions of her husband and not getting answers. Her belief was now reinforced to conviction, averred. *"Bertie know what him be talking bout. Him is a man of the world, who has seen the world and wise to her ways."* This in rebuttal to kin, who tried persuading differently. Even as they tried isolating her from him, in vain. Sensing she was mentally fragile, close kin and relatives came to live with her. Giving emotional support, help caring for young daughter, Madeline. A humorous side to this is. Bertram having convinced Barbara on extent of his wisdom. Tried doing same, regarding taking his brother's place in her life. She threw him out of her house, faster than overnight chamber pot of festering you know what. Funny ended when HOA threatened fine for littering. Edicted her to clean or be fined, plus cost of debris removal. Clement Jackson lived with his parents and extended family in Allapattah, Miami. Crossed paths with Madeline, who lived in Broward County, when both were preteens. Time marched on. Clement frequented a place where boxers sparred, and began training in the sport. Madeline tried talking him out of this vocation, to no avail. Listened, when she told him they didn't have a future together. Asked to give reason why, she told him. Someone told her, (Barbara did) a man, trained to beating someone until they're unconscious. Won't know the difference, when he's home. At slightest provocation, will do same to a wife. With even less regard for a sweetheart. So, it's bye bye good luck. For a month she didn't see, hear about or from him. He turned up at her house one evening. Had twelve dollars from sale of his gloves and other training gear. Would like to buy her a ring, if she said yes to be his girlfriend. In time they married, lived in Barbara's house, taking care of her as health waned. Too soon and unexpected. Madeline says her mom gave up will to live and that was only affliction. For which there was no medical cure. Madeline and Clement Jackson had five girls, of which, Barbara doted first two. Passing before others came to be. Oh, I should mention. Madeline worked at County hospital of her name and Clement at Port of Miami. Madeline's first two children were by natural birth. Next two by Caesarean section. Doctor suggested she should take steps to not get pregnant again, as there could be complications. For a while, she seemed to have heeded advice until. Worried now, she consulted wise old aunt, who being very knowledgeable about most things. Told her, all she needed was a good girther or belly band. Madeline had her fifth child. Husband Clement, was smitten with this baby, in a way he just could not explain. Hastened to name her Clementine for his self. Madeline objected, that name's era long gone and now seen as outdated. ***"Who in this day and age in right mind, name girl child, Clementine?"*** She asked her husband, who dug his heels in with firm resolve. Madeline grudgingly accepted and said, she would add Josephine to honour her father. Clement didn't like the name, but yielded. Saying, they came out even, and that was that. You think? Not so fast. Serious squabbling began, over which name should be horse's head. Which would end up as it's ass. Where do people come up with these things? You might ask. Willie Brannan and wife Georgette, were going to stand as godparents. Resolved impasse by getting both parents to abide his solution. Drew circle and a line on two bits of paper, turned them face down. Then got ready to flip a silver dollar. Told each parent to choose between head or tail. Gave them a slip of paper matching their choice, then flipped the coin. It came down in Clement's favour and that was that without recourse. See how simple, difficult situations can be remedied? Just about here, Madeline suggested to Clement they refurbish the house. Add another bathroom and convert the kitchen to an eat-in. Clement said, there could be no refurbishing, it had to be a rebuild. Infrastructure, such as plumbing, wiring, windows and pitch patched roof, all needed replacements. Never mind present distance but given time, Overtown would creep right up to annex Brownsville. Madeline was anchored to, and wanted to preserve that house in parent's memory. They bought a later built house, having less anomalies and moved to Richmond Heights. Years went by. Clementine silently hated her names. Thought about changing them at adulthood. Acknowledged, emotionally tied to both names. Seeing they honoured a father, she loved dearly and grandfather she never knew. In time, she met Robert Hargreaves. Neighbourhood wonder lad, everyone called Bobby. That boy was so cutely handsome, he got labeled "a pain in the neck." Because, young women snapped heads around, staring at him on first glance. He was cool as a cucumber. Tall, athletic, with smile that charmed. Although not yet married. Clement referred to Robert as one of his five sons-in-law. And the living was easy. Be it summertime, and all other seasons. Until a year and some after Robert and Clementine got married. Remember now, Clement adored Clementine. And this adoration naturally shone on Robert, moreso than other four men in his daughters lives. Suddenly, without known explanation there was obvious thaw between Robert and Clement. Formality was new order, introduced by the young man. His father-in-law followed suit. Without bothering to probe reason for diplomatic fallout. Madeline did not like ripples upsetting calm in her family. She firmly urged her dad to have a sit down with Robert to fact find. This, after she had done just that with Robert. He denied there being rift of any kind. Clement told his wife, he can get by without kissing Robert's ass, because he wears his own boxers. Never having to borrow those of young man. He was stubborn personified. When they met by forced chance and exchanged greetings.*"Morning Pa Clem."* Who replied. **"Howdy Bobby."** Then came escalation. Clementine said to her father. *"Dad, don't take this any ways. Bobby would rather you called him, Robert. Says he has now outgrown, aka Bobby."* Clement told his daughter. **"That's okay by me, because me don't have to call him, period."** See how the rut gets deeper? At a family gathering of eating, drinking and merrymaking. Someone said they had to go to gas station and get more ice.

Madeline said out loud, freezing chill in house was coming off Robert and Clement. Hence, person could save trip and chip ice needed, from them. There was uproarious laughter. Robert and Clementine did not see the joke. Her venturing to whisper, maybe mom had had too much of something. Clementine's first child was christened, Madison Robertha. Maintaining trend of honouring parents or grandparents. It goes without being said, if dad has favourite child. Her child will inherit, be favourite grandchild. Clement never set up college fund for Clementine. Did so for Madison, and much more. In fairness to him, when Clementine was born there was sparsity of resources. Compared to when Madison came to be. He wanted everything for little Maddy. Going to college, he was going to buy her a car. There was no end to what he would do. And then she came home from college. Sat with grandpa and told him, among other things. She was not done with school. All she has, is bachelors and must go on to Grad school. Her degree today, is worth less than when he graduated high school back in the day.Then she got suddenly serious and said.*"Gramps, I want to ask you something, and I want an answer. Look at me Gramps. I love and respect you deeply. We are adults and should be able to talk like adults. What is this thing, between you and daddy Bob? I won't tell anyone. But you've got to tell me, for my own peace of mind."* She stared him in the face, saw him at juncture, undecided where to go. She added the kicker.*"You know Gramps. I would have come out of college with higher pass marks. Had my head not been crowded. Trying to understand this simmering thing between you and my dad."* He sighed and remained silent. Stared at her, then said. **"Truthfully, I don't know for sure what is, but can take a guess. Because, your father's drawers began squeezing his balls one Saturday. After I sat down and had a chat with** my daughter, your mother. So maybe, good place for you to start would be with her." Madison is on discovery mission, goes to her mother. Repeats her talk with, and Gramps' response. Clementine asks her daughter. "You ever heard saying. Let sleeping dogs lie?" Madison quickly shot back. *"Yes mom, over and over, but guess what. While dog sleeps, it's fleas are making life miserable for those nearby."* They stared at each other, burst out laughing. Mother said to daughter. "You spend too much time with your grandfather. If I was blindfolded, I wouldn't know which of you were talking." Corralled by two women he could not say no to. Clement agreed to sit down at Larry and Penny Thompson Park. Clementine turned to Madison, in her dad's presence and began. "This thing started before you and your siblings were born. Matter of fact, there was a time. You all would have to be born to other parents, beside us. Because, your father and I not only stopped talking. But were on verge going separate ways, and this woman wasn't worried. Because after all, I am woman. So in short run, common sense prevailed. We decided not to talk about it ever. And here we are, one big happy family. Until you got infested with fleas." Not knowing where flea input came from, a startled Clement blurted. *"Where you go and get dog flea? Tell you bout them college, with all sorts of people from all over. Mingling and sleeping in same room. That's why me and…"* Both women yelled with one voice. "Dad! *Gramps!"* Madison told him. *"Slow your shake, rattle and roll. Nobody has fleas, it's a metaphor, figure of speech."* Everyone observed minute's silence. Clement was still dumbfounded. Kept exchanging stares with both women, jaws hung slack in a droop. Clementine resumed speaking, slowly and in very soft voice that compels attention. "It was

Saturday, I drove to pick up your grandfather at work, because we only had one car. I took him to work, then took mom to mall, supermarket, and both of us to hairdresser. On way home, I said to dad. "Do you know where "Mobile Home Village" is?" He thought for a bit, then said, no. He didn't. We came home. Robert was polishing his motorcycle for tenth time that day. Every time he finished and walked away, admiring his work from a distance, he saw new flaw. Had to go back at it. Now that I was home, motorcycle no longer had top billing. Your dad and I just sat down in the living room, when dad came. Beckoned me out on the porch. He asked. "What you was asking bout "Mobile Home Village?" I said. Robert was telling me about it and said some comes in doubles. Way they're comfortably laid out, you wouldn't know you're not in an average house. I was thinking I would go down there. Look the place over for myself, tomorrow after church. Dad got upset and said. "Whether you want to call it, "Mobile Home Village" or whatever, it's a dam trailer park. I busted hump to raise you and your sisters in a proper house, with room and space to grow. No man not going come and take my daughter, to live in no dam trailer park. No matter what y'all want call it, so it sounds all nice and cozy. Read my lips, it's a friggin' trailer park, if you will pardon my French." I sat there stunned. Before I could say another word, dad got up and stormed off, mad. How was I to know Robert was eavesdro….Well, shouldn't really call what he heard as, eavesdropping. Because dad, as your grandma would say. Was not talking with water in his mouth. Nothing he said was garbled, it was loud and clear. I honestly didn't know Robert was in on the conversation. So, later I said to him, we should put off going to the

village. I needed time to think things over. Then he said. "You know Clem, it's great to love parents. I love mine too. But when you're thinking about marrying another man. You must first divorce your father from your life and make your own decisions." I closed the room door, we had our fight, he stormed out madder than your grandfather. So now, two men who meant much to me in different ways, made me out to be their enemy. Only reason both are still in my life. I should say, our lives. Is because they both love me and would not give me up for anything. But, you know what? The hatchet gets buried today." Everything on this earth, has a beginning and an end. Sometimes it takes eternity, but there's always end. Clementine took out her cellphone, brow furrowed. Called her husband and asked if he was still at the gym. Could he come over to the park and take a look at the car. He tried to find out what was wrong with the car. She told him to just come and take a look at it. Well, he would call a friend and bring with him. His skill being limited, hence he wanted to know how was it acting up. **"Bobby, it's a simple thing that's beyond me but you can get it fixed. I wouldn't call you if I thought it was beyond your expertise. Who knows a husband's skill level better, than a wife? Just take a look at it. I haven't got all day, the park might close early."** Bobby arrives, slowly walks to the trio with that lazy gait that shows, he's thinking. *"What the hell going on?"* He says hello and asks Clementine. ***"What's problem with the car?"*** She says. **"Did I tell you anything was wrong with it? I said come and take a look at it. Now that you have looked, sit down here. Madison knows there's silent war between you and her grandfather. She wants it ended now. There's no "Or else" She just wants two grown men she loves**

dearly. To end this thing between them that started even before she was born. Gee, it's old enough to vote and very soon, can walk up to the bar and buy liquor." Clement stepped aggressively towards Robert, who backed off a step, caught by surprise. ***"Robert."*** He began, paused and continued. ***"Madison is your daughter. You love her and wants best things that life has to offer. As well as your other children. Now tell me, oil swimming truth, fair and square. Madison brings a man to your house. Tells you they're going to get married and go live in trailer park. Would you smile and give them your blessings. Or would you tell her, she got to be out of her cotton picking mind? Take your time, don't rush this. Because you have to fair and honest with yourself."*** All four stood staring at each other in silence. Then Robert held out a hand to his father-in-law who took and shook it. Robert hugged him, opened the embrace and drew in his wife and daughter. All four stood in a silent circle, no need for words. You know Charmin hug that lasted too long? This one eclipsed it until they finally broke. Robert looked at his wife with jestering side sneer and said. ***"Come look at the car, or else the park will soon close? You wily Devil, but you're my angel and I love you."*** And both shared their own hug as Madison and Clement looked on with broad grins. Now would you believe, when hugging was done. Each was dabbing corner of their eyes? Clement became conscious of his action and said. ***"It really getting late, see Sandfly come out already. Screech Owl next."*** Others, in chorus replied. **"Yes. Right. Sandfly get in your eyes."** Then all four laughed up a storm. Family foibles with orchestrated happy ending. Not always guaranteed a given but just this once, it happened. This one undoeth the done.

Behind Closed Windows-33

At PSE&G, Al Parsons successfully bids, Tuesday Saturday shift. Allowing him Mondays off to see doctors, and take care of business. If you are new to Miami-Dade County. Here's a basic rule of navigating surface streets. CRAP and STLouis. Forget lower case letters. CRAP is Court, Road, Avenue, Place, Path, and they all run North to South, in that order. STL is Street, Terrace, Lane in that order, East to West and includes Drive. Miami Avenue is dividing line between East and West. Flagler Street divides North and South. From Flagler, numbering starts at one going North as NW to abut Broward County and SW going South, abutting Monroe County. From Miami Avenue, numbering starts at one going East as NE to the ocean and SE going South. In this seamed layout of corridors, you will find Avenue Road, Circle Place, Circle Lane, Street Road and Street Circle. Icing this cake we add Blvd, Way and Trail but these are exception than rule. Cities within County sometimes have a different numbering and directional system, as obtains in Hialeah. Where non-residents cringe, at daunting challenge finding addresses there. At workplace, Saturdays were dubbed "discover the County" day. Monday thru Friday, about thirty C&D technicians covered Miami-Dade County. Reduced to about ten on Saturdays. Each technician, covering wider and quite often, unfamiliar territory, working tickets before expiry. Customer pays bill at four on Friday. PSC rule. Must be reconnected within twenty-four hours of paying. This was the usual hectic Saturday, chasing numerous time sensitive tickets. Miles apart with little time between to get them. Didn't help, Al searched an address at 104 Street that was Avenue. Here's Al at targeted address. Quick visual, showed open socket on East side, next to window. Toting replacement meter and yellow tape, he begins socket check. Connections secure and torqued, voltage each leg, good ground and possible remote back feed. Overheard male and female voices in rebuke and dialogue. *"I really can't understand, why you getting your ugly ass out of shape about no cold beer. You knows my shit been turned off since...."* Male interrupts in low tones. Female retorts. *"And I went down and paid it. I gots the paper somewhere here. Man I spoke to, says he will try for today, but cannot guarantee. If you'd a done what you suppose to do. You'd a have your cold beer now, instead of trying to stress me with you crazy shit."* Male says. *"You didn't have to wait on me. Coulda gone and borrow from your momma or sister. They gots a good thing going."* Female guffaws, pffft. *"Yeah, I coulda but I didn't. Wanna know why? Cause they woulda looked at you like some trifling low life. Who can't even keep his woman's lights on. So I kept our business to ourself. Dragging your lame ass around in 300 with 26's. And your beer not cold, cause you can't pay your bills. That's a messed up picture if I did see one."* Male seeks understanding. *"Look Cherie, you know I a hard working, trying dude. But I got lots of responsibilities, and I need for you to understand. You know? Cut me some slack. But every time I walk in, you got your hand out and your palm open. You need to..."* He just lit her fuse. *"Oh no Rick! You, you did not just freakin' go go there. Ain't nothing wrong with that. I'm your woman. Every time you walk in here, you gots your fly open and your Dick out. Do I complain? No. I just doos what I gots to do. Handle my business and you walk away happy as the cat that....You know what? Right now I feels like telling you, take your raggedy ass outta my house. Go sit on the shi shi shit hill. Come talking bout. I gots my hand open and my palm..... I can't even get your trifling shit right. You you you need to, to get, get your ass up and outta here."* When a woman stutters, watch out. *"Because, am fixing to to smash something over your dam head now."* Instead of running for the door, he pleads. *"But Cherie, I am just asking for a little understanding here. A little you see my side and I see yours, that's all I am..."* She gives second warning. *"Yeah, I see what, and I understand. That's why am telling you. Git your ass going and if you can't hear me. You'll hear the rescue siren before you pass out."* This guy isn't aware what he's up against. *"Ah Babe, you know we been places, we got further..."* Al slaps meter into socket. Silence deafens for just a brief moment. Female voice enquires. *"Who dat?"* **"PSE&G"** Al replies. She seeks confirmation. *"You said PSG? Thank you sir. See? God answers prayers, when you don't ask for much. And I was sitting here..."*

A pregnant pause follows, accompanied by male's voice in low murmur to female, who audibly responds. *"How am I going to to know that? Ask him. He a man, you THE man. Shiiit, if you was the man. You would not have to be here with me, having this argument. Wondering how long he been out there. Come talking bout, I gots my my hand up and palm down. I'm a going hurt you for that Rick. Your good, church going wife go needs pray hard for you. You shoulda thunk it and not say it. Trifling corn head Nigga, comes in my house and..."* Male interrupts with a low murmur. Female responds. *"How would I know? If he still there, he be handling his business. He gots no time to be paying attention to you and your trifling shit. And, like I says. You'd a taken care of business, he not need to be here. And let me tell you something else..."* Al steps off towards his truck. In case anyone gets idea. Al hung around to eavesdrop, even after installing the meter. Please put that thought to rest. Absence regulated can cover, he had to criss cross install, temporary secure barrier. Using yellow, industrial vinyl adhesive tape and post mandated "Caution" tag. These tasks have to be done in manner that emphasizes and enhances SAFETY. See how People at Play can get into situations? And we sing. *After the love is gone what used to be right is wrong.* Applies after lights get disconnected too. When a man cannot cool his mental imbroglio, he loses grip and reaches into the "never say" vault. Brings out a scroll and begins reciting. Usually, in such instances, do not talk to a woman. Let woman talk to you. She might be kind and talk "with" you.

Intimacy remorse:-34

Is an angst suffered mostly, if not totally by women. We were at graveside her father's funeral. Boyhood family friend, Reverend Pennycooke officiated. Waxing warm on long acquaintance with and spiritual guidance of family, Howsens. Shelly Witherspoon had bridled countenance. Scoffed loud and hissed teeth, causing me to look askance at her. *"I can't believe I allowed that sleazy pile of dog shit to screw me. And then get away to marry Jeanette Blount."* Taken aback, I silently stared at her. She went on. *"We used to be inseparable high school sweethearts, or so I thought. Until we graduated. He went to seminary school. First Christmas, I went and asked his mom for his address. Sent him an expensive card, expressing heartfelt emotions. He never replied. Sent instead, message through his snob of a mother. Saying they're so holy and dedicated to theology. There's no time to focus on, I guess, worldly distractions."* She's royally pissed, having allowed him to play in her romper room. Now back from college and married with a family. Greeted her with a smile, then rubbed salt in wound by telling her. *"I can't wait for honour, having you exchange vows with a lucky young man. Hope when it happens, he'll appreciate you for all that you are, as well as what you are not."* Never wanted to reminisce on their times together. Which began, night of his sister's wedding, When Shelly was fifteen and through to her, near eighteenth birthday. Women take sex seriously, it is a rite they engage in with intense emotion. In most situations, there is expectation it is first step of lifelong adventure together with the One. Filled with those blissful unforgettable memories. When this does not come to maturity, rancour and hatred of other person sets in. Not to mention levels of self disdain. Often this comes about, when male takes non-achiever's mantle. Outlaw or society misfit and female regrets. Having to accept, he found succor in warmth of her bosom. In similar situation of subjects reversed. Male revels in knowledge, he nibbled at apple before it got invaded by pests. Now devoid of blue ribbon quality, by them that knows. It's elation experienced, when basking in secret mountain spring, before discovery by safari visitors.

It is not YOUR money:-

And you cannot want it now. Came to my attention recently. Child was bitchin' with purpose, to other sibling. Regarding parents' nest egg. Supposedly coming to her upon their death, and having temerity to declare. *"I want mine now to do what I want with it. I don't want to wait for them to go, whilst opportunities pass me by."* Went on to express frustration with Korean hoopty she drives to work, and inability to take a vacation. Well, I've got news for her and others like minded.

As a responsible parent, my focused onus was, preparing you for life in a challenging world. Provided sustenance, shelter and education, so that when you reached adulthood. You were equipped to step out and make your mark. Whilst taking care of you, I was also stowing Acorns for Summer and Autumn of my life. When I would not be able to forage for myself. Not wanting to sponge off you and yours. Now that you are faced with similar task providing for your family. Pursuing goals for them, as I did for you. That's the cycle, and each generation is supposed to take the mantle a step farther. Today's families talk about, and encourage what is called. Creation of generational wealth. What I hear coming from you, is fixation with squandering. I recognize, you could have generous tendencies towards me that your spouse might not readily embrace. Would hate to be source of tension in your home. My wealth such as it is, of whatever proportion.

Was not created to be passed on to you. It is there to pay medication, hospital stays, food, living and final expenses until the day, and after I die. Then and only then, **IF** there's anything left, it will be divided with you and yours. So don't make my resources, a focus of your expectations. And wanting to grab it now, rather than when I go. You should rather, focus on possibility. I could outlive my wealth and as a good child. You might have to take up where the wealth crumbs ends in the forest. However, if you put me in the poorhouse. Barring senility, I will accept, understand and not be discontented. Then again, I might be beyond being aware or caring. So there. Thought that needed saying, on behalf of us relics, so everyone understands and curbs disillusioned expectations. Ere it festers and prompts evil thoughts, acted on to create heinous deeds. Media tells chilling events, arising from similar impatient mindset, at times.

Reader's Vox populi:

Reader sent email, without referencing any chapter or section of book content, yet virally castigating. ***"You Islanders are so promiscuous it boggles the imagination. To think how y'all get sexually involved with anything of opposite sex. Wouldn't come as any surprise, my finding the term "loving your pets" have different meaning."***

I emailed her back saying. *"If we pay attention to news items and other sources of information. It will be overwhelmingly established, this was not behaviour confined solely to island life. It is of humans living and cohabiting, found on every continent, and here in our United States."* When it comes to sexual co-mingling between peoples. Lure of deviant pursuit arises, because there are those, who want to depart from tradition. There's always quest for more pleasure from sexual encounters. Franny is still in quandary as to whether or not her father was her uncle. Whose head her mother bashed in and maybe still in prison for the deed. When it comes to sexual preferences there are men who draw invisible line in the sand. Mortimer declared in slurred inebriation, three women he would not have sex with. Were his mother, daughter and sister Underscored his statement adding. ***"In that order."*** Sister was not in a safe place, if push came to shove. Tales of incest is common occurrence in some countries. Notable exceptions are, where this is punishable by castration or ultimate beheading. A friend was recruited to work in Mideast for top dollar. But was warned not to engage in illicit sex with native women. He being an infidel in eyes of the law. If caught, punishment was beheading after prayers at sundown. Despite which, end of his contract and back in the US. He boasted how many women in secret cahoots, he fraternalized with. Fiction becomes reality, everyday by way of our media. One high profile family member went Hunting for intimate companionship and found this with wife of his recently departed brother. He could have gone farther afield but was already close to grieving widow. Not to mention his nieces and nephews. How will children reconcile scenario of uncle, whooping it with mom after dad passed? Remember now, around this time another woman was breeding for him, that he tried denying until science nailed him. So to "RK" of Lehigh, it is not an island thing. It is rather a people thing. So long as there are people, this will be existential fact..

TS of St. Petersburg writes: You put so much effort, promoting *inherent wisdom* and unequalled, superior qualities of your gender. It escapes your not recognizing, how convincing liars women are. This book is case in point. You make lies believably factual.

Quote Note: Page 127 carries following lines, DJ modified. Verbatim lines are reproduced in Italics. *'At the gates of the Temple. I purified my lips with sacred fire, that I might speak of love but when I opened my mouth to speak, I found myself mute'*..."Khalil Gibran

Afterword

What follows is a stop-the-press comment on all that's been said before. It's been two years and some, editing punctuation and font properties. As numerous pause breaks arise in course of the process. Not taking into account, dislocations arising by way of pandemic protocols and need to isolate and be wary. Which at any rate, is must do, to attain perfection and accuracy. This is never achieved by continuous process. Because, eyes refuse to focus and even when they are coaxed into doing so, brain does not absorb and process. So in taking a pause, I decided to go shop for groceries and wended my way two plus miles each way, for benefit of exercise. When you engage sedentary occupation, a chance for prolonged ambulating has to be taken. If only to get ticker out of lethargic repose. We live in unsettled times where racial kerfuffles are to forefront of daily existence. Outcry, most driven by heavy handed and sometimes unnecessary restraining force. By law enforcement, against citizens, especially of colour and minorities. Whilst protests and demonstrations rage in our cities and towns. There is latent under current of racial tension, that lies dormant like some volcanoes. For different reasons, sometimes for none whatsoever. There are people who just don't like other people. It is common knowledge there are blacks who don't like blacks. Whites who don't like blacks, whites and colours or races in between. Against this realization, I am taken aback by incident witnessed on my walk. Amazed it did not morph out of control. Methinks it was totally unnecessary, felt relief when aggrieved persons exercised restraint. At a shopping centre, as I walked on piazza towards food store. There was combo of musicians and singers, performing from the sidewalk in front of a sports bar. I should say a trio as there were two male guitarists, one of whom was singing, backed by female vocalist playing tambourine. Three or four parking spaces were "caution" taped, tents and seats set up for audience as they imbibed and enjoyed presentation. Yours truly stood a ways off on sidewalk. Jiving to rhythm and feeling the groove. I should tell you, there were sound equipment and cables snaking from bar across sidewalk, supporting the gig. I heard from behind me a strident command. *"Watch it pops."* Or maybe, it was more a *"Stand back pops."* Simultaneously, Joe Black hustled past me and declared. *"This ain't the f..ing arena."* Taken by surprise, I watched him striding and hoped against hope, he was not intent on doing what he did. Walked right through performers and their equipment. One player steadied equipment stack. Seemed Joe Black's feet snagged cables and…. Man under tent sprang to his feet and yelled. *"What the f… is going on?"* By then, Joe had made passage and gone. Performers played on, some in the audience sat, mouth agape in disbelief. Yeller fixed me a leer, probably figured I was bent passing through in like mode. Daring me to do so. I backed away and went round the tents, going my way. Thought to myself. *"Joe Black caught them off guard and got away with his shenanigan. Hope he knows better than trying return by same route."* Methinks, common sense should have dictated Joe Black not have done what he did. Whether or not he thinks, pedestrians has absolute right of way, there should not be encroachment on sidewalk. Denying his access to free passage. For whatever reason, promotional or otherwise. It is never always about being right or wrong. It sometimes is about common sense, being smart and not throwing matchstick in a hay bale. See how easily that can become an out of control conflagration?. Paradise, California was lost in November 2018 and 84 souls perished in wildfire, ignited by single spark. Yes, it is metaphoric but illustration is starkly realistic. Locale is overwhelmingly white, as were audience and performers. Question asked and not answered, yet known as fact. In predominantly black neighbourhood, given similar scenario. Could white dude dare trample through and emerge unscathed? The answer goes without need to say. Fifteen or more years ago I was employed to power company, working fringes of Liberty City at Miami's Pork and Beans, black community. Street was blocked by men, who were promoting their Barbershop opening .Music blared, large crowd made merry. Aromatic smoke rose from makeshift barbecue drums with slow cooking meat. Having work to do in the area, I honked horn for passage. Only to have a dude come by vehicle's window and advise. ***"Back up before your tires lose shape and can't roll."*** No skin off my face I parked at safe distance and simply endorsed tickets. "CGI-Street blocked." Soon after police arrived and had street reopened amid strident objections by organizers. We can enforce rights with caution and not end up "dead right." One of many wise advice my father gave was to always assess a situation before acting and ask myself. *"How can this go wrong?"* Better than after fact question. *"How could this have been avoided?"*

Footnotes: Diction of dialogue depicts quoted speaker's verbatim comfort vocabulary. Folks, rural and urban, have parochial English adaptation. This generic lingo at times excludes, proper parsing and grammar usage. Some words and commentary are in dialect, slang, adage and patois of times past. Still maintained in perpetuity by tradition. Editing to scholastic standards would emasculate and divest events, of inherent, natural harmonic syntax. In other words, grammatical imperfections reproduced verbatim. Lends authenticity to the story. Giving insight into a people's culture and their way of thinking. Assessing situations and ultimately that unique adaptation of English, with snippets of Spanish unwittingly thrown in. The author welcomes your comments. Please see contact information. Publishers joins the author expressing sincere appreciation for your purchase of this book, and trusts you found literary satisfaction. Would introduce you to other books by Colleen G. Lowe. These are available at Amazon/Kindle or at. www.theglenwoodcollection.com. Where there are excerpts and full chapters of selected books. Following pages introduces ShaunaKay Gabriel Harrison. She is aide who mixes paint, selects brushes for the artist. Sometimes, she fills in clouds, or greenery in a landscape. Time is on her side and whatever vocation she pursues. This author wishes her tremendous success. Her first tenuous step forward as a fledgling author.

RAGING FIRE

Prologue: All my life, I have seen love. But never felt it. Have seen the heart of childhood, and have envied it. I have witnessed the vibrant sounds of joy. Have seen the radiant smiles of children, competing with the sun. I am however, robbed of all these things.

My heart is like a vast open plain. Which is exposed to the erosion of life. My soul is the Amazon forest without rain. My spirit aches daily with the pain of hatred. Not hatred towards others, but from those around me. I rarely hate, but mostly fear. I tremble from my exposure to the Lions. Yes, they feed me to the Lions. They do this and they laugh. Laugh as if the devil himself was sitting in their hearts. I sometimes feel a fire within me, which is quenched by my tears. It leaves me dry. Like someone drained the ocean of all it's water. It leaves startled fishes and nothing but the salt it contains. It is a fire of hopelessness, fear and pain. Very little or no faith at all, and nowhere near love. I sometimes wonder if that fire is hatred toward others. Whether it is or not, it's only a matter of time before that fire rages wild. My name is Samuel Levi and this is my story.

Chapter One: I closed my eyes against the brazen sun. I tried to imagine myself in a world far away. The day was golden, as I sat in the honeycomb sunlight. How I wished this land was real. I saw myself looking down at this wonderful place. This Samuel was not troubled. His breaths were even and sure. He was lying on the finest Rose petals. But then the fear in me came over this Samuel. He sensed the danger too, and as the Rose petals turned to blood. Terror rinsed over me. I felt a sharp pain on the side of my face and quickly opened my eyes. ***"What are you doing, wasting time out here?. You are to be doing your chores like I told you. Not spinning around like a buffoon. Do I make myself clear?"***. Those eyes, filled with anger belonged to my father. Whom was most responsible for the dim life I lived. I hurried to my feet and stood as a soldier would to a drill sergeant.

"Do I make myself clear?!". My father repeated the question.

"Yes Sir!". I answered. Having relocated my voice box. I stood like this until I was sure my father was out of sight. And then plopped down into the muddy surface of the farm. I was dizzy from the blow I had received and couldn't seem to stand right. I tried to get up again but was stopped short by a back breaking weight on my hand. A sneering voice became audible.

"If I were you I'd stop daydreaming and get on with my work". It was my brother Noah. We had been abused together, starved together. And yet still he was a very comforting companion. In fact, he was one of my worst nightmares.

"I'm done!".

"You're done?. Oh really?. Well what's that I see over there?". I followed his pointing finger to see that he had turned over all the grains I had collected and scattered them about.

"You bastard!". I stood up to shove him, but he only pressed harder on my hands.

"Well watcha gonna do about it?. You ain't got no one to tell, do you!". He let go of me then, and walked off cackling. The bastard…but he was right. I had no one. I sighed despairingly to myself and got up. I found that not only had my brother made a fool out of me. But may also have broken a few fingers as well. I didn't make a big fuss out of this, or at least I tried not to. I was somewhat used to this by now. I went through it every day. I have to say though, that the pain was excruciating. My hand was throbbing and would not stop. My fingers were numb and it took me ages to collect the grains.

It was nerve wracking, just thinking of how many snakes could be around me without me knowing. When I was done, I tip-toed my way through the house to the room in which my brother and I stayed. It wasn't even fit for one person. As I passed the old grandfather clock, and headed up the stairs. It decided to take me on for being outside so late. One…two…three. *Three A.M..,* that is. I sighed as I climbed the last two steps and walked through the gloomy passageway. Slowly, I put my hand on the cool bronze knob, and pushed the heavy Oak door open, then peeked in. I was surprised to see my brother sitting on the bed staring. And became frightened when he spoke.

"What are you doing, playing hide and seek?".

"N-n-no". I stammered. I made my way past my brother carefully. In case he stayed up to break more of my fingers. I made my way to the cabinet in the corner of the room. Turned my back to my brother. Got a cloth from the cabinet and began wrestling with the cloth to bandage my hands as tight as possible.

"Father's gone out to drink again". My brother said.

"Uh huh". I did not really care for what my brother was saying. Our Father got drunk every day. I was so caught up in bandaging my hand. I did not hear when my brother came up behind. ***"What are you doing?".*** I turned to see my brother behind. I let out a nervous laugh, and hid my hand behind my back.

"Nothin'".

"Samuel Levi, if you keep lying to me. I'll break the other hand". I moved my hand from behind my back. He grabbed my wrist and clicked his tongue *I hated when he did that*....and reached into the cabinet. When stopped searching, he brought out another roll of cloth and wrapped it tightly around my hand. I stared at him disbelievingly. When he saw, he asked.

"What?".

"I thought you hated me". I was still shocked at his kindness.

"Where did you get that idea?". "You're always so mean to me". I was beginning to think he was messing with my head.

"I know I am". He replied.

"Not that I have a problem with this or anything. But why are you so nice now?".

"You're leaving Samuel". I could not believe my ears.

"I-I-I'm l-l-leaving….w-w-what d-d-do you m-m-mean?".

"I mean you are going to run away Samuel".

"Why?".

"Father may hurt someone tonight". He finished bandaging my hand and looked me in the eye. "Well what about you?. Won't he hurt you?".

"I'm not the one he wants to get rid of, it's you. I heard him talking to himself. Said it was the last straw for with what happened on the farm today. He said you had no use. He blames you for Mother's death. Even though it was her choice to give up her life for you. You have to leave now Samuel". I looked at my brother doubtfully, and he ruffled my hair. At that moment the door opened and closed. My brother grabbed my hand, and led me to the door. He looked both sides before dragging me into the hall and dashing down the stair. When we reached the back door, he hugged me and pushed me through the door.

"Noah!". My father's voice echoed through the house.

"Papa?!". My brother answered before giving me another shove.

"Go!". He whispered harshly……..

Epilogue: "Raging Fire" introduces Shauna-Kay G. Harrison at twelve years old. December 14th, 2010 during her class' second period. Scribbled an Acorn of her thoughts, which seed has remained dormant since. Kind of akin to an unfinished symphony. This is her work verbatim and unedited. Grammatical and other anomalies might be identified. However, this is as Virgin as the Sparrow taking it's first flight from the nest. It flutters erratically but soon straightens up and flies right. Who knows, she might get urge to fertilize and create a mighty Oak. We are both now, **"Unknowns".** Content to embrace each other and hopes for a ride on fame's Express.

Notes:

Colleen G. Lowe-April 2022

People at Play-Family Foibles-604-03-30-22-11 pt Times New Roman

The End

Colleen G. Lowe

www.ingramcontent.com/pod-product-compliance
Lightning Source LLC
Chambersburg PA
CBHW072318020726
47501CB00002B/554